Praise for Elaine Everest

'Heart-warming . . . a must-read'
Woman's Own

'A warm, tender tale of friendship and love'
Milly Johnson

'A lovely read'
Bella

'Elaine brings the heyday of the iconic
high-street giant to life in her charming novel'
S Magazine

'A feel-good summer read'
Bognor Regis Post

Also by Elaine Everest

The Woolworths Girls
The Butlins Girls

Ebook novella
Carols at Woolworths

Christmas at Woolworths

Elaine Everest was born and brought up in north-west Kent and has written widely – both short stories and features – for women's magazines. When she isn't writing, Elaine runs The Write Place creative writing school in Dartford, Kent, and the blog for the Romantic Novelists' Association. Elaine lives with her husband, Michael, and their Polish Lowland Sheepdog, Henry, in Swanley, Kent. *Christmas at Woolworths* is her third novel.

You can say hello to Elaine on
Twitter @ElaineEverest or
Facebook at www.facebook.com/elaine.everest

Elaine Everest

~

Christmas at Woolworths

PAN BOOKS

First published 2017 by Pan Books
an imprint of Pan Macmillan
20 New Wharf Road, London N1 9RR
Associated companies throughout the world
www.panmacmillan.com

ISBN 978-1-5098-4365-7

1 3 5 7 9 8 6 4 2

A CIP catalogue record for this book is available from the British Library.

Typeset by Palimpsest Book Production Ltd, Falkirk, Stirlingshire
Printed and bound by CPI Group (UK) Ltd, Croydon, CR0 4YY

Visit www.panmacmillan.com to read more about all our books
and to buy them. You will also find features, author interviews and
news of any author events, and you can sign up for e-newsletters
so that you're always first to hear about our new releases.

This book is dedicated to the many people who worked for F. W. Woolworths: Saturday staff, management, behind the scenes or on the shop floor. You all played your part in creating this iconic store. Thank you.

Prologue

~

June 1942

Sitting astride the powerful motorbike, Freda Smith removed a large leather gauntlet from her hand in order to pull tight-fitting goggles from her eyes. She rubbed her eyes with the back of her hand and yawned. Although only the first day of June, the air was sultry and not a day for being covered from head to toe in a heavyweight motorcycle uniform. Freda felt sweaty and would have loved nothing more than to pull off her jacket and feel the wind on her skin as she sped through Kent towards her destination. It had been a long day and no doubt many hours lay ahead before she would see her bed. Gazing towards an angry orange glow that could be seen even in the afternoon sky, she knew her journey was almost at an end. She was close to Canterbury.

Freda had always thought the notion of travelling to Canterbury appealing and she'd planned to visit this famous city just as the pilgrims had done centuries before her. Never in a million years did she believe her trip would be to carry important orders to the Fire

Service when Canterbury was under threat from the Luftwaffe. Ahead of her now was a city decimated by enemy action. As a volunteer dispatch rider for the Auxiliary Fire Service Freda had longed for excitement, but she now realized that what lay ahead was death and destruction for this beautiful Kentish city and many of the people who lived there. After nearly three years would this terrible war never end?

Freda fervently wished she was back behind her counter at Erith Woolworths, selling the popular Mighty Midget books and Lumar jigsaws that not only entertained the families but gave youngsters something to concentrate on during long nights when the country was under fire from the enemy. Life seemed so much easier then, even though she was often on fire-watch duties and had to sleep in her landlady's Anderson shelter on many occasions. Knowing how lucky she was had made Freda yearn to do more to help this beastly war come to an end. She wondered what she'd discover when she reached the city walls. How would she find the fire station, where she was supposed to report once she reached Canterbury? Fear urged Freda to turn back and not get any closer to the burning city.

The petite young woman gave herself a silent talking-to. Her job was important and lives depended on her handing over the instructions tucked safely inside the breast pocket of her uniform jacket. She was lucky to be able to work both at Woolies and be a volunteer in the Auxiliary Fire Service. Many people did not have a choice. Freda pulled the goggles back over her eyes and, slipping her small hand back into the gauntlet, she fired up the powerful Triumph motorbike. The bike had been assigned to her when she had completed her training only two weeks ago. Another fifteen minutes and she would reach her destination. Once her duties were complete Freda could do something about the worry that had been nagging at the back of her mind since she left Erith fire station. She would be able to look for her friends. The best place to start her search would be Woolworths. Surely someone could point her in the right direction?

'Thank you,' Freda said, as she was handed a tin mug containing piping hot cocoa along with a sandwich by one of the WVS ladies who were dispensing refreshments from a large van to the fire fighters, soldiers and the many civilians valiantly working to find those injured in the destruction of a once noble city and to dampen down the flames from incendiary bombs. Try as she might, Freda couldn't quite block out the sound of ambulance bells and the shouts for 'quiet' as men nearby dug with their bare hands, searching for people trapped in the rubble of what was until recently street upon street of fine shops.

'You look exhausted, love. Can you find somewhere to put your head down for a while before you head off again?' a WVS woman said as she wiped the counter.

Freda, who would have liked nothing more than to close her eyes and sleep for a few hours to ease her aching body after the long journey across Kent, smiled at the kindly woman. 'No, thank you all the same; I need to find my friends and put my mind at rest. Once I know they are safe I can head back home to Erith. Would you happen to know the best way to reach Woolworths? I'm sure staff there will be on fire watch duties and hopefully they can tell me where my friends are.'

The woman stopped and thought for a moment. 'I do believe that Woolworths is a couple of streets from here, but the road's been blocked off as there's an unexploded bomb. I doubt you'd get there anyway, what with so many shops and houses having been bombed. There's nothing but rubble. Hang on, I'll check with one of my ladies. She's a local and may know more than I do.'

Freda nodded her thanks and bit hungrily into the Spam sandwich while she waited for the woman to return. It had been an age since she'd last eaten, but the grey National bread with its scraping of margarine and thin slice of Spam tasted like a feast fit for a king. Since arriving in Erith from the Midlands at the end of 1938, Freda had come to enjoy her food after most of her childhood was spent going without. Her landlady, and grandmother to her best friend Sarah Gilbert, was a wonderful cook and Freda reckoned her mutton stews, fluffy dumplings and steak and kidney puddings wouldn't look out of place on the tables of any posh London hotel. Even with rationing taking a grip on the nation's food supplies, Ruby Caselton could be relied upon to conjure up a tasty meal for any occasion.

Freda had just swallowed the last of the cocoa when the WVS lady reappeared.

'I was right. You can't get to where Woolies is as the street's shut off. It seems the buildings down there have taken a bit of a bashing so I hope your friends are all right. Do they work there?'

Freda tried not to become alarmed. It wouldn't help matters. She made herself think of everyone back home who would be relying on her to stay strong. 'Er, no, but one of them is manager of the Erith branch and my other friend works with her. I just need to know they are not hurt. Would you know where I could possibly find them? That's if they are not badly injured or . . .'

The kindly woman patted Freda on the shoulder. 'Now, don't go getting yourself upset. Why, you're no more than a child yourself and riding that great big motorbike. You're a brave one and no mistake.'

Freda took a deep breath and composed herself. 'I'll be twenty-one later this year. I'm just a bit on the small side for my age.'

'Well, twenty-one or not, the world's a bloody scary place right now and we are entitled to be afraid. Just don't go bottling it all up. Scream and shout at the Hun if you want to. It does me the power of good, I can tell you.' She placed a protective hand on Freda's shoulder and pointed with the other. 'Now, if you take yourself off down that road and turn left, you will come across a church hall. It's being used as a rest centre as well as a first-aid post. I reckon you'll get news of your friends down there. Leave your motorbike and helmet here. You can park up behind our van. They'll come to no harm. I'll keep an eye on them for you.'

Freda thanked the woman and, after securing her bike, she hurried up the small road to the hall. Struggling to gain entry as the hall was full of people, she pushed and shoved her way through the crowd. So many looked to be in shock, wandering aimlessly about, no doubt looking for loved ones just as Freda was trying to do. Spotting an officious-looking ARP warden with a clipboard, she elbowed through the crowd. 'Excuse me, do you know if my friends, Miss Betty Billington and Mrs Maisie Carlisle, are here?'

The man ran his pencil down a list of names and turned a page. 'Here they are, Billington and Carlisle. Hmm,' he said, tapping the pencil on his teeth as he peered at the list. 'They've been moved to hospital. I assume they must be injured, but details haven't been noted. I do wish people would complete the forms properly,' he huffed.

Freda tried to stand on tiptoes to look at the list, but the man was having none of it and held it close to his body. 'What hospital would that be?' she asked.

'Margate General. It's not too far from here. Local hospitals are overstretched at the moment. Here, take a look at the map.' He pointed to a large map pinned to the wall.

Freda felt sick as she peered at it. Her head started to spin as she attempted to focus on where her friends had been taken and tried not to think too much about their injuries. They are still alive, she told herself as she thanked the man and rushed back to where she'd left her motorbike. Although now late afternoon, it was still warm and around her she could see men sweating as they pulled at bricks and masonry that had once been thriving businesses and family homes, seeking the living and the dead. Firing up the bike's engine, she headed off to find Betty and Maisie.

After being shown where to go by an elderly man in the gatehouse, Freda pulled up outside an imposing Victorian building. She stuffed her goggles and gloves into the helmet and tried to scrub her face clean with a once-white handkerchief. She loved to feel the wind and rain on her face when riding at speed, but the downside was a rather dirty face at the end of a journey. Maisie had suggested she carry her compact and a lipstick when on duty. Freda had laughed at the time as she wasn't one to worry about her appearance and very rarely wore make-up, much to her friend's chagrin, but Maisie had a point. Freda decided she would try to make an effort in future. She sighed as she pushed open a heavy double door, thinking of her vibrant, stylish friend, who might at this very moment be lying injured in this building, and stepped into a large quiet hall. The floor was covered with black and white tiles and the walls were painted a combination of pale green and cream. For a busy hospital it seemed extremely quiet. Perhaps she'd come to the wrong place?

'Can I help you?' a soft-voiced woman asked from a small cubbyhole in the wall.

Freda jumped. She hadn't realized anyone could see her as she'd gazed around the entrance hall trying to read the signs that indicated ward names and medical departments. 'My goodness, I never spotted you there!' Freda exclaimed, holding her hand to her chest to quell her fast-beating heart. 'You gave me such a start.' She peered through the hatch and saw that the voice belonged to a young woman dressed in a nurse's uniform.

'I'm so sorry. It happens all the time. I did suggest to Matron that we have a larger sign, but suggestions from trainee nurses aren't often taken on board.'

'It's my fault. I was rather daunted by stepping into such a posh building and I didn't have my wits about me,' Freda replied. 'I'm looking for my two friends that have been brought here from Canterbury. Their names are Miss Betty Billington and Mrs Maisie Carlisle. Would you know where they are?'

Freda watched expectantly as the young nurse checked paperwork and then looked up at Freda from her chair. 'They are both here, but visiting hours are over for today. Can you come back tomorrow?'

Freda looked sad. 'I came down from Erith on my motorbike. I had to deliver a message from our fire station; I'm a volunteer dispatch rider for the Fire Service. I have to be back at my proper job tomorrow at Woolworths. It would be days before I could get back to Margate, as I'd have to travel by train. Please, could I see them for a few minutes? I really need to know they are not badly injured. It's been such a shock, you see. I hadn't expected to hear they were hurt. I thought they'd be at Woolworths. Betty was going to meet Maisie there, you see . . .' Tears pricked her eyes and she couldn't speak another word. Distress overwhelmed her at being so close to her friends and not being able to speak to them.

The young nurse hurried out from a door close to the hatch and helped Freda to a nearby bench. 'Please, don't get upset. It's been an awful day. I know how you feel as my own parents live in Canterbury and I was beside myself with worry until I knew they were safe. Mummy managed to get through to the hospital from a telephone box to let me know they were fine and they'd be heading to my aunt's house near Dover. Thank goodness she phoned when she did as the telephones haven't worked for the past four hours.'

Freda wiped her eyes and gave the glimmer of a smile. 'Perhaps I could telephone the hospital tomorrow for news? I'm sure I could use the phone at Woolworths, what with Betty being our manager. I would think the telephones would be working by then.'

The nurse thought for a while. 'Look, I'm going back to the wards shortly. Why not come along with me and I'll make sure you can see your friends for a little while? What do you think?'

'Why, that would be wonderful, but I don't want to get you into any trouble on my behalf.'

'You won't,' the girl said as she rose to her feet. 'You stay there and I'll fetch you a cup of tea. One benefit of working in the reception office is that we have a gas ring and a supply of tea. Why, we even have sugar at the moment.' She bustled back inside the little room and left Freda to think about her day.

For Freda it had been a fairly normal Sunday. She'd helped Ruby with some gardening and rinsed out her underwear and hung it to dry on the washing line before heading to Queens Road Baptist Church. The Brownie pack and Girl Guide troop, where she helped out as Tawny Owl, were carrying their flags at church parade before marching behind the Boys' Brigade band through the streets of Erith. The younger girls were excited to be part of the parade, and although Brownies were not allowed to march like the older girls they walked proudly and kept in step. Apart from the flag falling off the pole there were no mishaps and after stowing away the equipment in the church hall she was able to join Brown Owl Charlotte Missons for a cup of tea and a chat. The news that Charlotte's daughter, Molly, would soon be on leave filled Freda with excitement. She'd got on well with Molly, who was close in age to Freda, and had been sad when Molly went off to play her part in beating the Germans by being a land girl on a farm in Suffolk.

Arriving back in Alexandra Road for her Sunday dinner, Freda found a note waiting for her. She was to report to Erith fire station as soon as possible.

'That can only mean something has happened,' Freda said, a thrill of excitement running through her as she headed towards her bedroom to change into the uniform of the Auxiliary Fire Service.

'The war can wait five minutes while you eat your dinner,' Ruby declared with her hands on her hips. 'I told the lad who dropped off the note that you were still at church parade so you're not expected this very minute.'

Freda knew better than to go against her landlady's words. She might have stood the same height as Freda, but she was a formidable force to reckon with. Besides,

Freda's stomach was grumbling and the aroma of roast meat was hard to ignore. 'You are right, Ruby, the war can wait for a few minutes. Who was it who said an army marches on its stomach?'

'I've no idea, girl, but he would have been right and no doubt it was a woman who cooked the food. Sit yourself down now before it gets cold.'

Ruby placed a plate in front of Freda, who gasped as she looked at the food. 'Roast beef? I've not seen that in a while.' She eyed her landlady warily. 'It isn't black market, is it, Ruby? I know a lot of people rely on black market goods to get by but it's not right. We should all work together to get through this war and if that means doing without, then so be it.'

A morning spent in church had made Freda more than a little righteous, but Ruby was having none of it. She went to pull the plate away, but Freda hung on to her food. 'I'll have you know I come by that beef honestly. David popped by with a hamper from his mother. She's a generous woman. What I wouldn't do to live on a farm and be able to eat like we used to.'

'Your Pat lives on a farm and we don't go short,' Freda pointed out.

Ruby looked a little shamefaced. 'Yes, and she's supposed to declare every chicken and egg. But who's to know if there are a few extra birds around the place,' she added as Freda scowled. 'Now, Freda love, don't you go looking at me like that. You've been having some strange opinions since you started going to that Baptist church.'

Freda laughed. She knew well Ruby's views on the smaller churches, as she called them. 'I only go when we have church parade with the Brownies and Guides. By the way, Molly is coming home on leave soon,' she said as she tucked into her meal.

Ruby watched the girl as she enjoyed the food in front of her. Freda was nothing like the scrawny, frightened child who had arrived in Erith in 1938. 'I wish I could make Yorkshire puddings but they never rise with powdered egg . . . Sorry, love, I was miles away. It'll be nice to see Molly again. You two got on like a house on fire. It must be hard for you now Sarah has baby Georgina, and Maisie has her own home and husband David to care for. I like the Misson family. No airs and graces there even though they own a big shop in Pier Road – and I'd lay money on the idea that Norman Misson's doing a bit of ducking and diving to keep his shop afloat!'

'Oh, Ruby,' Freda laughed, getting up to take her plate to the sink. Not everyone is ducking and diving, as you put it. As for your Yorkshire puddings, why not use one of those black market eggs from your Pat?' Freda ducked and ran for the stairs as Ruby threw the tea towel at her.

'I can take you up to the ward now,' the young nurse said, shaking Freda from her thoughts. 'Follow me. Your friends should both be in the same ward. You won't be able to stay long, but at least it will put your mind at rest and I would think your friends will be pleased to see you.'

Freda crept as quietly as possible into the ward. Aware that her boots made an awful noise on the polished tiles, she tried to walk on her toes, chewing her lip in consternation at each squeak from the new leather. She was told they would wear in after a few months but at this moment she wished they were much softer – and silent. There were screens around several of the beds and nurses in crisp starched aprons moved from bed to bed settling their patients for the long night ahead. The young nurse stopped to talk with a colleague before leading Freda to a bed further down the ward. 'Here you are,' she said, stopping at the foot of a bed. 'Mrs Maisie Carlisle. I'll leave you for a few minutes, but remember you can't stay long.'

Maisie's eyes flickered as Freda sat by the bed. Her face was pale with the remains of her make-up smeared across it. It looked as though she'd been crying for a long time. Even her usual perfectly coiffured hair appeared not to have seen a brush for a while. 'Oh, Freda. I'm so pleased to see you. How did you know we were here?' she asked as she started to sob.

'It was the postcard you sent to Ruby, where you mentioned you'd be popping into the Canterbury branch, that made me think to look for you. I was sent to Canterbury fire station with some important documents and to tell them we were sending reinforcements from north Kent. Knowing you would be in Woolworths, I set out to find you. If the pair of you hadn't thought to send that message, I'd not even have thought to check if you'd been in danger. Were you hurt in Woolies? Has the store been damaged? How is Betty?'

Maisie sniffed into her handkerchief. 'We never even reached the store. There was an explosion just after we got off the bus. Betty went head over heels as we hurried to the public air-raid shelter. I twisted me ankle trying to 'elp 'er to 'er feet. I've ruined me bloody shoes as well as me last pair of decent stockings.'

Freda smiled. Even in a distressed state Maisie was worried about her clothes.

'Don't worry about your clothing, at least you are all right – you are all right, aren't you?' she added as Maisie's face crumpled and she began to sob once more.

Freda held her friend close, gently rocking her and allowing her to cry. Once the heartrending sobs had subsided Freda tried to get her to talk. 'Please, Maisie, you've got to tell me what's wrong. Is it Betty? Is she seriously injured?'

'Oh, Freda, I really haven't got a clue,' Maisie said as she wiped her eyes and gave a small hiccup. 'I've not seen her for such a long time and no one will tell me a dickie bird. But there's something else . . .' Large tears formed in her eyes before falling onto her pale cheeks.

'Come on, Maisie, out with it. I can't help you if you keep crying now, can I?' Freda begged, unable to stand seeing her friend so distressed.

'I don't think anyone can 'elp me this time,' Maisie whispered as she shuddered and even more tears flowed. 'I think I might have really 'urt myself. The doctors won't tell me anything and if that's the case . . . well, David will never forgive me . . .'

1

Easter 1942

Betty Billington shooed the last of her staff out into the
darkening night before turning her key in the shiny brass
lock to the door of the F. W. Woolworths store. She
always found this time of day rather sad. Her staff would
be going home to their families and loved ones and no
doubt looking forward to two days off work, the next day
being Easter Sunday. Sundays used to be full of possibil-
ities. But what did she have to look forward to now?
Granted, her friends always included her in their plans
and would invite her for a meal, but deep inside she felt
as though something was missing. Betty had always
planned to have a large family, but the Great War had
put paid to that when her fiancé Charlie perished at
Ypres in August 1917. They hadn't made it up the aisle,
but Betty considered herself a war widow and remained
faithful to her first and only true love. To this day she
wore the wedding ring he'd purchased in anticipation of
their wedding when he was next on leave on the third
finger of her right hand. It had never felt right to wear it

on her wedding finger. She would go home to her little house in Cross Street, only a street away from Woolworths in Pier Road, and try to keep herself busy until the store opened on Tuesday morning. Today would have been Charlie's birthday. She would indulge herself, reflecting upon what might have been and how they'd have celebrated the occasion. Then, she'd do her utmost to pull herself together so she could return to her role as the ever-efficient Woolworths store manager.

Regardless of the war now being in its third year, there was always something to celebrate or look forward to. Today she'd heard her staff speaking hopefully of the war ending by the Christmas of 1942, now that the Americans were on board. They all seemed to agree that as bad as the bombing of Pearl Harbor had been, the idea of the Yanks joining our lads to fight Hitler, and the Japs, had cheered everyone up no end. Betty thought they were more than a little over-optimistic, but then they all had their dreams to hold on to.

Waving to the last of her girls as they left Woolworths and set off down Pier Road towards their homes, Betty checked the front of the store, making sure that each set of glass-fronted double doors was securely locked. The Easter display was bright and pretty with fluffy chicks sitting between painted eggshells on nests of straw. It had been young Freda's idea for the scene and they'd searched high and low for yellow and brown wool to make the fluffy balls that would ultimately become the little chicks. Betty smiled to herself as she recalled the day Freda Smith arrived for an interview back in

November 1938 and met Sarah Caselton and the glamorous Maisie. Who'd have thought the three young women would become such good friends, and also include her in their family life?

Despite the recent bombing of the nearby Thames-side docks that led up from the Kent town of Erith to the port of London, not one window in the popular store had suffered.

'Hey, Betty! Wait for us!'

Betty turned as she made to cross Pier Road, where the Woolworths store was situated. 'Why, Sarah, Freda, is there a problem?'

'There will be if you don't come with us to Nan's,' Sarah said breathlessly. 'She's made a meat and potato pie.'

'Enough to feed an army. We've been sent to invite you for tea. Please say yes or we will be eating it in our sandwiches for the next week,' Freda begged.

Betty laughed, all thoughts of her long-lost love forgotten for the moment. 'I'm interested to know how Ruby came by so much meat,' she said, raising her eyebrows.

'Goodness, there is little meat in the pie. It's just that she was busy arguing with Vera from up the road and peeled too many spuds. Not that we wouldn't have invited you anyway,' Sarah added quickly in case Betty was insulted. 'Nan had to add another can of corned beef otherwise it would have been a spud pie,' she explained.

'I could always donate a can or two of snoek,' Betty suggested, to which both girls shrieked in horror.

'Please, no!' Sarah said with a look of distaste. 'Even if I was starving, I couldn't eat the stuff. Why, it's revolting.'

The girls tucked their arms through Betty's and set off for Ruby's home in nearby Alexandra Road with its terrace of Victorian bay-fronted houses that had stood firm through two wars and where the girls were always welcome. It was as they turned the corner into the High Street that Sarah looked back and spotted the man. He stood on the pavement in front of Woolworths, where Betty had stood only minutes earlier and was watching Betty intently. Sarah knew she had seen him before. With a cold chill running the length of her back, she turned away and joined in the chatter about their friend Maisie, who was babysitting Sarah's adorable daughter, Georgina.

'You say you've seen the bloke before?' Maisie whispered as she dipped her hands into the washing-up water and retrieved a fork, then checked her nails. Maisie wasn't one for washing up as a rule, but the others were listening to a play on the radio so she'd had no choice but to volunteer after the grand meal Ruby had provided for them all.

'Yes, I remembered just now,' Sarah whispered back. 'It was in Woolies a couple of days ago. I was helping Betty collect takings from the tills and he was there, at the corner of the haberdashery counter. I called out to Deirdre to serve him. You know how that woman likes to chat. The last thing I wanted was to have to pacify a customer if she wasn't doing her job. But he walked away and headed for the door. A couple of minutes later I spotted him watching through the window.'

Maisie snorted with laughter before clapping her hand over her mouth in case the others heard. 'Come off it. You're 'aving me on . . . Why, he could 'ave been a normal customer thinking about a purchase. You've got too much time on yer 'ands, my girl.' She snorted again, having adopted one of Ruby's favourite sayings that she used in jest as her granddaughter, along with her mates, were doing more than their fair share of war work along with their everyday jobs at Woolies.

'I'm serious, Maisie. I really do think that man is watching Betty.'

'So, what can we do about it?' Maisie asked. She knew better than to joke about something when Sarah looked so serious.

'What's all this?' Ruby asked as she entered the kitchen with a pile of cups and saucers on a tray. 'Anyone would think the pair of you have a secret.'

Maisie and Sarah looked at each other and Maisie sighed. 'It's your idea so you explain to Ruby. I'm not so sure it's not all in yer 'ead.'

Ruby frowned. 'Come on, spit it out then. I haven't got all day. You can wash these cups and saucers while you talk. Give me the tea towel, Sarah, you won't dry a thing twiddling it between your fingers. So, what's the problem?' Ruby asked as she started to dry a dinner plate.

Sarah explained how she thought a man in a dark brown overcoat was following Betty and where she had seen him. 'Do you think we should tell her, Nan?'

Ruby thought for a moment as she stacked the dry

crockery on the shelves of the pine dresser that covered the wall of the small kitchen. 'I'm not so sure you should say anything at this moment in time.'

Maisie grinned. 'See, I told yer she wouldn't believe you, Sarah.'

Ruby looked seriously at Maisie. 'Oh, but I do believe Sarah. I'm more concerned that Betty, living alone as she does, would feel frightened.'

'Perhaps we could lie in wait and catch the man next time we see him?' Maisie suggested.

'And what if we are wrong? We'd be the ones locked up. Leave it with me. I'm popping over to see Sergeant Jackson later on. I've saved him a plate of meat and potato pie. I can ask his opinion while I'm at it.'

'Is Sergeant Jackson's dad staying with him?' Maisie asked with a glint in her eye. 'I heard he was coming back to Erith.' Maisie nudged Sarah and the pair of them fell into a fit of the giggles.

Ruby's cheeks turned a light shade of pink and she puffed herself up to her full height. Even so, she was shorter than the two girls, who were now laughing un-controllably. 'Stop it now, the pair of you. I've known Bob Jackson far longer than you've both been on this earth. He was a good friend of your grandad's, Sarah, and his son, Sergeant Jackson, went to school with your dad so you can stop all this right now. He's an honourable man, being a retired policeman, and Mike Jackson is following in his footsteps. There's no harm in offering a bite to eat to a neighbour, is there?'

'No, Nan,' Sarah said, trying to keep a straight face.

Ruby looked from Sarah to Maisie and sighed

dramatically. 'I think I'll take that food over the road now. I'm probably more welcome over there and won't get laughed at.' She opened the door to the stone pantry and lifted down a plate covered in a tea towel. 'Yes, I'll go right now and the pair of you can stop your silliness. Sarah, you might want to relieve Miss Billington of young Georgina. The face that kiddy was making just now makes me think she's filled her nappy.' She grinned at her granddaughter. 'Ha, that's wiped the smile off your face,' she said, heading for the front door.

'So, what do you think, Mike? Are the girls making a mountain out of a molehill?' Ruby asked as she watched Mike Jackson and his father, Bob, tuck into the meat and potato pie.

'I'd say be cautious at this time, but until the man has done something wrong the police have nothing to go on.'

'So, you do think it's something and nothing?' Ruby said, spooning the last of the pie onto his plate.

'What I think, Mrs Caselton, is that you can't keep feeding Dad and me all the time. However do you manage, what with rationing being what it is?'

'Oh, it's nothing illegal, if that's what you're thinking, Mike. Corned beef and potatoes with a few vegetables chucked in from my garden and the allotment. In fact, your dad helped grow some of 'em as I'd no idea about growing such things. I'm learning quickly, though,' she added in case Mike and his dad, Bob, thought she was asking for him to do more. She'd rather fend for herself and wasn't one to ask for help ordinarily.

'And very tasty it was too, Ruby,' Bob Jackson said, wiping his mouth with a handkerchief. 'You've got to admit, Mike, it's far better than eating at the police station or down at the Civic Restaurant in Slades Green.'

'You're right there, Dad,' Mike agreed. 'No offence meant, Mrs Caselton, but you'd be surprised what people are up to these days to get more than their fair share of food.'

'None taken, Mike. Now, you must come to tea tomorrow afternoon. Our George and Irene are coming up from Devon. Irene wrote to say they have some news. I'm at a loss to know what it could be. I hope they don't want to take Sarah and young Georgina back with them. I'd miss them so much. It's comforting to know they live just around the corner with Alan's mum, Maureen. If, or rather when, Alan gets called back to his squadron, Sarah will need her family and friends close by her.'

'That would be grand, Ruby. Cheers!' Bob Jackson replied. 'Do you think he'll be called back to duty soon, Ruby?'

'My George reckons it's on the cards. He can talk to the boy about such things more easily than I can. Our Sarah does get upset at the thought of losing him, after his accident. All we want for little Georgina is her daddy safe and at home. Now Alan's working out of the Gravesend airfield he is home most nights, which is a blessed relief to us all.'

'He had a nasty scrape, though. What a lucky bugger he is getting off light with just a leg injury. It must have been a worry being stuck on the other side of the Channel for so long. Many haven't been as fortunate,' Bob said, getting up to clear the table.

'Sit yourself back down, Bob Jackson, and let your food digest. I'll put the kettle on when I've washed up the plates. That's if you've got time to stop and drink it? I don't see much of the pair of you these days. I thought you was retired, Bob?'

'No one retires these days, Ruby. Not while there's a war on. I've been busy with the ARP, and I've also been helping out down at Erith police station. We still have criminals, even in wartime.'

Ruby wrinkled her nose in disgust as she headed towards the kitchen. 'And don't I know it. If it hadn't been for your Mike arriving at my house, I could have been bumped off along with half my family and a few of my friends by one of those criminals.'

Both men roared with laughter. 'I doubt that very much, Mrs Caselton. You are a force to be reckoned with,' Mike called back.

Ruby smiled to herself as she poured hot water from a kettle into an enamel bowl in the sink. She reckoned she was. If only she could get her hands on that Adolf, she'd show him a thing or two.

Irene Caselton kissed her mother-in-law on both cheeks. 'Goodness, what a journey we had. I'm thankful we won't be doing that for much longer. But I'll leave that news until later,' she added quickly as she saw the frown appearing on Ruby's face. 'Here, I have a little contribution for our tea. A couple of days late but I'm sure they will be welcome.'

Ruby opened the tin that Irene held out. Inside were a baker's dozen of hot cross buns. 'Why, I've not seen sight nor sound of these for a year or so. Even Betty hasn't had any for sale in Woolworths. I shouldn't ask, but how did you manage to get your hands on these beauties?'

Irene gave a throaty laugh as she removed her coat and the glossy fox fur from around her neck. 'It's nothing illegal, if that's what you are alluding to. We have a delightful little bakery in a village close to our house and I put in my order long ago just so my granddaughter could enjoy her Easter.'

'That's good of you, Irene,' Ruby said. 'Now, hang your coat up and let's find you a seat. You'll find Betty and the girls in the front room playing with your granddaughter. Alan and David seem to have escaped their wives and are in the back garden having a smoke while putting the world to rights.'

Irene laughed. 'My George headed straight out there. He likes nothing more than chatting about the war. He more than plays his part working at Vickers all the hours God sends, but I swear he'd love the chance to be flying a plane and taking potshots at the enemy like Alan or working behind the scenes like David. I still can't understand how Maisie caught the eye of such an important man as David.'

Ruby shuddered. 'There are more than enough men in this family laying their lives on the line for our country. Let's try and keep George's feet firmly on the ground, shall we, eh?'

'I'm with you there. Now, do you have a plate we can put these hot cross buns on?'

'I can do better than that,' Ruby said as she bent to open a door in the kitchen dresser. 'Let's use my best cake stand. It's something to celebrate when we have buns for our tea in wartime.'

'I can add something to that,' a voice piped up from behind Irene, who was standing in the doorway to the kitchen. 'I have real butter and eggs to contribute to the feast.'

'Well, blow me down,' Ruby said, passing the cake stand to Irene and reaching out to the woman, who was standing there grinning like a Cheshire cat. 'Pat, it's wonderful to see you. What are you doing here? The last time you wrote you were down in Cornwall with the kiddies.'

Pat, Ruby's youngest child, pushed past her sister-in-law and hugged her mother until the pair could hardly breathe. 'I came home to see John as I missed him so much. The kiddies are still down there,' she added as Ruby looked past Pat hoping to see her grandchildren.

Ruby's heart sank. It had been a year since she'd set eyes on her youngest grandchildren. Ruby had supported Pat's husband when he said he wanted his loved ones in a safe place, away from the bombing, and where safer than Cornwall? He had relatives down that way who had suggested Pat and the children stay. It had been a resounding success with the youngsters who attended the local village school and settled in to living on a farm, as just they might with their own father all but running Moat Farm on the outskirts of nearby Slades Green.

'John hasn't been able to leave the farm to come and

see us and I missed him so much, Mum,' Pat said beseechingly, not knowing how Ruby would take the news of her leaving the children behind.

Ruby thought for a moment. Was there more in this than what her youngest was telling her? 'You know what's best for your family, Pat, who am I to judge? Now, let's get this tea party underway before the buns go dry.' Ruby turned away to remove her apron and straighten her Sunday best dress before picking up a tray that held her best teapot and headed towards the front room.

Pat raised her eyebrows at her sister-in-law, who looked equally puzzled.

'I do declare the old girl is going soft in her old age,' Irene whispered as they followed Ruby.

'Come in, Mike and Bob, I think you know everyone,' Ruby called out as the police sergeant and his father walked in through the open door. 'Let's find you a comfortable chair, Bob. Tea is about ready. Mike, would you give the men a shout before all the grub's gone? They're in the garden gassing about something or other. Freda, clear me a space on the sideboard to put this tray down and, you young ones, budge up and give Bob somewhere to rest his bones.'

Maisie jumped to her feet and shook out the skirt of her summery frock. With her blonde hair pinned high on her head and her lips painted deep red she looked the picture of health. 'Here you go, Bob, 'ave my seat. I can perch on the arm of the sofa or sit on David's lap when he returns from whatever he's up to in the back garden.'

Vera, Ruby's friend from up the road, rushed over to the vacated seat. 'There's plenty of room for two. You can sit with me, Bob,' she said, patting the seat beside her.

'I'll ask you not to rush about my front room, Vera Munro, you nearly knocked over Rover.'

Maisie and Sarah grinned at each other. Rover was Ruby's best chalk dog that she'd won at last year's Erith Show. It had taken them all umpteen goes on the side shows to have enough vouchers for the large ornament that so resembled Ruby's dog, Nelson. 'Where is Nelson, Nan?' Sarah asked, hoping that Ruby would stop glaring at Vera in such a territorial way as Vera patted Bob's knee, much to his embarrassment.

'He's out the back. I asked your Alan to keep him there in case he pinched our grub. You know what he's like when there's food about. Now, let's all tuck in before the sandwiches start to curl. Would you like to pour the tea, Sarah?'

Maisie nudged her mate as she got to her feet to sort out cups and saucers and pour the amber liquid from her nan's best teapot. The pair of them were aware that Vera from up the road had set her cap at Sergeant Jackson's father now he was back home and living in Alexandra Road. Even if Ruby wasn't aware of it yet, she too had a soft spot for the amiable man, whose eyes followed her as she handed out food and made sure everyone had a fair share to eat.

2

With the delicious Easter tea over and done with and not a crumb remaining of the hot cross buns, the men in the family set to with the washing up while the women waved goodbye to Pat, who wanted to get back to her husband, and Vera, who was none too keen on taking a walk.

'Let's take Georgina to see the window display in Woolworths,' Freda said as she tucked her arm through Sarah's. 'The woollen chicks look so cute in amongst the eggshells and straw.'

'Here, darling, let me push my beautiful granddaughter. I don't get to see her nearly enough,' Irene said as she took control of the pram. 'I must say, this knitted cover is delightful. Is it your handiwork, Freda?'

'No, I worked on a pink blanket for the little bed that Alan made. It's ready for when she is big enough. This is all Maureen's doing. She does have a clever nanny, don't you, my sweetie?' Freda said as she leant over and tickled the little girl under the chin, before realizing what she had said. Alan's mum, Maureen, was a lovely lady but Irene could be a little prickly at times. She felt Sarah nudge her side but it was too late, the words had been said.

Fortunately Maureen was at hand and heard Freda speak. 'My goodness, don't look too close, Irene, or you will see where I dropped a stitch. If anyone is clever, it is you for finding such a smart new pram for our little angel. Why, there's nothing new to be found for youngsters these days.'

'You've all been so generous with gifts for Georgina. I'm truly grateful and I know Alan is too,' Sarah added quickly.

'Actually, the pram isn't new,' Irene admitted nervously.

'Well, blow me down with a feather,' Maisie declared before putting her hand to her mouth as she realized what she had said. It was common knowledge that Irene always purchased the best products and the word second-hand was never found in her vocabulary. 'I'd never have known,' she added quickly.

'I wouldn't have purchased it from just anyone,' Irene said, pulling on leather gloves before taking control of the pram. 'Lady Clairmont, from the golf club, had bought the perambulator for her daughter to use when she came to visit. Sadly her daughter has taken the children to Canada for the duration so it has had little use.'

'Lucky for our Lady Georgina,' Sarah said with a grin. 'Fancy you riding in a pram meant for royalty.'

Irene sniffed. 'Hardly royalty, Sarah. Lady Clairmont's husband made his fortune in industry. Do you think we should start our walk before it gets dark?'

Maisie grinned at Sarah as they linked arms and

followed the entourage of women down the road of bay-fronted terraces towards the town of Erith. 'She never changes, does she?'

'Oh, I don't know. I feel she has mellowed in some ways. Look how she is with Georgina and she loves wearing those siren suits you made for her so that she's just like the rest of us when we are down in the Anderson shelter.'

'Has she always been posh?' Maisie whispered as Freda joined them.

Sarah laughed. 'I've never really known her any other way. Mum just wants what is best for Dad and me. I've not long realized that.'

'I like your mum, Sarah. You get what you see with her and she's always there for you regardless of whether she's wearing a fur coat or not,' Freda said wistfully. 'You are lucky to have such a caring family.'

'Have you heard anything from yer mum?' Maisie asked. They'd met Freda's brother, Lenny, not long after Freda started work at Woolworths but knew little of her mother.

'Not a peep since I left home in 1938. We were never close, especially after my dad died and she took up with her current husband. As you know, I send her a few bob in a Christmas card but there's never a word from her. Lenny sends her money since he's been in the navy, but she's not replied to him either.' Freda shrugged her shoulders in dismissal. 'That's life, I suppose.'

Sarah felt so angry. It wasn't fair that Freda should be treated so badly by her mother. Freda was such a sweet girl and everyone who met her said what a delightful person she was. 'We are your family now, Freda, so no need to be sad. Why, Georgina looks on you as her aunty and you are her godmother, just as Maisie is. Even Nan treats you just like another granddaughter. You too, Maisie,' she added.

'We were certainly lucky the day we bumped into you at Woolies,' Freda said, a smile brightening her face. 'Goodness knows what would have happened to me if I'd not been told they were advertising for staff for the Christmas period and decided to turn up on the off chance they would take me on.'

'And looking like a right ragamuffin, gawd luv yer,' Maisie said, giving her a hefty shove with her elbow. 'Look at you now,' she added, so proud of how Freda had turned into a pretty young woman.

Freda stopped and spun around. 'All thanks to you two,' she said as her pretty floral skirt flew out from her neat waist. 'Have I said thank you for passing this on to me, Sarah?'

'Only about ten times,' Sarah laughed. 'It's best going to you as the waistband is just too tight since I've had Georgina.'

'And taking it in means there were a few scraps of material for the patch pocket on your blouse,' Maisie said, admiring her handiwork.

'Well, I'm grateful to both of you,' Freda said, making one more delighted spin as they reached the end of Alexandra Road and turned left towards the shop-lined streets that formed the centre of Erith. 'I owe you lots of favours for this and will look after Georgina any time you want to go out. You too, Maisie, when the time comes.' She almost skipped as she went ahead to join Ruby, who was chatting to Betty as they followed Maureen and Irene with the pram.

Sarah noticed a shadow pass over Maisie's face. 'It'll happen soon enough, Maisie,' she said softly. 'You've not been married a year yet.'

'But I 'ad that scare at the end of last year. What if I can't 'ave kids? I'd never forgive myself. David wants them even more than I do.'

'It's not going to happen if you keep worrying. I remember Maureen saying that to one of the women at Woolworths and she's had three since then. So, you never know what's around the next corner, do you?'

'I s'pose yer right,' Maisie said although she didn't look convinced.

'Look, Alan's taking me to the pictures tomorrow evening. Why not come with us? There's a musical on at the Odeon. It's a Busby Berkeley. You like them.'

Maisie shrugged her shoulders. 'Ta, but no thanks. David is back on duty the day after so I really want to make the most of having him to myself if we are ever to 'ave a kiddie of our own.'

Sarah flinched. Even now she wasn't used to the way her friend spoke sometimes. 'We'd best hurry up, the others are so far ahead of us.'

'You've certainly done wonders with your window display, Betty. Wherever do you get your ideas, let alone the materials?' Irene said as she stood gazing into the windows of F. W. Woolworths. Even with the crisscross of sticky paper over the windows, to limit damage if enemy action should shatter the glass, the wonderful Easter scene could be seen.

'All praise must go to Freda,' Betty replied proudly. 'She has such wonderful ideas. Head office sent a photographer down last week to take a photograph for the staff magazine. We've not featured in *The New Bond* since Sarah was carnival queen in 1939. The journalist interviewed Freda about her ideas so I do hope it is published. Staff need a boost at the moment with this awful war going on for so long.'

'I certainly agree with you there, Betty. In fact, that is why I accompanied George this weekend. We are house hunting,' Irene said.

Sarah, who was standing just behind, shrieked with glee. 'You're moving home?'

'It's hardly home, Sarah. Our home is in Devon, not Erith,' Irene corrected her daughter.

'Why now?' Ruby asked. She was trying to keep a straight face as the relief that Irene was not taking Sarah and Georgina back with her was hard to hide.

'George is to work more hours at Vickers in Crayford, so it makes sense for us to move up this way. We will rent a house for now and let our own home out to one of his colleagues. I accompanied George to make sure he found something presentable.'

'There's an empty house near me in Crayford Road,' Maureen suggested.

'I saw an advert in the tobacconist for rooms in West Street,' Freda added.

Irene wrinkled her nose. 'No, I was thinking of

somewhere in Crayford close to St Paulinus Church. It would have to be something tasteful.'

Maisie grinned at Sarah. 'What was that we were saying about snobs?'

'Shush, she will hear you,' Maureen hissed. 'I'm sure wherever you live you'll make a beautiful home for George,' she said, turning to Irene. 'Crayford isn't far for you to visit the family.'

'Or for them to visit me,' Irene smiled through thin lips. 'It will be a novelty to have my daughter step over the threshold of her parents' home once again.'

Sarah didn't know what to say. Her mother had never understood why she'd preferred to move to Erith and work in Woolworths rather than stay in Devon and be introduced to umpteen chinless offspring of Irene's friends at the golf club. Maisie, however, had plenty to say.

'Come off it, Irene. Sarah's had a lot on her plate since moving here. She has an important job and a baby, and don't forget that her husband was missing in action for a good few months. Besides, most of her family live in this neck of the woods now . . . and she always sees her dad when he's working at Vickers.'

Irene adopted an injured expression and sighed. 'I suppose I am only your mother, Sarah.'

'For goodness' sake, Irene, I thought we were here to look at the window display, not talk about your social arrangements,' Ruby snapped. 'I for one think it is exceptional and if the people at Woolworths decide to publish a photograph, I'd like a copy to frame and hang at home if that is possible. I'm very proud of all of you.

Now, shall we move on and take Georgina to watch the boats on the river before it's time for her tea?'

A rather subdued group of women followed Ruby, who had taken over the pushing of the pram containing her great-granddaughter. Chin held high, she marched across Pier Road and down the High Street to the banks of the River Thames.

'I love coming here,' Maureen said as she breathed deeply, taking in the river smells. 'I feel so lucky to live in Erith. I couldn't imagine moving away. Even with the barrage balloons hovering over the river and the threat of air-raid warnings at any time, it is still a great place to live.'

'I'm with you there, Maureen,' Ruby agreed. 'I'll be here until they carry me off to join my Eddie at St Paulinus.'

'Oh, Nan, don't be so miserable. That won't be for many a year,' Sarah admonished Ruby as she lifted her daughter from the pram and held her up to see the busy river. 'Look, Georgie, boats!'

'Ships, Sarah, they are ships,' Irene said, 'and how boring they look all painted in the same awful grey. However can anyone be excited about such a scene? It's just the same boring river it has always been.'

Georgina replied by excitedly chuckling and pointing as a nearby tug sounded its horn, which made the women laugh.

'I do wish the grandchildren were here with us. I do miss them. They must have grown a foot at least since I last saw them.'

'It's safer for them down in Cornwall, Ruby. Look at

how close the farm was to those incendiary bombs that landed at Slades Green sidings last year. If it hadn't been fer some of the locals putting out the fires, the whole area would have been blown sky high,' Maisie reminded Ruby.

Ruby nodded thoughtfully. 'You're right there, Maisie, but it doesn't stop me missing them.'

'Perhaps you could visit them,' Freda suggested.

'What? All the way down in Cornwall? It might as well be the end of the earth for all the chance I'd get to travel there,' Ruby laughed. 'No, I'll just have to wait until the war is over and Pat brings them home,' she added, looking sad.

Freda gave her landlady a big hug. 'Never say never, eh, Ruby?'

'I'll keep it in mind, love, but for now all I can think about is a nice cup of tea. I don't know about you lot but I could do with putting my feet up for a while.'

'Let's get Georgie back in her pram. I don't think she can walk all the way home just yet,' Sarah said, as she lifted her daughter. Georgie immediately started to grizzle as she preferred to toddle unsteadily, holding on to her mum's hands.

'Georgina is a perfectly good name. I see no reason for you to shorten it, Sarah,' Irene sniffed, as she headed away from the river and up the High Street.

The women were quiet as they headed back to Alexandra Road with Georgina still complaining in her pram. Ruby had just put her key in the front door of number thirteen when they spotted Vera, Ruby's friend from up the road, heading towards them. Maisie, who had taken over pushing the pram, steered around the woman, intent on getting the child inside the house and cheering her up.

'You're quite a hand at looking after a kiddie, Maisie. I'm surprised you haven't got one of your own by now,' Vera said pointedly. 'Our Sadie is courting and I'm sure she will have a family as soon as she's walked down the aisle. In wartime it's a woman's duty to bring more children into the world to make for a better future for our country.'

Maisie lowered her head and dashed into the house, only stopping to let Freda take hold of the pram. Sarah rushed after her friend and closed the front door. Ruby could hear Maisie's sobs from outside the house.

'Why, Vera Munro, that is the most hurtful comment I've ever heard you say,' Ruby scolded her neighbour. 'Why don't you stop to think before you open your big mouth and let your words spew out? For all you know Maisie may have problems and words like yours can hurt someone's feelings.'

'Is she having problems then?' Vera asked with interest.

'It's none of your business if she is. Not that she is having problems,' Ruby added quickly in case Vera probed even more. 'Now, what can we do for you?' she asked, folding her arms across her chest and giving the woman a hard stare.

'I just thought I'd pop down and spend a neighbourly hour with you,' Vera said.

'I'm in no mood to be neighbourly,' Ruby said, with a stony expression. 'So, you can go back home to your

Sadie and her young man. You must have a lot to discuss if there is a wedding in the offing.'

For a moment Vera looked puzzled before turning away and heading back up Alexandra Road to her own house.

'Well I never. That woman has the nerve of the devil sometimes,' Ruby huffed as she opened the front door that Maisie had pulled shut behind her. 'As for her Sadie, the girl only volunteered for war work to get away from Vera, and if she does have a young man he must have met her in a blackout!' She hurried into the house leaving Irene, Maureen and Freda lost for words.

'So, George, how are things at Vickers?' David Carlisle asked as he passed a pile of plates to Alan to put back on Ruby's dresser. He was aware that careless talk cost lives, as the posters were always reminding them, but with just himself, George and Alan on washing-up duties while Bob Jackson and his son spent half an hour in the garden sorting out the weeds from the vegetables, he knew it was safe to talk.

'More work than we can cope with at the moment, David. Even taking on extra staff we are pushed to meet the demands the government has set. That's what made me decide to move up this way, rather than travel back and forth from Devon so much. Apart from petrol rationing, it's hell travelling. I've wanted to move home for a while now but our Irene would miss her social life, committees and the golf club.'

'The war comes first, George,' David replied. 'I've

been trying to talk Maisie into moving in with my mother, but she won't leave Erith and her friends or her job.'

'She's safe here, David, and Ruby will look out for her,' Alan pointed out. 'She's near enough family.'

'Even though we live several streets away? There are times when I'm away and I hear about air raids and can't stop wondering if she's all right. Maisie is my life and I don't want to lose her,' David said desperately.

'We all feel the same, lad, and it makes no difference where our family is. We can only work to get this war over and done with as soon as possible.'

Alan, who had been washing up at the sink, placed the last cup on the draining board and dried his hands on a towel hanging behind the kitchen door. 'I'm thinking of putting in a request to go back on active duty for that very reason. I don't feel I'm doing enough at the moment.'

George, who had pulled his pipe from his pocket and was about to place it in his mouth, stopped what he was doing. 'Why, Alan? You are doing an admirable job teaching young pilots to fly. Why would you want to put yourself in danger again?'

Alan sighed. 'I don't feel as though I'm doing enough in this war. I'm not blowing my own trumpet when I say that I'm a good pilot and if we are to win this war, we need good pilots who can go out there and beat the enemy at their own game.'

'Now's not the time to discuss this. The women will be home anytime soon and we don't want them upset, do we?' David said.

'That sounds like them now. I'd better help them in with my daughter,' Alan said as he left George and David alone.

'I don't like to ask but is there anything you can do?' George said.

'As you know, George, I can pull strings in my job, but I'm not sure I can put Alan in a safe job. And anyway, is anyone safe in this war?'

Leaving instructions to chase the men out of the kitchen and put the kettle on, Ruby entered her front room to find out what the problem was with Maisie. She had a good idea why there were so many tears, but wanted to get the news herself from the horse's mouth. 'Now, what's going on here? You left me to sort out Vera and that wasn't nice, was it?' she said with a smile.

Sarah, who was sitting next to Maisie on an over-stuffed sofa, looked at her nan with worried eyes. 'Why is Vera Munro so horrid, Nan? There was no need for her to pry into Maisie's private life like that. None of us would ever ask such a question and we are all friends.'

'She's a nosy so-and-so, that's why, and never happy unless she's poking her nose into other people's business. She'll never change,' Ruby huffed as she pulled back the heavy green velvet curtains and let some light into the room. 'That's better,' she declared, looking approvingly around her 'best' room, 'although the aspidistra looks a bit on the dry side. Remind me to give it some water, Sarah love, and perhaps when you've time you'd wipe the leaves over with a drop of milk. They seem to have lost their shine.'

Sarah nodded in agreement as she continued to hug Maisie, who was still sniffing into her handkerchief. 'I'll do that shortly, Nan. Can you tell me why Vera Munro is your friend if she is so nasty to people? You don't usually give people like her the time of day.'

'I always give her the benefit of doubt, love. Vera's had a hard life and if anyone is entitled to be bitter then it's her.'

Sarah was puzzled by Ruby's words. 'I don't understand, Nan. You are always calling her names and hardly a day goes past without you both having words. How can you still be friends?'

Ruby sat at the other side of Maisie and brushed away a few stray hairs that had stuck to the girl's tear-stained face. 'Vera's not had a good life, but she is a good woman underneath all her nosiness. Have you ever wondered why her granddaughter, Sadie, lives with her?'

Sarah screwed up her nose as she thought hard. 'No, I've never given it much thought. It's always been just Vera and Sadie living up the road. Not that we ever see much of Sadie. What happened, Nan?'

'Let's just say that Sadie's mum was no better than she ought to be. She preferred to entertain men down at the docks rather than earn a decent living and that's how she met a sticky end. Vera was always a strict mother, perhaps that's why Doris went off the rails as she did, but that was no reason for people to turn their backs on Vera. That's why I've stuck by her all these years.'

'Oh, Nan, that's such a sad story. No wonder Vera is

like she is. I'll do my best to put up with her from now on as long as she doesn't overstep the mark with my friends. Thank goodness Sadie had Vera to take care of her. No child deserves a mother like Doris.'

Sarah's words brought on another wave of sobbing from Maisie.

'There, there, love. Don't let on so. You'll have your babies one day and what beautiful kiddies they will be,' Ruby said, enveloping Maisie in her arms. 'Ignore Vera and her sharp words. I'm right? That is what has upset you? Now, I'm going to get you a hot drink. That'll see you as right as rain in no time,' she continued, pulling herself up and stretching her back. 'You sit there a while and chat with our Sarah,' she added, patting Maisie's shoulder gently.

Sarah waited until Maisie's sobs subsided and she'd wiped her eyes.

'Nan's right, Maisie. You'll make a wonderful mum.'

'I don't deserve to have kiddies. You know what happened just before Christmas.'

'If you mean you lost your baby, it can happen for many reasons. It don't mean you don't deserve to have another child.'

Maisie's eyes flashed with anger. 'But it does. You see, I was no better than Vera's daughter. I used to earn money from men just like she did and now I'm being punished.'

3

Betty looked up from her ledgers, disturbed by the sound of tapping on her office door. She valued these quiet moments tucked away in the office on the first floor of the Woolworths store in Erith. She was so behind with her work and being understaffed on the shop floor didn't help at all. There was an overall hanging on a hook by the door and she was seriously contemplating pulling it on and helping out downstairs, before they received complaints from shoppers who were tired of queuing in order to feed their families and didn't expect to face yet one more queue in Woolworths.

'Come in,' she called with a sigh, hoping it was nothing terribly important.

Freda put her head around the door. 'Can you spare me a couple of minutes please, Betty?'

'Of course I can, Freda. Move that pile of overalls and sit down. Is there a problem?' she asked, noting Freda's expression.

'No . . . no, not a problem as such. It's just that I've been thinking about war work.'

Betty held her breath. Please, not another staff

43

member leaving, she thought as her heart plummeted to her feet. 'What has made you think of this, Freda?'

Freda sighed. 'I love my work here at Woolworths, but I don't feel I'm doing much to help us win the war. I'd rather find work I enjoy before I'm given something awful to do. I don't want to sound ungrateful,' she added quickly.

Betty nodded in agreement. Her mind went back to when Freda left her job in Woolworths to work in Burndept's factory on the other side of Erith and the night the whole of town seemed to be alight when the factory caught fire after enemy action. They'd all been worried until Freda appeared only a little worse for wear and later resumed her job in the store. 'We will miss you, Freda, but I do understand how you feel. I've been tempted to volunteer myself, you know.'

Freda raised her eyebrows in surprise. 'I never knew you felt like that. Whatever would Woolworths do without you?'

'It's very kind of you to say such a thing but, like you, I feel I'm not quite doing all I can to bring this war to a speedy conclusion.'

'Why, Betty, if Woolies wasn't run properly, the whole town would suffer. Even when we only have canned snoek to sell, you are the person who shows our customers how to serve the awful stuff,' Freda insisted.

Betty smiled. 'The recipe competition was a good idea, but I can't take all the credit for that. We have many staff members who are adept at making a meal out of only a few ingredients. Now, tell me, which war work has taken your fancy?'

'I read in the *Erith Observer* about a need for more people to join the Auxiliary Fire Service. I made enquiries at Erith fire station and they said it would be possible for me to fit my shifts around working here. That's if you approve?'

Betty thought for a moment. She was thrilled that she wouldn't be losing Freda completely. 'Why, I think that's an admirable idea but I don't want you wearing yourself out. You still help out at the Brownies, as well as giving Ruby a hand around the house.'

'I feel I'd be able to cope, if you agree ... ?' Freda held her breath as Betty considered the situation.

Betty thought for a moment longer. 'No, I don't think it would work.'

Freda's face fell. 'But ... '

Betty raised her hand, silencing Freda. 'It would be better if you reduced your hours here; that way you could concentrate more on being a firewoman. We could always reconsider the arrangement at a later date.'

Freda could have hugged the rather stern woman sitting in front of her. So many of the staff were slightly afraid of the temporary manager of Woolworths, but Freda and her friends had got to know Betty Billington quite well since the Christmas of 1938 when she'd first hired them. Although they always called her Miss Billington in front of other staff she preferred to be called Betty in private. 'Thank you ... oh, thank you, Betty. I'll work extra hard when I'm here to make up for my lost hours. I promise.'

Betty smiled at the young girl. It was hard to believe how shy and timid Freda had been when she first joined the company. 'Now, one more thing before I send you back to the shop floor. I assume you will be working some late shifts?'

'Yes, I believe I will and of course there will be times when I'm working late due to any fires that have to be put out. Is that a problem?'

Betty dug into one of her desk drawers and pulled out a key. 'I don't like the idea of you walking through the streets late at night. Here is a key to my house. Now, I live only yards from the fire station so you're welcome to come to my home and sleep there. But please discuss this with Ruby as I'd hate her to be up all night fretting when you don't arrive home after a shift. In fact, why not tell her you will always stay with me when you have to work late at the fire station?'

Freda rushed around the large wooden desk and hugged her friend. 'Betty, you don't know what this means to me. Thank you. Oh, thank you.'

'It's wonderful to get you to myself for a few hours,' Alan said, putting his arm around his wife's shoulders as they settled back to watch the Pathé News before the main feature started.

'Perhaps we should think about finding our own place, Alan, then we can be together more often,' Sarah said as she snuggled as close as she could, given there was an armrest between them.

Alan stared ahead at the cinema screen and remained silent.

'Alan?'

'What about my mother? Would it be fair to leave her alone in her house while we have air raids and black-outs?'

Sarah had a feeling that Alan might mention Maureen. 'We could find somewhere close by. I've heard there is a house to rent about twelve doors up from her in Crayford Road, so we would be very close by in case something should happen.' She longed to create a cosy home for Alan and their daughter and after over two years of marriage the longing was growing stronger day by day.

Alan shook his head. 'No. I'd then be worrying about two households – three if you count your nan's house. I can't do that while concentrating on flying.'

'But, Alan, you are on the ground more than in the air now you are teaching new pilots. Whatever do you mean? What are you saying?'

From the dim lighting in the Erith Odeon Sarah could see the firm line of her husband's jaw as he continued to stare ahead at the screen. 'Alan, please speak to me.'

'There's nothing to discuss. I'm simply thinking ahead. It's something I've been taught to do,' he whispered back.

'But Alan . . .'

An annoyed 'shh' from the row behind silenced Sarah as the lights went out and the film began. In the darkness Alan raised Sarah's hand to his lips and gently kissed her fingers, before squeezing her hand and holding it tight throughout the film. Everything will be fine. Alan will not leave me again, she reassured herself.

*

'*You stepped out of a dream . . .*' Alan sang as he held Sarah at arm's length then spun her around and waltzed her across the pavement in front of the Odeon and into the darkness.

'Alan, do stop it. People can still see even if there is a blackout.'

'Why shouldn't I sing to my beautiful wife? You are as beautiful as Hedy Lamarr and Lana Turner any day. You could hold your own in *Ziegfeld Girl* and any other film come to that.'

Sarah laughed and pushed him away. 'You daft thing. I'd look a right so-and-so dancing across the screen in my Woolworths uniform and holding Georgina in my arms,' she giggled.

'You can dance me off my feet any day, young man,' cackled an elderly lady who passed them by with her friends, who all joined in with the friendly banter.

Sarah playfully punched her husband on his chest. 'See, people can see us even in the dark. It must be all those carrots we eat.'

Alan took her hand and pulled her down the side road of the cinema and into an alley before wrapping his arms around his young wife. 'They can't see us now,' he murmured before claiming her lips.

Sarah closed her eyes and enjoyed her husband's embrace. They had so little time together these days. She felt as though they were courting once again and revelled in the memories and the thrill of those first fleeting kisses when they met back in 1938. She felt the roughness of Alan's RAF jacket on her face as the kiss ended and he held her close.

'I do love you, Sixpenny,' he murmured into her hair. 'To me you are more wonderful than any film star on the silver screen.'

Sarah smiled to herself. Alan had never forgotten the nickname he gave her the very first time they'd met when she was applying for the job of saleslady and Alan was still a trainee manager. In fact, she still wore a silver sixpence on a chain around her neck, a gift from Alan when he returned to her after many months apart when she felt she'd lost him forever. She stood on tiptoes to kiss him as a torchlight shone on them.

'Time to be on your way home,' a familiar voice said in a formal voice.

Sarah and Alan both blinked to make out who was speaking. As the torch beam was lowered they could see it was Sergeant Jackson. Sarah was so embarrassed to think their family friend had found them in a compromising situation. 'Hello, Sergeant Jackson,' was all she could think to say.

'Why, Mr and Mrs Gilbert, taking the air, I presume? I'll bid you goodnight.' Nodding his head and giving Alan a wink, he went on his way.

Sarah giggled as Alan took her hand and they headed towards Maureen Gilbert's house in nearby Crayford Road.

'It's not as glamorous as the *Ziegfeld Girl*, but Mum will have the milk on for our cocoa and no doubt our darling daughter will still be awake.'

'It sounds wonderful to me,' Sarah said as she hurried to keep up with Alan's long strides. 'By the way, Judy Garland . . .'

Alan stopped and looked down at his wife. 'What do you mean, Judy Garland?'

'If I had to be a film star, I'd rather be Judy Garland and sing "*I'm always chasing rainbows*", just like she did in the film.'

'Then never stop chasing them,' Alan said as he kissed the tip of her nose before they hurried home.

'Nan, is Mr Jackson here?' Sarah asked as she let herself in, using the key tied to a string and hung inside the letter box of number thirteen. After hours on her feet serving customers, she was relieved that her nan's house was only two streets away from Pier Road and Woolworths. For a while Ruby Caselton had removed the key, as she had feared Hitler's soldiers would invade and find a way to break into her home. However, when she had become shut out of her own home after forgetting to put a key in her bag, she had decided to risk a visiting German and replaced the key, leaving the handle to an old broom behind the door so she could see off unwelcome visitors.

Ruby looked up from where she was rolling out pastry for a pie topping. It was much thinner than her usual offerings as the pie had to be big enough to feed six people. She'd offered a meal to Bob Jackson and his son, Mike, and Freda and Betty would be round once Woolworths had closed for the day. 'He's up the garden putting in some broad beans. I said I could cope with doing that but he wouldn't listen. He's a good man. What do you want to see him about?'

Sarah shrugged her shoulders. 'Something and nothing,'

she replied, stepping out of the open back door and winding her way down the garden to where Bob Jackson was forking over a pile of compost.

Ruby frowned. There was something afoot there. She could feel it in her water.

'Hello, Sarah. If you've come to give me a hand, you're too late,' he said with a grin as he pointed to the neat vegetable patch.

I'm sorry, Bob. If I'd known you were helping Nan out, I'd have come over earlier. Maureen is looking after Georgina, so I thought I'd make the most of the opportunity and pop round to have a few words with you. Sergeant Jackson said you were here.'

Bob Jackson put down the garden fork and leant against a nearby fence. He looked at the young woman, who at that moment wore a serious frown. He had a soft spot for Ruby's granddaughter, but then, just like her nan, she had a steely glint of determination in her eye along with a cheery disposition, so what wasn't to like?

'Do you have a problem, Sarah?'

Sarah chewed her lip. 'Not really a problem, Bob, but I was thinking of volunteering to be an air raid precaution warden. I've heard they take women, but I wasn't sure what the procedure was and if I'd be good enough. I thought I'd ask you for advice as I know you run the local unit.'

Bob thought for a moment before speaking. He was aware that many people would have an opinion on whether Sarah had the time to be an ARP warden, which could be a dangerous job. 'What does your husband think about this idea of yours?'

Sarah's cheeks turned bright red and she looked a little ashamed. 'I've not spoken to him yet.'

Bob tutted. 'Perhaps. . .'

Sarah interrupted the old man. 'Please don't think I'm going behind Alan's back. I didn't want to talk to him about it until I knew if it was something I was capable of doing . . . and if they'd accept me,' she added quickly.

Bob nodded his head. 'I can see the sense in that. Let's sit down for a few minutes and I'll give you an idea of what we get up to. You do understand that being an ARP warden can be hard work and at times traumatic?'

Sarah nodded her head so hard her shiny chestnut-coloured hair bounced on her shoulders. 'I'm not afraid of hard work, Bob, and I know I could see some awful sights. I've heard about the injured and those who lose their lives and how the ARP wardens have to dig people out with their bare hands at times. I'm not saying I won't be scared and upset, but it wouldn't affect the way I worked. I'd give it my best shot,' she said with a defiant tilt of her chin.

'I'm sure you would, my girl. Now, sit yourself down on this bench and let's have a chat,' Bob said as he patted the wooden seat next to him and Sarah sat down quickly, keen to learn all she could. She knew she would have opposition from Alan, so needed to find out all there was to know about being an ARP warden if she was to convince her husband.

'Apart from wearing a rather smart helmet with a W on the front, you get to shout a lot,' Bob said with a grin. 'Do you think you can do that?'

Sarah laughed. 'Do you mean, PUT THAT LIGHT OUT?' she bellowed.

Bob clapped his hands together. 'Spot on, love, you'll do well.'

'Come on, Bob, there's more to being an ARP warden than that. What else would I have to do and would I have to give up my part-time job at Woolworths? Please don't think I don't like my job at Woolies but, like everyone else, I want to play my part in bringing this war to an end. When I think what my Alan's been through and all I've done is serve behind a counter and give birth to Georgina, it doesn't seem enough.'

'There's some what would say that's more than enough. I'd be glad to have you on my shift for as many hours as you can spare.'

Sarah flung her arms around the old man's neck as Ruby appeared from the kitchen wiping her hands on a tea towel. 'Whatever was all that shouting? I could have sworn someone bellowed "Put that light out" when it's only mid-afternoon.'

'It was Sarah here,' Bob said as he untangled himself from the younger woman's arms. 'I've agreed she can join my shift and train to become an ARP warden. That's if the Labour Exchange agree. You'll have to register with them, you know.' He directed his words to Sarah, who was now watching her grandmother's face.

'Don't look at me like that, Nan. You know we've all got to pull our weight. Why, you've joined the WVS and look at all you have to do.'

'I don't have a young child to care for or a husband who could fly off anytime with the RAF. What if something was to happen to you? What would Alan and Georgina do without you?'

'Oh, Nan, Alan's safe now he is a flying instructor at Gravesend airfield and there are plenty of family around to care for Georgie while I'm on duty.'

'That wasn't what I was saying and well you know it. You could be killed at any time. Why, the ARP wardens are the last down the public shelters and they are often the first to help the injured and the dying. You've not thought this through properly. Why not join the WVS with me?'

Sarah wrinkled her nose. 'No offence, Nan, I'm no good at what you do and I'd find it boring serving tea and organizing jumble sales. No, I want some excitement.'

Ruby went a little red in the face. 'Excitement? I'll let you know there's more to the WVS than tea and jumble and well you know it.'

Sarah looked shamefaced. 'Sorry, Nan, I got carried away. I know you work hard with Vera and the other ladies.'

Ruby nodded but wasn't convinced. 'If you want some excitement, you can get yourself down the garden and stop Nelson digging up Bob's compost heap and then you can get the tin bath and give him a good scrub. I'm not having him in the house. He'll stink the place out.'

Sarah rushed down the garden calling out to Ruby's dog, who by this time was wriggling on his back amongst the rotting garden waste.

'Sorry, Ruby, the girl was so enthusiastic it was all I could do to tell her what the job entailed,' Bob said, looking shamefaced.

'You're not to blame, Bob,' Ruby said, patting him on the shoulder. 'When that girl sets her mind on something there's no talking to her. She reminds me very much of her grandad.' She smiled to herself at the memory of Eddie Caselton.

'It's good to be reminded, Ruby. My Mike reminds me of his mother at times. It can be a comfort.'

'It can at that, Bob, but I think sometimes we should move on. There's no good dwelling in the past all the time. Now, how about you scrub your hands clean in the kitchen sink and I'll put the kettle on? It won't be long before everyone arrives for their tea and I'm nowhere near ready.'

Bob rose to his feet and stretched his aching back. 'I'll give you a hand. You can rely on me, Ruby,' he said as he followed her into the house.

Freda bounced into the kitchen with a bright smile on her face and headed to the sink to wash her hands.

'You look full of the joys of spring considering you've been on your feet since this morning,' Ruby said as she nudged her aside to strain a large pan of cabbage through a colander. 'What's made you so chirpy and where is Betty?'

'She's following on. There was a telephone call just as she was leaving Woolworths so I rushed on ahead to give you my news.'

Ruby held her breath for a moment. Whatever Freda's news was she had a bad feeling about it. 'You've not gone and joined up, have you?' she asked, trying hard not to look worried. 'You might set about mashing those spuds before they get cold.'

Freda rolled up her sleeves and set to with the large pan of potatoes. 'I have in a way. I'm going to join the Auxiliary Fire Service. I've completed the forms and handed them in at Erith fire station. They reckon I'll get taken on there as an auxiliary. Isn't that wonderful?'

Ruby huffed as she dolloped large spoonfuls of cabbage onto six plates. 'You think it's wonderful? I think it's foolhardy. What about Woolworths? You've a good job there and you want to throw it away fighting fires? Why, you could be killed.'

'I won't be allowed to fight fires, Ruby. Only fully trained females can do that. I'm part of the auxiliary service who do the backup work, but I'm sure it will still be hard work and I won't be leaving Woolworths.'

Ruby stopped what she was doing and stared at the young girl. 'Well, I'll be blowed. How you can be a fireman and a shop assistant at the same time? Giving up sleeping, are you?'

Freda giggled. 'No, Betty has said I can work part-time at Woolies and fit my hours around my fire duties. That's part-time as well, but I may be working night shifts at the fire station.'

Ruby sighed. 'Life was so much easier when you girls just worked at Woolworths and I knew you'd all be home for your tea. Nowadays I have no idea what's happening. Even with our Sarah living with her mother-in-law, I like to know she's home and safe . . . well, as safe as you can be with Hitler trying to kill us all. I'll be glad when this bloody war's over.'

Freda put down the potato masher and went round the table to hug her landlady. 'Oh, Ruby, we all want this war to finish. That's why we are doing our best to join in and help it along. I promise I'll be careful and Betty was going to speak to you about that, but I'll tell you now as you are upset. As I'll be occasionally finishing my shifts quite late, she has offered me a bed so as not to be wandering the streets of Erith late at night or have you sitting up worrying about me. With her house being only yards from the fire station it seems ideal. However, I'm worried you'll be on your own at times. What do you think?'

'Oh, I'm just a daft so-and-so getting so upset. Betty's offer of a bed is very good of her. Of course I don't want you wandering in the blackout at the dead of night. As for me, I'll lock the doors and have my trusty frying pan to hand in case anyone breaks in. I'm capable of getting myself down the Anderson shelter if the sirens start. I may even see more of Sarah if she becomes an ARP warden, as she'll be working just up the road a bit. If truth be told, I'm a little envious of you girls with all your get up and go.'

Freda laughed. 'No one will approach you if you have that pan in your hand. Why, I still can't believe how you bashed that crook over the head and rescued our Lenny. Are you sure you are all right with me joining the Fire Service? If I don't join something, there's the likelihood I'll get drafted into the services or sent for munitions work. I'm old enough for that. If Burndept's hadn't burnt down, I'd probably still be there now, and between you and me, it wasn't nice work. I'd have stuck it out, though,' she added quickly.

Ruby patted the young woman on the back. 'I know you would have, love. I'm right proud of you all. It's just that I'm getting that bit older and don't like change. Now, let's get this food on the plates before it gets cold. They'll all be banging on the door soon and we won't be ready.' Ruby returned to dishing up the vegetables, feeling just a little lonely and thinking she ought to do something more towards the war effort.

4

George scratched his chin thoughtfully. His only wish was to have a quiet hour to himself while he read his newspaper before heading into work, but his mother had started chatting as she cleaned the kitchen. 'Cornwall's a long way off when you're worrying about someone, Mum. Why didn't you have a chat with Pat while she was here visiting John?'

Ruby sighed and thought for a moment. 'Because I didn't get the chance, that's why, George. With so many people coming and going, this house is like Charing Cross station at times,' Ruby said as she sat down at the kitchen table. 'I've never even got time to think some days. The one time we were alone she danced around my questions like I don't know what and before I knew it she'd left Slades Green without even a goodbye. Didn't even tell me how she got on with that husband of hers.'

'Now you know that's not true,' George said, taking his pipe from his pocket and starting to fill it with tobacco from a leather pouch. 'Our Pat popped her head in before she left for the train station. In fact, if you recall, I walked her there myself and carried her case.

She reckoned, depending on bombing raids, it would take her nigh on a day to get back to the farm. More if the train is stopped because of air raids. Would you want to travel for that long and to a place you've never visited? To my knowledge you've never left Kent in your entire life.'

Ruby ignored her son's jibes about her being a home bird. Why, she'd been to London a few times with Sarah and her friends to see the shows, and hadn't she been down the Thames on the Sawyer family's paddle steamer to the seaside at Southend? That must have been outside of Kent, surely? 'Did Pat say anything to you about what's eating her? You've got to admit she's not the same girl who left here a couple of years back. You mark my words, George, there something not right in our Pat's world.'

George sighed to himself. He knew his mother of old and once she had something wedged in her mind there was no talking to her. 'She was full of how much it meant to see her John again and how she'd be pleased to get back to the farm in Cornwall to see her children.' George didn't let on that he agreed that his younger sister was not telling all of what was on her mind. He'd put it down to the war and how it was changing people, but he wouldn't let on to Ruby that he was worried or she'd be like a terrier with a juicy bone. 'I'll put my thinking cap on, Mum, and see how we can have you chat to Pat on the telephone so you can put your mind at rest. Now, I'm going to sit out in the garden and smoke my pipe. I have some paperwork to read before I go into work.'

Ruby nodded. Her George was a hard worker and she could tell from the greyness around his eyes that the job he did was preying on his mind. Whatever his work was, she knew it was important to the war effort. No doubt once he and Irene had moved up here from Devon he'd be working even longer hours, but at least he wouldn't have all that travelling every other week.

'You go have your smoke while it's quiet. I promise not to go on about our Pat.' She grimaced as she heard someone pull the key on its string through the letter box and the front door being opened.

'Cooee, it's only me, Ruby, and you'll never guess what's happened?' she heard Vera from up the road announce in a flustered breath.

'You best hop it into the garden or she'll have you involved before you know it,' Ruby told George. She needn't have spoken as her son had already seized his cup of tea and briefcase and was hurrying out of the back door.

'So you see, I'm in a right two and eight, Ruby,' Vera declared as she took the official-looking letter back from her friend.

'I just can't have strangers living in my home,' she said sadly. 'I did tell them our Sadie would be home someday and she wouldn't take kindly to having had someone we don't know sleeping in her bedroom. She's particular about things like that.'

And don't we know it, Ruby thought to herself. Not a day goes past without Vera proudly announcing another of her granddaughter's foibles as if they were gifts from above.

'I wondered if your George could have a word with someone in authority?'

'I'm not sure someone who works at Vickers in engineering has any clout with the government, even if his work is valued. Did I tell you that George and Irene are moving back up this way?' Ruby added, trying to change the subject.

Vera was having none of it. 'Then Maisie's David, he has an important job. It's well known that he had a finger in finding out what had happened to Alan when his plane went down.'

'I doubt whether the RAF can help you, Vera, even if you had the whole of the Luftwaffe sleeping in your back bedroom.'

'But there's no room in my Anderson shelter. What if we have another air raid? The person may get there before me and I'd be blown to kingdom come in my own garden! It's just not right of them men in parliament to tell us to take in strangers. I could be killed in my own bed. Goodness knows who they will send to Alexandra Road,' she wailed.

'Your shelter's the same size as mine and if ours can hold the family, then so can yours; not that we've needed to use them these past few weeks. No, I'm afraid you're just going to have to do your bit for the war and take in some paying guests, Vera. Some people are having a worse war than we are and it's only fair we do our bit.' Ruby was getting annoyed with her friend. She knew that Vera was decent in so many ways, but when she got the bit between her teeth there was no letting up.

Vera was thinking. 'Paying guests, you say? I hadn't looked at it that way. My Sadie will just have to bunk in with me if she comes to visit and she'll have to realize that we all have to play our part. I'll write a few words to Mr Churchill and say I'm more than willing to help out under the circumstances and suggest he sends me a couple of genteel ladies who have fallen on hard times . . . but not so hard that they can't pay their rent. I'm glad I thought of that,' she said, rising to her feet. 'Well, I can't sit here nattering all day long. Some of us have war work to do.'

That put me in my place, Ruby thought with a grin as she saw her neighbour to the front door. 'Don't forget we have WVS duties this afternoon. There's fresh clothing needs sorting as well as umpteen other jobs.'

'I'll knock for you on my way down,' Vera called back.

'I'm sure you will,' Ruby muttered to no one in particular. You don't miss a chance to feather your own nest, Vera Munro, she thought, you never have.

Freda had no sooner stepped inside the crumbling building that was Erith fire station and climbed the rickety stairs to where the office and a staffroom were situated when she was issued with her orders for the day from the officer in charge. He was sitting at a small wooden desk set beside a large window, from which could be observed two fire tenders ready to head out whenever a call came from the concerned public. Freda took a deep breath. She could just about catch the smell of straw from when the horses, which used to pull the old tender, had their feed stored in this very loft of the old fire station building in Cross Street.

'Now then, young Freda, there's a pile of papers on that desk that need filing away, but first you can put the kettle on and make a nice cuppa for the shift.'

Freda nodded her head and set to with her duties. She had been with the Fire Service for one week and was becoming more concerned by the hour as to how her filing paperwork and making copious amounts of tea could help win the war. The past two years had seen rationing introduced and, along with the rest of the household, she'd more than done her bit to put food on the table that was filling and nutritious. Even visiting the cinema there were tips and recipes which Freda and her friends took home to Ruby to try out. Not all were a success, but they were eaten nonetheless as food wastage was now a criminal offence. She'd closed her ears to the jokes about young girls like her working for the Service and soldiered on despite her disappointment. She'd had hopes of doing something worthwhile, but instead was bored out of her mind and, more to the point, had cut her hours at Woolworths at a time when Betty was worried about a lack of staff. So many of the younger women who'd not joined up had gone into the factories where the pay was so much better, as were the perks. Only last week George had regaled them with news of the lunchtime concert at Vickers in Crayford, where he'd seen his favourite comedian, Tommy Trinder, perform live to the factory workers. It had certainly boosted morale. If she could have turned out a tune and looked as pretty as Maisie or Sarah, she'd have joined ENSA and spent her time entertaining the workers or even travelling overseas with a variety show to entertain the troops.

As she dreamt of singing her heart out like Vera Lynn and bringing a tear to the eye of the soldiers who were missing their loved ones, the large black Bakelite telephone started to ring. Without thinking, she reached out and picked up the heavy receiver. 'Erith fire station, how may I help you?'

'Now that's a voice I haven't heard before,' a cheery woman said as Vera picked up a pen ready to take down any information.

'I'm Freda, part-time auxiliary and tea girl,' she replied before silently scolding herself. The woman might have an important job and not be impressed with what Freda had just said.

'Not another one. We lost the last girl to the navy when she found out she wouldn't be putting out fires. You've got to stick to your guns and not let the old boys leave you with the housekeeping duties. I bet you've got a pile of papers to tidy, haven't you?'

'Yes, and the kettle's about to boil and I've yet to wash the cups from the last round. I reckon they leave the washing up for when I arrive.'

'Chin up, ducks, and don't let them get to you. You should find a stack of papers I sent to your fire station giving details of worthwhile jobs for women in the Service. I doubt the old codgers have filed them away as we both know that's not a job they think of as men's work.

If you come across something you feel you are suited to, then telephone me. My name's Enid Roberts.'

Freda was thrilled to think she wasn't just being selfish and that at least one other woman had felt as she did. 'Thank you, Enid, I'll do just that. Thank goodness I answered the telephone when it rang.'

'I take it they don't let you do that often either?' the woman laughed.

'No, it's far too important for the likes of me. I'm supposed to call someone to tell them it's ringing. You'd think I'd never seen a telephone before, let alone know what to say. Why, I'm always taking important calls at Woolworths when I help the manager in her office,' she said with a small laugh. It wouldn't do to be moaning too much to someone she'd not met. They'd think she was a right misery guts. 'Is there something I can help you with?'

Enid laughed. 'That's me all over. I chat that much I forget to convey the message. There's a dispatch rider due to arrive at your station soon. Can you ask her to get in touch as there's something needs collecting and brought back here.'

Freda dutifully noted down the telephone number and put a copy of it into the pocket of her skirt before bidding goodbye to Enid. A female dispatch rider, how exciting! That's a job she'd love to try her hand at. She quickly made a tray of tea and took it outside to where uniformed firemen were busy polishing the brass on the fire engines. The vehicles that were present at fires and the aftermath of air raids in Erith and the surrounding areas gleamed in the sunshine. Freda could see her face in the bodywork. Hurrying back inside, she began sorting the pile of paperwork with renewed vigour and gave out a whoop of delight when she came across a box containing information about working in different sections of the Fire Service.

Freda slipped a few of the leaflets, aimed at women workers, into her gas mask case to read later. In a happier frame of mind, she continued with the duties that had been assigned to her for that day.

It was quiet in the yard of the fire station when, an hour later, Freda heard the powerful roar of a motorcycle. There was no one else there as all the on-duty staff were now out attending a serious fire down near the docks. She slipped out of the office and headed downstairs to where a woman, no older than herself, was removing her helmet and shaking out her jet-black shoulder-length hair. Freda marvelled that the woman still had perfectly painted red lips.

'Hello there, I was told you were on your way. It's only me here at the moment. Do you have time for a cup of tea? There's a fresh supply of biscuits as well. They won't last long once everyone gets back here.'

'Thanks awfully, darling, a cup of cha would just about hit the spot. Lead on!' she replied in a plummy voice.

Freda showed the woman up the stairs to the staff-room, where a kettle was bubbling away on top of a small gas stove ready for when the workers arrived back from fighting the flames. 'I'm Freda, by the way. I've only been a volunteer for a couple of weeks. How long have you been riding your motorbike?' she asked as she held out her hand.

'Barbara Grosvenor,' the other woman said, pumping Freda's hand up and down with a firm grip. 'The amount of bruises I have on my you-know-where, it feels like I've been riding for a year when in truth it's just one week since I've been out of training school.'

Freda looked wistful. 'I'd love to do something worth-while. How do you become a dispatch rider?'

'Like most things connected to this war, I filled out a form and never looked back. Thanks awfully,' she said as Freda placed a mug of hot tea next to where she'd sat down and offered a tin of biscuits for Barbara to dip into.

'As simple as that?' Freda said dreamily, her imagin-ation already placing her astride a bike with the wind in her hair as she delivered important information that would help win the war.

'It helps if you can ride a motorbike,' Barbara pointed out, bursting Freda's bubble in just a couple of words.

'Oh,' Freda mumbled, disappointment showing all over her face. 'That's put paid to that idea!'

'Don't be so despondent. Surely you have someone who can show you how to ride one? I grew up with four brothers so I mucked in with what they did and became a bit of a tomboy. Riding a motorcycle was part of my life once my older brother built his own.'

Freda thought hard. 'My brother, Lenny, is in the navy and only ever had a second-hand pushbike. My best friend's husband has a motorbike, he calls it Bessie,' she added with a grin, 'but she's been put away for the dur-ation.'

'Have a word with him. It's not hard to learn. Just stay on and steer the machine in a straight line and bob's your uncle, you'll be an auxiliary dispatch rider in no time.'

Freda nodded in agreement. Barbara's advice seemed straightforward enough. Yes, she'd do just that and the firefighters of Erith could make their own tea. She was going to follow her dream and there was no stopping her. As long as Alan agreed to show her how to ride his beloved Bessie, that was.

'Why, it's the first time in an age since I've seen the three of you here together.' Betty smiled as she walked into the Woolworths staffroom and found Sarah, Maisie and Freda taking their break together.

'Aint it just?' Maisie said with grin. 'And with Maureen behind the counter serving up decent grub it's just like the old days when we started work together.'

'Not quite the old days, Maisie,' Betty replied with a hint of sadness. 'Back then I didn't have to think of window displays to rally support for the war and Woolworths' own Spitfire campaign.'

Sarah glanced at Maisie. She may be cracking jokes as usual but she doesn't fool me, she thought to herself. A bit of rouge and an extra layer of powder didn't quite cover her pale expression and the shadows under her eyes. She wished Maisie would talk about her fears of not having a baby. What she'd mentioned the day that Vera upset her had shocked Sarah. Did Maisie mean she'd been a good-time girl? She needed to sort this out before Maisie had a breakdown or it caused a rift with her new husband, David. The last thing Maisie needed was to lose another husband.

Betty collected a cup of coffee from Maureen and joined the girls.

Sarah wrinkled her nose. 'Ew, Camp Coffee, how can you drink that stuff?'

'I've come to enjoy the taste. It makes a change from tea but, if truth be known, I'd kill for a decent cup of coffee.'

'I'll have a word with my friends on the docks,' Maisie said with a wink.

Betty looked more than a little horrified, but Sarah noticed that she didn't refuse the offer. The war had certainly changed people's views of what was right and wrong. Goodness knows how many times she'd heard customers say that, if it didn't hurt anyone, it was all right to have something on the black market.

'Now, while I have you all together, I wondered if we could put some thought to our window displays? I feel it is important we continue to raise money towards the war effort without rattling collecting tins under our customers' noses. If we could possibly make the display entertaining and raise morale, all the better. I've been offered the loan of a wing from a damaged Spitfire. Do you think we could make use of this for a display?'

Maisie was thinking hard. 'P'raps we could add straw and some of our gardening tools, along with packets of seeds and stuff, to make it look like the plane came down in the countryside. We could 'ave a bucket to collect coins as well.'

'How does that boost morale?' Sarah asked. 'It would upset me to see it and think Alan or his comrades may have crashed.'

'I think it may have been the wing of a German aircraft now I come to think about it,' Betty said, looking confused. 'How can anyone tell the difference between all the different planes?'

'Haven't you seen the leaflets and posters showing their planes and ours?' Freda asked. 'We could have some of those in the window as well.'

'What about that poster that shows a bombed-out German Woolies with the words underneath, "If you think we're suffering, take a look at theirs." It would look good alongside the wing of that German plane?'

'This all sounds extremely positive. Thank you, girls. Please let me know if you have any other ideas. I'll speak to all the staff about this. We need a team effort to raise funds.'

'What about a dance?' Freda asked.

'What, in the shop window?' Maisie laughed.

'No, I mean what about asking if we can use the hall at the Prince of Wales and sell tickets? We could ask head office for some prizes and perhaps scrape enough together for a bit of a buffet.'

Betty thought for a moment then smiled. 'I think it's an admirable idea, Freda. Can I put the three of you in charge of organizing things?'

'Count me in as well,' Maureen called from behind her counter. 'I'm not missing out on a bit of fun.'

The girls headed back to their counters full of ideas for the dance.

'We could have spot prizes like we used to at the Woolies Christmas parties,' Freda said.

'But we need a dance band. Maureen may know who we can ask. She knows a lot of people and used to sing at dances when she was younger. Alan told me she would have been a professional if she'd not met her husband and settled down to family life.'

'Lucky her,' Maisie mumbled as they reached the door that led to the shop floor.

Sarah caught Maisie's arm and held her back from following Freda through the door. 'Can I have a word, Maisie?'

Maisie nodded her head. 'I thought you'd want to after my little outburst. It is that, isn't it?'

'Yes, I've been so worried about you, Maisie,' Sarah said as she sat on the bottom step of the stairs that led up to the office and staffroom.

Maisie squeezed onto the step next to her friend. 'I didn't mean to worry yer. It's just that I can't believe me luck being married to David and finding friends like you and Freda after everything that went on before.' Her eyes took on a distant look. 'What if me life went pear-shaped and I lost David and ended up on me own, all through something I did just to survive? I should 'ave told him but it was a long time ago . . .'

'What did happen, Maisie?' Sarah asked. She wasn't sure she wanted to know the nitty-gritty of her friend's former life but felt it would help if she unburdened herself.

'It was after I left home and earned a living working in bars and then at that cafe over Deptford way. The owner of the cafe forced 'imself on me one night when he'd had a few. He said that if I fought too much, he'd have me out on the street by the morning and tell folk I'd been on the game.' She looked at Sarah beseechingly. 'I didn't 'ave anywhere to go. What choice did I 'ave?'

Sarah wrapped her arms around her friend as she wept silently. 'Shh, I'd have done the same and so would many other women. Men can be such bastards,' she exclaimed bitterly.

Maisie gasped. 'Why, Sarah Gilbert, I've never 'eard you say such a word.'

Sarah smiled guiltily. 'I don't ever think I've used it word before. Can it be our secret?'

Maisie nodded. 'But secrets can be our undoing. He chucked me out when he found I was in the family way.'

'Oh no,' Sarah murmured. She didn't want to hear what happened next.

'Yeah, I ended up on the street and with a bun in the oven. I got myself a live-in bar job pretty quick. The landlord took a fancy to me and before I knew it he was leaving his wife each night to visit my bed. I hated myself but I 'ad a plan, see.'

'Go on,' Sarah urged.

'I waited fer a night when he'd had a bit too much ter drink and I nicked the takings and legged it. I 'eaded out ter Woolwich dockyard where I'd heard about a woman who helped girls like me. Mind you, I walked out of her place with me 'ead held high, determined to make a fresh start, and I never gave it another thought until recently. I met my first 'usband, Joe, not long afterwards.

I reckon losing our baby last Christmas was God's way of punishing me. I'm never going to 'ave David's baby.'

As horrified as Sarah was by her friend's confession, she knew that Maisie was a good person deep down. She couldn't and wouldn't dwell on the baby. Maisie was more than suffering for what she did and who was she to judge? 'Please, Maisie, don't say such things. If God does have a hand in things, he will know what you've been through and he'll know you feel guilty enough for what has happened. Time to move on, eh?'

'But, David . . . I feel I should tell him.'

'Not now, Maisie, you've not been yourself for a few weeks. Get yourself strong again and then think about the future. Promise me?'

Maisie nodded slowly. 'I will, but it's got to be done before too long, regardless of what 'appens to me.'

'But promise, no running away if things get bad?'

Maisie nodded her head but didn't answer.

'I've been thinking about your Pat,' Bob said as he carried in a bag of vegetables he'd collected from the allotment he shared with the Caselton family. Ruby had been more than grateful when Bob offered to take on their gardening chores. What with Freda hardly seen these days since she started her duties at the fire station and also working as many hours as possible at Woolworths, and Maisie and Sarah no longer living at number thirteen, Ruby had been finding it hard to keep playing their part in the Dig for Victory campaign. The girls, as well as

George when he had time, did give a hand, but life was so busy now the war was well into its third year.

Ruby looked into the bag that Bob had placed on the kitchen table. She would put some of the veg aside for Maureen and Maisie, she thought to herself, before moving a few items from the sink so Bob could wash his hands. 'I've done nothing but think about her, Bob. I know she never said anything, but I've a feeling so strong that something might be wrong. What if she was planning to bring them back home? I know they say that if a bomb's got our name on it we could die anywhere, but it's nigh on safer down in Cornwall than it is up here.'

Bob nodded in agreement. 'I was thinking the same as I was working on the allotment. That's when the idea hit me.'

'Well, cough it out. I can't stand here chatting all day. I've a list as long as my arm of things to do and that's without queuing for some fish for our tea.'

'I was thinking you should get yourself down to Cornwall and check things out for yourself. At least then you'd have peace of mind.'

'What? Me go all the way to Cornwall?' Ruby scoffed before frowning at Bob. 'I wouldn't even know how to get there.'

'They do have trains that go to the South West.'

'On my own you mean? Why, I don't even know my way to London. Anything north of Woolwich is a foreign land to me. Even when I'm with one of the girls, I'm that worried I'll get lost and never find my way home.'

Bob looked at Ruby. He had such admiration for the woman and was surprised to see how worried she appeared and also how vulnerable. He'd always considered her to be such a strong person and the kind of woman that would stand up to whatever was thrown her way. Even Hitler didn't stand a chance with the likes of Ruby Caselton. He was proud to know the woman and more than a little in love with her. 'There's no need for you to worry about travelling alone, Ruby.'

'Ask one of the girls, do you mean? I'm not sure they would be able to spare the time to accompany an old woman on a silly whim.'

'It's not a silly whim, Ruby. You have concerns for a member of your family and you miss your grandchildren. There is someone who could go with you and make sure you reached your destination.'

Ruby screwed her face up as she considered who it could be. 'I suppose I could go to Devon with George and then travel from there. It's not so far, is it? No, I don't mean to sound ungrateful, but I'm not so sure I could live under the same roof as my daughter-in-law for too long. Why, she might take me to that golf club she's always going on about and introduce me to her posh friends. No, I couldn't be doing with that.'

Bob laughed. 'Oh, Ruby, you'd be a breath of fresh air to your Irene's friends, but I agree, it's not my cup of tea either. Besides, George and Irene's home is still over a hundred miles from where your Pat and the kids are staying. No, I thought I'd be the right person to accompany you and make sure you reach your destination in one piece . . . and get home again,' he added with a smile.

Ruby was pulled up short by Bob's suggestion. She needed time to think. Picking up the used cups and saucers, she placed them in the sink and poured the remaining hot water from the kettle onto the crockery. 'I couldn't ask you to do that for me, Bob. Why, you are as busy as the girls, what with you ARP work and helping out down the police station. You said yourself that once a copper, always a copper, and your Mike relies on you for help with them being so short staffed. Then there's the gardening and we mustn't forget your work with the Home Guard. Didn't you say there were going to be some special manoeuvres before too long?'

He shrugged his shoulders. 'Even in wartime people deserve a holiday, Ruby. You'd be safe travelling with a man and I'd never forgive myself if you or one of the girls came to harm when I'm able to accompany you,' Bob said softly.

Ruby sat back down deep in thought as she wiped her hands on the hem of her apron. 'It does make sense, Bob, but I'm not sure we'd get much of a holiday. I'd be down there and back in a couple of days. I only want to make sure those children are happy and give them a big hug. I miss them so much.'

Bob reached across and squeezed her hand. 'You must do. I was the same with our Michael when he was up here in the thick of things and I was down in Margate. We always will worry about our kith and kin. It is only natural.'

'But you was the one who was bombed out. Alexandra Road has survived so far.'

'Do you think the Luftwaffe would dare drop explosives on Ruby Caselton?' Bob joked, trying to lighten the mood. 'However, you do know you'll be gone longer than a few days? It will take that just to get yourself down to Cornwall.'

Ruby shook her head slowly. 'I had no idea. There was me thinking I'd pop down there and see my Pat and then catch the next train home.'

'Do you have a map?' Bob asked. 'If not, I have one at home you could look at.'

Ruby thought for a moment before going to the sideboard and opening one of the polished mahogany doors. 'I thought so. I've still got our George's geography books from when he was at school.' She pulled out a shabby atlas with a broken spine and laid it in front of Bob. 'Cornwall must be in there somewhere.'

Bob flicked through the pages until he came across a map of England. Pointing to north Kent and then to Margate, he looked up at Ruby, who was peering over his shoulder. 'Can you see the distance between where we are now and where Margate is?'

'It's no more than half an inch,' Ruby whispered. 'Who'd have thought that? Why, it took a good couple of hours to travel to Margate when we used to go on the paddle steamer down the Thames on our days trips. Now, show me where Cornwall is.'

Bob pointed to the most western county in the country. 'It doesn't help that Pat is on the Lizard Peninsula, which is the southernmost point of England. It'll take days to get there, especially if we have to travel through bombing raids and on damaged train lines. It's a shame we can't drive down, but with petrol almost unobtainable it's nigh on impossible.'

'I'd not wish to waste petrol on visiting family even if

we could get hold of it, Bob. The war comes first in this household.'

Bob nodded in agreement. 'We could get there by train. Many trains. Let me be your companion, Ruby. I'd feel a lot happier that you were in safe hands.'

'I'll give it some thought, Bob. Thank you for thinking of my safety. It's a great comfort to me. Now, I need to dash off to the fishmonger and see what I can get for our tea.' She patted Bob on the shoulder. 'You're a good man, Bob Jackson, and a good friend to this family.'

'More than a friend, I hope, Ruby,' he said as he got to his feet and reached for his overcoat. 'I'll wait for your answer but don't take too long as you never know what Hitler's got up his sleeve next.'

Bob was thoughtful as he left number thirteen. He decided to check up on travel routes and what was happening in the South West of England, as the last thing he wanted to do was to take Ruby into danger. That's if she agreed to him being her companion. He dearly hoped she would.

5

'There's another pile of clothing over there that needs sorting, Vera. If you come across any bedding, can you put it to one side? We have two families who've been bombed out and are in urgent need of any household items we can lay our hands on. I'm thinking bedding comes pretty near the top of the list. I know I'd want a bed if nothing else if I was bombed out of my home,' Ruby said as she stopped to wipe her brow. It might only be May but already the days were becoming warmer.

Vera had been no help as she moped about. 'I'll get around to it soon, Ruby. I'm not feeling my best today.'

Ruby stopped what she was doing and placed her hands on her hips. 'Now look here, Vera Munro, if everyone was as much use as you are today, we'd soon lose this war. Stop being such a limp lettuce and get working. The sooner our work is done, the sooner we can go home,' Ruby said. She had no time for people who couldn't turn their hand to helping others. Looking around her, she could see fellow Women's Voluntary Service members hard at work going through donated items for those less fortunate due to this awful war. It was warm in the old church hall and with so many piles of unwashed clothing, as well as a few hot helpers, there was an odour it was hard not to turn her nose up at. In the corner a tea urn was bubbling away ready for a tea break and Ruby was more than in need of a drink. When that was done there would be a meeting to go over duties for the rest of the week. Life was never quiet in the WVS and she'd have it no other way. They all had to play their part and the only one not doing that was Vera.

'I've received another letter,' Vera said as she picked up a pillowcase from a pile of donated items and wrinkled her nose as she checked it over. 'I've been told in no uncertain terms that I have to take in two evacuees whether I like it or not. No amount of me explaining how I've more than done my bit for the war effort could convince them that my home was not the place for strangers. Why, even telling them I was a leading light of our local WVS couldn't sway them.'

Ruby tried hard not to snort with laughter and had to turn away for a moment to compose herself. 'They most likely thought you were the kind of person to make someone welcome in their hour of need due to your work in the WVS,' she suggested.

Vera visibly brightened. 'I'd agree with that, Ruby. No one's more welcoming than me,' she said, throwing the pillowcase into a box marked for rags.

'Good afternoon, ladies, 'ave I caught you shirking yer duties?'

Ruby looked up to see Maisie with two bulging bags. 'Chance would be a fine thing, love. Vera here was just saying how she was looking forward to welcoming two evacuees into her home.'

'What, they're evacuating people here? I thought they sent the 'omeless to the countryside, not to Vera's.'

Ruby burst out laughing. Maisie was a real tonic after having worked with Vera for a few hours. The two women usually ticked along together fine, but when Vera had one of her moods on her time could drag on forever. 'I suppose these would be adults who have lost their homes. Does it say much in the letter, Vera?' Maisie asked.

Vera pulled the letter from her pocket and passed it to her. 'Check it for me, love, I'm rather busy at the moment.'

Maisie grinned at Ruby before scanning the letter quickly. 'Doesn't give much away 'ere, Vera. You'll have to wait and see what turns up, won't yer?'

Vera nodded thoughtfully. 'Knowing the top-secret job our Sadie does, it'll probably be someone important. They'll need somewhere respectable to place people like that.'

'You could be right, Vera. What have you got for us today, Maisie?' Ruby said as she looked at the bags Maisie placed on the table.

'This bag has items of clothing. There are a few women's skirts as well as children's dresses and some overalls fer smaller boys. The other bag is full of scraps that were left over after I turned the clothing you gave me into useful bits and bobs. Can someone use 'em to make rag rugs?'

'Rag rugs? Now's there's a thought. They'd be just the ticket for people who are trying to set up home again after being bombed out,' Ruby said, half to herself. 'If only we knew how to make them, we could set up a group for women wanting to learn.'

'It would make a change from knitting,' Vera added as she peered into the bag of clothing and pulled out a flower-patterned skirt. 'Do you think this would fit me?' she asked, holding the skirt to her ample waist.

'Perhaps thirty years ago it would have done, Vera. Now put that skirt back where it came from. Maisie made those for women who have lost all their possessions, not for you to regain your youth.'

'I know how to make rag rugs. It's something I grew up doing. It was that or walk on bare boards in my home. If you can get hold of some sacking for the back of the rugs, it'd take no time at all to get going,' Maisie said. 'Perhaps you could start a rug-making group. There are always rags to be found.'

'Leave it with me, Maisie; I'll soon get the group up and running. Welcome to the WVS.'

Maisie was secretly delighted to be accepted and to be able to do more to help the less fortunate, but she was unsure how she could fit this into her life. She'd felt so tired of late and something was nagging at the back of her mind. She brushed it aside and smiled at Ruby. She didn't want to upset the woman who had done so much for her in the past. 'Thanks, but I'm not so sure about wearing one of them green uniforms.'

'Whoa there. Slow down a bit or you'll have me falling off!' Alan shouted above the roar of the engine of the beloved motorbike he called Bessie. 'If I'd known you would be so reckless, I'd have said no to your request,' he continued in a loud voice.

The motorbike came to a halt in front of Ruby's house and Alan climbed from the pillion seat. The driver dismounted and held on to the handlebar of the bike, unsure what to do next. 'How do you park this thing?' Freda asked as Alan wiped his brow and took control of Bessie.

'You done very well for your first attempt, girl,' Bob called from where he was watching Freda's riding lesson. 'I reckon another couple of lengths of the road and you'll have the hang of things,' he added, grinning at Alan, who looked rather pale.

'Don't encourage her, Bob,' Ruby scolded as she waved to a woman from across the road who had been peering from behind net curtains at the goings on in front of number thirteen. 'The neighbours are starting to get a bit twitchy with all the noise and shouting.'

'Tea's up,' Sarah announced as she carried a tray into the small front garden and perched it on the wall. 'How is Bessie faring?' she asked her husband. 'And more importantly, how is Freda faring?'

Alan patted the seat of his prized possession before kicking the stand lever down with his foot and leaving the bike to rest, then reaching for the much-needed tea. 'Freda is doing very well. I'm surprised how brave she is. Bessie's not so bad considering she's been covered in a tarpaulin in Mum's shed for the past couple of years. The tyres required pumping up and I needed to clean a spark plug, but she's running like a dream.'

Sarah frowned. 'I'm surprised there was any petrol.'

Glancing at Bob for help, Alan looked a little sheepish as he confessed, 'Er, I had a can hidden in the shed for emergencies . . .'

Sarah was shocked. 'Alan, really! We are not supposed to stockpile petrol. To think that's been in Maureen's shed all this time. Why, if anything had happened in an air raid the shed could have gone up in flames and taken the house with it, along with your blessed Bessie.'

Bob felt sorry for Alan. 'We all do it, Sarah love, there's no harm in a little drop here and there.'

'Not you as well, Bob Jackson. How can we win a war when men are squirrelling away petrol all over the place?' Ruby said, giving Bob a stern look. 'Don't you all realize this is part of the black market? All the time it is going on you are denying supplies to our troops and the war isn't being won.'

'Do you want me to take back the sugar I brought over this morning?' Bob said as he stirred his tea.

'I'd best take that packet of tea home as well,' Sarah said, trying hard not to smile at her nan's shocked face.

'Not you as well?' Ruby said. 'You've really shocked me, Bob and Sarah. Well, I thought you'd been brought up to be honest and not break the law.'

'Nan, I only bought a packet of tea without asking any questions. We all do it. The stuff is still coming in at the docks despite enemy action. I think of it as a perk of having friends who have friends who can lay their hands on essential items. It's not as if I stole the Crown Jewels.'

Ruby tutted loudly as she picked up the tea tray and headed indoors.

'Perhaps it's best not to mention to your nan where you get the odd packet of tea from in future, Sarah. What she don't know won't hurt her,' Bob said, noticing Sarah's glum face. 'Now, young Freda, what about showing us how you can ride up and down the road without Alan sitting behind you? Standing here drinking tea won't make you a dispatch rider for the Fire Service.'

Freda gingerly pushed the motorbike onto the road and, once seated, turned on the engine. With a quick glance back at Sarah, who gave her a thumbs up sign, she set off, keeping the bike in a straight line, until she reached the top of Alexandra Road. Turning slowly, she headed back down the road before stopping in front of number thirteen. 'I did it,' she grinned. 'Now I don't feel so bad about telling the Fire Service I can ride a motorbike. Hopefully they'll allow me to go on their training course to be a dispatch rider. Can I ride Bessie round to the fire station and show them I'm capable of attending the training course?'

Alan grimaced. 'As long as I'm riding pillion. I don't want to let Bessie out of my sight for more than a minute.'

Maisie and Sarah were enjoying a rare visit to Mitchell's tea rooms, across the road from Woolies. 'It seems an age since we've had a chat without some kind of interference. Even the Luftwaffe's behaving itself for once,' Sarah said as a waitress in her smart black dress and white frilly apron placed a pot of tea in front of them, along with a plate of rock cakes.

'Hmm, I've seen better cakes from 'ere. There were times when Mitchell's was the best place for afternoon tea in these parts,' Maisie said as she lifted one of the rock cakes and dropped it back onto the plate with a heavy thump. 'It's saying something when I could make a better effort than this and provide some better tunes as well.'

Sarah had to agree with her chum. The music being played by four elderly ladies seated in one corner of the tea room was slow and more than dreary. 'The ladies are doing their best, Maisie. Perhaps you should jump up and give them one of your songs?'

'Ter be 'onest, I don't feel up to it, Sarah. I've been like a limp lettuce these past weeks.'

'This war's dragging us all down, Maisie. What you need is a little break away from Erith. Can David take you away for the weekend?'

'It's not that. After all, many people have got it worse than me. At least I get to see my 'usband and I have a job as well as a roof over me 'ead. No, it's something else.'

Sarah held her breath for a moment, dreading what could be wrong with her friend to have her so down in the dumps. 'Whatever it is, you can tell me, Maisie. I won't say a word to anyone, I swear.'

'I've missed me monthlies fer a while and . . .'

Sarah reached across the table and grabbed her friend's hand. 'Why, that's wonderful news, Maisie. Have you been to see Doctor Greyson yet and what has David said? He must be over the moon – he will make such a wonderful father,' Sarah said as her words of happiness over her friend's news tumbled out one after the other.

Maisie looked embarrassed. 'Please don't get so excited. You're the first person I've told. After last time I don't want to make a fuss. What if it's a false alarm or something goes wrong again? I couldn't bear it . . . I just couldn't,' she said, her voice breaking into a small sob as she reached for her cigarettes with a shaking hand.

'Everything will be fine, Maisie. You weren't to blame for what happened last time. These things happen. You need to speak to Doctor Greyson first and then tell David. Make an appointment and I'll come with you. That's if you want me to?'

'I'm so frightened,' Maisie said as she lit her cigarette. 'I spoilt everyone's Christmas and disappointed David. What if it does happen again?'

'Come on now, Maisie, chin up. It wasn't to be last time and you can stop saying it spoilt our Christmas. Yes, we were sad for you and David, but as Doctor Greyson said, you are young and healthy and the babies will come along soon enough.'

Maisie nodded. 'Yer right. I was just feeling sorry for meself. I'd be grateful, though, if you would come with me to see the doc. I'll not say anything to David before I know if I'm expecting or not. You won't tell anyone, will you?'

'Of course I won't. Your secret's safe with me,' Sarah said. 'Now, let's have a cup of this tea before it becomes stewed. I don't know about you, but I'm going to attempt to eat one of these rock cakes even if they have hardly any currants and are as heavy as bricks.'

'Yer right, as usual.' Maisie smiled sadly as she reached for one of the cakes.

Sarah nodded and grinned. 'And just think, by Christmas you could have cause to be celebrating. Wouldn't that be wonderful?'

Ruby climbed the steep steps from the Anderson shelter and looked around at the dew-covered garden. The signs were there for a lovely spring day and her garden still looked a treat due to the hard work of Bob and Freda. She stretched her arms and rubbed her back. However many home comforts she added to the shelter, she remained stiff and slightly sore after a night spent in a hole in the ground. At least it had been a quiet night despite the all-clear not sounding for many hours. There was no sign of smoke clouds, so with luck no one in Erith had suffered at the hands of the Luftwaffe during the dark hours of the night. She'd found it lonely in the shelter as Freda was on duty at the fire station. Granted, she'd had Nelson down there with her, but the dog simply climbed onto the bed next to her and snored the night away. At least he would be handy to see off any rats that came from the railway line that ran from the nearby docks. Vera reckoned there were hundreds of them. Ruby wasn't sure if she'd ever get used to the knowledge that Freda was on duty when most people in the town were huddling down in the shelters waiting for the all-clear siren. If anything happened to her, she'd never forgive herself for not putting her foot down and stopping this notion of riding a motorbike. Why, that was men's work. This war had a lot to answer for. Would things ever be the same again?

Unlocking the back door, she checked that she had water flowing from the tap and filled a kettle. After an air raid there was always the worry that water or gas lines had been ruptured. Today was a good day and she prayed it was the same for others. Hearing the rattle of the letter box, she collected two envelopes and placed them on the kitchen table. One was for Freda; Ruby recognized the handwriting as that of the girl's brother, Lenny, and put it to one side. The other was from Pat. She'd make her tea and a slice of toast before settling to read what her daughter had to say. There was just about time before she started her many duties of the day. 'At least this war keeps me busy,' she said to herself.

No doubt Pat would have something to say about her travelling to Cornwall and would try to put her off attempting the long journey. Bob had looked into how they could obtain travel permits and her family was resigned to Ruby travelling across the south of England. Bob had even looked into where they could stay so they were not imposing on the farming family who had put up her daughter and children this past two years. The day before they were to leave she would send a postcard to Pat informing her they were on their way. However, there was something that played on her mind about her long journey to Cornwall with Bob. It wasn't something she could talk about with her daughter-in-law or grand-daughter or, God forbid, Vera. Perhaps Betty Billington would be the right person to advise her? Yes, she would pop into Woolworths on her way to the WVS later that afternoon after she'd tidied the house and changed the beds. Hopefully Betty could spare her a few minutes for a chat. She could invite Betty round for a bite to eat as well. She'd been so good to young Freda, putting her up when she had a late shift at the fire station.

Nelson snuggled up to her leg and gave a pitiful whine. 'Now, whatever is wrong with you, you silly old thing?' Ruby said as she scratched his ear. 'Hungry again, I suppose? Let's see what I can find for you then we can take a walk up to Vera's and see how she's faring. I've not seen hide nor hair of her for a few days. It's unlike Vera to be so quiet.'

Delving into the pantry, she pulled out a dish containing a few spoonfuls of rice pudding that had been saved for the dog and added a crust of bread that had seen better days. Scraping the rice from the bowl into one that was kept just for Nelson's use, Ruby then broke up the bread and added a little cold milk. 'You are a spoilt dog,' she said and she placed the bowl onto the floor and stroked his head as he tucked into his food. 'Times might be hard, boy, but I'll not see you starve.'

Returning to the table to finish drinking her tea, Ruby opened the envelope. Thankfully Pat seemed resigned that her mother would be visiting and had given a telephone number for the farm, which Ruby was to ring when they arrived at the station. It seemed that Ruby would be sharing Pat's bedroom at the farm and the barn had been cleared for Bob's use. 'That answers one of my questions,' Ruby thought to herself with a wry grin.

Strolling up Alexandra Road with Nelson ambling by her side, Ruby found herself thinking how the rows of houses on each side of the road had escaped Hitler's attempts to bomb the area. Granted, some windows were still boarded up from the blasts and a few families had moved away to the country, but all in all the road of bay-fronted homes had withstood the constant aerial attacks of the war. But for how much longer? she asked herself. At least it hadn't been as bad as the Blitz and for the moment the smaller towns along the banks of the River Thames were surviving. 'We've had some near misses, though,' she muttered to Nelson, who cocked his head as if listening to his owner as she thought of Betty and Sarah caught up in the oil bombing of the Bexleyheath branch of Woolworths, and of how they all thought Maisie had been killed when the Running Horses pub had been bombed. 'We should be grateful for small mercies, Nelson,' she said with a sigh as they arrived at Vera's gate. 'Now, let's see if Vera's heard from the ministry about her putting up a homeless family.'

Nelson curled up on the pathway next to Vera's front door as Ruby gave a sharp tap on the brass knocker. He knew he wasn't welcome in the home of the woman who never spared him a biscuit or a fuss.

Vera opened the front door slightly and peered through the gap. 'Oh, it's you, Ruby. I thought perhaps it was them arriving. Get yourself inside and that dog can stay there. I don't want hair or fleas on my furniture.'

Ruby bristled at her friend's comments but decided not to bite back. Freda had recently bathed Nelson in the back garden and there was still a pleasant aroma of carbolic when he walked into the room. As for fleas, didn't all dogs carry the odd one or two? 'Now, tell me what's been happening? I've not seen you for a day or two. You didn't turn up for your shift at the WVS yesterday. We could have done with an extra pair of hands as we were packing comfort boxes. I stayed on for an hour just to see the job finished.'

Vera sat down in an armchair and indicated for Ruby to do the same.

It was a pleasant room, Ruby thought, but not as homely as her own best room as there was a lack of family photographs and a distinctive unlived-in atmosphere. Each to their own, she thought as she tried in vain to plump up an obstinate cushion.

'The powers that be are having none of it and told me in no uncertain terms that not only was I to take in a family, but they suggested I do more war work.' She pulled a handkerchief from her sleeve and sniffed into it. 'I really don't know what to do. You know as well as I that I work every hour God gives and I'm not one to shirk my war duties. Why, I'd go down the mines if it wasn't for my fear of the dark.'

Ruby kept her grin in check and tried to look sympathetic. 'Perhaps you could put in a few more hours at the WVS and I know they are shouting out for more help at the British restaurant that's not long opened in Slades Green. Maybe they'd be more sympathetic then. Is it really such a bad thing to help out a family who've been made homeless because of this war?'

Vera shot her friend a filthy look. 'A fat lot you care. Why, you could take in someone else now your Sarah's living with her mother-in-law and your George won't be staying with you now he's renting that house in Crayford. I've heard that costs a pretty penny?'

Ruby didn't bite. It wasn't anyone else's business how much her son paid to rent the house up near St Paulinus Church in Crayford. Ruby was more relieved that he no longer had to travel from his home in Devon when his presence was required at the big Vickers factory in Crayford. No doubt her daughter-in-law had been showing off yet again and Vera had been a more than interested listener. 'That's their business, Vera, and yes I have thought about taking in someone else now my son isn't staying in my home when he's up this way doing his important war work. Why, I've not even changed the sheets on the bed yet. Give us a chance. Now, tell me, what's happening?'

'They are coming today. I thought it was them when you knocked on the door.'

'They? Do you have some idea of who "they" are?'

Vera sniffed dramatically and picked at an invisible mark on the arm of her chair. 'All I know is that it could be a family or even a couple of men working at one of the local factories. I just hope it isn't men, what with me being a woman living on my own.' She looked horrified at the thought. 'They wouldn't do that to me, would they?'

'Calm down, Vera, I'm sure whoever they send to live with you will be respectable and you'll get on with them like a house on fire. Don't forget, you'll also be paid for taking them in.'

Vera visibly brightened. 'Well, that's as maybe, but what if they eat me out of house and home?'

Ruby sighed. This was hard work. 'Whoever they are, they will have their ration books and will have to abide by the ration regulations just like the rest of us, so stop your worrying. Now, I wanted you to know that I'm going to visit my Pat down in Cornwall for a while. Will you keep an eye out for Freda and Nelson while I'm gone? There shouldn't be any problems, but I'll feel better knowing someone's watching number thirteen while I'm away. If there's a problem, you can always give Sergeant Jackson a shout.'

Vera forgot her own problems for a while and showed interest in Ruby's news. 'A holiday, is it? It's all right for some. I can't think of the last time I had a bit of a holiday, what with the war and everything.'

'It's not really a holiday. I'm missing my grandkids and want to see them before they grow much older.'

'I wouldn't call it essential travel,' Vera said. 'I'm surprised you managed to get a travel permit or did your George have a hand in it? Or perhaps it was Maisie's husband? They both seem to be able to pull strings when they need to.'

Ruby stood up to leave. Sometimes there was no talking to Vera and today was one of those times. 'I'll leave you to it as I've a lot to do today, just as I know you have. Thank you for the offer of a cup of tea, but I don't have that much time to sit about chatting. Idle hands and all that . . .'

It was as she closed the door that Vera realized she hadn't even put the kettle on, let alone offered her a cup of tea. She didn't understand Ruby at times.

6

'You look exhausted, Freda,' Sarah said to her friend as she stopped at her counter. It was a quiet afternoon in Woolworths and Sarah was able to have a few words without disrupting the girl's work. She'd taken on Betty's job of inspecting the shop floor and keeping an eye on the staff so that the manager could try to catch up with her paperwork.

'I must say I've felt brighter,' Freda said with a grin. 'But last night was the last of my shifts at the fire station and I'm off on my training course from tomorrow. I can't wait. In two weeks' time I'll be an official dispatch rider for the Fire Service.'

'I'm surprised you'll have time to work at Woolworths, what with dashing off on a motorbike all over the place. Who'd have thought when we first met that the shy young thing I knew then would turn into such a brave woman?'

Freda stopped polishing the glass at the front of her counter and looked earnestly towards her friend. 'You'll never know what it meant to me to meet you and Maisie that day I turned up for my interview. It changed my life.

I'd never leave Woolworths. The company has been too good to me to do that. But all the time we have this war to fight I feel I have to play my part. I'm just fortunate that Betty is allowed to let us work odd hours so we can join the services and fight Hitler.'

'I'm with you all the way there, Freda. That's why Bob is training me to be an air raid warden. I can be of use, keep my job here and take care of Georgina – with help from the family.'

'What did Alan say about you joining the ARP? It can be a dangerous job.'

Sarah gave a small smile. 'He was none too pleased, but we had a long chat about things and he realizes now I have to play my part, just as he does. As long as Georgina is cared for he is happy enough.'

'But what if he has to start flying again? He is almost over his injuries so I don't suppose he will be able to teach the young pilots how to fly Spitfires for much longer,' Freda said.

Sarah looked glum. 'I know. It's been playing on my mind for a while now. Part of me knows he should fly again and I know he wants to, but I'm so afraid of losing him.'

Freda slipped from behind the high mahogany counter and hugged Sarah. 'Just remember that lightning doesn't strike twice. Alan will be fine.'

Sarah nodded her agreement, but deep inside she felt that even her darling husband would have trouble avoiding the German planes and getting home safely to his wife and child.

After composing herself, Sarah moved on to where

Maisie was beckoning to her by waving a roll of paper above her head. She was busy working on a window display they had discussed with Betty, which showed a section of an aeroplane wing, along with patriotic posters and several collecting tins. The people of Erith had been most generous with their donations to raise money to build new fighter planes. 'My goodness, whatever have you got there?' she asked as she took the poster from Maisie and unrolled it. The picture showed a photograph of a bombed-out Woolworths store somewhere in England with the words, 'If you think we're suffering, take a look at theirs.' 'My goodness, whatever next,' she grinned.

'That's not what I called you over for,' Maisie whispered. 'Look behind you over by the knitting-wool counter.'

Sarah peered to where Maisie was pointing. 'Is that . . . ?'

'Yes, it is. I spotted him outside the shop and now he's crept in. He doesn't seem to be looking at the goods but is keeping an eye on the staff door.'

'Hmm, do you think he is up to something?' Sarah asked with a frown on her face.

'Don't be daft. We've seen him a few times now and it is always Betty he is watching. I reckon he's got a good idea of when Betty is on the shop floor and that is why he is here. He could be after robbing us when we empty the tills.'

A smile crossed Sarah's face at her chum's words. 'Honestly, Maisie, you've been watching too many of those Clive Danvers films at the Odeon.' The friends were big fans of the handsome spy and made a point of watching the films whenever they came to Erith.

'We've seen him outside the store, don't forget, and didn't Freda say she saw him standing across the road outside Misson's ironmongers the other week as we were shutting up shop?'

'It does seem a bit of a coincidence now you come to mention it,' Sarah agreed. 'But what should we do about it? We can't really call the police just because we recognize a man.'

'No, but we can have a word with him. Look, he's moved over to the door of the staffroom. Let's go nab him. We can grab Freda on the way. Follow me.'

'But . . .' Sarah was too late to stop Maisie and had no choice but to follow her along the polished wooden shop floor, past counters and the occasional shopper. She caught her beckoning to Freda as she headed towards the tall, distinguished man, who now had his hand on the handle of the staff door that led upstairs to the offices and canteen. Perhaps Maisie was right after all, she thought.

'Excuse me, sir, can we help you?' Maisie said in a stern voice.

The man froze. A look of horror crossed his face. 'I . . . er . . .'

'That door leads to a private part of the store, sir,' Sarah said, trying to sound authoritative.

'I was looking for a Miss Billington. I need to talk to her about something private,' the man said as he tried to compose himself after being confronted by three female shop staff. He started to open the door.

Maisie took him by the arm and almost pushed him through the doorway. Freda took his other arm and Sarah closed the door behind them so as not to attract attention.

'If you would follow us, please, sir,' Maisie said as she guided him up the steep stairway and towards Betty's office.

'Be ready to call the police,' Sarah whispered to Freda as they followed behind. 'This is most peculiar.'

Maisie knocked on Betty's door and walked straight in without waiting for an answer. She pushed the man into a chair and stood in front of him. The look on her face defied even the devil to move from the spot. 'Miss Billington, we've spotted this bloke hanging about the shop more than a few times and we think something fishy's going on.'

'Now, look here,' the man said, trying to stand up before Sarah and Freda, who were standing behind him, pushed him back into the seat.

Betty brushed a stray hair from her face and removed the spectacles she used when working on the heavy ledgers. She looked from the serious faces of the three staff members to the man, who by now was very flustered. 'Can someone explain exactly what is going on here?'

'We've seen him casing the joint. I think he's out ter rob Woolworths,' Maisie said with a gleam in her eye.

Sarah sighed inwardly. Maisie seemed to be acting just like Clive Danvers. They could all be in terrible trouble if this man was innocent.

'I think the very least I need is an explanation,' Betty

said, 'both from you, Maisie, and you, sir,' she added as she leant both elbows on the desk and laced her fingers together, giving both an icy stare.

Sarah looked towards Freda and raised her eyebrows.

'Don't think you two are getting off scot-free,' their boss and good friend added.

'Well, it's like this,' Maisie said. 'We've all seen 'im hanging about either in Woolies or out in the street. He even followed yer down the road the other day till we all caught up with you. Then he scarpered. We' – she looked at Sarah and Freda – 'all think he's up ter no good and we think yer in danger.' She smiled in satisfaction as she finished speaking.

Before Betty could speak the man roared with laughter. 'Nothing could be further from the truth,' he exclaimed.

Betty frowned. 'My staff have made a serious allegation. I hope, for their sake, that they aren't correct. However, I would like to hear your reasons for allegedly loitering in my store?'

'And outside,' Maisie added quickly, which resulted in Betty awarding her a stern look.

The man straightened his tie and coughed. 'My name is Douglas Billington . . .'

Betty frowned as he spoke and the three girls looked at each other in surprise.

'He has the same name as Betty,' Freda said in a whisper to Sarah.

'I wondered if you would recognize my full name,' he said gently.

'I do but I don't know from where . . .'

'I was a friend of your fiancé, Charles.'

'Oh my . . .' Betty mumbled, putting a hand to her mouth in shock. 'Please . . . please, go on . . .'

'I apologize for frightening your staff. If the truth be known, I've been rather a coward. Many times I've wanted to speak to you, but was never sure if you would want to revisit the past. For all I know you have forgotten about Charles and have a new life and family and what I have to say would not be welcome.'

Betty thought for a moment. 'Girls, I feel sure that I am quite safe and Mr Billington is not a threat to Woolworths or me. You can go back to you duties. Freda, perhaps you could fetch a cup of tea for Mr Billington before you go back to your counter?'

Maisie and Sarah followed Freda to the staff canteen, while she collected the requested tea.

'What do yer make of all that?' Maisie asked.

'I'm totally confused,' Sarah said, 'but I feel you did the right thing. Who was to know he is a relative of Betty's?'

'I think it is very romantic,' Freda sighed.

'How can it be romantic to meet a relative?' Maisie chuckled.

'But he's not a relative. He mentioned Charles and that was Betty's bloke who died in the trenches during the Great War,' Freda explained.

'Well, that's too confusing fer me,' Maisie said, pinching a biscuit from the tray where Freda had carefully placed two cups of tea and biscuits. 'You'll just 'ave ter 'ang about and listen when yer drop off the tea tray.'

'Sorry, I'm not going to be a nosy so-and-so just so

you know what's going on,' Freda said as she walked away with the tray.

Maisie nudged Sarah. 'She's dying ter know really.'

'I can't believe it. After all this time,' Betty said, reaching for a clean handkerchief in the top drawer of her desk. She always kept a fresh supply for when her female staff were upset.

Douglas Billington reached out and took Betty's hand. 'You have no idea how many times I wished I'd contacted you.'

They both glanced up as Freda entered with the tea tray. Freda's eyes grew wide as she surveyed the scene before quickly leaving.

'I hope your staff are discreet. I'd hate to have put you in a compromising position,' he said apologetically.

Betty smiled. 'There's no fear of that. Freda is a good friend and most reliable. Please, have your tea before it gets cold.'

They both sipped their tea in silence before Douglas placed his cup and saucer on Betty's desk and cleared his throat nervously. 'I want to apologize for lurking in your store . . .'

'And outside from all accounts.' Betty smiled. 'I'm sure you have your reasons, Douglas.'

He nodded. 'As I said before, I have been trying to find the right time to speak to you and also work out how to say what I know without distressing you or your family unduly.'

Betty did her utmost to hold her emotions in check.

It didn't do to let a stranger see how his announcement had affected her. It was beyond her wildest dreams to hear about Charlie after all these years. 'As you can tell by my surname, I never married. After Charlie died my life was over. My future life as a wife and mother had been cruelly taken from me.' She paused for a while as her thoughts went back to the day she heard that Charlie would not be returning.

'I'm sorry if my coming here has distressed you,' he said gently, bringing Betty back to the conversation.

'No, I'm pleased you are here. I've not spoken of my past for a while. I may have been young, but I knew the love I had for my Charlie was for life. It took several years, but once I learnt that happiness lay in my own hands and staying at home with my parents and weeping wouldn't help matters, I decided to find a job I would enjoy. That is when I entered the retail world. So, please tell me about Charlie and how you knew him. Did you attend school together?' She really wanted to know about Charlie as a little boy and to be able to add to her memories. That thought brought tears to her eyes. Would their children, the children she was denied, have looked like her lost love?

Douglas took a moment to answer before stumbling over his first words. 'How I wish . . . how I wish we had been school friends. No, I only got to know Charlie in the last weeks of his life, but it was a time I will never forget.'

'You were at Ypres together?'

Douglas nodded his head in agreement. Words were not needed.

Betty was frightened to ask her question. 'Were you with Charlie when . . . ?'

He reached for both of her hands and held them reassuringly. 'I was beside him when it happened. Please believe me when I say it was over quickly and he would not have suffered.'

Tears ran silently down Betty's cheeks. 'I always wondered but we never knew,' she whispered.

Douglas released her hands and passed her her handkerchief that had dropped onto her desk, then watched as Betty held it to her eyes and silently wept. 'I'm dreadfully sorry to have upset you so. That was not my intention. In fact, that was one of the reasons I have held back from seeking you out for so long.'

Betty slowly composed herself, then, squaring her shoulders and sitting upright in her chair, she spoke. 'I'm sorry for my display of weakness. I am truly grateful for your visit and can now see why you faltered when trying to contact me.'

'Dear God, woman, you are not weak. Look at how strong you've been and how you have turned your life around. I have nothing but admiration for you. After hearing of your career I expected to see some kind of bossy tyrant in front of me, not a beautiful woman who is in control of her life.'

Betty felt her cheeks start to burn. 'Mr Billington, you flatter me. I simply got on with my life like any other woman would have done.'

Douglas smiled. 'Perhaps we should agree to disagree?'

Betty laughed. 'Perhaps, but it is not important. The

reaction of my family did not surprise me. My parents disapproved of my choice to earn my own living. They have passed away, though, and I only have a couple of cousins now living. I fear their views are similar. However, it no longer bothers me. Tell me, you mentioned another reason for not contacting me sooner?'

'Like many soldiers, I shut my mind to what I witnessed during that time. I came home, went back to my job and in time met the lady who became my wife and who gave me two beautiful daughters.'

'Oh, you have children, how delightful. That is my one disappointment. Does your wife know you have been seeking me out?'

Douglas's eyes clouded over. 'Clementine died three years ago.'

It was Betty's turn to reach across the desk and touch Douglas's hand. 'I'm so sorry for your loss. I've carried my grief for over twenty years and know how you must be feeling.'

Douglas could only nod his head in agreement.

'I think it is time we had fresh tea. I'll just be a few minutes,' she said as she made to leave the room.

'No, I cannot take any more of your time. You have your work to consider.'

Betty waved her hand, dismissing Douglas's words. 'Don't give it a second thought. Woolworths is my life and the company is aware of the hours I work.'

Opening the office door, she called to a passing staff member to take the tea tray and ask Maureen, who was working in the staff canteen, to send fresh tea. Sitting back behind her desk, she smiled at Douglas. 'Please tell me how you found me, and why now?'

'It was while grieving for my wife that I started to think how, if I'd lost my life in the last shout, I'd not have met her or been the father of young Clemmie and Dorothy. I pondered on the friendship I'd had with Charlie and how, if things had been different, he'd have stood by me as best man when I married and been a godparent to the children. Our lives would have inter-twined and, of course, you would have been a valued friend. It was only when Clemmie's friends from her schooldays wrote and told me about my wife's life before I met her that I realized I know things about Charlie that you may wish to hear. I found great comfort from her friends at that time and felt only sorrow that I'd not done the same after Charlie's death.'

'You would have had so much on your mind at that time, Douglas, please, please, do not blame yourself. Now, I'm going to make a suggestion that may sound rather presumptuous of me but I feel we have much to discuss. Would you like to come for dinner at my house? My home is not far from here – that's if you haven't already discovered where I live?' She smiled. 'However, I'd still like to know how you discovered I was in Erith?'

Douglas thought for a moment before replying. 'I'd be delighted to dine with you. As for seeking you out, I was told by your late parents' neighbour that you now man-aged a branch of Woolworths in the town of Erith so I did a little detective work. I'm just ashamed that my reticence in approaching you alarmed so many people.'

'Miss Briggs? I still correspond with her and exchange

cards at Christmas,' Betty said with a smile. 'So I shall see you tomorrow evening at seven?' She wrote her address on a sheet of paper and handed it to Douglas.

'Thank you, I'll look forward to seeing you then,' Douglas said as he got to his feet and buttoned up his overcoat before shaking Betty's hand. He opened the door just as Maureen appeared with the fresh tea. Maureen reported later that it was the first time she had ever seen the manager of Woolworths exuding such a warm glow.

'A very cosy home,' Ruby admitted as they finished Irene's tour of the house she'd found to rent in Crayford and followed her into the walled garden.

'It suits our needs for the present and isn't too far from George's workplace. Of course, our home in Devon is much larger.'

'Of course.' Maisie grinned at Sarah as they followed the older women. 'Where's yer Anderson shelter, Irene? You don't wanna get caught out.'

Irene turned to face Maisie. She still could not understand how such an attractive woman, who had made a most suitable marriage to David Carlisle, had not made the effort to improve the way she spoke. 'We have a reinforced cellar. It was what attracted me to the house in the first place, along with the sunny aspect of the landscaped garden.'

Maisie snorted with laughter. 'Isn't that why we all pick our 'omes?'

Irene gave Maisie a stern look and continued giving a

tour of the garden. 'I will have a man come in to take care of things. I can't expect George to care for it all, even if he could spare the time.'

'Dad does work long hours at Vickers, Mum. Please don't begrudge him a rest,' Sarah pleaded. 'Perhaps you could care for the garden? After all, you did say it isn't very large,' she suggested.

'Me? Garden? I'm far too busy, Sarah. I have the WVS to consider for a start.'

Ruby frowned. What did her daughter-in-law have to do with the WVS? 'You've joined the WVS, Irene?'

'I made enquiries the moment I knew we were moving here. Knowing I was leaving behind my charity work and friends, I thought it was time I did something constructive while George was away at work all day. I was accepted at once. No doubt because of the letter I sent explaining all my charity work. I'll soon have the Erith ladies shipshape.'

The smile left Maisie's face. She'd started to enjoy the hours spent helping out at the WVS and her rag rug-making group was making splendid progress. She couldn't imagine Irene joining in with that or sorting clothes for the bombed-out families. Come to that, she couldn't see her on tea-making duties or doing any of the hundred and one things the women of the WVS undertook to make life a little easier in wartime. 'Irene, you do know it's hard work in the WVS and isn't anything like yer fundraising dinner dances?'

Irene shuddered. 'I'm aware of that, Maisie, and that is why I have decided to make changes when I join the Erith division next week. We need to be a slick fighting machine and operate just the same as our fighting forces do. We have a war to win, Maisie!'

Maisie was spared thinking of a response to Sarah's mother's comments when Alan shouted hello as he came through the garden gate, followed by George.

'Hello, everyone. Guess who I found walking down the road?' George said as he kissed his wife's cheek, hugged his daughter, then swooped on Georgina, who'd been toddling on unsteady feet watched carefully by Ruby, who was worrying her great-granddaughter would fall into the rose bushes. 'How's my favourite little lady?' he asked.

Georgina gave her grandfather a toothy smile.

'I got off early and managed to get a lift into Crayford from one of the lads. I thought I could walk back to Erith with you after tea,' Alan said, raising his eyebrows at Irene.

'There's always room at my house for the RAF, Alan, especially an officer. In fact, you must all stay for dinner.'

'I'd like to, Mrs C., but I have to be somewhere in just over an hour,' Maisie said, glancing at Sarah.

'And I offered to go with you, Maisie, so we need to start getting Georgina dressed and in her pram or we will be late.'

'Let Georgie stay with me, Sarah,' Alan said. 'You've got enough on your hands, what with your ARP duties later this evening.'

Sarah kissed her husband's cheek. 'I knew there was a good reason I married you,' she smiled, brushing a hair from the shoulder of his uniform jacket.

Alan took her by the elbow and led her to a corner of

the garden. 'I did want to have a word with you. It won't take long. Something's come up at work.'

She looked into his eyes and realized the time had arrived when her world would again be turned upside down. 'I was going to take some flowers over to Grandad Eddie's grave before I left. Why not come with me?'

Making her goodbyes and telling Maisie to meet her at the lychgate in twenty minutes' time, she gathered up the bunch of blooms that she'd picked from the family allotment and took Alan's arm.

It was only a short walk to St Paulinus Church. The sun shone down just as it had on the third of September 1939, the day she'd married Alan. 'So much has changed since our wedding day,' she sighed, 'good and bad.'

'That's life, my love. Even if we didn't have a war to fight there'd have been many changes,' Alan said as he helped her walk through the lines of graves until they reached Eddie Caselton's headstone.

'And now you are going to tell me you are going away . . .' she said as she removed a few dead blooms and placed her own bouquet in the glass vase, not daring to look up at her husband.

Alan took her elbow and helped Sarah to her feet. 'I've been dreading telling you for fear of how you'd react after . . . after last time,' he murmured.

'Oh, Alan, you know I dread the thought of you being hundreds of miles away and quite likely in terrible danger, but I like to think I've grown up a little since last time you left, and I just know deep inside you'll come home to me and Georgie safe and sound.'

Alan pulled his wife into his arms and held her close.

He breathed in the smell of the soap she'd used that day and felt the softness of her hair against his cheek. As his lips sought hers, he wished with all his heart that he had her strength and fortitude, as he feared what lay ahead. Closing his eyes, he fervently hoped Sarah's wishes would come true.

7

Sarah sat nervously chewing her nails as she waited for Maisie. Doctor Greyson's surgery in Queens Road was situated on a floor of one of the grand terraced houses that overlooked the railway line, which stretched one way to the seaside towns of Kent and to London in the opposite direction. She thought back to family trips to the coast when staying with her grandparents. They would catch an early train and spend the day on the beach, before heading back through the Kent countryside, past hop fields and quaint villages, arriving home ready for bed. Often Grandad Eddie would carry Sarah home on his back when she was too tired to walk. Such happy memories.

They'd climbed the wide, steep steps up to an ajar door badly in need of a lick of paint and entered a hallway paved in diamond-shaped black and white tiles similar to the ones in Ruby's house. Although there was a small pebble-glassed window that must have opened to a receptionist's office, it remained closed so after coughing politely to let whoever was there know they'd arrived, they sat down to wait. A staircase wound up from the hallway and Sarah wondered if Doctor Greyson lived above the surgery. From below she could hear the distant sound of a radio broadcasting a news item and shortly after dance music. Did he have a maid or perhaps the basement was rented out? Whoever the person working below their feet was, they certainly enjoyed their vegetables as Sarah wrinkled her nose at the almost overbearing aroma of cabbage. She'd looked to her friend, who had removed her smart kidskin gloves, which Sarah knew to be a gift from Maisie's mother-in-law, and was gripping the handle of her handbag so tightly that her knuckles had turned white. Sarah had reached over and squeezed her hand. 'Everything will be fine, Maisie. Either Doctor Greyson will say you are expecting or you are unlucky this time and will have to wait a little longer to be a mother.'

Maisie had kept staring forwards but had nodded. 'I know I'm being daft to worry my guts out like this. But I can't help feeling I'm letting David down by not giving him a little kiddie. He's just plain dotty over your Georgie and to deny him that . . .' Her face had crumpled as she leant into Sarah to sob.

'Now, now, what's all this? Surely I'm not that scary?' Doctor Greyson had said as he appeared round the door of his surgery. He took Maisie by the hand and helped her to stand. 'Why all the tears, Mrs Carlisle? Let's take a look at you and see what's to do, shall we?'

Maisie had nodded and, without saying a word, followed Doctor Greyson. At the door to the examining room she'd looked back at Sarah and given a weak smile. Sarah had held up both hands and crossed her fingers.

Please let it be good news, she'd whispered to herself. Delving into her shopping bag, she'd pulled out her knitting and tried to concentrate on the balaclava helmet she was working on. Since Freda's brother, Lenny, had joined the navy she had helped her friend to knit items that could be sent to the brave sailors. As the needles clicked away she'd started to wonder where the lad's ship was in the world. Pathé News, along with radio reports, had told of some fierce sea battles and she knew that Freda was more than a little worried. Hopefully there would be a letter soon, which would put their minds at rest. Thoughts of letters made her realize that before too long she would be waiting for letters from Alan. It had been hard to put on a brave face when he told her he was leaving the comparative safety of training young pilots and would be heading off to fight the enemy. As they walked back to the lychgate of St Paulinus to meet Maisie, Alan had hinted that he would be based overseas, protecting a brave island of people.

Sarah followed the newspapers enough to suspect it might be Malta, but even there in the quiet graveyard of Crayford she didn't wish to speak of it in case they were overheard. Walls might well have ears, even in a churchyard. Instead they had spoken of how they could spend time together before Alan left to join his squadron.

Sarah was shaken from her thoughts as the door of the surgery opened and she heard Doctor Greyson's voice giving instructions to her friend.

Maisie appeared with a big smile on her face.

'I take it there was bad news?' Sarah grinned.

Doctor Greyson handed a fistful of papers to Maisie.

'Now, remember what I said. You are to take things easy and consider your child above anything else.' He shook Maisie's hand. 'Now, run along home and tell that husband of yours.'

'Yes, Doctor . . . thank you, Doctor,' Maisie burbled as she hugged the startled man and rushed towards Sarah. 'Guess what, I'm expecting!'

'I'd never have thought it,' Sarah laughed as she linked arms with her chum and they headed out of the surgery.

Outside the girls stopped and faced each other. 'Maisie, I'm so pleased for you, especially after what you told me.'

'I never thought it would happen and I'm going to take extra care so the baby is safe until it's born. I'm taking no chances this time. I shall be a lady of leisure until the birth.'

'You will?'

'Well, perhaps some sewing and housework, but you know what I mean,' she grinned.

'No more Woolworths?' Sarah asked.

'I'll miss Woolies but I can still visit, and once the little one arrives I'll do my best to work a few hours. I know how short staffed Betty is. You won't get rid of me that easily.'

'David is going to be so thrilled. When is he home?'

'He should be home tomorrow evening. I'm fortunate he ain't away all the time like some men. I'd best make sure he's sitting down when I tell him.'

'Will you tell him what you told me of when . . . when you lost your first child?' Sarah asked, worried that

Maisie would be annoyed with her for bringing up the subject.

Maisie sighed. 'I'll 'ave to one day but not now. You won't say anything?'

'Your secret's safe with me. I won't tell a soul. By the way, when is the baby due?'

'Around Christmas time. It's going ter be a great Christmas present,' Maisie grinned.

'It certainly is,' Sarah agreed.

Ruby rose from where she'd been sitting in Irene and George's garden. Although it soothed her mind to know her son no longer had the arduous journey up from Devon every month or so to the Vickers factory in Crayford, she was sad to think he would no longer be lodging with her in Erith. At the back of her mind was the thought she now had a spare bedroom and, like her friend Vera, she would soon be expected to take in a lodger of some kind. Possibly someone who had been bombed out of their home, or perhaps a serviceman working in the area. An idea had come to her during the afternoon, but she would need to speak to Maisie and David before making any decisions.

'Before you go, Mum, there's something I'd like to speak to you about,' George said as he took his pipe from his waistcoat pocket and turned it over in his hands, before leaning against a small wall that bordered the garden.

Ruby raised her eyebrows. She knew from experience that her son always fiddled with his pipe when he was nervous. 'Cough up, George. I've not got all day. Young Freda will be home soon and expecting her meal and I want to walk back to Erith with Alan and Georgina.' She also wanted to know where Sarah and Maisie had disappeared to. She knew something was afoot there.

'This will only take a few minutes, Mum. Sit yourself down and listen, please.'

Ruby frowned but did as her son requested.

'I'm worried about you travelling down to see our Pat. It's a long way from Kent to the other end of Cornwall.'

'Yes, but—'

George held up his hand to stop Ruby speaking. 'Let me finish, Mum. It's not a good journey, even in peacetime. Exeter had that bad air raid the other week, the one they're calling the Baedeker Raids. Who's to know if the Luftwaffe will target Truro or any other town in Cornwall and you will be stuck in the middle of it – and alone?'

'But George—'

'Mum, please. Why you've got this notion in your head to rush off to see our Pat and the kids I'll never know. Can't you write her a letter, or we could arrange a phone call? An elderly woman travelling hundreds of miles and in wartime is utterly ridiculous.'

'Listen, George—'

'For goodness' sake, Mum. Pat was here over Easter. Why couldn't you chat with her then?'

Ruby was becoming frustrated as she tried to speak to George. 'Now listen here, George Caselton, and stop interrupting me. The reason I couldn't talk to our Pat was because the rest of the family were at the house and she vanished as soon as she got wind of me trying to get her alone. No, it's my time to talk,' she said as he opened his mouth to continue. 'I've been down the farm to see John and, bless his soul, he is happy as things are and I didn't like to tell him I had my worries. So, yes, I am going down to Cornwall. The travel permits have been approved and we are going to stop off on the way down. Pat knows to expect us and our beds are ready and waiting for the end of the month.' She stopped to take a breath.

'Travel permits? Beds? So you're not going alone? Don't you think it's foolhardy to take along one of the girls? God forbid, what if you both get injured in a raid . . . or worse?'

'I'm not taking the girls with me. Not even one of them,' Ruby sighed.

'Then who?'

'For heaven's sake, George, let me speak. Bob offered to accompany me. He was worried about me and it seemed the perfect solution. And before you say another word, we will sleep in separate rooms and there is nothing between us. Trust me.'

'Mum, please . . .' George looked acutely embarrassed and glanced away. Whatever was his mum thinking? He'd admired her fighting spirit after his dad passed away and since the start of the war she'd been a tower of strength in the local community. And he liked Bob, but were they becoming too close?

Ruby could see Alan approaching the garden gate so, quickly plonking a kiss on her son's forehead, she pulled on her coat and reached for Georgina's pram. 'I'll be seeing you soon, George, and don't go worrying about me. I'll be safe with Bob wherever we go – and I'll enjoy his company,' she added before heading out of the gate.

Alan took control of the pram from Ruby as they headed up past St Paulinus Church and took the lane towards North End and Erith. 'Would you like to stop off and have a few minutes with Eddie?' he asked his mother-in-law. 'I'm in no hurry to get back.'

'I visited on my way here, love, and said all I had to say then.'

Alan nodded and took Ruby's arm as they crossed the road, steering the pram with one hand. 'I see George and Irene aren't living far from a golf club,' he said, nodding to where a clipped green could be seen.

'Irene will be pleased and at least if she gets her feet under the table there, she will leave our WVS section alone. She means well but, my goodness, she seems to get under people's skins. I've always said that one comes up smelling of roses whatever the situation. But I'm not being charitable. Irene loves our Georgina and I swear I've seen a softer side to her since the little one's come along.'

'You could be right there,' Alan agreed. 'She's always been good to me.'

'Of course she would be. You're a pilot officer in the RAF. She didn't stop bragging to her snooty friends when our Sarah introduced you.'

'I'd sooner still be a trainee manager for F. W. Woolworths than be fighting this war,' he said with a faraway look in his eyes. 'I've lost too many friends in the past few years.'

'No doubt the young men in that German plane said the same,' Ruby said, nodding to a rough area of the golf course where a Dornier had crashed two years previously. 'They're buried up on the graveyard of St Paulinus, you know.'

'You may think it strange but I went to pay my respects,' Alan said apologetically.

'Not at all. I like to think the Germans would do the same for any of our lads that are killed over their country. There are always fresh flowers on the grave and locals take care of them. I hope the two boys get to go home sometime.'

Alan nodded. 'It could be me one day. I'd hate to think of Sarah and Georgina not being able to visit my final resting place.'

Ruby reached for his arm to stop Alan pushing the pram. 'I just knew it. You're going to be flying again, aren't you? Have you told Sarah?' Ruby feared that her granddaughter would not take the news well after almost losing her husband in the early days of their marriage.

Alan pulled the hood of the pram up slightly to shade his daughter from late afternoon sunshine. 'She took the news well. A few tears but she's much stronger and our marriage is strong too, Ruby. I do need you to watch out for her and Mum, please. You will, won't you?'

'It goes without saying and your mum is as much family as you are, Alan, and will be taken care of . . . whatever happens.' She reached out and pulled him to her, giving the lad a hug. She wished she could keep this charming young man close to her forever – or until the damned war was over and done with. Looking over his shoulder to the distant church, she was sure that the loved ones of the two German pilots must have felt the same when they waved them off to war.

'Is that you, Ruby?' Freda called when she heard the key rattle as it was pulled through the letter box of number thirteen.

'It is and I hope you've got the kettle on,' Ruby called back. 'We walked back from George and Irene's and I'm fair parched. Alan's with me,' she added, pulling off her coat as she popped her head around the door to the kitchen. 'Any sign of Sarah?'

'I've no idea. I've only just got home myself. Didn't she go with you to see her parents' new home?' Freda asked.

'She did but then left early to accompany Maisie somewhere.'

Freda frowned. 'I shouldn't think they'd have gone into work. How strange,' she said, turning back to measure tea leaves into the pot, being very careful as every leaf was precious now tea was in short supply. She wondered for a moment what the secret was and why she hadn't been included. However, as she was halfway through her training course to be a dispatch rider for the Fire Service she was hardly home these days. Another week and hopefully she'd have passed the course and be back dividing her time between her job at Woolworths and the fire station in nearby Cross Street.

'Georgie's still fast asleep,' Alan said as he took the teapot from Freda and placed it on the kitchen table.

'I've left her in the hallway. I'll have this and then get off home before she wakes and wants feeding.' He looked at his watch. 'Mum will be home from Woolies and be preparing tea. God forbid if it spoils before we are home.'

'Make sure you have a few words with Maureen and tell her what's happening. She won't want to be the last to hear,' Ruby gently scolded.

Freda looked between the two of them, sensing something wasn't right. 'Oh, Alan, are you back on flying duty already?'

Alan nodded. He liked Freda; she was like a younger sister to them all. She'd grown up in recent years and Alan hadn't been surprised when she'd decided to ride a motorbike; he thought she'd be flying an airplane before long, like the women he'd seen transporting planes between airfields. 'Yes, but I wasn't called back on duty. I've volunteered for special duties,' he said as both Freda and Ruby opened their mouths to speak. He raised his hand. 'Don't ask. I can't say any more than that.'

'You're mad,' scolded Ruby.

'You're brave,' sighed Freda. 'You're going out to Malta, aren't you?'

'Freda, you know I can't say, and besides, you are making wild guesses.'

'I'm just putting two and two together. You know I hardly miss a news broadcast these days and always make sure I get to the Odeon in time to see the latest Pathé News. Besides, I think Lenny's ship's somewhere out that way,' she said defiantly.

'Lenny's not been silly and put something in his letters, has he?' Ruby asked. 'You know there'll be hell to pay if he has. I'd have thought he would have kept his head down after what he'd been through in the past . . .'

'He hasn't, I'll show you,' she ran upstairs and came down within minutes with a bundle of letters from her younger brother. 'Take a look,' she said, placing them in front of Ruby.

'Lovey, I don't want to read your private letters. I believe you,' she said, pushing them back to Freda.

'What makes you think Lenny's out there?' Alan asked. 'Don't tell me the pair of you have a secret code.'

Freda grinned. 'Nothing half as clever. It was only when I was steaming stamps off the envelopes to add to the Brownies' collection that I noticed something written underneath the stamps of Lenny's last three letters. Look.' She checked the dates of a few envelopes and held them up. 'I thought it best to keep the stamps to cover what he'd written.' She flicked back the half-attached stamp to show an M, an A and an L written on three of the envelopes.

'Silly boy,' Ruby huffed. 'I hope you're not doing anything as daft?'

'I just told him to try and let me know where he is,' Freda pouted. 'He's the only relative I have apart from Mum and she's not bothered about us, and hasn't been for some years since I moved south. You're more my family than she is,' Freda added sadly.

Alan smiled. 'I suppose you'll have to wait for the next letter to be sure, but to be on the safe side I'd burn the envelopes if I was you. No sense in getting in trouble or Lenny being put in irons for something silly like this.'

'He could always be signalling that he's got malaria,' Ruby said with a grin.

Freda giggled. 'By the time I received the final letter he'd be cured,' she joked. 'But seriously, Alan, be careful. From all accounts it's horrendous out there.'

'It horrendous everywhere, kid,' he said, using the affectionate name he'd given her since she first moved to Alexandra Road. 'It's called war.'

They were finishing their tea as someone hammered persistently on the front door, causing Georgina to awake and start to cry. Freda was the closest and rushed to soothe her goddaughter whilst reaching past the pram to open the door.

Vera pushed past the pram without a word to Freda and hurried into the kitchen, her face a mix of distress and anger. 'They've arrived and they're only bloody foreigners! I can't understand a word the woman said. I reckon I've got spies under my roof. What can I do, Ruby? Whatever can I do?'

Ruby encouraged her friend to sit down, pouring a cup of tea and sliding it across the table to Vera. 'Now, calm yourself down and tell me what all this commotion is about. You've given Georgina a fright banging on the door like you did.'

Vera's hand shook as she lifted the cup to her lips and grimaced. 'This is stone cold.'

'It's good for shock. Now, tell me what has happened?'

'They arrived. The people the government said I got to have sleep under my roof. Oh, Ruby, I'll be murdered in my bed. They've sent foreign spies.'

Freda looked puzzled. 'Are you sure about this, Mrs

Munro? We have many allies in the war from other countries. They aren't spies,' she said as she rocked the pram to pacify Georgina.

Vera shot her a venomous look. 'I've lived through one war already, Freda. Let me tell you there are spies everywhere and now there are some in Alexandra Road.'

'About these men – how many are there, where are they from and where are they now?' Alan asked as he took over rocking the pram from Freda.

Vera sighed. 'They are in my front room drinking my tea and eating my biscuits. I dare not show them I'm aware they are spies now, could I? I said I needed to borrow some milk and left as soon as it was safe to do so. You've got to come and help me get them out of my house! You too,' she said, glancing at Alan and Freda, who were trying not to laugh.

'I've really got to get Georgina home, she's not going to settle,' Alan said, 'but I'll follow you up the road to check all is well . . . just in case you're likely to be murdered in your bed.' He dared not look at Ruby and Freda or he knew they'd all laugh. Vera was known for her outbursts.

'I'll knock on Sergeant Jackson's door. We may need the long arm of the law if these men are spies,' Freda said, jumping to her feet and squeezing past the pram that still stood in the hallway.

'I just hope you're right, Vera Munro, otherwise this could be very embarrassing for those men. I'll get my coat.'

'But Ruby . . .'

'No more, Vera. Let's get to your house before they

steal your best china and plant a bomb,' she said, pushing her friend towards the door. 'Come on, Alan, let's get to Vera's house and save the country.'

Alan could see Ruby's face twitch as she pulled on her coat and they set off up the road. He was finding it hard not to laugh himself.

Vera let herself into the house and looked nervously over her shoulder towards her friends as they followed behind.

Ruby stepped boldly into Vera's front room. It was a mirror image of her own home but without a large aspidistra plant atop a polished sideboard. She stopped in amazement as she saw a dark-haired woman sitting beside a pale-faced young girl. Frowning at Vera, she said, 'I thought your guests were men.'

Ruby shrugged her shoulders. 'I didn't say who they were. Let me introduce you.' In a loud, slow voice she pointed towards Ruby. 'This . . . is . . . my . . . neighbour . . . Mrs . . . Caselton.'

The woman smiled and nodded. 'I'm very pleased to meet you, Mrs Caselton. My name is Gwyneth Evans and this here is Myfanwy but we call her Myfi. Don't we, *cariad?*'

The child gave a small smile but continued to cling to Gwyneth's arm, trying to hide. Large pale eyes followed Sergeant Jackson as he entered the room followed by his dad, Bob, and she shrank even further away as the men almost filled the room.

Bob knelt down in front of the frightened child and took her hand before starting to sing. '*Paham mae dicter, O Myfanwy . . .*'

Ruby smiled fondly. She'd forgotten that Bob had a beautiful singing voice. 'I recognize that song.'

'"Myfanwy" was always one of my favourite songs when I sang with the Police Male Voice Choir,' he said, 'although it's been a while since I've performed.'

Gwyneth looked tearful. 'Thank you, I've not heard my mother tongue for many months. Do you speak my language?'

'Sadly not, my dear, forgive an old man's ignorance. I do, however, have a fondness for the music of Wales.'

'Why, you are Welsh?' Ruby said as the penny dropped. The woman had a beautiful lilting voice. She could listen to her talk all day. Trust Vera to get the wrong end of the stick.

'Put the kettle on, Vera, and let's get to know our new friends, shall we?'

'I'm going to shoot off home, Ruby,' Alan said. He'd followed Bob and his son, Mike, into Vera's with Georgina in his arms.

Ruby waved to her son-in-law as he left and followed Vera to her kitchen at the back of the house. 'Now, whatever makes you think that lovely young woman and her daughter are spies? Are you going bonkers in your old age, Vera?'

Vera turned from filling the kettle. 'She's got a strange accent and I don't understand what she's on about when she talks to that young kiddie. She could be saying anything. I'm sorry, Ruby, I know you'll take in any waif and stray and not mind the consequences but I'm uncomfortable about them sleeping under my roof. I'm going to ask if I can swap them for people I can understand.'

Ruby would have laughed if she weren't so annoyed. 'I've heard some rubbish come out of your mouth over the years, but this takes the biscuit. What makes you think they want to stay here? I've no doubt that Gwyneth and Myfanwy would much prefer to be in their own home than here with you.'

Vera bristled indignantly. 'There's nothing wrong with my home. It's clean and respectable, I'll have you know.'

'I'm not arguing with you, Vera, I know you keep a respectable home, but you are none too welcoming, are you?'

Vera shrugged her shoulders. 'They can take it or leave it.'

'Then I suggest they leave it and come down the road and stay with me. I have a spare room now George has his house in Crayford. Forget that tea, I'll take them home with me right now, but think on. The government will be wanting you to take in others and they may not be as kindly as those two sitting in your front room right now.'

Not if I can help it, Vera thought to herself as she watched Ruby usher Gwyneth and the child out of the front door, followed by Mike Jackson, who had hold of their suitcases. 'Oh, Bob,' she called to Bob Jackson as he went to leave the house behind his son.

Bob turned abruptly. Although he hadn't been party to the discussion in the kitchen he had the impression that Ruby had fallen out with her friend and was still annoyed. He'd seen Ruby in a fighting mood in the past and could spot the signs – thin pursed lips as she tried not speak out of turn and flushed cheeks. My, she was a handsome woman, he thought to himself.

'Bob, I wondered if you'd had your tea yet? I have a bit of fish and it's too much for one,' she said coyly.

'Another time, eh, Vera?' he said as he let himself out the front door.

Vera smiled to herself. Oh yes, she would make sure there was another time. She'd set her cap at Bob Jackson a while back and by hook or by crook she would get her man. Married to Bob, she would invite his son to move in and then no government would be telling her to take in any Tom, Dick or bloody Blodwen.

8

'Here, let me take those,' Douglas said as Betty started to clear the table. He carried their plates to the kitchen and placed them in the sink.

'Thank you, Douglas, but if you don't mind, I'd like to hear what you have to say about Charlie. I'll take care of the washing up later. I've wondered about Charlie's last days for twenty-five years and can't wait a moment longer. Please, make yourself comfortable,' she said, pointing to one of two armchairs placed either side of the fireplace. The May evening was warm so the fire remained unlit. A wooden fireguard, embroidered with the image of a magnificent stag, hid the empty grate. A bunch of early summer flowers from Douglas were arranged in a cut-glass vase and stood on the mantel-piece.

Douglas took a large brown envelope from where he'd left it on the sideboard and sat in the proffered armchair. 'I feel quite nervous now the time has come to talk about my friend and your late fiancé,' he said apologetically. 'I never thought this would happen.'

'There's nothing to be nervous about, Douglas. Please

take your time and tell me how you first met,' Betty encouraged.

'We met on the troop ship heading over to France in late December of 1917. It was cold and snow started to fall as the ship left England, so it was not a day for sitting on deck. Conditions were cramped below deck and it wasn't long before a fight broke out amongst the men who'd been drinking.'

Betty drew in a sharp breath. 'But Charlie wasn't a drinker. High days and holidays he'd have one, but even then it was to be social or to toast the King.'

'Be assured that Charlie hadn't been drinking. In fact we'd been chatting about our home life and shared a laugh about your surname being the same as mine. He'd been keeping his own council until he felt it prudent to pull a couple of heavily built lads off another soldier and they objected with their fists.'

'Oh my!' Betty said. 'He never mentioned this in his letters.'

Douglas gave her a smile of reassurance. 'A true gentleman wouldn't wish to worry his loved one. We met when I helped pull him to safety and we sat together waiting to be patched up.'

'You were injured too?'

Douglas ran his finger up the side of his nose to a small bump on the ridge. 'For my sins I received a broken nose, whereas Charlie had two black eyes. You would have thought we'd been in the fight rather than acting as peacemakers,' he laughed. 'From that day on we found ourselves in each other's company and got on well. I mourned his passing as much as I would a brother, if I'd had one,' he said sadly.

'I suppose being thrust together as you were, friendships would have been made much quicker than before the war. Charlie was quite a reserved man. I have often wondered how he coped alone during the time he served in the army. It doesn't matter if I say now, so long after his death, that for some time Charlie had thoughts about not fighting in the war. However, he was aware his family would have suffered if he declared himself to be a conscientious objector.'

Douglas nodded his head in agreement. 'Charlie was not alone in thinking this way. I believe that is why we became firm friends. We weren't quite the sharp shooters the Rifle Brigade expected so until the time of fierce fighting we worked as stretcher bearers rather than killing the enemy.'

Betty flinched. 'I can't imagine my Charlie killing anyone. Even now with colleagues and friends going off to war it is hard to think they will kill fellow men.'

'It's a case of kill or be killed,' Douglas said gently. 'We didn't dare think we were dispatching someone's son or brother, or indeed a husband with a young wife and children back home in Germany. For my part, I can just say that having made friends with a comrade while in the trenches was a comfort and I hope Charlie thought the same. I have a few things here that may bring you some comfort.' He delved into the envelope and pulled out a small well-worn notebook. 'I kept a diary at that time, although there were days when, due to fatigue or being in battle, I didn't write.' He flicked through the pages. 'My words seem to be fading – perhaps it's for the best. Who wants to remember times like that when our beloved country is again at war? However, I'd like you to have it as I mention Charlie and our thoughts up to . . . up to the sniper ending his life so quickly.'

'A sniper?' Betty stopped midway through reaching out for the diary. 'I had no idea. Charlie's family did not say . . . but then they were in mourning and I was not accepted into the grief. My parents assumed I would soon find another beau or live the life of a spinster taking care of them into their dotage. I was to all intents and purposes told to pull myself together and forget Charlie.'

'My dear woman,' Douglas said, reaching across for her hand and squeezing it tightly. 'If only I'd been brave enough to find you and console you in your time of grief.'

Betty pulled her hand away, even though she took great comfort from the warmth of his fingers. 'Douglas, time has moved on and, if anything, Charlie's untimely death showed me I could stand on my own two feet and forge a career for myself. I have my little house and good friends. Why, I'm even a godmother. Here, let me show you a photograph of young Georgina. Isn't she pretty?' Betty smiled, gently running her finger over the image of the chubby-cheeked child before returning it to the sideboard. 'My only regret is not being blessed with my own children, but my friends, and young Georgie, more than make my life a happy one.' She picked up the notebook that Douglas had laid on the arm of her chair when he reached for her hand. 'May I borrow this for a while? That's if you can bear to part with it?'

'Please, take the notebook, Betty. I brought it for I'd

rather my memories lived with someone who was connected to that time.'

Betty smiled her thanks. It was the first time that Douglas had called her by her Christian name. She'd asked at the beginning of the evening if he would be less formal as calling each other by the same surname was somewhat confusing and a little comic. She liked him calling her Betty. It felt good.

'Now, young lady, have you fallen off your bike today?'

Freda kept quiet as the men of Erith fire station laughed at her discomfort. She'd managed to topple from her motorbike as it came to a standstill in front of the station on the first occasion she was allowed to ride the bike home from her training session. She'd have the last laugh when they realized that in less than a week she'd be a fully trained dispatch rider and not at their beck and call to make tea and answer the telephone every time it rang. Freda had been flattered when told she was trusted enough to take telephone messages, but the novelty had soon faded. In fact, she might even be stationed elsewhere so they'd definitely have to make their own tea then. She smiled to herself. 'I could ask if the wall at the corner of Erith Road was still in one piece?' she retaliated. 'But then I'm too much of a lady to mention such a thing.'

A roar of laughter followed her words and one of the men who'd been joshing her looked shamefaced as his colleagues laughed at his discomfort.

'I'm off home,' Freda announced. 'It's been a long day.'

She glanced at the clock; it was too late to head to Alexandra Road, as Ruby would have locked up for the night. She'd go to Betty's and use the bedroom that had been put at her disposal by the manager of Woolworths for when Freda's fire station duties ran into the night. She yawned. First she had to push her motorbike behind the fire station and cover it with tarpaulin, then she would cross the road to Betty's house and be in bed inside ten minutes. Reminding her colleagues to keep an eye on the motorbike, she bade them goodnight and headed outside. The watch had been a busy one with callouts to a house fire and an out-of-control bonfire. Thankfully no enemy action but even so, the air-raid siren went off in the early evening. It all made for a tiring night's work after a day spent at the motorbike training school in the East End of London.

A flash of light from a doorway startled Freda. Someone was lucky not to be in trouble with an ARP warden . . . but surely that was Betty's house? Whatever was she doing outside at this time of night? As she approached the little terraced house she spotted a man walking away . . . It was Douglas – and at this time of night! Freda thanked her lucky stars that she'd stopped for that last cup of tea, otherwise goodness knows what she'd have walked in on.

Betty rinsed the sherry glasses and placed them on the wooden draining board before turning off the kitchen light. She'd had such an enjoyable evening with Douglas as they had shared memories of Charlie. It was as if he was alive once more and the two people who cared for him most were able to fill the gaps in their knowledge of the brave soldier. They'd had so much to talk about that the evening had passed in a flash. A little thrill of excitement ran through her at the thought of seeing Douglas this coming weekend. She'd agreed to meet him to go dancing, something she'd not done with a man for a very long time. Raising her hand to her cheek where he'd kissed her goodnight, she gave a contented sigh and headed up to her bedroom. Because of Charlie, Douglas had come into her life. 'Thank you, Charlie,' she whispered as she made her way up to bed.

'It's only me,' Freda said as she let herself into Betty's house.

Betty walked back downstairs, pulling on her dressing gown. 'I'm not in bed yet, Freda. Would you like me to make you a cup of cocoa? I'm dying to know how you got on with your training.'

'That would be lovely, if you're sure you aren't tired? I thought I saw a light at your front door just now.'

Betty took milk from the pantry and poured some into a small pan. 'It was Douglas. We had such a lovely evening chatting about Charlie and how our paths have crossed. It's so strange to think Douglas and Charlie only became friends because of my surname being Billington.'

'And you're not related in any way?' Freda asked. She noticed that Betty had a glow about her that she'd never seen before with the Woolworths store manager. Surely she wasn't falling in love at her age?

'Goodness no, it is a pure coincidence,' Betty smiled.

Thank goodness for that, Freda thought to herself as

she removed her coat. She'd have hated anything to upset her friend and suddenly finding oneself in love, as that was the way she could see Betty's new friendship heading, would have been just awful.

Betty handed Freda a cup and saucer and they sat down to chat. 'You've had a busy day. If it was me, I'd be exhausted, but then I am older than you.'

'You're still a young woman, Betty, and you always work long days. I have to confess to flagging this evening, having had to work my hours at the fire station after a morning shift at Woolies and an afternoon on my training course.'

'So, tell me, what did they teach you today?'

'We had to listen to a talk about basic repairs to our motorbikes. It wasn't as interesting as learning about riding them. Tomorrow it is first aid.'

'I can see how that wouldn't be so interesting but both are worthwhile learning. Why, you could break down somewhere remote and not find anyone to help you. First aid is always useful, as you well know. You could pass on what you learn to the Girl Guides.'

Freda's eyes lit up. 'I hadn't thought of that. They will love to know about first aid and I've promised to take my motorbike to one of the meetings and give a talk about being a dispatch rider for the Fire Service.'

'When will you be operational?'

'Would you believe, the end of next week. The training course has gone so quickly. I'm just a little bit scared at the enormity of the job.'

'You will be fine, Freda. The Fire Service would not

have put you forward for the job if they didn't have faith in your abilities. I'm rather envious.'

'And I'm in awe of the way you run Woolworths, Betty. I just hope that when this war is over they don't demote you.'

'It may happen, Freda. After all, I stepped into the job so a man could go off to war to defend our country. Perhaps if my workload diminishes after the war, I'll think about another profession. I quite like the idea of riding a motorbike for the Fire Service like you or perhaps becoming an actress in the films.'

'I take it you are pulling my leg?' Freda asked with some uncertainty. She'd never known Betty joke about anything.

'It's a long time until I retire from Woolworths, Freda, and then I'll have more years spread in front of me with no family or job. Sometimes I wish I'd done more with my life,' she sighed.

'I've never heard you speak like this before, Betty. Does it have something to do with Douglas coming into your life?'

Betty, who had stood to collect the empty cups, stopped to answer Freda. 'I'd be lying if I said it wasn't. Douglas's appearance has made me think about the past and the hopes and dreams I held dear to me at that time. By rights I'd have been a wife and mother by now. I might even have been a grandmother. Yes, that does sound strange, doesn't it?' she said, noticing Freda's smile. 'That was my dream back in 1917 when Charlie died.'

'You can always have new dreams,' Freda said sadly. 'My dream used to be to run my own market stall and live with my parents, but after Dad died everything changed. The only reason I came to Erith in the first place was to look for Lenny when he went missing. Luckily I settled into a new life with my job at Woolworths, along with all my new friends. Until the war started I imagined a future where I would live here in Erith and work at Woolies. I just never thought things would change.'

'We are so alike, Freda.'

Freda nodded. 'We have Woolworths to thank for that. Just like Sarah and Maisie. It seems so much longer than four years since we all met.'

Betty placed the cups and saucers in the kitchen sink. They could wait until the morning. 'Tell me, Freda, do you like Douglas?'

Freda stopped to think for a moment. 'I haven't got to know him as well as you have, but he accounted for himself in a respectable manner the day we nabbed him in the shop and he doesn't come across as a ne'er do well, so yes, I should think he is a gentleman and decent enough. What do you think?'

Betty headed to the bottom of the steep staircase. 'I feel he is an admirable man and I hope to get to know him better.'

Freda smiled to herself as she turned out the light. Betty might just be about to have her life changed beyond recognition. She could think of nothing better to happen to her boss and friend, although she still felt Betty was a little old for such things.

*

'Now, have you got everything you need?' Ruby asked as she stuck her head round the spare room to see Gwyneth and Myfi placing their clothes into a large walnut chest of drawers. 'My, that's seen some clothing in it over the years. This was the first piece of decent furniture my old man and me bought after we married. We didn't have much back then, not that I've got much now, but we scrimped and saved for that chest of drawers.'

Gwyneth ran her hand over the polished surface. 'It is indeed a fine piece of furniture. I must say, it is very good of you to take us in, Mrs Caselton. I still don't know what we did to offend Mrs Munro,' Gwyneth said with a sad look on her face.

'Don't you be worrying about her, my love. The pair of you are welcome to stay here for as long as you wish. We can let the authorities know tomorrow and do all the bits and pieces then. Now, has the young lady everything she needs before she goes to bed?'

Gwyneth ran her hand over the child's dark hair. 'I'm thinking she has, Mrs Caselton. I'll be tucking her up in her bed soon.'

'When she's settled come downstairs and join me in the front room. I'll put the kettle on,' Ruby said before nodding to the child. 'Night night, sweetheart. Happy dreams.'

Gwyneth took the cup of tea from Ruby. 'There's nothing better, is there?' she sighed as she took a sip of the hot liquid. 'It's been a very long day.'

Ruby nodded as she watched the woman. She'd never

seen such shiny dark hair and vivid bright eyes. She didn't know any Welsh people but if they were all like Gwyneth, then they were a good-looking nation, she thought to herself. 'How did you and your daughter come to be in Erith?' she asked.

Gwyneth paused before replying. 'It's been a year now. We moved to Maidstone to be close to a family member, but after our rented cottage was damaged in an air raid we've moved from digs to digs. Thankfully, I managed to find temporary work but then we found ourselves homeless again. Once registered as homeless the officials found us digs with Mrs Munro. You know what happened then.'

'You couldn't go home to Wales or live with your relative in Maidstone?'

Gwyneth shook her head so violently that her beautiful hair flowed around her shoulders. 'No, it's not an option,' she said firmly before picking up her tea and drinking with shaking hands.

Ruby observed the woman's reaction and remained silent. Something was amiss and she'd bide her time before asking. She prided herself on being a good judge of character and Gwyneth seemed a decent sort. This war affected people in so many ways and if Gwyneth did have a problem, then who was she to judge? 'Well, you're safe here now and Erith is a pretty good place to live, though I do say so myself.'

'Do you live here alone, Mrs Caselton?' Gwyneth asked, having composed herself quickly.

'Goodness, no. I'm a widow, but this house is like Clapham Junction at times with all the toing and froing going on. My son, George, used to stay here when he came up from Devon for his work at Vickers, but he's moved to Crayford for the duration. George's girl, Sarah, is living with her mother-in-law just down the road – her husband flies Spitfires – and another lodger, Maisie, has married and lives with her RAF husband a few streets away. Freda still lives here but is away tonight on duty at the fire station. I'm sure you'll get on well with Freda.' Ruby stopped short of explaining about her friends and then chuckled.

'Whatever is so funny, Mrs Caselton?' Gwyneth asked in her lilting Welsh accent.

Ruby wiped her eyes and smiled. 'I just thought that if Vera was correct and you and the kiddie are spies, then I've just given away a hell of a lot of information. Goodness me, I'll be locked up in the Tower of London,' she chuckled.

Gwyneth laughed. 'Be assured that we are not spies, Mrs Caselton, but then I would say the same if I was,' she added with a smile.

'I'd soon find you out, love, we don't have any secrets in this house. Oh, and please call me Ruby.'

Gwyneth nodded but the smile had left her face.

'You've made a marvellous job of the shop-window display,' Betty declared as she stepped back into the store after checking the view from outside Woolworths.

'It's all thanks ter Freda really. It was 'er who mentioned she 'ad to learn about first aid and it got me thinking about how many people would want to know how to 'elp if there was a raid or an accident. Getting hold of those booklets and stuff was a good idea too.'

Freda shrugged her shoulders. 'Maisie was the brave person who went over to see one of the managers at Hedley Mitchell to ask to borrow a mannequin for the display. I wouldn't have dared do that. They are far too posh for me in that shop.'

Maisie laughed aloud. 'They all have ter use the lavvie, just like us.'

'Shh, Maisie, our customers may hear you,' Betty said. Personally she agreed with the girls. Some of the department heads at Hedley Mitchell did appear superior, but the majority of their staff shopped in the store she managed. If Hedley Mitchell was the biggest shop in Erith, then Woolworths was the most popular for ordinary folk, she liked to think.

'The mannequin they found for us at the back of their storeroom was bashed about a bit and not likely to be used again. There are chunks of plaster missing on all the limbs and it's bald,' Freda said glumly.

'All the better for us. We covered those parts with bandages. It looks healthier now than it did when we carried the thing over the road.' Maisie grinned.

Betty smiled at Maisie. The woman looked a picture of health now after having looked quite down for the past weeks. Maisie had asked for a meeting, and Betty felt she had an inkling of what Maisie was going to say. She checked the time on the wall of the store. 'I can spare a few minutes now to speak with you, Maisie. Let's go up to my office. Freda, take your break now. I hear that Maureen has been baking rock cakes so you may be lucky and nab one before the rest of the staff eat them all.'

The three women took a final look at the window display, which was already attracting attention from passers-by. Satisfied they'd done their best, they headed to the door that led upstairs to the staff area. 'Oh my goodness,' Betty declared, 'what a lovely surprise.'

Leaning against a wall by the door was a young soldier with striking red hair.

'Ginger!' Maisie screeched, giving the lad a big hug. 'I've not seen yer since me wedding.'

'I got home on leave yesterday and thought I'd look you all up,' he grinned.

'It's a pleasure to see you, Ginger. Come upstairs and have a cup of tea. The morning break starts soon and I'm sure everyone will be pleased to see you. Freda's going for her break – if you've forgotten your way, you can follow her. I'll see you after I've had a few words with Maisie.'

'I've not forgotten Woolworths, Miss Billington. In fact, it's thinking about you all that's kept me going at times.'

Freda glanced at Ginger as they headed up the stair-case towards the staff area. She could see he'd grown up and wasn't the young cheeky lad that she'd met on the day she arrived at Woolworths for her interview. There were a few lines around his eyes and his freckled face was thinner and paler than it had been when he'd been a trainee manager alongside Sarah's husband, Alan. 'You're in luck: Maureen has rock cakes fresh from the oven. We don't get as many treats these days as when you were here.'

'Don't tell me. There's a war on.' He grinned weakly as he stopped to look around the familiar room. 'Nothing seems to have changed.'

'Oh, but it has,' Freda said. 'Look at the cracks on the ceiling; we had a close call that day.' Ginger gave Freda a sad smile and she blushed. 'I'm sorry, you must think I'm a right ninny, what with you seeing action and all that. We're all trying to do our bit here, you know. Sit down and I'll get the tea.'

Tea took a little longer than usual as Maureen made such a fuss when she spotted Ginger. 'We're all going to the Erith Dance Studio on Saturday. You must join us. Alan will be there. It should be a good evening.'

Ginger looked at Freda. 'Will you be going?'

'I should be, unless I'm needed at the fire station.' It would be her last weekend answering the telephone, as she would be a dispatch rider by the Monday, all being well.

Ginger smirked. 'What's a little thing like you doing putting out fires?'

Freda tried hard not to bristle at his comment and instead slid his tea in front of him and started to explain how she and her friends were all playing their part in fighting Hitler.

Betty hugged Maisie close. 'I'm so pleased for you and David. It must have been hard for you after last Christmas. David must be so excited.'

Maisie extracted herself from Betty's arms and sat down. 'He's not back until tomorrow so he doesn't know.'

'Oh my, you mean I'm the first to know? That seems rather a strange way to go about things, Maisie. David deserved to know first. After all, he is your husband.'

'You're not the first ter know. Sarah was with me when I went ter see the doctor. I need ter ask you something before I see David.'

Betty sat down opposite the pretty blonde woman. Even in wartime Maisie looked perfectly turned out. 'Is there a problem, Maisie?'

Maisie shook her head. 'No, but I'm handing in my notice. I need ter be careful and if that means not working until the baby is here, then I'm sorry.' She raised her chin defiantly, expecting Betty to argue.

'I'm so proud of you, Maisie. Putting your child's well-being before anything shows you will be the perfect mother. I envy you.'

Maisie frowned. 'So it's all right that I'm giving up Woolies for now?'

'Yes, of course it is. I won't say it will be easy, but we will cope and I'm sure David will be relieved that you are cutting back for the sake of your child, and that is as it should be.'

Maisie was relieved that her boss understood her problem. 'Thank you. I'll still help out at the WVS and by doing a bit of sewing, so if there's anything you need altering or making, just shout.'

'It's funny you should say that as I've been invited to go dancing on Saturday and I'm not sure if I have anything suitable to wear. Can you help me?'

'Are you going to the dance at Erith Dance Studios?'

'Why, yes, I am.'

'I was going to ask yer to come along with us. What with Alan flying off God knows where and Freda most likely off on her motorbike, we thought it would be our last time fer a get-together.'

Betty had hoped to keep her friendship with Douglas a secret a little longer, but with most of her friends being at the dance she had no choice but to tell Maisie now. 'I've been invited to the dance by Douglas Billington.'

Maisie raised her eyebrows but said nothing.

'Please don't read anything into this. It is simply his way of repaying me for inviting him to dinner the other day. He is a widow with young daughters. He is simply a friend,' she explained.

And that's why you're blushing, Maisie thought to herself before beaming. 'Then let me help you find something to wear. There's no time to make something new, but I have an idea that will make Douglas have eyes only for you.'

Betty tried not to look excited at the thought of Douglas holding her in his arms as they danced. She had been worrying about her conservative wardrobe of clothes, but knew she could rely on Maisie to help her out. Saturday would be a day to remember.

9

Freda was late for the dance. The time on the Coronation Clock Tower in Bexleyheath showed it was almost six o'clock as she revved the engine and sped towards home. She desperately needed a bath to scrub the smell of oil from her body before stepping into her dance frock and preparing herself for a night of dancing. It had taken longer than she thought to collect the motorbike allocated to her and sign for the uniform of an Auxiliary Fire Service dispatch rider.

Turning onto the road that led through to Erith, she gasped in horror as an army lorry pulled out from a side road, giving her no choice but to swerve left towards a grassy field and allotments, where her bike bumped about on the uneven surface, throwing her onto a pile of compost. Before she knew it helpful hands were pulling her up from the warm mound. Feeling shaken and wondering how her bike had fared, it took a few minutes for her to realize the soldiers who had caused her to swerve were not British.

'Here you go, ma'am, let me help you out of that mess.'

Freda could just see a hand reach out to her through the muck spread on her goggles. Once standing on her own two feet, she pulled off the goggles and glared at the soldiers. 'Why ever were you driving like that? Not only were you going too fast, but you were on the wrong side of the road!' she bellowed.

'Whoa, ma'am, that's no way to welcome servicemen who are here to help you win the war.'

Freda stood, hands on hips, trying to calm down. She was always polite, regardless of whether someone was in uniform or not. Her years working in Woolworths had taught her not to show her anger under any circumstances. But this time she could not hold back. 'Rest assured we are grateful for you arriving here to join us in fighting the enemy, but it doesn't help if you go around trying to kill locals and ruining our vehicles. Anyone would think you were on Hitler's side, not ours!'

Four of the men stepped away from Freda, but she could see they were smiling and overheard one of them call her a 'firecracker'. She tried hard to keep a straight face until she saw one of the men wheeling her beautiful new bike from where it had ended up under a bush. Her face crumpled. How could she ride it now and however would she get home?

'There, there, honey, don't get upset,' said a serviceman who'd stayed by her side and didn't seem worried by her anger. 'We can help her, can't we, guys?'

'We sure can, Hank. It'll take some doing but we can make it look as good as new in no time.'

Freda wiped her eyes with the cuff of her jacket and looked more closely at the bike. The handlebar was now crooked, as were the spokes of one wheel. There were scratches everywhere. 'It's new. I only collected the motorbike an hour ago. I'm on duty on Monday,' she said with a shaky voice. 'Can you really fix it?'

'I promise it will look as good as new,' the soldier called Hank said softly, looking into her eyes. 'You can trust the American army.'

'Th . . . thank you. I'll get into awful trouble if not,' Freda said as she gazed back at the bluest eyes she'd ever seen.

'Don't give it another thought. Guys, get the machine on board and we'll have the mechanics start work within the hour. It's the least we can do after our bad driving. We don't want our British friends thinking we're rough-necks, do we?' He turned back to Freda, after watching that the bike was loaded onto the back of the army lorry. 'Now we need to deliver you safely home, ma'am.' He took Freda by the arm and led her to the vehicle, gently helping her onto a front seat.

'Thank you . . . Hank?'

He saluted her. 'Sergeant Hank Marshall at your service, ma'am.'

'Freda Smith at yours,' she said to the fair-haired man.

'Come on, you lot, there'll be no seats left if you don't get a move on,' Vera grumbled as she walked into Ruby's front room in Alexandra Road. 'And you could have got yourself home a bit earlier than this,' she sniffed at Freda, as Maisie dabbed powder on the girl's face to cover a scratch while Sarah brushed her short hair to a shine.

'Go on ahead if you're that worried, Vera,' Ruby said, feeling relieved that her nosy neighbour had missed seeing Freda dropped off by a group of handsome American soldiers. She noticed also that Freda had her head in the clouds, even though she was rushing to wash and get dressed for the dance.

'I'll wait if it's all the same,' Vera huffed as she re-arranged the fox fur draped around her shoulders. 'I thought I might ask Bob to escort me,' she smiled. 'A lady shouldn't have to walk alone in the dark.'

Ruby grinned to herself. So Vera still had designs on Bob, did she? She felt sorry for the man. 'You're out of luck then as he's gone to the pub for a quick half along with the other men. Irene and Maureen are with them. You'll just have to be brave and walk in the dark, not that's it's that dark this time of year, or you can wait and walk with us.'

Vera shrugged her shoulders and sat down. 'I'll catch him later,' she said, making the women present laugh gently amongst themselves.

'Yer know what this reminds me of?' Maisie said as she snapped her gold powder compact closed and placed it in a pretty black satin evening bag.

'Go on then, tell us,' Sarah muttered carefully, as she had several hairpins in the side of her mouth.

'Our first Woolies Christmas party and dance,' Maisie grinned. 'Surely you haven't forgotten that, Sarah?'

'As if I would,' Sarah said dreamily of that snowy

evening when Alan had held her in his arms for the first time.

'Alan kissed Sarah that night,' Freda grinned. 'I spotted them through the letter box.'

'You were a little minx then and you haven't changed much,' Sarah said, trying not to smile at the memory. 'And you're a good one to talk, what with being brought home by a lorry-load of American soldiers not an hour ago.'

'Shh,' Freda whispered as they noticed Vera listening. 'Ouch, that hurts. I'll not bother having my hair clipped up if it's all the same, Sarah.' She gave her friend a wink, but already Vera had turned her attention to Gwyneth, who'd just entered the front room.

'You look beautiful,' Ruby exclaimed. 'Red really suits you with your dark hair. Turn round and let's see the back view.'

Gwyneth spun round and the full skirt flew out around her ankles in ripples of light organza. 'It's a wonderful dress but I feel a little exposed,' she said in her soft voice as she raised her hands to her bare shoulders.

'Wait here a minute,' Freda said as she jumped from her seat and dashed from the room. 'I have just the thing,' she called over her shoulder as she bounded up the stairs.

'I hope she doesn't wake up Myfi and Georgie,' Sarah sighed. 'It took an age to get Georgie off to sleep. She's only known Myfi a few days, but she simply adores her and to be sleeping in the same room has rather over-excited her.'

Vera sniffed and glared at Gwyneth. 'Leaving your

young child here to care for a baby, are you? She couldn't even call out if there was a problem. Mutes shouldn't be left alone with babies. Anything could happen.'

Silence filled the room, with all eyes turning towards Vera just as Freda returned. 'I have this shawl that would be perf . . .' She looked at Ruby, who charged towards Vera. 'Is something wrong?'

'Out now before I do something I'll regret. You can walk yourself to the bloody dance and if Hitler himself jumps out and grabs you, I'll be buggered if anyone here will bother saving you.'

Vera dashed from the room, making sure not to get too close to Ruby as Gwyneth sat on the vacated chair and covered her eyes with her hands, the full skirt of her pretty dress spreading out around her. 'I knew I shouldn't have come here. It's happening all over again,' she cried.

'Whatever was that all about?' Freda asked as she wrapped the soft black shawl around the woman's shoulders and held her as she cried.

'Never you mind about Vera, she can be a nasty so-and-so sometimes. Your girl will speak when she wants to so don't go upsetting yourself, my love. Many a child's been shy and got over it. The pair of you have settled in well here and we want you to stay, whatever happened in the past,' Ruby said, wondering if Gwyneth would explain what she meant by 'it's happening all over again'.

Gwyneth nodded and wiped her eyes. 'I should be used to people saying nasty things by now and in a way Mrs Munro is right. Myfi can't, or I should say she won't, speak,' she said, nodding her thanks to Maisie, who held out a clean handkerchief. She looked up to Ruby, who was pulling on her coat. 'You're a good woman, Mrs Caselton, but I don't want to be the reason you fall out with your friend. Do you think we should tell Mrs Munro that you have someone sitting with the girls?'

'No, let her stew for a while. It'll be good to see her squirm when she knows she was wrong. As for your troubles, if you want to speak to me about them, you'll find me a good listener. Don't let her spoil your evening.'

Maisie, who'd been silently watching what had gone on in front of her, decided to speak. 'Don't let 'er get under yer skin or it'll eat you away. She said some bloody awful things ter me a while back about me not 'avin 'ad a baby and it made me think badly of myself.' She looked to Sarah and gave a small smile. 'A friend stood by me and give me a good talking-to and now I can prove Vera wrong. Not that I want 'er knowing me news just yet.'

'Oh my goodness,' Freda shrieked and hugged Maisie tightly. 'How marvellous!'

Ruby wiped her eyes and when Freda stepped aside she hugged the girl she thought of as a granddaughter. 'I just knew things would work out for you. I'm bloody pleased. Tonight we will have a big celebration,' she told the girls.

'Please, can you pretend you don't know? David really wants to make a big announcement. He thinks Sarah is the only one to know as she was with me when I went to see the doctor. He'd be disappointed if he knew I'd told everyone and spoilt his surprise.'

'I think we can fake our surprise,' Freda said.

'Just don't squeeze me so blooming tight next time. Now, are we all ready ter go? They'll be playing the last waltz before we've even walked in the door.'

'And I've got to protect Bob or Vera will have her hooks in him,' Ruby added, picking up her handbag and gas mask.

Gwyneth followed Maisie out of the front door and pulled it closed behind her. 'I'm really pleased for you,' she said. 'A child is a great blessing. If I can help in any way, please do say. Everyone's been so good to me, and Myfi.'

'Erith folk are a good sort.' Maisie smiled at the girl. 'I don't know what I'd do without them.'

'Did you know that Freda insisted we swap bedrooms, as hers is bigger and would give us more room?' Gwyneth said as she closed the wooden gate.

'I think of Freda as a kid sister,' Maisie smiled.

'Then you lent me this dress. I've never worn anything so grand in my life. I'm truly blessed.'

Maisie walked in step with the Welsh woman. 'Had it bad, have yer, love? My life wasn't that great before I came ter Erith. Now I'm a new woman with a happy future ahead of me. Life can be good, even in wartime. You can keep the dress, I doubt it'll fit me again.'

Gwyneth stopped walking and took Maisie by the hand. 'You really mean it? My goodness! Don't forget that if you ever need any help, whatever it is, just ask. You don't know what this means to me.'

Maisie winked at the woman. 'You shouldn't 'ave said that as you've given me an idea. Now, come on, let's catch the others up.'

The women hurried on, crossing Manor Road and passing the Co-op before heading past the Odeon cinema and along the road to Erith Dance Studio, situated above shops in the High Street.

'Can you see my 'usband?' Maisie asked Freda as she caught her up.

Freda pointed through the crowd to where David Carlisle was talking with Alan, both smartly turned out in their RAF uniforms. She could see Ginger nearby, leaning against a wall smoking a cigarette. Why was it that the British army uniform was not as smart as the American version? she thought to herself, remembering Hank's blue eyes and strong hands as he helped her from the lorry when it parked in front of Ruby's house only hours earlier. Pull yourself together, she thought as she walked over to greet the young man.

Entering the large ballroom, they spotted Maureen and Irene waving to them from across the dance floor. They hurried over, minding the chairs piled high with bags and coats. George got to his feet, then hugged his daughter and mother before disappearing to buy everyone drinks.

'Don't be too long, George, the band will be starting the first dance soon and I don't wish to sit here like a wallflower,' Irene called after him.

'That's not going to happen, Irene,' Ruby said, sitting next to her daughter-in-law. 'Not in that ball gown.'

Irene patted the voluminous skirts of her turquoise frock. 'This old thing? Why, I've had it years.'

'It's very nice, Mrs Caselton,' Freda said. 'Did Maisie make it for you?'

She raised her eyebrows. 'Certainly not. One of my friends at the golf club owns a couture establishment. This is a one-off, I'll have you know.'

'Thank goodness for that,' Ruby muttered to no one in particular.

'What did you say?'

'I said, the band seems to be warming up,' Ruby said.

'Thank gawd for that.' Maisie grinned at Ruby and they burst out laughing.

'I do hope they speed up the tempo or we'll be doing slow foxtrots all evening,' Irene sniffed.

'Have you met, Ginger, Mrs Caselton? He's home on leave,' Freda said, nudging the lad sitting next to her to shake hands with Irene.

'I do believe I know you from somewhere,' Irene said with a disdainful look at the young soldier.

'I worked at Woolworths with your son-in-law. No doubt we'll be back there once this war's over,' he said as he picked up his pint of pale ale and took a mouthful.

'My son-in-law is an RAF pilot. I doubt he will return to such a mundane job,' Irene replied.

'Oh, I do hope he does,' Sarah joined in. 'I want everything to be as it was before the war. Not to see Alan at work every day is too terrible to think about. Besides, F. W. Woolworths are paying the men's wages all the time they are away serving their country. I think that's rather splendid of them. To not return to work after all that is absolutely not on.'

'Oh, I do hope Alan returns to Woolworths. I'm sure he will one day have a store of his own to manage. He has such a bright future with the company,' Betty Billington announced.

Sarah turned round to welcome Betty and gasped. Her boss looked wonderful in an oyster satin gown that looked familiar. As the penny dropped she saw Maisie give their boss a wink. Of course, it was the gown Maisie had worn to their very first Woolworths Christmas party four years previously. 'Why, Betty, you look wonderful.'

It was true. Betty's eyes were shining as she stood there still holding the arm of Douglas, who was looking extremely smart in his best suit. 'Hello, everyone, may I introduce Douglas Billington?' Douglas shook hands with the ladies and asked if they'd like a drink.

'Thank you very much, but Dad's getting a round in,' Sarah explained, before adding, 'I do hope you will accept our apologies for the way we manhandled you when we first met?'

Douglas laughed loudly. 'Apology accepted. If it wasn't for you, I'd still be loitering outside Woolworths.'

'My goodness,' Irene declared. 'Sit here and tell me all about this handsome man. I take it he is a relative?' she asked as she moved her handbag from the chair next to her and patted the seat for Betty to sit down. 'And where did you obtain that delightful gown? I so love oyster satin and the button detail is just beautiful.'

Betty ran her fingers across the soft skirt. 'This is one of Maisie's creations that she kindly lent to me. I'm not one for going out much so don't have a wardrobe of party frocks. She came to my rescue when Douglas invited me out.'

'You look lovely. The best-dressed woman here,' Ruby

said. 'I'm always telling Maisie she should make her living from dressmaking.'

George and David arrived at that point, balancing trays of drinks and dodging couples who were now on the dance floor waiting for the band to start playing.

'I've said the same, Mrs C., but she's not interested. No offence, Betty, but she's not making use of her talents stuck in Woolworths behind a counter,' David Carlisle said.

'I like Woolies and I like a bit of dressmaking for meself and friends,' Maisie said, looking embarrassed by the attention. 'Betty was welcome to the dress. It only needed bit of altering, what with 'er being shorter than me. Besides, I'm never likely to fit into it again,' she added, patting her stomach gently.

'Oh my, you're not . . . are you . . . ?' Irene said with delight, rising to her feet to give Maisie a hug before looking pointedly at Vera. 'I'm sure everyone is really pleased for you.'

'I think a toast is in order,' George said as he passed drinks around the table. The men and women present raised their glasses and toasted David and Maisie Carlisle.

'Good health to you, Maisie, and may your children grow up in peace,' Betty said as she wiped a tear from her eye. 'You have no idea how envious I am of your good fortune.'

'You never know what lies ahead, Betty,' Ruby said as she looked to where Douglas was gazing at their friend with adoration in his eyes.

*

'It's been a lovely evening and thank goodness there were no air raids. I wouldn't have fancied going down the public shelter in my best outfit.'

Bob steered Ruby passed a couple of dancers who were blocking their path around the dance floor. The lights had been turned down for the last waltz as the band played 'Who's Taking You Home Tonight?' 'You look a picture and give the youngsters a run for their money.'

Ruby slapped his shoulder. 'Don't be a daft 'a'porth. You're as bad as my Eddie saying such things.'

'Then I'm in good company. He was a good bloke was your husband. Do you think he'd have approved?'

Ruby looked puzzled. 'Of what?'

Bob sighed. 'Of us, Ruby. Do you think he'd have liked me courting his wife?'

'Is that what you're doing, Bob? I thought we was just having a dance.'

'Come off it, you know what I mean. After all, we do see quite a lot of each other.'

'Don't make too much of it, Bob. I like you a lot, but I'll love my Eddie until the day I die.'

'And that's as it should be. I feel the same about my old girl, but they've gone now and it would be criminal not to make the most of the time we've got left, wouldn't it?'

'I suppose it would . . .' Ruby said as the music came to an end and the light came back on.

Bob's face lit up. 'So, do you think . . . ?'

'I don't think anything, Bob. I'm just saying.'

'I'll take that for now,' he grinned.

Ruby smiled to herself. Bob was a good sort and she'd become fond of him. Perhaps Eddie would have approved? If the boot had been on the other foot, she'd have wished him to find love again. Love? Is that what she was feeling for Bob Jackson?

'Well, well,' Bob said as he led Ruby back to her seat.

She looked to where Bob was gazing at his son. Mike Jackson was still on the dance floor with his arm around Gwyneth and both were in deep conversation, appearing not to notice what was going on around them. 'She's a nice woman, Bob. Mike could do a lot worse. I've only known her a few days, but I pride myself on being a good judge of character.'

Bob nodded thoughtfully. 'Our Mike's always been one for his work. He's walked out with a few women over the years, but never found one he wanted to settle down with or who wanted to settle down with him.'

'Perhaps now's the time?' Ruby said as she reached her chair and sat down.

'I'd like to know a little more about her first,' Bob said.

'Come off it, Bob, your Mike's the same age as my George and he's a grandfather. Some would say your Mike's got off light so far. You can't wrap them in cotton wool forever. All the same, I'll have a chat with Gwyneth and let you know if there's anything untoward. I would like to know why her daughter's like she is. The poor mite's not spoke one word since she crossed my threshold.'

'She's not wearing a wedding ring either.'

'So you're already keeping an eye on her?'

'Once a policeman, always a policeman,' Bob laughed.

'I'll keep that I mind if our Nelson goes missing. I take it you coppers still look out for lost dogs?'

Bob roared with laughter. One thing was for sure, Ruby was a good laugh.

'I thought your mum and dad would have come back for a cup of tea?' Ruby said as she sat down to take off her shoes and rub her toes. 'I can't remember the last time I danced so much. What do you make of Betty and her beau?'

Sarah looked over her shoulder in case her nan had been heard. Fortunately there was too much chatter from the front room for anyone to have noticed. 'I'm not sure that Douglas is her beau, Nan. Mum and Dad didn't want to miss the last bus back to Crayford. Douglas went to Betty's for his dinner so they could talk about Betty's fiancé who died in the last war. Douglas was in the trenches with Charlie and saw him die. They have shared reminiscences, that's all.'

'Shared reminiscences, you say? Hmm.'

'Oh, Nan, you're getting as bad as Vera,' Sarah said as she placed cups and saucers onto a tea tray. You'll be planning a wedding next.'

'Stranger things have happened, my love. Now, before I forget, will you pop round and check things are all right here while I'm away visiting your Aunt Pat? I know Freda can take care of the house, but she's so busy these days and I'd hate Gwyneth to have a problem while we aren't around to help. I've shown her where everything is in case we have an air raid.'

'Of course I will. She's going to look after Georgie one evening while I go out with Alan. Now he knows when he is off on duty again we want to make the most of things and have a few hours together. She did offer to have her while I went to work, but I don't want to impose too much.'

'She's a good one, but I wish I knew why young Myfi doesn't talk. Don't think I'm being nosy, but can you ask her? I was going to have a chat myself, but it may come easier from someone who isn't her landlady.'

'If the opportunity arises, I'll do my best. Now, let's get this tea handed out before it gets cold.'

'Blimey, you took yer time making that. I'm parched. I thought you'd gone to pick the tea leaves,' Maisie chuckled.

'Not so much of your lip, madam,' Sarah grinned. 'Just because you're a lady of leisure now don't expect me to wait on you hand and foot.'

'No need. That's what I've got an 'usband for,' Maisie retorted, looking up adoringly at David, who was perched on the arm of her chair. 'That reminds me. Betty, are you still needing sales staff?'

'I am but surely you aren't thinking of returning? You only left yesterday,' Betty replied with a worried look on her face.

'I'm not but Gwyneth is looking for a job.'

The Welsh woman looked up from where she'd been deep in conversation with Mike and his father, Bob. 'Why, that would be wonderful, but only if you think I'll be up to it. I have done some shop work but not in a Woolworths store.'

'Why don't you come in and see me on Monday morning and we can have a chat?'

'I'd like that, thank you, Miss Billington,' Gwyneth said with a shy smile.

'I thought you wasn't coming,' Ginger said as he threw his cigarette stub to the ground and stamped on it with one booted foot. 'The film's about to start and I'm getting wet waiting here for you.'

'Some of us have work to do,' Freda retorted as they joined the queue at the doors of the Erith Odeon. 'How have you spent your day?' Ginger was good company, but Freda couldn't get the thought of the handsome American serviceman out of her mind. Ginger had changed in many ways since joining the Royal West Kent Regiment – not just in appearance, having filled out considerably, but his merry disposition had all but disappeared. She forgave his moodiness, as no doubt he'd experienced hostile situations while serving his country. However, she felt bad for not telling Ginger the truth – that she'd not been late because of work, but instead had hung on at home waiting for her motorbike to be dropped off in case Hank delivered it and she had a chance to talk to him. Instead it had been two of his comrades. Ruby had been enchanted by the men and accepted their gift of a box of groceries. Freda, after thanking the men profusely, had taken the bike to the fire station, where it was to be stored, before dashing off to meet Ginger.

He was silent for a moment, contemplating Freda's question. 'This and that,' he said with a shrug.

Standing next to him as he paid for the two tickets, she could tell he'd been to the pub as apart from the smell of his damp uniform and cigarettes, she could smell beer. Freda had been looking forward to seeing the film and felt quite excited as they filed into the darkened cinema and were directed to their seats by the beam from the usherette's torch. The latest Pathé News had just started and Freda was keen to know if there was any update from where she believed her brother Lenny's ship would be. She sat on the edge of her seat clutching her handbag and holding her breath with her eyes glued to the large screen. Please God, keep Lenny safe, she silently prayed.

Ginger nudged her arm and offered her a cigarette. She waved him away, her eyes still firmly fixed to the screen and her thoughts hundreds of miles away with her much-loved brother.

He gave an exaggerated sigh. 'A barrel of laughs you're gonna be.'

Freda placed her bag on the floor by her feet and leant back in her chair as the titles appeared on the screen for the 'B' film. It was a Clive Danvers spy story and she was a fan of the actor who appeared as the handsome secret agent. The film had barely started before she felt Ginger's arm reach along the back of her seat and touch her shoulder. She did her best to ignore him and watch the film, wriggling a little to dislodge his hand, but his grip tightened as he pulled her closer to him. Freda froze. What should she do? Not only was she uncomfortable with the arm of her seat digging into her side but she wondered what was going on in Ginger's mind as he started to grope her leg, raising her skirt, at the same time pulling her head towards his and doing his utmost to kiss her. The grip on her shoulder was such that she couldn't pull away. 'Stop it,' she hissed and slapped his hand, turning her face to the left to avoid the overbearing smell of cigarettes and beer.

Ginger pulled her closer still. Freda gasped in pain as his hand moved to her right breast and squeezed it tight. What the hell was he up to? She yelped in pain and distress as she heard the fabric of her blouse tear.

'Young man,' a voice from the seat behind said loudly and Ginger jumped, releasing Freda from his hold. He swore and turned round.

'What's up with you, Grandad?' he retorted, glaring at the elderly man.

'I don't think the young lady wishes you to treat her so disrespectfully,' he said pointedly.

'Mind yer own business. I paid for her ticket so what we do is up to me,' Ginger hissed back.

Finding herself free of Ginger's grip, Freda grabbed her handbag, along with the gas-mask bag she'd tied to the handle, and ran from the cinema, tears blinding her eyes. The dim light in the foyer startled her as she headed towards the main exit where a staff member was standing by the door allowing latecomers in. He nodded to Freda. 'The film not to your liking, miss?'

Freda sobbed, 'No,' and ran from the cinema, not noticing the man's concerned face. Not wishing to head home and worry Ruby or go to Sarah's house with Alan bound to be at home, she decided to walk the short distance to Maisie's as she knew David was away on duty. She would die of embarrassment if she had to explain to a man why she was so upset. With her head down to hide her tears she rushed across the road, dodging a drayman's horse and cart and a couple of women on bicycles who called out to her to be careful.

'Oi, Freda, wait up!'

Freda stopped dead in her tracks as Alan caught her up. 'Where are you off to in such a rush? I've just been to the chip shop as Maureen heard they had some rock salmon in,' he said. 'There's enough here for four so why not come home with me and join us?'

Freda took a deep breath to calm herself and turned to face her best friend's husband.

The smile dropped from Alan's face. 'Aw, kid, what's happened to you?' He noticed how she was trying to hold her blouse together to hide the tear.

Try as she might, Freda couldn't hold back her tears and with a gut-wrenching sob she blurted out, 'Ginger.'

10

Sarah handed Freda a cup of tea and sat down beside her. The girl was still shaking, even with the blanket that Maureen had wrapped round her shoulders when Alan had brought her into the house. 'Here, sip this. I've added three spoons of sugar.'

'Sarah, you can't go giving me your sugar allowance. I'll bring you some round tomorrow to replace this.'

'Oh no you won't. It'll be a sad day when I can't help a friend when she needs something sweet. It's supposed to be good for shock. Alan has gone upstairs to put Georgie to bed and Maureen said she'd work to do in the kitchen so we can be alone to talk about what happened.'

'But what about your supper? It'll get cold. I'll drink this and be off out the way. I don't want to spoil your evening. You haven't got long before Alan goes back on duty to goodness knows where. You should be with him, not taking care of me. I'll be off home as soon as I've drunk my tea. And you wasted your sugar ration on me . . .'

'Stop right there. Freda, you are my best friend. In

fact, you're the sister I never had. Alan did right to bring you to our home. We all want to help you.'

Freda felt her eyes start to water and quickly took a mouthful of tea while she blinked the tears away. 'Thank you, I'm being daft. I'd like to tell you all what happened so please ask Maureen and Alan to come and listen.'

Sarah called out to her mother-in-law, Maureen, and then ran upstairs to speak to her husband. Once everyone was seated Freda explained what had occurred in the Odeon cinema.

Maureen, who'd started to weep as Freda told what happened, hugged Freda. 'What a brute. Thank goodness the man seated behind you spotted what was happening. I dread to think what would have happened if Ginger had followed you from the cinema and you'd not bumped into Alan like you did. Thank goodness I fancied chips for my supper.' She looked towards her son, Alan. 'It could have been so much worse if you'd been alone.'

'He used to be such a sweet lad,' Sarah said. 'I wonder what's happened to him?'

'It's this damned war,' Maureen said passionately. 'It's turned the world upside down.'

'You can't blame the war for this, Mum. Some men just . . . well, let me say that some men are not so good deep down inside. Ginger's not been the same since he signed up. I thought he wasn't himself last time I met him when he was on leave. Far too cocky for his own good and he's started to like the drink too much. He wasn't very happy at the dance the other night either.'

Freda nodded. 'If it hadn't been for you and George,

I'd have not danced all evening. I only agreed to go to the pictures with him as he was so grumpy. I wish I hadn't now.'

'Sorry, kid, I should have kept an eye on you and this wouldn't have happened,' Alan apologized.

Freda gave him a shaky smile. 'Don't blame yourself, Alan. Perhaps I'm not meant to meet a decent bloke like Sarah and Maisie have. I'll end up on the shelf like Betty and live out my years working for Woolworths.'

Sarah roared with laughter. 'I do hope that was a joke, Freda? You're still not twenty-one and Maisie and me could both tell you tales about failed romances. Believe me, one day you will meet the right man and be blissfully happy. You may even meet him at Woolworths,' she added with a smile.

'And even our Miss Billington seems to have a spring in her step since Douglas came on the scene,' Maureen added, 'so I'd not write her off just yet.' She'd have liked to add that Ruby was also smitten with a certain retired policeman, but she wasn't sure anyone else had noticed. 'How about we all wipe away our tears and have a bite to eat? I put the fish and chips in the oven to keep warm and I've buttered some bread.'

'You get started. There's something I've got to do,' Alan said as he pulled on his jacket and headed towards the door. 'I won't be long.'

'Alan . . . don't . . .' Sarah called out, but it was too late as the front door banged shut behind him. 'I hope he isn't going to do anything stupid,' she said.

Maureen served up the meal and placed Alan's portion back in the oven with another plate on top so the chips didn't dry out too much. Despite their worries they started to eat, although each of them kept looking towards the clock on the mantelpiece as time ticked by. 'The chips will be past saving before too long,' Maureen observed.

They'd all but finished when they heard a key in the door. Sarah was on her feet in seconds and hurrying to the door. 'He's all right,' she called out as they both came into the room.

'Sit yourself down and eat, we can hear what you've been up to afterwards. I take it you found Ginger?'

Alan grinned at his mum. 'I thought you said I was to eat first?'

'I'd like to know if that's all right?' Freda said. She was worried that Alan would be hurt if he went to find Ginger. Although short in stature, Ginger's sturdy build could have done serious damage to Alan's slimmer body.

Maureen fetched Alan's supper and placed it on the table in front of him. 'You can eat and talk just this once,' she indicated to her son. 'Usually I'd not allow bad manners at my table,' she said to Freda, 'but this time I think we all want to know what happened.'

Alan cut into the crispy batter and chewed a mouthful of food before speaking. 'I thought he might still be at the cinema. He's so cocky he could have stayed to watch the film. However, just as I got there Sergeant Jackson and another policeman came out of the Odeon. They had Ginger between them and carted him off. I asked what was going on and was told Ginger had started a fight when an usherette asked him to leave. There'd been a complaint made about him after you rushed off.'

Freda sighed. 'Did he hurt anyone?'

'I don't know much more than that, but I do feel you should go to Erith police station and tell them your side of what happened.'

Sarah squeezed Freda's hand. 'He's right, love, its best you speak to them.'

Freda looked horrified. 'What if they think I was the cause of this? They may think I let men touch me like that and that Ginger and me have . . . Oh no, I couldn't go to the police station. I'd rather die first.'

'There's no need to get upset, Freda. I have a better solution. Alan and Sarah can walk you home when you're ready and if you see a light on at Mike Jackson's house, you can knock and ask to speak to him. If not, it can be done in the morning. He's a decent bloke and will advise you on what's best. I suggest Sarah lends you a blouse so you look respectable and don't worry Ruby. It's up to you if you tell her what happened, but don't do it while that nosy so-and-so Vera is about.'

'That does make sense,' Freda said. 'I can't really go home wearing this blanket.'

'I'd rather have punched him on the nose,' Alan muttered before spearing a chip with his fork.

Ruby picked up a broom and swept a pile of used bedding across the hall and into the yard behind the building. Returning to the task of sorting donated clothing, she spotted Vera arrive in her smart WVS uniform.

'Watch out, this pile of bedding is hopping with fleas. I've started a pile for burning out in the yard. You'd best use a broom rather than get too close or you'll be scratching for weeks to come.'

Vera just gave a sniff and walked past Ruby without a word, heading towards the table where Irene was sitting overseeing that day's work for members of the WVS. She'd taken to her work like a duck to water, but today she would encounter Vera for the first time.

'Oh, Mrs Munro,' Irene said as she pointedly checked the clock on the wall of the church hall. 'Thank you for joining us. I had planned for you to join the canteen van today but unfortunately it has just left. Instead would you help Mrs Caselton sort out the bags of donated items?'

Vera was confused. 'Mrs Caselton? Do you mean Ruby or yourself?'

Irene sighed. The voluntary job hadn't been what she'd expected. Her supervisory skills had not been accepted as joyfully as she'd anticipated and it was only with much persuasion that had she managed to wangle a desk job for a few days. Come next week she could be sorting flea-infested clothing with her mother-in-law.

Vera sniffed. 'I thought with new members joining the WVS those of us who had been long-serving members would have been promoted?' She looked pointedly at Irene and the empty chair beside her.

'Mrs Munro, there is only so much administration to be done. At some time we will all have to head to the coalface and do our best for King and country.'

Vera wasn't exactly sure what Irene was talking about.

'I've never been near a coalface in my life and I'm not about to start now. So, if you don't mind, I'll get sorting the clothes that have just come in. You can let someone else work with the coal . . . unless of course there's a free scuttle of the stuff going begging?'

Irene sighed and wished she were back in Devon amongst the women she called her equals. 'Thank you, Mrs Munro. Now, if you don't mind, I have work to get through before my shift comes to an end.' Taking a discreet look at her watch, she was pleased to see there were just a few minutes left before she could retrieve her coat and escape.

Vera wandered over to where Ruby was throwing some old clothing onto a pile on the floor. 'Are they for the rag-rug group?' she asked, bending down to pick up the pile of tattered rags. The group had grown since Maisie had volunteered to show the women of Erith how to create colourful rugs for their homes. They'd also made rugs for families who'd lost their homes in the bombings.

'Don't touch them,' Ruby bellowed a little too loudly as other WVS volunteers turned to see what the shouting was about.

'There's no need to speak to me like that,' Vera snarled back. 'You've changed, Ruby Caselton, and it ain't for the good. Why, you've even set your sights on the man I plan to marry . . .' she blurted out before stopping dead in her tracks as she realized what she'd said.

Ruby roared with laughter. 'You daft bugger, Bob's never shown any interest in you. Why, it's all in your mind. Pull yourself together, woman.'

In her heart Vera knew that Ruby was right, but she'd dreamt so often of having a husband who was devoted to her and who she could care for and Bob Jackson fitted the bill, not that she was going to admit that to Ruby. 'Please yourself, but there wasn't any need to holler your head off.'

'Well, if you want to be hopping with fleas, why should I care?' Ruby said, turning away so Vera didn't see her laugh.

'What do you mean?'

'That pile of old clothes you picked up. It's running alive with 'em. I was sweeping them out the door to put on a bonfire.'

Vera shrieked and started flapping her arms about, jumping from foot to foot. 'I'll be infested and this is my smart uniform. What shall I do?' she moaned.

'Let me take this lot out and put a match to it while you take off your mac and give it a good shake. Chances are you'll have a few bites on your legs, but no one's died from a flea bite.'

Vera eyed Ruby suspiciously. 'Are you sure?'

Ruby nodded. 'Sort yourself out and then we can have a tea break. Irene brought some cake along . . . unless it's all gone,' she added.

Vera needed no second bidding and shook her mac and headed to the kitchen before Ruby put a match to the bonfire.

Freda tapped nervously on Sergeant Jackson's front door. She'd sat in the bay window of Ruby's house watching from behind a heavy green velvet curtain, keeping an eye on the house across the road until she'd seen his father, Bob, heading off to the allotment, going by the clothes he was wearing and the spade in his hand.

'Why, Freda, what a lovely surprise. What can I do for you?'

'I wondered if I could have a word with you, Sergeant Jackson?'

'Come on in and, please, my name is Mike, we've known each other long enough not to stand on formalities.'

Freda followed Mike into a front room that was the mirror image of Ruby's home. 'Actually, it's not really a social call. I have a little problem and I'd like your advice,' she said nervously.

'Advice, eh? That sounds serious. Would you like a drink while we chat?' he offered as he showed her to a comfy armchair placed by the fireside. Mike sat in an identical chair opposite.

'No thank you. I had one with Ruby before she went off to her WVS meeting. I've got to be at Woolworths in an hour for my shift.'

Mike nodded. 'So what can I help you with?'

Freda felt her cheeks start to burn. 'It's a little embarrassing.'

'Let me help you then. Would it have anything to do with young Ginger being arrested yesterday evening?'

Freda hung her head in shame. 'Yes, it does, and I'm afraid I'm involved. It may even be my fault he was arrested.'

Mike nodded his head. 'I was told a young woman was

seen with him earlier. What makes you think you're to blame?'

'Well, he tried to kiss me and I wouldn't let him and he became rather insistent. I left the cinema as I was upset and bumped into Alan, who took me back to his mum's house.'

Mike looked concerned. 'Did he hurt you, Freda?'

'No, although he ripped my blouse. It was an old one so doesn't matter, although I'd be a fool if I didn't say he frightened me. He used to be such a sweet lad,' Freda said as a large tear dropped onto her cheek.

'There, there, don't you go upsetting yourself, Freda. I shouldn't really tell you this, but Ginger was arrested because he started a fight with another man. It was nothing you did.'

'But there was a man who told Ginger to stop upsetting me,' Freda said, brushing the tear away with her fingers. 'I'd hate to think I caused a fight and a person was hurt. Ginger seems to be so grumpy these days and not anything like he used to be when we all worked together at Woolworths.'

'The war affects people in different ways, Freda, and Ginger will learn from what happened once he has time to think about his actions. If it's any consolation, he is nursing a cut lip and a dented ego today. He came off worse, as the man he upset was a boxer in his youth and can still throw a punch.'

Freda smiled. She'd like to have seen that. No doubt Ginger would have been surprised after the way he spoke to the man in the cinema.

'We won't be pressing charges as he is due to return

to his regiment later today, so you won't see any more of him around town for a while,' Mike assured her. 'So no more tears, eh?'

'That's a relief,' Freda sighed. 'I just wish . . .'

'What do you wish, Freda? Are you unhappy?' Mike liked Ruby's young lodger. He'd watched her grow up in the years since she'd arrived in Erith as a frightened child and had been on duty when her brother turned up in the town. He wondered more than a few times what would have happened if she hadn't been given a job at Woolworths and made friends with Sarah and Maisie. She was a plucky kid, which was proved by her eagerness to join the Fire Service, even if it meant learning to ride a motorbike.

Freda sighed. 'I just wish I had a nice boyfriend and was looking forward to settling down with my own home and a family. Do you think I'm daft to feel this way, Mike?'

Mike ran his fingers through his short hair. 'I wouldn't say you're daft. Isn't it what we all want? It's the natural progression of things. Some of us just don't achieve it.'

Freda put her hand to her mouth. 'I'm sorry, Mike. Here's me going on about my own dreams and never thinking that perhaps you wanted to marry and settle down.'

Mike shrugged his shoulders. 'It just never happened for me. I had my chances but I've never met anyone who wanted to be a policeman's wife.'

'You'd have made a good father, Mike. I've seen you

with the youngsters in the street – you've got time for everyone.'

'I could have been a grandfather by now,' Mike said ruefully.

Freda's eyes opened wide. 'You could?'

'I was at school with Sarah's dad. Granted, he's a couple of years older than me but close enough not to make any difference. Look at him, he has a married daughter and a granddaughter.'

'You look so much younger than George. No one would think you could be a grandfather,' Freda said, looking at the tall dark-haired man with the athletic build. In comparison Sarah's dad was already grey-haired and approaching old age. Perhaps it was the responsibility of his job at Vickers that had aged him. Sarah had hinted that her dad did important war work. 'Never say never, Mike.'

Mike laughed. 'Well, if you don't find yourself married by the time you are thirty, come and knock on my door and I'll get down on one knee and propose. That's if I can get down on my knees by then,' he laughed.

'Oh, Mike, you're a right tonic and I promise to keep that in mind,' she laughed as she rose and headed to the door. 'I'd better get going as I've a busy day ahead and I don't want Betty reprimanding me for being late.'

Mike watched as Freda headed back across the road to Ruby's house, stopping to talk with Gwyneth, who was just leaving. Now, there's a woman a man could settle down with, he thought to himself as he recalled holding the rosy-cheeked woman in his arms only days before at the Erith Dance Studios. He'd wished there could have been more than one dance but as a single man he was honour-bound to ask the other ladies present to take a turn around the floor, and before he knew it they were playing the last waltz and Gwyneth was in the arms of another. 'You daft bugger,' he muttered to himself. 'As if a beautiful young woman would be interested in a duffer like you.' He raised his hand in greeting to Gwyneth as she passed by, before closing the front door and going to the kitchen to prepare his solitary meal.

'Come in and take a seat, Gwyneth,' Betty said as the nervous woman knocked on the open door of the temporary manager's office. 'No doubt Maisie would have told you about the interview procedure at Woolworths?'

Gwyneth nodded enthusiastically, sending her shiny shoulder-length hair waving around her shoulders. She wasn't going to tell Betty Billington how Maisie, Freda and Sarah had giggled about their interview at the store on the day they met and how Sarah had helped the others with the arithmetic test. She'd sighed when Sarah told how she also met Alan at the store. She would love to have some romance in her life. It had been a long time since . . .

Betty took several sheets of paper from a file. 'I have an application form as well as an arithmetic test for you to complete. As you are on your own I'd usually say you could sit here in my office to complete the paperwork, but I have a meeting in ten minutes. So, I'll take you through to the canteen and organize a cup of tea. Maureen is preparing staff lunches and will take care of you. You can sit there and complete the questions. There's no rush as I'll be the best part of an hour. Come along,' she said as she hurried from the room.

Gwyneth grabbed the papers from Betty's desk and, picking up her handbag and gas mask, she hurried after the store manager. She'd been warned by Maisie that Betty was a different person when at work and, as she was ushered to a table in the corner of the staff canteen, Gwyneth could see the difference between the efficient manager and the woman she'd met at the dance in her beautiful oyster-coloured gown, who had gazed adoringly at the handsome grey-haired man who didn't leave her side all evening.

'Hello, my love,' Maureen said as she wiped the table-top where Betty had seated Gwyneth before rushing off for her meeting. 'There you go, all nice and clean so you don't get your papers messy. Sarah said as how you were going to join us at Woolies. Now, how about a cup of tea and a slice of my homemade bread pudding?'

'That would be lovely. Thank you, Mrs Gilbert,' Gwyneth said as she reached for her purse to pay.

'I'll have none of that,' Maureen said, raising her hands in horror. 'Why, you're one of us now and it would be a sad world if I couldn't give someone a cuppa and a bite to eat when they come along for an interview. You get writing and I'll make a fresh pot. Why, I might even join you. I've got a little time before the lunch rush starts. That's if it's all right with you?'

'Please do,' Gwyneth said with a smile before pulling a sheet of paper towards her and thinking about the arithmetic questions. Thankfully she was a dab hand with giving change and adding up pounds, shillings and pence from the jobs she'd had working in a butcher's shop and recently at a busy greengrocer's. By the time Maureen appeared balancing two steaming cups of tea and a plate with chunks of bread pudding Gwyneth was chewing the pencil and looking at the application form with a worried look on her pretty face.

'Having problems with the adding up, are you?' she asked, passing a cup of tea to Gwyneth.

'No, I've completed them. It's the application form I'm having problems with. I didn't know that Woolworths would want to know so much about me,' she said glumly, pushing the paperwork away from her with a sigh. 'I'll tell Miss Billington that I've changed my mind and don't want the job after all.'

'Oh, don't do that,' Maureen said sadly. 'I'm sure we can sort something out. What's the problem?'

'It asks about next of kin and children.'

'I can't see that being a problem. Just add an adult relative and write down young Myfi's name under the part where it asks for details of your children.'

Gwyneth shook her head. 'I'd rather not write anything about Myfi.'

Maureen frowned. 'Why ever not? Is there a problem with the child? I hope you don't mind me asking, only I've noticed how she never speaks. Is she poorly, love?'

Gwyneth nodded, a look of sorrow spread across her pretty face. 'In a manner of speaking she is. She's not spoken since she saw her mother killed in front of her two years ago.'

'Her mother? You mean she's not yours?'

'No, Myfi is my niece. She's my late sister's daughter,

183

but I love her as if she were my own child and I'll protect her until my last dying breath.'

'But your surname . . . ?'

'Myfi took my name. I thought it best at the time and as she doesn't speak it didn't seem to be a problem.'

'Then I suggest you write the child's name on the form. The paperwork is just a formality and it's not as if you've abducted her, is it? You haven't, have you?' Maureen added as an afterthought.

'No . . . no, I haven't abducted her. I'm just keeping her safe from—'

Both women jumped as two cleaners entered the staffroom and headed towards the counter.

'Let me go and serve these two and then we can chew over your problem. Your secret is safe with me. Don't worry about what you write on that form. It's not as if it will do any harm, is it? Now, drink up your tea before it gets cold and stop your worrying. You're amongst friends now and there's no need to be afraid.'

Gwyneth nodded and picked up the pencil, quickly writing Myfi's name in the required box. She was sick of the pretence and had hoped that now she'd moved to an area where she wasn't known she could start life anew. Albeit it with a new identity and free of her violent husband. As much as she loved Myfi, it was a godsend that she never spoke. Come the day she did, they would have to move on again before anyone heard the truth.

'I thought we could start you on the crockery counter,' Betty said as she showed Gwyneth through the busy

Woolworths store. 'It was Maisie's domain and I'm sure she will be able to give you a few tips about how she ran things. We will miss her, but I'm relieved we have a friendly face to take over.'

Gwyneth hurried to keep up with Betty as she strode through shoppers heading to where flower-covered cups and saucers could be seen carefully stacked on the glass-fronted mahogany counter. 'I haven't had experience of selling china,' she said, wishing she'd worn more comfortable shoes as it felt as though a blister was already forming on her left heel.

'Oh, it's not just crocks,' Betty said, looking over her shoulder. 'We've amalgamated the pots and pans with the crockery as supplies aren't as reliable as they used to be.' Betty waited for Gwyneth to catch up. 'You'll need to wear comfortable shoes if you intend standing on your feet all day,' she said, noticing how Gwyneth limped behind her.

Gwyneth nodded politely, but inside she was thinking that at least her painful feet would take her mind off the fact that her past might very soon catch up with her, and it could be as soon as Christmas.

11

'Cooee!' Maureen called out as she left Woolworths and spotted Irene and Ruby up ahead. 'Wait up!'

Irene sighed and looked at her watch. Ruby noted that her daughter-in-law did this quite often. Why was it she was always in a rush but never really getting anywhere? 'I really don't have time to stop and chatter. George will be home for his tea soon and will wonder where I am.'

'He knows you don't sit at home waiting for him, Irene, and besides, I didn't bring him up to be useless. He can roll his sleeves up and peel a few spuds if needs be. Hello, love,' she added as Maureen caught them up and held on to Ruby's arm while she caught her breath.

'That nigh on puffed me out,' she gasped. 'I've been on my feet all day cooking for the staff. I'm not sure I can keep doing it for much longer.'

Ruby grinned. Maureen carried a little weight regardless of, as she said, being on her feet all day, but it suited her even if she was rosy-cheeked and out of breath for the short run along the High Street. 'You'll never leave Woolworths. You love working there. I'm surprised you've not offered to transfer to the shop floor, what with

Betty being so short staffed. I've never known so many girls leave at the same time.'

'To be honest, I've thought about it. I fancy myself as a supervisor. After all, I put in the years working at the Dartford Woolies. There's nothing I don't know about selling biscuits and cakes. Why don't you both come back to mine and we can have a cup of tea and a catch-up? It seems an age since we've had a nice chat. Sarah's off to her ARP warden duties so we'll have Georgina to ourselves to spoil.'

Irene's eyes lit up. 'It would be wonderful to see my granddaughter for a little while. It'll only take me twenty minutes to walk home to Crayford.'

'Our granddaughter,' Maureen laughed, 'and Ruby's great-granddaughter. That's makes us all related in a way.' She linked her arm through Ruby's and the three women set off on the short walk to Maureen's house in Crayford Road.

Sarah was pulling her jacket on as the three women entered Maureen's two-up, two-down close to the Prince of Wales public house. Although the weather was warming up as May crept towards its end, she knew she'd be home late from her ARP duties and there could still be a chilly breeze blowing from the nearby River Thames.

'Shooting off so soon, Sarah?' Maureen asked as she took coats from Ruby and Irene. 'I thought you'd stay and chat to your mum for a few minutes?'

'I daren't stop,' she said in between kissing hello her mum and nan. 'It's just Bob and me on duty this evening so it wouldn't be fair on him if I was late. I'm hoping for a quiet evening.'

'Sod's law there'll be a raid now you've said that,' chuckled Ruby. After almost three years of war the women could joke about their situation even though they secretly worried about their loved ones.

Irene was alarmed. 'I'm not so sure about you being alone with just an old man if there is an air raid, Sarah. However will you cope?'

Sarah could see her nan was getting annoyed. She was aware Ruby had a soft spot for Bob, but then he was a likeable man, as was his son, Mike. She was pleased Nan had a good friend. 'Mum, Bob takes good care of me. I'm the liability in our team as I have no idea what to do and Bob has to tell me everything. Now, I must be off or I'll get the sack.' She waved goodbye to her good-natured daughter, who was sitting on a blanket on the floor playing with a knitted teddy bear, picked up her gas mask and tin ARP helmet and hurried from the house.

'Sit yourself down and I'll stick the kettle on. Would you like a slice of bread pudding? I brought home what was left over from the batch I made at Woolies. Betty had two slices as well.'

Irene waved her hand to decline the pudding. 'I'm surprised Betty can eat that much. It's rather stodgy,' she said, wrinkling her nose.

'No doubt she will share with Douglas when he goes for his tea,' Maureen called as she busied herself in the tiny kitchen.

'They are becoming rather cosy,' Irene said as she

watched Ruby take a big bite of the brown spicy pudding. 'I'd have thought at her age she wouldn't be bothered with male callers.'

Maureen burst out laughing and Ruby joined in, sending a spray of crumbs in Irene's direction. 'I wouldn't mind a bit of male company,' Maureen called out, 'if only to help around the house with the papering and painting. Not that we can get any decorating things these days. I've got a problem with my guttering. I may have to call on your Bob for a helping hand, but I'd better get in quick before the two of you head off to Cornwall.'

'He's not *my Bob*, Maureen.' Ruby glared a warning at her friend. 'He's a good neighbour. Besides, his son went to school with George and we've always known the family. This is lovely bread pudding, Maureen. You should try some, Irene.'

Irene took no notice of her mother-in-law's attempts to change the subject. 'Cornwall? What's this all about?'

'I'm going to visit our Pat. I miss my grandchildren. There's nothing to make a fuss about.'

'Bob is going with you?' Irene persevered.

'He is,' Ruby said, trying not to be drawn into explaining herself.

Irene frowned. 'Does George know about this?'

'He knows I want to go and see my family and he was happy to know I'm being accompanied rather than travelling alone, if that's what you mean?'

'It seems a little . . .' – Irene tried to find the right word – 'a little unusual for an unmarried man to be accompanying you.'

Ruby could feel her hackles rising. 'Bob is a widower, as well you know. He respects the memory of his wife, just as I hold dear my memories of Eddie. This is no different to you playing golf all day long with men down in Devon whilst my son was up here working for King and country.'

Maureen watched the exchange between Ruby and Irene. 'You'd both best drink your tea before it gets cold,' she said, passing over her best cups and saucers with the steaming brew. She always got out her best crocks when Irene visited. Considering they'd first met when they both worked as shop assistants in nearby Dartford and back then Irene was as common as the rest of them, she had certainly put on some airs and graces.

The two girls had met on the cheese counter and had bonded over their dislike of what must have been the smelliest job in the store. Irene had an eye for the boys and was never short of an escort. Whenever she went dancing with a boy she made sure her new friend came along and there would always be a lad available to dance with Maureen. That was until George Caselton came on the scene. Irene could see even then that the quiet, studious man was going places and she made sure she would be the woman by his side. Before too long Irene started to talk as if she had a plum in her mouth and gradually the girls drifted apart. It had been a surprise when young Sarah turned up to live at her nan's house in Alexandra Road and she fell in love with Maureen's son, Alan, when they met at Erith Woolworths. It's certainly a small world, she smiled to herself.

She was jolted from her revelry by the whine of an air-raid siren as it wailed louder and louder.

'Bloody hell, that's early. Hitler's on the ball today,' Ruby said, grabbing her coat and picking up her hand-bag.

'Oh my God,' Irene said, her face going a ghostly white. 'Where is the shelter? I take it you do have one?' She dashed to pick up Georgina and looked around des-perately. The youngster started to grizzle, picking up on her grandmother's fear.

'There's no need to panic, Irene. Ruby, can you take them down to the cellar while I grab a few things?'

'Follow me, Irene, and mind the steps, they're a bit on the steep side.' Ruby picked up a torch that was hanging on the doorknob and guided her daughter-in-law down to the cellar below Maureen's house. 'It's a bit snug, but Alan's done a good job making it cosy.' The walls were whitewashed and on the floor he'd laid a piece of lino-leum bought cheap in the second-hand department of Mitchell's. Two benches ran along the walls, which were wide enough to double as beds if the need arose. Bright-coloured rag rugs were scattered on the floor, courtesy of Maisie's classes, and Maureen had put blankets and cushions on the benches. In a corner was a small cot for Georgina along with a box containing some wooden toys to keep her amused.

'It's not much but it's home,' Maureen said as she fol-lowed them down and closed the door behind her. 'I've turned off the gas and left a note on the table. Thank God the kettle was half full and didn't take long to boil so we have tea to drink to while away the time. Stick the

Thermos on that shelf, Ruby, while I light the hurricane lamp. There are also candles on the shelf if we should need them.'

As the women settled themselves and kept Georgina cheerful, they could hear the rumble of enemy aircraft overhead.

'They're off to London by the sound of it,' Ruby said, looking up to the low ceiling of the cellar. 'Let's hope they aren't successful and our boys send them packing.'

'Whatever happens, some mothers will lose their sons today, whether they are on our side or the Germans',' Maureen said fearfully.

'How do you know they're not our planes?' Irene asked.

'When you've listened to as many planes as we have and had the Battle of Britain raging over Kent, let alone living through the Blitz, you know what they sound like. Why, we used to stand in the garden and watch the dog fights. I can't believe we were so bloody stupid,' Ruby muttered. 'You got off light living in Devon for so long.'

Irene nodded her head. 'I know I've been lucky. That's why I wanted to do something to help now we're here for the duration. But I'm not sure the WVS is for me. The women seem to hate me.'

Maureen couldn't help but laugh. 'I take it you've crossed swords with Vera?'

'Yes, this afternoon; she doesn't seem to like taking orders,' Irene said sadly. 'Then, when the other ladies saw her answering me back, they decided they preferred to do the jobs of their choice rather than follow my carefully planned rota.'

Maureen and Ruby laughed and Irene joined in when she noticed Georgina was laughing with them.

'Things tick over nicely, Irene; we don't need rotas or telling what to do. We get on with things that need doing and don't wait for people to give us jobs.'

Irene sighed. 'Then I'm superfluous to requirements. I shall have to think of something else to do towards the war work.'

'Don't be so hasty, love. You could always set up a children's clothing exchange. It's very popular from what I've heard from other WVS divisions. To be able to exchange clothes for growing children is a big weight off a mother's mind. They have enough to think about with trying to put food on the table each day. In fact, while I'm away in Cornwall you could take on the sorting of the donated clothing. It would give me peace of mind knowing it was in good hands while I was visiting our Pat. It doesn't sound like much of a job, but with people losing everything they've got there's always a need for bedding and clothes. I like to get the stuff sorted, washed and turned around as soon as possible so as to help folk.'

'I'd feel useful doing that,' Irene agreed. 'The clothing exchange would certainly help families.'

'Then there's Woolies. Betty is so short staffed these days,' Maureen said.

'Or you could join the ARP,' Ruby suggested. 'You've seen for yourself how much they need volunteers.'

The women fell silent as they thought of Sarah and Bob out in the open when God knows what was going on outside.

A resounding thud shook the house. The women

could hear the sound of breaking china and taste dust in the air. Maureen reached down, took Georgina in her arms, and started to sing. '*Pack up all my cares and woe . . .*'

The little girl beamed with joy and waved her arms as Ruby and Irene joined in. '*Bye bye, blackbird.*'

Their mood lightened as they sang song after song, trying to blot out the sound of planes. After a rousing chorus of 'Bless 'Em All' they listened in silence.

'I think it's over,' Maureen said. 'Let's break out the tea ration, shall we? I'm parched after all that singing.'

Georgina started to wave her arms about and cried out in annoyance.

'Do you want another song, darling?' Irene said as she took her granddaughter from Maureen and jiggled the toddler her on knee. '*Knees up, Mother Brown, Knees up, Mother Brown . . .*'

Maureen looked at Ruby and they both burst out laughing before joining in. The war's a great leveller, Maureen thought to herself. Perhaps there was still a spark of her old friend deep inside?

Sarah peered out from the entrance of the public shelter. It had been the first time she'd had to count in the civilians and her hands had shaken as she ticked off names on a clipboard. Each shelter had a list of locals who were supposed to use it.

'All right, love?' Bob asked as he joined her.

'No, there's a family missing.'

Bob took the clipboard and rubbed his chin as he glanced down the list, adding up the residents who should be in the shelter. 'You're right, we are five people short. The family live in rooms in Queens Road. I'll pop up there and check they're all right.'

Sarah looked skywards as the German bombers appeared further down the Thames. 'I'll go. Someone's propped a bike up over there by the wall. I'll borrow it and be there and back in five minutes. You are best staying here as you can calm folk down if they get worried.'

Bob looked concerned. 'I don't know. I did promise your nan that I'd not let you do anything dangerous.'

Sarah laughed as she headed towards the bike. 'Oh, Bob, there's a war on and my husband is up there fighting the enemy. Why, even Freda is doing her bit volunteering for the Fire Service. I'm sure I can ride a bike a few hundred yards without causing myself an injury. I'll be back before you can say Winston Churchill.'

Bob shook his head before heading down to the steps to the shelter and closing the door behind him. He could never understand women. It was best not to argue.

Sarah pedalled furiously up Pier Road, past Woolworths, which was locked up for the day, and turned left into Queens Road. She slowed down, trying to look at the house numbers as enemy planes became larger in the sky.

Spotting the correct number, she hopped off the bike and propped it against a brick wall. The fancy iron railings that once were a feature of the long elegant rows of Victorian town houses had long disappeared, no doubt to one of the many scrap-metal drives that were organized in order to build planes and tanks.

She raced down the steep steps to the basement, where the McKinley family rented their rooms, and banged on the door; the drone of German aircraft was deafening and they were so close she could hardly see the sky. Ack-ack guns up the Thames were in action and the sky seemed full of planes, barrage balloons and smoke from the guns as the early evening sky darkened and night approached.

Sarah hammered on the door and called out, 'Mr and Mrs McKinley, please open the door. We need to get you to the air-raid shelter. Please, oh please, open the door.' She knelt down and peered through the letter box. Listening as hard as possible, as the drone of the planes didn't help, she thought she heard a baby crying somewhere inside the house, but it could have been a cat. Please God, let someone be at home, she prayed to herself. It was then she spotted the piece of string. Just as her nan had always done, the McKinley family also kept a key attached to the letterbox by a piece of string. As quickly as her trembling fingers would allow she pulled the string through the letter box and inserted the key into the keyhole. Why now, after a quiet time and with just a few false alarms, did the enemy suddenly appear and why did this family not go to the communal shelter?

Aware that at any time the enemy overhead could drop their bombs, she flung open the door and called out loud and clear, 'Hello, is anyone at home? Mr and Mrs Mc . . .' The overpowering smell of smoke stopped Sarah dead in her tracks. There was a fire somewhere in the house and it wasn't a cosy coal fire. Rushing along a narrow passage, she stopped at a closed door and listened. Yes, it was a baby crying. Whatever was happening?

She carefully opened the door as thick smoke belched out into the hall. 'Hello . . . !' she called, but was met with silence. Crawling below the smoke, she spotted the wailing toddler in a wooden pen. On a nearby sofa two older children slept – or were they dead? Sarah thought as she reached for the youngster. She hurried back outside and looked up and down the road for help. Anyone with any sense was in a shelter. She placed the baby onto the concrete floor of the basement area and dashed back inside. Reaching the two children, she shook them roughly. There was no time to be gentle. She tucked the smaller of the two under her arm and, grabbing the other by an arm, pulled them both out to join the baby, who was crying fit to burst. The children seemed groggy, but the fresh air was bringing them round.

With no time to spare Sarah hurried back inside, but could not see the parents in the living room or the two bedrooms that led off the hallway. That just left the kitchen, but she knew that was where the fire had started, going by the sounds from behind the wooden door. If she opened the door, the fire would spread. Not sure what to do, Sarah returned to the children. A little girl was crying and her older brother was staring blankly. She knelt down in front of them. 'Where are your mummy and daddy?'

'I put some milk on the stove for Shirley and went back to finish reading my book,' he mumbled.

Sarah's heart broke for the young lad as silent tears ran down his grime-covered face. 'I need to find your parents,' she said clearly and calmly, frightened that they were somewhere in the burning house but not sure where. 'Can you tell me where they are?'

He thought for a moment. 'They went down the New Light ages ago. Dad said it would only be for a quick half and they'd be back before we knew it. But our Shirley was hungry so I thought I'd do some milk for her just like Mum does. I'll get a hiding when Dad finds out what I've done.' The lad started to cry silently.

Sarah thought for a moment. At least Mr and Mrs McKinley weren't in the house; she could forget about them for a while. First she needed to get help to put out the fire. Closing the front door and removing the key so the children would not be able to go into the burning building, she helped them up the steep steps to the pavement. 'I want you to sit here and cuddle your sisters. I'm going for help. You are not to move an inch. Do you understand?' she said sternly to the boy. Now wasn't the time to be soft. She had to make him understand.

'Yes, miss,' he said and placed his arms around his sisters.

Climbing onto the borrowed bike, Sarah headed back down Queens Road and into the town, making her way towards the fire station in Cross Street. Somewhere behind her she heard an explosion. Had the raid started? Approaching the fire station, she breathed a sigh of relief. There was still a fire tender at the front of the building and nearby she could see Freda's motorbike parked close to the door. Throwing the bike to the ground, she hurried through the door and bumped straight into her best friend. 'Oh, Freda, I've never been so glad to see you. There's a fire in Queens Road. I've pulled out three little kiddies, but their parents are missing. I've left them on the pavement while I came for help.'

'Sit yourself down and catch your breath,' Freda said, pushing her towards a battered wooden chair. 'I'll get things underway. There's some tea in the pot that should be warm. Pour yourself some and take a spoonful of sugar. It's good for shock and once the chaps know we have a supply it'll be gone in minutes. You might as well have the benefit.' She grinned, before heading off to summon her colleagues.

Sarah took a few minutes to calm down and then poured herself a mug of tea. It tasted like nectar. She must look a fright, she thought, but thank goodness for her ARP overall. Pulling the ARP helmet from her head, she shook her hair free of the snood and pins that kept it tidy while she worked and wished there was a mirror to check how dirty her face was. At once she felt guilty. There were three little children sitting on a pavement in shock and here she was thinking of her looks. Quickly draining the mug of tea, she placed the helmet back on her head and ran back to the bike. She'd done all she could to get help. Her place was now with those little children until their parents could be found.

Ruby breathed a sigh of relief as the all-clear sounded. As much as she loved her daughter-in-law there was only so much time she could spend in her company. There were glimmers of the old Irene, the girl her son had first brought home to meet his parents, but they were soon replaced by the social-climbing, golf-playing show-off. In some ways she wished that her George had married Maureen and then chided herself, as if things hadn't worked out as they did, their Sarah would never have met Alan Gilbert and fallen in love and she'd not have had her adorable great-granddaughter to dote over.

Maureen stood up and stretched her arms above her head before picking up the empty flasks. 'We could have done with more tea to pass the time. I like to drink when I'm playing cards. It helps me think better.'

'You didn't do so bad considering,' Ruby laughed. 'You won most of the jar of buttons. If it had been money, we'd both be in your debt.'

'If we'd been playing for money, I'd have concentrated more and wiped the floor with both of you,' Irene interjected. 'Playing gin rummy for buttons isn't the same as being in our local whist drive league. I've won the best female shield more than once.'

'Not for your big head then,' Maureen muttered to Ruby as she headed up the stairs to the cellar door.

Ruby sucked her cheeks in hard so as not to chuckle out loud. Maureen could be a right laugh at times.

Maureen rattled the handle a few times then thumped the door with her fists. 'The bloody door's stuck,' she declared, coming back to where Irene was picking up a sleepy Georgina.

'Do you think someone has locked us in?' Irene asked with a worried look on her face. 'I've heard of looters visiting houses during air raids. Did you leave the key in the door and make it easy for them,' she added accusingly.

Maureen glared at Irene. 'Do you think I'm daft or something?' She held up a bunch of keys. 'The house is secure and the cellar door was unlocked so we can get out in an emergency.'

'But we can't get out,' Irene said as she hurried up the staircase and rattled the door handle.

'Now she doesn't believe me,' Maureen said in exasperation. 'It was exactly the same when were younger. Always correcting me and then pinching my boyfriend.'

Irene stomped down the stairs and faced Maureen. Before she could open her mouth to retaliate Ruby stepped in. 'Come on, ladies. We're all a little tired and hungry. Someone will come along and rescue us soon.'

Irene looked shamefaced. 'You're right. I apologize for my behaviour.' She held out her hand to Maureen, who shook it without saying a word.

'Now, let's put our thinking caps on. Who is likely to know we are stuck down here?' Ruby asked.

'George will wonder why I'm not home,' Irene suggested.

'Would he know you were at my house, though?' Maureen asked.

'He would check at my house but it could be hours before he realizes something is amiss,' Ruby added. 'Sarah will be home before then and find us.'

Maureen sighed. 'She's on the night shift with Bob at the ARP station, so we will have to wait a long time to be rescued.'

'We'd best break out the buttons and have another game of gin rummy. A shame we didn't think to bring food down with us. There was a time when we were prepared for everything but of late, with not so many air raids, we've become lazy.'

'Hang on a minute,' Maureen said with a sudden grin. She went to the shelf where she'd put the flasks of tea and lifted down a tin. 'We have bread pudding. All is not lost.'

'We also have this,' Irene grinned, pulling a bottle out from a corner close to where she'd been sitting. 'Do you have any sherry glasses?'

12

Maisie threw down her sewing. 'I'm bloody bored. I've done nothing but sew all day long and 'aven't poked me nose out of doors apart from our dash ter the air-raid shelter. If I don't go out, I swear I'll go mad and chuck this sewing machine out of the window!'

David Carlisle put down his newspaper and smiled adoringly at Maisie. Since hearing she was carrying their child, he'd made sure his pretty wife put her feet up as much as possible and not worried about a thing. 'It's for the best, darling,' he smiled. 'We don't want a reoccurrence of what happened last year, do we?'

Maisie looked sad. 'Yer don't need to remind me we lost a baby. A day doesn't go past when I don't wonder if it was my fault. Yer told me to give up work and I didn't and look what 'appened.'

David crossed the room and knelt before her, taking both her hands in his and tenderly kissing her fingers. 'Don't ever blame yourself, my love. The doctor told us these things happen, but this time we will do all in our power to have a healthy baby.'

'I know yer right but I'm still bored,' she sighed, stroking his cheek.

'I know. Why don't we walk down the road to the Prince of Wales and have a swift half?'

Maisie wrinkled her nose. 'I never thought I'd hear meself say this but I'd rather not. The smoky bar makes me stomach churn. I'd rather go and see Freda and Ruby and also find out what 'appened to Gwyneth at her interview with Betty.'

'Then a walk it is. I'll get your coat and we can be off. I may just leave you there and pop to the pub. You can chat all you want then without a man to put you off.'

Maisie laughed and threw a cushion at him. 'I love yer, David Carlisle, and I still can't believe a posh bloke like you is married ter someone like me.'

'I'm the fortunate one, Maisie, and don't you ever forget it. As for posh . . . well, none of us can choose where we come from. I'm just glad we met through my cousin Joe.'

Maisie's ready smile dropped from her face as she thought of her late husband, Joe. 'He was a good bloke was Joe. This bloody war! Life just ain't fair.'

David helped her to her feet and wrapped his arms around her. 'I think Joe would approve of us being together, don't you? We've both got our memories and Joe will always be remembered in our home.'

Maisie forced the tears not to fall. 'Yer right, we're the lucky ones. Come on, let's get a move on or you'll never get that drink.'

'I was thinking,' David said as he locked the door behind them. 'Why don't you go away for a few days? I have a colleague who owns a guesthouse down near Margate. I'll have a word and see if he has a room. It'll do you good to get some sea air.'

Maisie wrinkled her nose. 'What, on me own?'

'You know I'm away for a couple of weeks otherwise I'd jump at the chance of taking my wife on a trip. Why not ask one of the girls to accompany you?'

'I could ask Betty. She was saying the other day that she'd not had a break for a while.'

'That's a good idea. I'll sort out the details tomorrow.'

The couple walked arm in arm down Avenue Road past the Prince of Wales pub and the Royal Arsenal Co-op before heading down Manor Road into Alexandra Road, where Ruby had lived since the first years of her marriage to her late husband, Eddie. Getting close to number thirteen, they spotted Sergeant Jackson leaving his home and crossing the road towards them.

'Hello, Mike, not on duty tonight?' David asked.

'No, it's one of my rare nights off. I'm just returning Ruby's pudding bowl in case she needs it. The woman's a marvel. She can make a steam pudding out of nothing,' he said by way of making an excuse when in truth he was hoping for a quiet word with Gwyneth. He'd thought perhaps she would go with him for a drink to celebrate passing her interview for a job at Woolworths. However, now there were visitors to number thirteen he was unsure of what to say to the woman to whom he'd taken such a shine. Pull yourself together, man, he silently told himself. You're a grown man, not some lovesick youngster. She probably doesn't even know you exist.

'I do miss her grub now I don't live here,' Maisie said.

'I'm always grateful when Ruby invites us round fer a meal. We'd starve to death otherwise.' She hooted with laughter.

'We don't do so badly, my love,' David said, opening the gate and ushering his wife in front to walk up the short path and knock on the door.

'Only because your mother sends us the occasional hamper and you've shown me what ter do,' Maisie sighed. 'Goodness knows how this little blighter's gonna survive,' she added, gently holding her stomach.

Gwyneth opened the door. 'Oh, I thought you were Ruby. But then again she'd have had her key,' she added, her Welsh accent making it hard for the trio to understand.

'Is something wrong, Gwyneth?' Mike Jackson asked. 'You look concerned.'

They followed Gwyneth into the front room as she explained. 'We expected Ruby home hours ago, didn't we, sweetie?' she said to young Myfi, who was sitting in an armchair playing with her doll. The child looked up and nodded shyly. They'd become used to the girl's lack of speech by now. 'She went to her WVS meeting and should have been home for her tea but we had the air-raid warning and . . . and I've been worrying something rotten that she's been hurt and is lying injured somewhere.'

Mike frowned. 'Yes, there was an air-raid warning but no bombs fell. The planes were heading up to the capital. Ruby should be safe, wherever she is,' he assured Gwyneth.

Maisie sat down next to Myfi, a worried look on her

face. 'She's never gone anywhere without telling someone what she's up to. I've got a feeling in me waters that
things aren't right.' She looked at her husband and Mike.
'Can't you do something?'

'Perhaps she's at Vera's house?' Mike suggested.

'No, she wouldn't be there. They've had a bit of a
falling-out and the last I heard Vera wasn't talking to
Ruby. I've no idea why,' Maisie said.

'It may be worth checking,' Mike added, turning to
leave the room.

Gwyneth reached out and took his arm to stop him
leaving. For a moment she looked into his eyes before
coming back to her senses. 'No, I looked out the front
before going into the shelter and I could see Vera hurrying up the road to her house. She was alone.'

Mike coughed to cover his confusion. He could gaze
at Gwyneth all day long. 'Then where can she be?'

'Perhaps she went to Woolworths?' David said.

'They've been closed a while now,' Maisie said, chewing her lip as she worried about the older woman. 'But
Betty may still be there. You know what she's like after
an air-raid warning. She'll be catching up on her work
after being stuck down in the cellar fer so long.'

'I'll go now,' David said. 'Do you want to come with
me, Mike?'

As much as Mike Jackson wanted to stay with
Gwyneth, he agreed and the two men headed off to
Woolworths to see if there was news of their friend.

'There's no one here,' Mike said as he peered through
the glass doors into the darkened store.

'Betty may be up in her office,' David said, knocking

insistently on the doors. They both listened but could hear nothing from inside the large store. 'I'll try the staff door,' he said, heading to the side of the building and again knocking hard on the door before calling out the manager's name several times.

Again they stood and listened. This time they could hear footsteps approaching and a key turning in the lock. The door opened and Douglas Billington looked out. 'Hello, Mike, David,' he nodded. 'Is there a problem?'

'We're looking for Ruby Caselton. She hasn't arrived home and we're somewhat concerned,' David said. 'We wondered if she'd stopped off here to see Betty.'

Douglas thought for a moment. 'I've not been here long. I'm collecting Betty to take her to meet my daughters. She's just finishing up some work before we leave. I've not seen Mrs Caselton but Betty may know something.'

'What do I know?' Betty asked as she walked down the corridor towards the men.

The men said hello to the store manager. 'Ruby hasn't been home since midday and it's unlike her not to tell anyone where she has gone, and her WVS duties finished hours ago,' Mike explained.

Betty frowned. 'It's certainly uncharacteristic of Ruby. I wonder if Maureen Gilbert has seen her. She did say she had some of her delicious bread pudding for the family. Do you think she's been round to Ruby's?'

'Gwyneth didn't mention seeing Maureen. Perhaps we should check at Maureen's place?' Mike said.

'It's worth a try, but Ruby is hardly likely to be chatting with Maureen when she was due home hours ago,' Betty pointed out.

'There's also the public shelter,' Douglas added. 'There may be an ARP warden who can say if she was there. I believe they keep lists?'

'That's a splendid idea, Douglas,' Betty said with a beaming smile. 'I feel we should help look for Ruby. I'd never forgive myself if she'd come to harm and we'd done nothing to find her.'

'We need a plan,' Mike said. 'There's no point in us all going to the same place to search. I could check at the police station to see if they have news and also telephone Erith Cottage Hospital for anyone who's been taken in since this afternoon. Let's hope Ruby isn't amongst them.'

David nodded. 'I'll go to the public air-raid shelter and see if she was there.'

'I could use my office telephone to contact Irene Caselton. Fortunately the house she and George rent has one installed. Perhaps Ruby may have decided to visit.' However, as the words left her lips, she knew it was highly unlikely.

'You never know, our paths might have crossed and she is now safely at home,' Mike said. He looked at his wristwatch. 'Let's meet back at number thirteen in twenty minutes. Hopefully one of us will have good news.'

Betty and Douglas watched the two men set off on their quests, both walking in different directions. 'Come on, Douglas. Let's see if we can get hold of Irene. I must say I'm rather worried. Ruby Caselton is not one to go off on her own without telling someone.'

'I suggest, my dear, that we also let Clemmie and

Dorothy know that we may be late. Your friends are important to you and I'd not wish to whisk you away when you are worried about them. I'm confident my girls will understand.'

'Douglas, you may whisk me away anytime you wish,' Betty said shyly as she turned the key in the door.

For once the much-admired Woolworths manager was not on view to the public as Douglas pulled her close and kissed the woman he had come to love. 'I hope I didn't startle you, Betty?' he said, still holding her close.

'I have to confess my heart is beating a little faster than usual,' she replied, 'but I'd be lying if I said I hadn't been hoping for this to happen and knowing you were taking me to meet your daughters, I did wonder if your intentions were honourable,' she added with a smile.

'I've never taken another woman home to meet my daughters,' he said seriously. 'In fact, I've never entertained the thought of being close to another woman since my wife died. That was until I met you.'

Betty sighed with delight. 'I hoped beyond hope that you felt as I did, but with me being an older woman and you having had a loving marriage with two young daughters I felt it was just a foolish notion.'

'My love, if you are foolish then so am I. I can think of nothing better than spending the rest of my life with you by my side.'

Betty stepped away from Douglas in shock. 'Please, Douglas, you are assuming so much after one kiss. Why, you have your girls and I have my work. Can we take things a little slower and get to know each other?'

'Forgive me, my love. I do apologize for being so forward. I will agree to whatever you suggest as long as you don't send me away?'

'Oh, Douglas, I'd never do such a thing, but something does worry me.'

Douglas frowned. 'What would that be?'

'It's Clemmie and Dorothy. Perhaps we should not tell them we are close at the moment? Let them get to know me first and I to know them. Am I asking too much of you?'

'Betty, you could ask me to fly to the moon and back and I'd agree.'

'Then let's leave it there and get on with helping with the search for dear Ruby, shall we?'

'I do understand,' Douglas replied, leading her towards the stairs and her office. 'My daughters must always be my first concern. I owe that to their mother.'

'Bob! I'm glad I caught you,' David said as he spotted Mike's father outside the entrance to the public air-raid shelter.

'Hello, David, nothing wrong I hope? We've just been having a bit of a tidy-up. It can get terribly stuffy down there with so many bodies close together for a few hours. 'Sarah,' he called down the steps, 'we have a visitor.'

'There's a problem,' David tried to explain, as Sarah appeared at the entrance to the shelter, her face streaked with smoke.

'A problem? It's not Maisie, is it? Please tell me she's all right,' she asked as a look of panic crossed her face.

'No . . . she's well. Sarah, it's your nan. We can't find her anywhere and we're worried she may be hurt. We're out looking for her and I thought you might have seen her, Bob. Did she come to this shelter when the siren went off?'

Bob took off his ARP helmet and wiped his forehead with a handkerchief. 'Now you've got me worried, lad. I've not seen her since she dropped over a bit of food for us earlier today. I'll come and help you look for her. It won't take a minute to lock up here.'

'I think I know where Nan may be,' Sarah said with hope in her voice as she looked at the faces of the two men. 'She was at Maureen's when I left to come here. Mum was with her as well. They were going to have a cup of tea before going home. I would think they were still there when the air-raid siren went off.'

'It must have been an hour since the all-clear. Wouldn't she have set off for home since then? I'd have thought Mum would have done as well?'

'Betty is going to use her telephone to contact your mum. We thought perhaps Ruby might have gone home with her.' David knew it sounded ridiculous as the words left his mouth.

'I doubt it,' Sarah said. Perhaps they just got to nattering and haven't noticed the time passing. Maureen's cellar is very cosy so they'd be all right down there. Come on, let's go and find them. At least we know they're safe as there weren't any bombs dropped.'

As the trio hurried towards Crayford Road they spotted Betty and Douglas up ahead.

'I have to report that George answered the telephone

and he is as perplexed as we are, as it seems Irene is not at home either. We were on our way to Alexandra Road to report our findings. George is on his way over to number thirteen on his bicycle to help with the search,' Betty said, her face flushed not just with hurrying from Woolworths but with her inner joy that she feared would bubble over at any moment.

'Sarah believes we will find them at Maureen's house,' David explained.

'That's good. I suggest Douglas and I head to Ruby's house and let Gwyneth and Maisie know what's happening. We can wait for George and Mike and let them know where you are.'

'There's no need to wait for me,' a voice said from behind them as Mike appeared on a borrowed bicycle and pulled up beside the group of concerned friends, who updated him on what they'd discovered.

'Then let's get cracking and track down our prey,' he grinned as he dismounted from the bike and walked alongside his dad the short distance to Maureen's home. It was as they turned the corner by the Prince of Wales that the small group stopped and gasped. Glancing up at where the chimney stack of Maureen's house had been, all they could see was a gaping hole in the roof slates.

'But there weren't any bombs dropped,' Sarah cried out as she ran across the narrow road, wondering if the female members of her family were still alive. And her daughter . . . Pulling a key from the pocket of her ARP overall, she inserted it into the lock but the door wouldn't budge. There was something leaning against it.

She sank to her knees and sobbed in frustration and

fear as David and Mike helped her to one side, before putting their shoulders to the door and forcing it open. What faced the friends was the complete destruction of Maureen's front room. Bricks, rubble and broken black slates. The dust in the air made them cough as they fought their way across the room to the kitchen, where a still tearful Sarah pointed out the entrance to the cellar hidden behind a pile of bricks.

Bob stepped forward. He'd seen this kind of obstruction many times in his work as an ARP warden. 'Come on, Sarah, this is perfect training for you. That's if you really do wish to be part of my team? You've saved three children already so what about doing the same for your own family?'

Sarah didn't need any second bidding. She cuffed her eyes, smearing dust and smoke over her face. 'Sorry, Bob, I don't know what came over me. What should we do next?'

Bob liked the plucky young woman. Now wasn't the time to tell her that he too had shed tears over the sights he'd seen but would try to bottle it up in front of the public, who waited to see their loved ones fit and well. Sadly, that wasn't always the case. 'We need to make a chain so we can pass the bricks and rubble out of the way, then we can release the women and young Georgina.'

Quickly the men and Sarah lined up and set to, passing from person to person and out to the small front garden, where Maureen's neighbours joined those helping to rescue the trapped women.

'Shh! Quiet, everyone,' Bob shouted out. 'I can hear something.'

'. . . *Roll out the barrel, we'll have a barrel of fun . . .*'

Bob grinned back at the row of brick-dust-covered helpers. 'They seem to be in good spirits.' He banged on the part of the door he could just about reach and called out. 'Can you hear me, Maureen?'

Everyone held their breath and waited for a reply to Bob's words.

'Maureen, tell me who is down there with you,' Bob shouted clearly.

The singing stopped.

'Bob, is that you?' Maureen shouted back from the other side of the cellar door. 'I can't seem to get the door open. I think it's jammed.'

Bob repeated his words. 'Who is down there with you?'

'I have Ruby, Irene and Georgina down here. We are all well but a little fed up,' she replied.

'We're bloody hungry!' Ruby bellowed. 'Is that you, Bob?'

'Yes, love. We'll have you out in next to no time. Just keep clear of the door in case we have to break it down,' Bob said as a big smile crossed his face. Thank goodness they were all well. The amount of damage to the house had him worrying that those in the cellar would be hurt . . . or worse.

Sarah pushed past Bob and shouted to the women. 'Is Georgina all right?'

'She's fine, love. We've been singing to her to keep her amused. She'll be glad to see her mummy, though,' Ruby called back.

The rescuers set to with gusto, clearing as much as

possible so that the women could not only exit the cellar but would also be able to get out of the house. Half an hour passed before it was deemed safe enough for the three women and Georgina to escape from their underground prison. The door to the cellar was opened and willing hands helped the ladies out of the house to the pavement just as George arrived on the scene, huffing and puffing from the cycle ride from Crayford. Sarah hugged Georgina close and murmured words of endearment as the child clapped her chubby hands in glee to see so many people calling her name and clapping in their delight to see that all four were safe.

Maureen stood looking up at the roof of her terraced home. 'Oh my, I didn't realize the damage would be this bad. There's no way I can sleep in my bed tonight.'

Mike Jackson put an arm around her and sympathized. He wasn't about to tell the woman he'd known for many years that her bed was in pieces, having crashed through the floor with half a chimney stack on top of it. 'We need to find you somewhere to sleep tonight while we make your home safe. A tarpaulin over the rest of the roof will keep it water tight.'

Maureen nodded, too stunned to argue. 'Can you let my landlord know? He will have to do the repairs. We've been telling him for ages that the roof's been leaking and the chimney stack needed repointing. He can't turn a deaf ear now.'

'That Ken Barnham's always been a tight bugger. No doubt he'll blame this on the enemy rather than him being a bad landlord, just so he gets the government to cough up for the repairs,' Ruby said indignantly.

'Don't you worry about it, Maureen,' Bob said, patting her shoulder as the woman looked about to burst with anger. 'I'll make a point of writing a report and watch him closely while he gets the work done. What we've got to sort out now is a bed for you, as well as Sarah, Alan and the little one.'

'Don't you worry about a thing,' Irene said, stepping forward to take command. 'We have two large spare bedrooms at my house. You can all come and live with us in Crayford. Don't you agree, George?'

George could see the look of horror on his daughter's face and Maureen's wasn't very happy. 'Don't be too hasty, Irene love, they may have other ideas about where they will live for the foreseeable future. After all, our Sarah does work in Erith, as does Maureen. The journey would be hard for them and of course that would leave you caring for our Georgina every day.'

Irene blanched at her husband's words.

Sarah could have hugged her dad. As much as she loved her mother, the thought of staying under the same roof didn't bear thinking about.

'There's no need to worry about where to lay your heads when I've got room at number thirteen,' Ruby said, halting the conversation. 'In fact, let's get back there now and put the kettle on. I'm fair parched. Your sherry was tasty, Maureen, but after that long underground only a strong brew will hit the spot for me. Are you coming back with us, Bob, Mike? I was going to do a bit of dinner for us all.'

'I'll stay here and check everything's secure, Ruby. I'll

see if I can get hold of some clothes for you all,' Mike said.

'I'd be grateful for Georgie's pram if it's still in one piece,' Sarah said. 'Thank goodness we left some of her bits and pieces at Nan's.'

Ruby and Bob headed the crocodile of people making their way back to Alexandra Road. All were weary and covered in dust of varying depths. 'I feel you've been a little overenthusiastic inviting Sarah and Maureen to live with you,' Bob said gently, not sure of how Ruby would take his words.

'I know,' she answered back, checking that no one was within hearing distance. 'I'd forgotten Gwyneth and Myfi were staying with us.'

'We have a spare room. They'd be welcome to stay with us if you'd rather have family in your home?' Bob suggested gently.

'That may not be a good idea,' Ruby whispered as they reached the gate of number thirteen. 'Gwyneth needs women around her at the moment. Something's not right with her and that poor child. I'd like to keep an eye on them, if it's all the same with you. Also, I've noticed your Mike has more of a spring in his step when Gwyneth's in the room. Perhaps it's best not to force them together. I smell a possible romance and it may not blossom if they live under the same roof.'

Bob tapped the side of his nose and winked. 'Bob's yer uncle!'

'He's also a very good friend and I'd be lost without him,' Ruby replied, giving the man a hug. 'I have an idea how we can squeeze everyone under my roof.'

'Let me know what you have planned and I'll give you a hand. I'll leave you here for a while and pop home and have a wash. See you shortly, love,' he said, giving Ruby a peck on the cheek. 'I'm glad you wasn't hurt.'

'Me too, Bob, me too!'

Freda let herself into number thirteen. It had been a long shift and all she wanted was a bite to eat and her bed. She stopped dead in the hall, blocked by Mike Jackson pushing the end of a bedstead up the stairs. From the voice above her it was Maisie's David holding the other end. 'Whatever is going on?' she asked no one in particular.

'There you are, Freda. I was beginning to think you'd gone missing as well,' Ruby said as she stuck her head around the door of the front room. 'Come in here and I'll get you up to speed. Once Mike's out of the way I'll fetch your dinner. I've kept it warm on a pan of hot water. I'll pour you a cuppa, the teapot's still warm.'

Freda perched on the arm of the settee, enthralled as Ruby and Sarah told her all that had happened since the afternoon. 'So, it means deciding who sleeps where until Maureen has a roof back on her house and we've sorted out the mess,' Ruby explained.

'Alan will be off with his squadron by next week so we thought, if you don't mind, that we'd take over your room and you could go in with Gwyneth and Myfi for the time being,' Sarah said.

'Myfi can climb in with me. There's plenty of room,'

Gwyneth explained. 'But you may not want to share with a stranger so in that case we can find other lodgings. I don't wish to impose,' she added, looking at Ruby.

'Don't be daft,' Ruby and Freda said in unison before bursting out laughing.

'Gwyneth, the girls all lived here before some of them went off and married. Even then Sarah returned to live here when Alan was missing in action. This house has been fit to bursting at times, but we all rub along together so I'll not have you say you're leaving us. Why, I'd miss the pair of you even though young Myfi never utters a word. You're staying and that's the end of it.'

'So you don't mind us sharing a bedroom?' Gwyneth asked Freda.

'Not at all. It'll be fun and I'm sure you don't snore like Maisie did when we shared a room.'

Freda ducked as Maisie pretended to throw her shoe at her. 'I'll 'ave you know I don't snore,' she scolded.

'Don't throw your shoe away,' David said, 'we need to make tracks for home. You, my love, need your beauty sleep.'

Maisie snorted with laughter. 'Gawd, I must be a fright, what with snoring and needing me beauty sleep.' David helped her into her coat as they made to leave. 'Don't forget, Maureen. Pop up to ours tomorrow and I'll have some bits and bobs for you to wear. I can make some alterations at the same time. They'll do until we get yer own clothes washed and mended.'

'Mike's been a diamond going through the mess and getting me some clothes and stuff.' Maureen smiled to where Mike was now sitting on a rug in front of the unlit fire after setting up the single bed in Ruby's bedroom.

'I did get some funny looks pushing Georgina's pram round the road piled high with Maureen's worldly goods,' he laughed.

'But where will Maureen sleep?' Freda asked.

'In with Ruby, that's where Mike and David were putting the bed when you came home,' Sarah explained. 'Thank goodness Nan has three bedrooms or someone would be sleeping in the Anderson shelter. I'll go up and make it now it's assembled,' she said.

Freda jumped up. 'I'll do it as soon as I've eaten my dinner. You must be shattered after rescuing those three kiddies out of that fire this afternoon, Sarah.'

Ruby looked between Bob and Sarah. 'Fire? Is there something the pair of you haven't told me? I thought you said you'd take care of my granddaughter, Bob?'

'I wasn't in danger, Nan. The Fire Service did all the hard work.' She raised her eyebrows at Bob, warning him not to elaborate on what really happened as it would worry Ruby. 'I sat with the children until the fire brigade arrived and their parents were located.'

Ruby frowned. 'I'm not sure you're telling me the complete truth, Bob Jackson. I'm sure you are leading my granddaughter into danger. Goodness knows what the pair of you will get up to next.'

13

'A few days away from work sounds ideal,' Betty smiled after Maisie outlined David's suggestion. 'Thank you for inviting me, Maisie,' she said, opening her diary and flicking through a few pages. 'There's nothing here that can't be rescheduled or dealt with by someone else. Of course, we do have our staff dance before then, but I know my girls have planned everything perfectly. We should raise a tidy sum towards another Spitfire.'

'I'm looking forward to it,' Maisie said, 'although I'll not be dancing as much as I usually do. The old man's already put his foot down. Blimey, he's wrapping me in cotton wool.'

'And so he should, although I would think a slow waltz wouldn't be a problem. Life will be so busy before we head off on our little trip. I'm wondering if perhaps I'll be able to visit a couple of our stores while we are away. It would be most pleasant to meet my fellow managers.'

'I know it's short notice, but David's colleague has a room going begging and I thought it would be ideal for us to share. It won't be long before I'm waddling like a duck and won't feel like travelling, let alone enjoying a few days by the sea. Not that we can go paddling or anything,' she laughed.

Betty smiled. Even if she did waddle like a duck Maisie would still look beautiful. Pregnancy suited her and the girl was absolutely blooming. 'I will enjoy your company. Tell David that I shall not allow you to overdo things and will make sure you arrive home in the best of health. Now, I need to rearrange my work roster and make sure my most reliable supervisors are on duty while I'm away enjoying myself. Can I offer you some tea?'

'No thanks, I'm off to Ruby's to help Maureen repair some of her clothes that were salvaged from her house.'

'A most unfortunate situation. I wish we could do more to help. Please tell her that her job will be here waiting when she is ready to return. Already we miss her cooking.'

'I'll do that, Betty. Bob's been a blessing chasing up her landlord. He's made the bloke pull out his finger and get cracking with the work. He's quoted all kind of official stuff at him. Why, the bloke's feet 'ave hardly touched the ground. Bob reckons it'll be months before she's back in her home, though.'

Betty clapped her hands together in delight. 'Well done to Bob. We need more people like him running our country. Perhaps we should encourage him to enter politics.'

Maisie hooted with laughter. 'Bob Jackson for Prime Minster. I'm not sure Ruby will like that, especially if he gets to smoking one of those big cigars just like Churchill does.'

Betty smiled. 'She is rather fond of Bob, isn't she?'

'Yeah. It would be lovely to see them get together, but she is always telling us she is a one-man woman and that man was her Eddie. Sarah's told us a lot about her grandad and it sounds as though he'd take some beating. It makes yer think, though, doesn't it?'

Betty frowned. 'What do you mean?'

Maisie shrugged her shoulders. 'I know I was lucky to marry David not long after I lost my old man, but when we get older can we be bothered with all that courting lark and marrying someone else? Ruby must be set in her ways by now, so why take up with another bloke?'

Betty was about to answer when one of her staff knocked on the door.

'I'll be off and let you get on with yer work. I'm pleased you can come away with me, Betty. I'll keep yer posted when David tells me more about where we're staying.'

Betty said goodbye to Maisie and quickly dealt with the staff query. Getting up from behind her desk, she stood looking out of her office window through the crisscross of paper stuck to the panes of glass. Outside, locals were getting on with their daily routines, working around air raids and their war duties. Was she too old to take up with courting and possibly marriage? After all, she was over forty years of age and considered very much an old maid in the eyes of many people. Was she taken up with the dream of being with Douglas and not thinking of her responsibilities? She had still to meet his daughters after cancelling their get-together on the day Maureen's roof collapsed. Perhaps it was fate intervening and telling her to stop being such a fool as to have feelings for Douglas. She would reconsider her life whilst away with Maisie. Douglas's presence made it hard to think straight and she certainly needed to think of her future. As much as she was attracted to the handsome man and the links he had with her past, she must be careful or she could be making the biggest mistake of her life.

'Up a bit ... to the left ... Perfect!' Maisie called to Sarah as she watched her chum pinning bunting to the walls of the hall in the Prince of Wales pub. 'It looks a little skew-whiff but it'll do. I think we've done a good job,' she said, looking around the drab hall that was now bedecked with bunting of all colours of the rainbow. 'Where did you get it from?'

'Alf, the landlord, found it in the cellar. He reckons it's been there since the coronation.'

'Queen Victoria's going by the dust on it,' Freda added, brushing down her dress. 'If I'd have known I'd have got this mucky, I'd have worn my Fire Service overalls.'

'Can someone help me down from this ladder?' Sarah called to her friends. 'Goodness knows where Alan and David have got to.'

'I'll give you one guess,' Maisie said, pointing to the door that led through to the public bar. 'They said they'd go and sort out a barrel for the dance. I reckon they've stopped to test the stuff. What I wouldn't give for a drop of gin right now. Watching you two work is making me thirsty.'

'Now, now, Maisie, think of the baby,' Freda scolded as she held the ladder steady while Sarah gingerly made her way back down to the floor. 'We can't have you staggering home and having a fall or something, can we?'

'As if I would,' Maisie hooted out loud. 'I'll have a drop of muvver's ruin later. It'll perk me up.'

'Here we are, ladies,' Alan announced as he pushed through the double doors into the hall balancing a tray full of drinks.

'Gosh, Alan. That's rather a lot for a lunchtime. Are we celebrating something you've not told me about?' Sarah said as she took a glass of shandy from the tray and handed the same to Freda.

Alan's smile dropped as he turned to place the drinks on a nearby table.

'Alan, no!' she cried out as an awful thought hit her. 'Not yet. I thought we had few days more together.'

Maisie nodded to Freda and the pair crept from the hall, leaving Sarah and Alan alone.

Alan hugged his wife close, wishing he could stay like this forever. 'Sarah, they've cancelled all leave.'

'But you've not been on leave. You've been working really hard teaching those lads to fly. You've not even had time with us . . . I thought we might have been able to go away for a few days . . . Perhaps down to Whitstable, where we had our honeymoon,' she added hopefully, looking up into his eyes. 'Please, Alan, let's at least have that.' She kept talking as Alan shook his head in a silent no. 'They can give us a few days, can't they . . . please?'

'Shh,' he soothed her as she finally broke down and

the tears came. 'Do you remember how Betty once told you how you have to make memories and hold them close to your heart when times get hard?'

Sarah mumbled her agreement into the jacket of his RAF uniform as he stroked her back and ran his fingers through her hair. He never wanted to let her go. She smelt good: a mix of soap and rose water. Tipping her chin up so he could look at her flushed face, he whispered, 'Remember this, my love,' as his lips met hers.

Time stood still as the couple clung to each other until Sarah pulled away. 'When . . . ?'

'This evening. David pulled a few strings so I could be at the dance for a couple of hours and we can enjoy ourselves before I head off to . . .'

Sarah put her hand across his mouth. 'Don't tell me. I don't want to know.' He took her hand and kissed each finger one by one. 'Careless talk?'

'No, I want to believe you are only ten miles away at Gravesend airfield and that you could walk through the door at any minute and we'd be a happy family without a care in the world. If I had to think of you hundreds of miles away and in constant danger, I wouldn't be able to go on living. I couldn't go through what happened last time. Not again, Alan.'

He smiled at his wife, wiping a stray tear from her cheek. 'I promise I won't leave you ever again. I'll write as much as I can and, if you have any concerns, you are to speak to David. You have no idea how important a man he is in the RAF.'

'I don't care about anyone else but you, Alan. The

King himself could walk through that door right now and I'd not take any notice. It wasn't by chance that you were there at Woolworths the day I went for my interview. It was meant to be and it's meant to be that you come home to me and our Georgina and we live happily ever after.'

'Oh, Sarah,' he groaned before kissing her gently until she could feel her knees buckle beneath her.

They both jumped as the doors crashed open and David walked in. 'Christ, I'm so sorry,' he apologized before turning to leave. 'Please forgive me . . . pretend I'm not here.'

Sarah burst out laughing. 'Oh, David, you are a tonic. Do come back in, and call the girls as well.'

David frowned. 'It's all right?'

'Yes, Alan has told me. Thank you for managing to give him a few hours more. It means a lot to me.'

'Anytime,' he smiled. 'And remember that if you have any problems, just ask. You are like a sister to my Maisie and I know you'd both do the same if the boot was on the other foot.'

Sarah stood on tiptoe and kissed David on the cheek. 'I'm a lucky woman to have so many people who care.'

'Hurry up, you two, or we'll miss the first dance,' Freda called upstairs to Maisie and Sarah.

It had been a rush with so many getting ready at number thirteen. Ruby and Maureen, who shared the front bedroom, had not taken so long with their preparations and had handed over their room for the younger women to put on their best dresses and do each other's hair. In the weeks leading up to the Woolworths fundraising dance everyone had been busy selling tickets to customers and thinking about what to wear. Gwyneth had been a problem as she only had one best dress and Maisie deemed it not quite right for the dance. She rummaged through her own wardrobe as well as Sarah's, and jointly they decided that they'd alter the bridesmaid dress that Sarah had worn at Maisie's wedding. Gwyneth was delighted and with a pretty silver clip in her dark shiny hair and a little red lipstick on her lips she looked charming.

'That'll make Mike Jackson's eyes light up,' Maisie whispered to Sarah.

'He's certainly smitten with Gwyneth,' Sarah agreed, 'but is she free to be courted? We don't really know much about her past, do we?'

'P'raps we should ask her?'

Sarah chewed her lip as she thought of Maisie's suggestion. 'I'm not so sure. We don't want her to think we are prying. It's not as if she has confided in us, is it? The last thing we want to do is to make her think we are being nosy.'

'But we are being nosy,' Maisie laughed.

'Shh, she will hear you,' Sarah said, looking worriedly towards the closed bedroom door where their new friend was settling Myfi down for the night. 'I must say you look lovely. No one would know you were carrying.'

'That was my aim,' Maisie said as she twirled around in a pale pink full-skirted dress with a sweetheart neckline and short puffed sleeves. 'Do yer recognize the material?'

Sarah frowned. 'I do, but for the life of me I can't think where I've seen it before.'

Maisie laughed. 'I was hoping you'd say that. It was that horrid off-white wedding dress we picked up at a jumble sale before the war. I unpicked the seams and washed the pieces of fabric and then put it away and forgot about it.'

'But it's pink. How did you—'

Maisie interrupted her friend. 'Beetroot. Bob gave me a couple from the garden and I simmered the veg along with the fabric. Do you think anyone will know?'

'Only if you get caught in the rain and the colour runs.' Sarah grinned, remembering when they'd both used gravy browning on their legs when they didn't have a pair of decent stockings between them and Maisie's contact down the docks had been nicked.

'Come on, you two. I've been ready for hours,' Freda said, sticking her head round the bedroom door. 'Sarah, you've not even done your hair yet. I'd have thought you'd have been the first at the dance considering it's the last time in a while you'll be able to do a quickstep with Alan.'

Sarah picked up her hairbrush and quickly ran it through the glossy chestnut waves. 'I'm leaving it straight this evening. I have to pin it up so often under my ARP helmet that it'll make a nice change to have it loose around my shoulders.'

'I still like that dress. It's the one you wore when Alan first kissed you, isn't it?'

Sarah grinned. 'Yes, I'm hoping he remembers. I'm surprised you do, Freda.'

'I was peering through the letter box,' she said with a giggle before running downstairs.

'Gawd, yer wouldn't believe that girl drives a motor-bike for the Fire Service, would yer? She still acts like our little kid sister. If yer ready, let's go dazzle our men-folk.'

The band started playing the first dance as the girls entered the hall. Ruby and Maureen waved to them from where they'd saved a couple of tables and beckoned them over. 'Sit yourself down here, Maisie, and take the weight off your feet. You don't want to be standing more than you have to in your condition.'

'I'm not ill, Ruby, I'm just having a baby and it's not coming along until Christmas. I'm fighting fit.' Maisie said but sat down all the same.

'You want to be careful,' Vera chipped in from her seat in the corner, 'I knew a woman who—'

'Shut up, Vera. Maisie don't want to know about these people you always go on about. She's a sensible girl and will tell us if she's not feeling well. You will, won't you?' she added, turning to Maisie, who was swaying along to the tune 'In the Mood' and gazing across to the bar look-ing for her husband, David.

'Of course I will, but yer might want to go and boil some water to be on the safe side,' she called across to Vera, before hooting with laughter.

'Oh, you're a right tonic,' Ruby said, wiping her eyes

after she stopped laughing. 'What would we do without you?'

'It's more what I'd do without you,' Maisie said without a hint of a smile. 'You're the family I've never really had.'

'It's the same band that used to play for the Woolworth staff parties,' Maureen whispered to Sarah. 'They've requested that I sing with them later. I've not done that for a while – in fact, not since Maisie's wedding in this very hall.'

Sarah gave her mother-in-law a hug. 'This place holds many memories for me too.' There'll be another this evening she thought to herself. Alan would be leaving before the last waltz was played in order to join his squadron. They'd agreed to say goodbye quietly and without any fuss. Maureen knew her son was leaving and had already said her goodbyes with more than a few tears. Fortunately Georgina was far too young to understand. 'Now, tell me what you intend to sing?'

Maureen gave a secretive smile. 'It's a secret, you'll know soon enough. Now, why don't you go and find my son and have a dance. If you don't, I'll grab him for myself.'

Sarah needed no second bidding and headed to where Alan was talking to a couple of Woolworths colleagues who were home on leave. She took her husband's arm and led him to the dance floor. 'I'm not leaving your side this evening.'

'That suits me fine,' Alan said as he took her in his arms and moved to the mellow tones of the saxophonist, as the lights dimmed and he played 'Red Sails in the

Sunset'. 'I'll be home before you know it,' he whispered in her ear. 'Nothing will keep me away from you longer than is necessary and when I'm back we'll look for our own home and perhaps plan a brother or sister for Georgie.'

Sarah felt her skin prickle with excitement as she thought of the future and of Alan. 'First just stay safe for me,' she whispered. 'We can think about the rest when you are home for good.'

Alan spun her round as the music finished and the lights were turned full on. There were cheers as Betty stepped onto the small stage and the pianist played an intro to the popular Woolworths manager. She raised her hand to quiet the audience. 'Ladies and gentlemen and employees past and present of F. W. Woolworths, thank you for purchasing a ticket to this wonderful fundraising dance. Like many people in Erith, we are doing our best to bring this war to a speedy end. By raising funds alongside other Woolworths stores we've so far been able to pay for two Spitfires, which help our brave lads fight the enemy. This evening's fundraising event has been organized by three of our Woolworths Girls: Maisie Carlisle, Freda Smith and Sarah Gilbert, who, I have no need to remind many of you, is the wife of Alan, an RAF pilot who flies the very planes we are raising funds for this evening. Alan was, until war broke out, one of our trainee managers. He is leaving us this evening to rejoin his squadron.'

The room erupted in wild cheers for Alan and there was much backslapping and many wishes of good luck.

Betty waited for the room to quiet down before

speaking again. 'It just remains for me to remind you all that we have a bumper raffle as well as a prize bingo during the interval, with gift donations not only from F. W. Woolworths but some of the local traders in Erith, so please dig deep into your pockets to support our worthy cause. Oh, and in the event of an air-raid warning, please follow our ARP wardens to the public shelter.'

This final comment met with many good-natured boos and hisses by those present before the band struck up a lively dance number and Betty left the stage.

'Well done, my dear,' Douglas said as he gave her a hand to step from the stage.

'Thank you, Douglas,' Betty said and she reclaimed her hand. He looked so smart in a black tailored suit that wouldn't look out of place in a posh London hotel. As she caught the citrus scent of his cologne she felt herself weaken. She was so attracted to him but was doing her utmost to be strong and not be swayed by the thoughts of his kiss. She was not a love-struck young woman. She was a responsible manager of a busy Woolworths store. There was no time for her to fall in love and act like a fool. She was far too old for such things. She must distance herself from Douglas Billington.

Douglas took her arm as they walked across the room towards the bar, stopping from time to time to speak to staff and friends. She wanted nothing more than to remove herself from his hold and move away, but it would be so churlish and besides, it was comforting. What harm would it do?

Douglas handed her a small sherry. 'I thought we

might reschedule that dinner with Clemmie and Dorothy. They've been asking when they will meet you. How about Sunday afternoon? If the weather is fine, we could take a walk over the heath at Dartford if you wish?'

'I'm sorry, Douglas. It isn't possible,' she replied, knowing now was the time to step away from this handsome man before she got tangled up in his family and before he stole her heart completely. 'I'm not so sure it's a good idea for me to meet your family. Besides, I'm going away for a few days. It's time I took a break from work. I'm looking forward to some time alone!'

Douglas looked confused. 'I had no idea. Have you told me and I've forgotten? I do apologize if that is the case.'

Betty felt awful, but she couldn't change her mind now. Douglas would soon get over her and perhaps even find a younger woman who might marry him and be able to give him another child. She knew he doted on his daughters from what he'd told her. 'It's only just been planned. I'm going to the Kent coast with Maisie for a few days. We leave tomorrow afternoon. I'll also be having a meeting with the manager at Canterbury while I'm away. It will be good to meet a fellow colleague,' she added, defiantly holding her chin a little higher. 'I'm looking forward to it.'

Douglas stared at Betty without saying a word, his eyes scouring her face for a sign that she didn't realize how harsh her words had been.

The seconds ticked past as she wondered whether she should say something but then he spoke. 'I'm sure you deserve a trip away from Erith. I do hope you'll have a good time. Now, if you'll excuse me, I'd like to speak with Alan before he leaves.'

Betty watched as Douglas turned his back on her and walked over to the bar, where Alan was talking with David and Mike. She felt awful. Whatever had she done? The man didn't deserve to be rejected like that. She would have to try to apologize but not now. Perhaps wait until they were alone – but would he want to speak to her after the way she had acted?

The evening was lively with staff and their friends forgetting the war for a few hours to enjoy themselves. Maureen introduced Gwyneth to staff she'd not had a chance to meet since starting work at the store and when the women heard about Myfi there were invitations to meet so the children could play together. Gwyneth thanked them all, but wondered how to explain that the child wasn't able to speak so it was unlikely the other children would wish to play with her. She made her apologies and joined Ruby, who was uncovering the buffet table. As usual Woolworths head office had made a splendid contribution to the fare, supplying hard-to-come-by ingredients so that their staff canteen cook, Maureen, had been able to prepare a tasty spread.

Ruby gave Gwyneth a sympathetic look as she passed Spam sandwiches across the table to the hungry dancers. 'Something bothering you, love?'

Gwyneth nodded. 'Yes . . . but I don't know where to start.'

'Now's not the time or place. Let's have a little chat tomorrow before you head off to work, shall we?'

Gwyneth nodded, a small smile of relief spreading across her face. 'That would be nice, thank you. I'm really fortunate to have met you and your family, Ruby.'

'I'm glad to have met you and your lovely daughter as well,' Ruby said as she slapped the hand of a young lad who was about to help himself to another dish of jelly. 'Now, I do believe the band is about to start up again and there's someone wanting to dance with you.'

Gwyneth turned to see Mike Jackson standing awkwardly close by. 'I'm not much of a dancer, but I can manage a foxtrot of sorts if you'd care to, Gwyneth?' he said.

'You're a good dancer, Mike, as you know very well. Why, you never left the dance floor when we went to that dance at Erith Dance Studio recently. You spun me around the floor more than once.'

Mike had the good grace to blush. He did enjoy dancing but never had much of a chance and the last thing he wished to do was to show off to Gwyneth. 'You've caught me out, but I still don't reckon I'm much of a dancer. I have flat feet from too many years walking the beat. Perhaps I should start again and just ask you to dance?'

'There's no need, Mike. I'd love to dance with you.'

Ruby nodded knowingly to herself as she watched the policeman escort the young Welsh woman to the edge of the floor before taking her into his arms and gliding off to the sound of a well-known Fred Astaire song.

*

With a roll of the drums the leader of the dance band stood to his feet. 'We've now reached the time in the evening which has become quite a tradition at Woolworths staff dances. Please welcome Maureen Gilbert to the stage to sing a few of our favourite songs. Come on, Maureen, let's be having you.'

Maureen waved to the happy crowd as she climbed up the three steps to the stage before whispering in the ear of the bandleader, who nodded and turned to his fellow musicians to tell them what Maureen intended to sing.

Maureen stood behind the microphone. 'Thank you all for your wonderful welcome. Isn't this a fantastic dance? I bet there's nothing like this over in Germany.'

The room erupted with cheers and loud comments.

'Settle down now. I see we have many service men and women here this evening. Let's all join together and sing that well-known favourite "Bless 'Em All".'

The band played the first notes and Maureen's clear voice could be heard throughout the Prince of Wales pub and to the street beyond.

Alan put his arms around Sarah and Freda as they joined in with the singing. '. . . *so cheer up my lads, bless 'em all.*'

Maureen continued with 'It's a Long Way to Tipperary', quickly followed by 'Pack up Your Troubles in Your Old Kit Bag' before stopping to take a sip from a glass of shandy that was passed to her from the side of the stage. Fanning her hot face with her hand, she beamed at the audience. 'More?'

The crowd cheered. 'I think it's time someone else had a go and let me take a rest.' Her happy face looked sad as she gazed into the crowd. 'There's someone here this evening who will very soon be saying goodbye to his family to fly off and fight for his country. We've had the pleasure of his company for the last few months, but as much as we want him to stay here in Kent, he is needed for his skills as a pilot. I know many of you have said goodbye to loved ones since this bloody war started, so please indulge this old woman for a few minutes if you will. This man can turn out a reasonable tune so I'll not apologize for calling my son, Alan Gilbert, to the stage. Come on up, Alan.'

Alan joined his mum on the stage, giving her a kiss as she stepped aside for him to take over the microphone. 'I've not done this for a while so bear with me,' he said to riotous shouts from the audience. 'As Mum said, I'll be off shortly, but the memory of seeing you all here this evening will remain with me all the time I'm away. There are a few people I'm especially sad to be leaving behind. Mum, our Georgina, and of course the in-laws,' he added with an embarrassed laugh. 'But my songs are dedicated to my wife, Sarah.' He nodded to the band-leader and the music started. '*I want a girl, just like the girl that married dear old Dad* . . .' Alan sang before leading the audience into a rousing rendition of 'I'll Be Your Sweetheart'.

'Thank you,' he said as the last strains of the music died away. 'It's probably still a little early in the evening to be singing this next song, but it's very special to me and the wife so please indulge us a little.'

Applause started as Alan sang his final song of the evening. '*Goodnight sweetheart, till we meet tomorrow* . . .'

Gwyneth joined Sarah and Freda, who stood close to the stage. 'Your husband sings very well,' she said with admiration.

'He takes after Maureen,' Freda added proudly. Alan was like a big brother to her and although she was sad to see him head overseas she was so proud of him she thought she would burst. If only she could find a boyfriend like Alan, she would never moan again about being on fire duty or peeling sprouts for dinner – two of her most hated jobs.

'The song is special to you?' Gwyneth asked.

'We've danced to it at many special moments in our life,' Sarah said with a slight wobble to her chin. 'Do you and your husband have special songs?' she asked.

Gwyneth gave her a blank look before recovering herself. 'Oh, you know what Welshmen are like. They never stop singing,' she replied before wandering over to stand with Ruby.

Freda nudged Sarah's arm. 'That was a little peculiar.'

Sarah, who was trying to listen to Alan as the song came to an end, just nodded and whispered quickly, 'She never mentions her husband. I assume she has one, but then she doesn't wear a wedding ring although she has a daughter.' She left Freda to head towards Alan as he jumped down from the stage and joined his mum.

'Take care of yourself, Mum, and look after my girls for me.'

'It goes without saying, my love. Don't worry about us, we can look after ourselves. You just concentrate on finishing this war off once and for all and get yourself home in one piece. Do you know how long you'll be gone?'

'They say it'll be six months this time. I hope it's not any longer.'

'So you'll be home for Christmas?' Maureen asked hopefully.

'What's this about Christmas?' Sarah asked as she joined them.

'David tipped me the wink that they expect this tour of duty to be over by Christmas. I could be home to see you and Georgie open your presents.'

Sarah's eyes sparkled. 'That would be wonderful, but I don't need presents. I just want you home in one piece so we can start our happy ever after.'

Maureen kissed her son's cheek and slipped away. There were times when a mother should leave her son alone.

Alan nodded to where David was waving to him. 'It's looks as though I've got to go, Sixpenny.'

Sarah's hand went to her throat where the silver sixpence he'd given her hung on a chain. She slid her arms around his neck, oblivious to the crowded hall, and kissed him gently. 'Goodbye, my darling,' she said, fighting back the tears she promised would not fall.

'Come and wave me off,' he said, grabbing her hand and hurrying her through the dancers before anyone stopped them to talk.

Outside the warm May day had turned a little chilly as night had set in. Sarah shivered in her thin dance frock. Across the road she could just see a truck painted in camouflage colours. Behind the wheel a man in RAF uniform was smoking a cigarette and talking to David, who'd left the hall ahead of them with Maisie by his side. 'No limousine for you then?' she said, trying to keep the atmosphere light.

'It's all the same in the blackout,' he grinned back. 'I'm going to miss you, Sarah,' he whispered as he pulled her close to him.

She detected a break in his voice and steeled herself not to cry. 'It's Sixpenny to you, young man,' she said sternly. 'Sarah's a married woman with a child and responsibilities. Sixpenny is the shy young thing who fell in love with her Woolworths boy, remember?'

'How could I ever forget?' he groaned as his lips found hers and the two young people, who by rights should have lived out their lives in their hometown if it wasn't for Hitler intervening, made their goodbyes.

'If I was you, I'd be a wreck right now,' Maisie said as they watched the lorry turn a corner at the end of the road and disappear.

'I promised myself I wouldn't cry. I didn't want to upset Alan. But if you don't mind, I need a shoulder to cry on now he's gone,' Sarah said as she started to sob uncontrollably.

'You cry all yer want to. No one can see you out here. Just remember he'll be home by Christmas. It won't be that long.'

'It's going to feel like years,' Sarah hiccuped, trying to control herself.

'Chin up, Christmas will be here before we know it so let's put our best foot forward and prepare to welcome

Alan home, and also to give a big welcome to my little one, shall we?'

'I can't wait,' Sarah said, looking over her shoulder to the empty road as Maisie led her back towards the hall.

14

'Let's have that chat, shall we?' Ruby said to Gwyneth after waving off the rest of the household to their various jobs. 'I enjoy having a house full of people, but just sometimes it is nice to sit down and take a rest and have a chat with a friend.'

Gwyneth smiled at her landlady. She'd never known anyone quite as busy as Ruby Caselton. Already she had made sure everyone staying at number thirteen had a filling breakfast inside them before they went about their day and before she set off for Cornwall with Bob after they'd had their Sunday dinner. 'You deserve a rest, Ruby,' she said, putting a cup of tea in front of her.

'Let's not beat about the bush with small talk,' Ruby said kindly. 'What's bothering you, love? I get the impression not all is happy in your life.'

Gwyneth sighed. The time had come to tell a lady she respected that she'd not told all the truth about her life. Or, to be more accurate, she'd kept something to herself that she should have shared with the people who had been so kind to her and Myfi. 'I've not been completely honest with you, Ruby,' she said sadly.

Ruby just nodded and sipped her tea. Sometimes it was best not to comment and just let the person talk.

'There's a reason I'm in Erith with Myfi rather than back home in Wales and it's also the reason why Myfi doesn't talk. We are on the run from my husband.'

'You won't be the first woman who's had to leave a bad marriage, Gwyneth, even if it does mean your daughter doesn't get to grow up living under the same roof as your husband.' She'd wanted to ask about the young girl and why she didn't speak, but knew that she'd have to bide her time until the child's mum was prepared to confide in her. Young Myfi had blossomed living at number thirteen. She was like a big sister to Georgie, who adored her in return. Already Myfi was settled in the small local school. Ruby wasn't sure what the pretty Welsh woman had said to the teacher by way of explaining Myfi's silence, but the little girl seemed happy and went skipping off each morning eager to see her new friends, who appeared not to be concerned that the little girl could not speak.

Gwyneth stopped to take a gulp of her tea. Her hands shook as she put the cup back in its saucer. 'Myfi's not my child, Ruby,' she said apologetically.

'There's no shame in being a stepmother,' Ruby consoled her. 'It can be just as rewarding as having given birth oneself.'

Gwyneth shook her head. 'I'm not her stepmother either. She's my niece.' She felt relief for finally having blurted out the truth. She hadn't expected to have carried her secret for so long, living in fear that if Myfi started to speak again she would have to move on and give herself another identity in case they were found.

Ruby frowned. She was confused. 'I think you'd better start explaining, don't you?'

Gwyneth nodded her head. 'You have no idea how much I've wanted to unburden myself.'

'You must have your reasons,' Ruby said as she waited for Gwyneth to say more.

'I made a mistake and it has followed me around for the past two years. I just wish I could wind back the clock and start all over again,' she said sadly. 'It's just been me and Myfi facing the world on our own.'

Ruby remained quiet, waiting for Gwyneth to continue. For a rare moment you could hear a pin drop in the living room of number thirteen.

'Myfanwy,' she said, giving the child her full name, 'is the daughter of my sister. When she died during an air raid it was only right that I took her under my wing.'

'Was there no husband?'

Gwyneth shook her head. 'No, he left her when Myfi was a baby. To be honest, it was a relief as he wasn't a good man. My sister had her head turned by his flash ways. Things changed when he had to marry her and he didn't take kindly to the responsibilities of a wife and baby. He left her before Myfi was three months old.'

'My, my,' Ruby said. 'I can never understand why some men don't take to marriage and rearing kiddies. I still thank God my Eddie loved us all. But go on. I don't want to stop you talking. Your sister died, you say?'

'Yes, she'd been a nurse and had followed her husband to London, hoping to convince him to return to Wales and face up to his responsibilities. Of course, he wanted nothing to do with her and rather than face the shame of returning to our village in the Welsh Valleys without her husband, she took a job at the Royal London Hospital as a ward sister. She dared not tell them she had a child, so it was kept quiet and a neighbour cared for Myfi while she worked.'

'That's a responsible job. Did you not follow the same profession?' Ruby asked, forgetting that she wanted Gwyneth to tell her story uninterrupted.

'I didn't have the calling or the passion like she did. I'd always wanted to be a wife and mother and was more than happy to work in an assortment of shops until that magical day appeared.'

'It didn't?'

Gwyneth gave a harsh laugh. 'Oh, I married early on when I was twenty-five, but the children never came. He blamed me for that but we soldiered on. I lived in hope and he . . . well, he lived mostly at the pub when he wasn't working long shifts down the mine. We lived almost separate lives, although to the outside world we were a happy couple who had never been blessed with children.'

'You're still young. How old are you? Thirty, thirty-five? You've never said where your husband is now. I take it he is serving his country somewhere? When he's home again who knows, that baby may just come along. Why, our Pat was a late baby. She arrived when our George was almost eleven,' Ruby said with a smile. She loved a happy ending.

'I'm thirty-six,' Gwyneth replied, 'but I've given up all

hope now. Some women just aren't blessed with children. There are worse things that happen at sea, as they say,' she said with a wry grin. 'Myfi is as much a daughter as I'll ever have and I truly love her as if she were my own.'

'But your husband . . .' Ruby nudged her, wanting to know why he wasn't considered in her plans for the future. She couldn't even think about Mike Jackson and how it was obvious he doted on the woman. He'd be brokenhearted knowing there was a husband about, as it had been assumed Gwyneth was a widow. Hadn't Maureen said as much?

Gwyneth took a deep breath and looked Ruby in the eye. 'My husband is not serving his country, Ruby, he is languishing in prison. He is not someone to be proud of and, as evil as it makes me appear, I wish he were dead.'

Ruby considered she was able to cope with most things but to be faced with such a statement was a shock. 'I think we need another cuppa, don't you? Do you want to tell me any more? Feel free to tell me to mind my own business if you think I'm poking my nose into your affairs.'

Gwyneth picked up their teacups and, following Ruby to the kitchen, she filled the large kettle and placed it on the stove while Ruby drained the now cold teapot and stepped outside the back door to empty the dregs onto Bob's prized compost heap.

'I'd like to tell you everything,' Gwyneth said as Ruby returned to the kitchen. 'It feels good to get things off my chest. You've been good to the two of us and it doesn't feel right to live a lie and deceive you as well.'

'You must do what you feel is best for you and the

child. I'd think no worse of you, but you know what they say: a problem shared is a problem halved.'

'It isn't fair to give you half my problems. Idris Jones is a nasty, bitter man and the last thing I need when he comes out of prison is for him to find out where I'm living and turn up here causing trouble for my friends.'

Ruby glanced to where a large iron frying pan hung above the stove and thought that it had come in useful once before and would do so again if trouble came knocking at her door. Then she frowned. 'Jones? Your surname is Evans. Is there something else you've not told me?'

'There's a lot still to tell,' Gwyneth said, looking shamefaced. 'I'm not Gwyneth Evans.'

Ruby poured boiling water into the large brown earthenware teapot before swishing it round and tipping it into the stone sink. Adding two teaspoons of leaves plus one for the pot, she poured water on top before placing on the lid and covering it with a tea cosy that had been a gift from Freda. It was made from odd lengths of wool and Ruby loved the colourful cosy. It cheered up the gloomiest of mornings when the house was cold and she yearned for that first cup of tea of the day. The remains of the hot water were poured into a bowl, where Gwyneth rinsed their cups and saucers.

Going to the pantry, Ruby brought back a slightly battered tin and opened the lid. 'Good, there's a couple of slices of cake left. Now, I suggest we settle ourselves down and you start from the very beginning.'

'But I have to collect Myfi from Sunday school in three-quarters of an hour,' Gwyneth protested.

'Then I suggest you talk quickly,' Ruby prompted with a small smile. She wanted to know what was happening in this girl's life so she could do her best to help.

Gwyneth placed a milk jug on the table and sat down to tell Ruby about her life before she arrived in Alexandra Road. 'I was flattered when Idris set his cap at me. He was a handsome lad and was popular amongst my friends. My sister hadn't long married and I dreamt of walking down the aisle dressed in white just as she had. I've always been the twin who didn't do as well as her sibling. Yes, I was a twin,' she added, seeing Ruby's face light up. 'At school, and then when we started our working lives, I was the one who wasn't quite as bright. I walked in my sister's shadow. When Idris proposed I was the happiest girl in Wales and made sure my wedding was bigger and better than my sister's had been, but then she announced she was expecting and her news over-shadowed my own day.'

'That wasn't a nice thing to do,' Ruby said, sympathizing with the girl.

'My parents were as much to blame as they couldn't contain their excitement when they were told. Anyway, my sister soon moved to London and we got on with our lives. Did I tell you that Idris was a miner?'

'Yes, that must have been a hard living,' Ruby said. She'd read about life in the mining areas of Wales and watched Pathé News films. She knew there were even coal mines in Kent and in northern England. She'd not have liked to live like that, but it was honourable work and she admired anyone who did a proper day's labour.

'Yes, he was a hard worker, but as news of war became more of a reality and talk in the pub turned to men earning more in the forces than down the mines, he became unsettled and spoke of joining up. By then we'd been married a good while and he was beginning to insinuate that it was my fault he didn't have a son.'

'That must have hurt,' Ruby sympathized passing a cup of tea across the table along with a slice of sponge cake.

'It did but I'd grown a thick skin by then. Anyhow, he decided he was going to join the army and I did nothing to discourage him, even though mining was a reserved occupation. I was looking forward to being free of Idris for a little while when he went off to war with his friends. Then things went from bad to worse. When what he thought would be his call-up papers arrived he was informed that his request had been refused. To add insult to injury he was not only going to remain a miner, but was being moved to a mine in Kent, as there was a shortage of skilled coal miners there with so many having gone off to fight.'

Ruby bristled. 'There's nothing insulting about working in Kent.'

Gwyneth smiled at her landlady. 'I agree with you. I've come to love this county almost as much as my homeland. But Idris is fiercely patriotic. Get a few pints of beer inside him and there's no stopping his rage, as I found out to my cost.'

'He used his fists on you?' Ruby asked, fearing for the girl.

Gwyneth undid the top two buttons of her blouse and exposed her shoulder. Ruby could see an angry-looking red scar of around two inches and felt tears in her eyes that a man would do such a thing to a beautiful young woman. 'The bastard,' she muttered before apologizing for swearing. 'How did he talk his way out of that?' she asked, feeling angry that any man would raise a hand to a woman.

'He told anyone who asked that I'd tripped and fallen while carrying a tray of cups and saucers to the kitchen. In truth, I'd said that moving to Kent wouldn't be so bad and we'd get to like it. He'd grabbed me by the hair and screamed horrid things in my face before pushing me across the room. How I didn't fall into the fireplace I don't know. Instead I fell on the broken china, which had been a wedding present, and cut myself. He forbade me from going to see our doctor in case questions were asked and the wound took an age to heal and has not improved these past few years.'

'So you moved to Kent with him?'

'I had no choice. My parents would never have believed me if I'd said that Idris was such a brute and by then my sister had her own problems, having to rear a young child and work full-time. It was simpler to move to Kent with Idris and hope for a better future and that he'd be a happier person. However, it didn't work out like that. No, it grew progressively worse. Amongst the other miners were a few fellow Welshmen who were just as unhappy as Idris to have been sent so far from home and they would drink together and be vocally open about their hatred of their fellow workers and the bosses.'

'How about you? Did you fit in with the other wives?'

'It was hard but I made the decision not to work close to Betteshanger. It's a mining village near Deal on the coast of Kent,' she added as she noticed Ruby's puzzled look. 'Instead I caught a bus each day into town, where I worked in a dress shop. If I'd worked local to the village and the mining community, I know I'd have suffered for being married to such a bigoted man. Of course, Idris was horrid to me for not being home with a meal on the table and he began to use his fists on me more and more.'

Ruby sighed with frustration. She'd love to get her hands on this man and give him what for. 'I'm lost for words and that doesn't happen often. I take it you ran away?'

'I didn't run but I did plan my escape. I decided to head to where my sister lived on the Isle of Dogs in the East End of London, but I needed to have money until I could find a job and support myself.'

'You had your wages, though . . .'

Gwyneth nodded. 'Yes, but I had to hand them over to Idris every Friday night. He left me with just a few shillings for personal bits and pieces. Fortunately for me my boss spotted the bruises Idris left after one of his drunken rages and she was most sympathetic. She'd experienced the same and helped me plan my escape.'

'Thank goodness for that,' Ruby sighed. 'Did it take long before you could do a runner?'

'A month and funnily enough it was Idris that helped

in my escape.' She laughed at the memory. 'He had a habit of rolling home drunk and would turn out his pockets before falling into bed. I'd wait until he was snoring his head off and then I'd help myself, but always made sure not to be too greedy in case he noticed. That covered my train fair up to London. Meanwhile I would put an item of clothing into my shopping bag and leave it at work so he wouldn't notice me with a suitcase. I picked up a second-hand one close to where I worked.'

'But what about money to live on? A few pinched coins wouldn't last long?'

'My manager held back some of my money each week. One time I told Idris it was because I'd damaged an item of stock. That earned me a thick ear. Another time I told him the extra would be added the following week as my manager had taken the shop's takings to the bank without holding enough back for staff wages. I hated lying but I had no choice. I'd planned that the following week I would take my wages and leave the area for good. However, I didn't expect Idris to be arrested for near on killing a man in a brawl and to be called as a witness. That put paid to my escape until he was locked up and the key thrown away.'

'How long did he get?'

'Three years; he's out just before Christmas.'

'But it's not your concern, is it? That part of your life is over and done with.'

'Not quite. He'd got wind that I'd gone to my sister's home and made sure I knew that he'd find me and kill me for giving evidence against him in court that meant he'd never be able to find work as a miner again.'

Ruby looked horrified. 'Oh my!'

'So there I was living with my sister as I'd planned but fearing for my life.'

'Is that when you changed your name?'

'No, that was a year later. There was an air raid. Gwyneth and Myfi were caught in it and Myfi watched as her mum died,' Gwyneth said with a shaky voice. 'Myfi hasn't spoken since that day.'

'Hang on a moment,' Ruby said with a puzzled expression. 'You said that Gwyneth was killed but you are . . . ?'

'I'm Gwyneth's identical twin sister, Gladys. God forgive me but I took on my sister's identity hoping that Idris would never find me. In a way I thank God that Myfi has never spoken a word since that day as she is the only one who knows I'm not her mother. That is . . . apart from Maureen, but I've not given her any reasons. She was present when I filled out my application form to work at Woolworths and could see I had a problem. She doesn't know about Idris.'

There was silence as Ruby absorbed this information. 'There's one thing that troubles me with all this,' she said with a frown. 'I can excuse you not giving any of us your right name, but it's the thought your poor sister has been buried under another person's name. It's just not right.'

'I agree with you. Gwyneth has been laid to rest under her own name. Her headstone can prove that. I wouldn't dare do otherwise. It was only after the funeral, and knowing I was now caring for her daughter, that I thought it might help me avoid Idris if I pretended to be my sister.

We looked so alike. I've even grown my hair longer so no one who knew us would be confused.'

'Your parents?'

'My parents know the truth. They wanted us both to return home, but it would be one of the first places for Idris to look for me.' She looked at Ruby, beseeching her not to give them both away.

Ruby reached across the table and squeezed her hand. 'Your secret is safe with me. I'd have most likely done as you did if I'd been in the same situation. I may be worried about my Pat down in Cornwall, but at least I know she doesn't have a vengeful husband after her.' She looked at Gwyneth and cocked her head to one side thoughtfully. 'You don't look like a Gladys. To me you'll always be Gwyneth.'

'My second name is Gwyneth. My mother was in a quandary when we were born as both our grandmothers insisted we carry their names. I was baptized Gladys Gwyneth and my sister vice versa.'

Ruby burst out laughing. 'I've heard everything now.'

Gwyneth smiled. She was so grateful to this woman for not only taking her in but also believing her story. At last she could sleep at night and hopefully prepare for her future. But what should she do about Mike Jackson? She had warm feelings for him but didn't want to allow him to think there was a future for them.

Maisie ran up the staff stairs in the Woolworths store and tapped on Betty's office door before entering. 'Are you ready? David's begged a vehicle from God knows where so we won't have ter take the train. It'll save absolutely hours. We may even be able ter get some sun on our faces this afternoon despite not being able to get onto the beach anymore.'

Betty closed her powder compact after checking her lipstick and smiled at the excited woman. 'Why, Maisie, you look splendid. Is that a new suit?'

'Nah, I've had it a while now but there were generous seams so I was able ter let out the waistband on the skirt and move the buttons over on the jacket, so it's good for a month or two yet. Waste not, want not, eh?'

'You are wasted working for Woolworths. By rights you should have your own establishment and be making couture gowns.'

Maisie screwed up her face and shook her head, causing the small pin curls on top of the elaborate French pleat to bounce about. 'What, me own a posh shop? Heaven help us. Can you imagine all those rich women coming ter me for a dress?' She snorted with laughter. 'I'm happy making stuff fer me friends and besides, I'll be busy with this one before too long,' she said, patting her stomach protectively.

'I don't think you'll be hanging up your Singer sewing machine just yet, Maisie,' Betty said as she checked her desk was tidy before picking up a small suitcase that stood by the coat stand. 'Right, I'm all yours. Let's get going, shall we?'

Betty stopped to talk to staff, as she followed Maisie towards the large glass double doors at the front of the store. Looking back before leaving, she was satisfied that all was as it should be. The counters were tidy and well stocked, the mahogany woodwork polished and shining. If it wasn't for the crisscross of sticky paper on the windows and doors, and the knowledge that stock wasn't as plentiful as she'd like, no one would even know there was a war on. It was business as usual at Woolworths.

Betty enjoyed the drive down to the Kent coast. She liked David and Maisie Carlisle's company. They were a devoted couple and Betty could only hope that this time their wish for a healthy baby was answered by whatever god looked after pregnant women. She could still recall the day just before last Christmas when Maisie lost her baby – it had been such a sad time.

The sky was clear and the sun shone down as the friends travelled through the towns of Dartford, Gravesend and Rochester before hitting the countryside of Kent. Betty marvelled at the open spaces and for once they ignored barrage balloons and other signs of war and enjoyed the best that the county of Kent could offer. David pulled up outside a small pub on the outskirts of Faversham, where they enjoyed a quick bite to eat before heading on to Margate and the seafront guesthouse owned by David's colleague.

'This is a bit of all right,' Maisie exclaimed as she collapsed onto her bed after saying her goodbyes to her husband. 'I can see still see the sea when I'm lying down.'

'We must make sure the blackout curtains are in place this evening. I'd dread to think a chink of light from our room would guide the enemy in from across the Channel,' Betty said, looking worried as she inspected the curtains that hung each side of the large bay window of their second-floor bedroom.

'I wouldn't worry too much. It's been quiet lately. What say we have a lazy day tomorrow checking out Margate before we catch the bus to Canterbury the day after to visit the Woolworths store and have afternoon tea with the manager, unless you want to go there tomorrow while the store is open? Seems a bit on the strange side to visit Woolies when it's closed. Whatever you decide, we can spend the rest of the day shopping.'

'Sunday would suit me better. I'd rather like to visit the cathedral if you don't mind.'

Maisie shrugged. 'I'm not a religious person but I'd like to say a little prayer to end this bloody war.'

'I'll most definitely join you,' Betty said as she opened her suitcase and started to place her clothes and soap bag into the bottom drawers of a large walnut chest of drawers set in the bay window. 'I've left you the top two so you don't have to bend too much,' she said to Maisie, who looked comfortable spread out on the bed. 'Shall I unpack your things then I can slide our cases under the beds? It'll keep the room spick and span.'

'Cheers, Betty. To be honest, I could do with forty winks. I must be getting old as all I want to do at the moment is snooze.'

'In that case the unpacking can wait until later. I'll take a short walk along the seafront and leave you to have a nap.' She removed Maisie's white sandals from her feet and covered her with a candlewick bed cover. 'I may pick up a few postcards to send back home.'

'Get me a couple, please, Betty. The funnier the better,' Maisie mumbled as she drifted off to sleep.

Betty walked down the steep steps from the front door

of the guesthouse, stopping to breathe in the fresh sea air and gaze past the barbed wire and gun emplacements to where a few fishing boats bobbed about on the calm sea. Margate was still a beautiful place regardless of the war. She decided there and then that she'd not be a stranger to this pretty seaside town. The golden sands must be a wonderful sight in peacetime, she thought to herself. As she set off along the front at a sedate pace, enjoying the sun on her face and bare arms, she felt the tension of the past weeks fall away from her shoulders. At last she had new staff in the store and at least one would one day make a supervisor if she continued to work hard. Yes, she liked Gwyneth and hoped that the pleasant girl from Wales did not leave Erith once the war ended – when it ended, she sighed to herself. There didn't seem any let-up in hostilities, even though they didn't suffer so many air raids in Erith, thank goodness.

Walking further along the seafront, Betty stopped at the entrance to Dreamland. To think this used to be the place to head to when one went on a day trip to Margate. Now requisitioned by the army, it was no longer open to the public. Maisie had told her, on the long journey down from Erith, that she'd heard they still held dances and were visited by many well-known entertainers. How wonderful to think that famous show business people that she'd heard on the radio and seen in the cinema had walked on the very pavement where she was standing now!

Moving on down the seafront, there was a sign for Lyons Tea Rooms with steps that led upstairs above a row of shops. Looking upwards, Betty could see a veranda where diners were seated. It would be the ideal place to enjoy afternoon tea. Perhaps when Maisie was up and about they could visit. Yes, it would be her treat to say thank you to her friend for inviting her along on this trip. Turning off the seafront, she walked up the High Street looking out for a shop that sold postcards. Lo and behold there was an F. W. Woolworths. Betty smiled to herself and crossed the road to enter the store. She'd not introduce herself to the manager, as she didn't feel it was the right thing to do. When she travelled to Canterbury to visit the town's Woolworths store it would be a business appointment to discuss stock and the war effort. The manager at the Canterbury store was expecting to see her sometime during her holiday to this part of Kent. Besides, she wasn't dressed appropriately today, wearing, as she was, a simple pale green floral patterned cotton sundress and sandals with a cardigan over her arm in case the day turned chilly.

It was like coming home, Betty thought to herself, as she breathed in the same aroma of floor wax and furniture polish that the company used to keep the stores looking shiny and clean. If she closed her eyes, she could be back at the Erith store.

Finding a rack of postcards, she chose one of the beach to send to Ruby and Freda and another of the Woolworths store to send to her staff. Betty thought it would make them smile. Perhaps when they visited the Canterbury store she could send one from there as well?

Deciding it was time for refreshments, she headed out of the store and back towards the seafront, stopping only to browse through a small selection of postcards outside a shop selling tin buckets and spades, even though there was no access to the sandy beaches for holidaymakers. Maisie was sure to like some of the cartoon characters with sketches of overweight wives and puny husbands accompanied by risqué jokes. Paying for her purchases, Betty crossed the road to a small tea shop and ordered a pot of tea for one and a currant bun. Perhaps she should treat herself to trips more often. She rarely left Erith on her day off and Kent was such a lovely part of the country regardless of the war. Perhaps Douglas and his daughters would join her in a trip to Margate? They would be sure to love it here ... It was then that she realized her mistake. Douglas was no longer in her life. She'd as much as shown him the door at the staff fundraising dance the other night. She would never meet his two daughters or have wonderful day trips to the coast. There was never going to be a happy relationship with the first man who had made her heart flutter since her Charlie died. She put down her cup and pushed away the plate with the uneaten bun. 'Oh, what a fool you've been, Betty Billington,' she muttered to herself. Large tears dropped silently as she gazed out to sea, but she didn't notice a single thing being so deep in thought.

15

'That was a rare treat, David. You must remember to thank your mother for me. In fact, I'll write her a letter if you leave me the address before you go home,' Ruby said as she left the last of the pans to dry on the wooden draining board.

'It's my pleasure, Mrs C.,' David Carlisle said, untying an apron from around his waist. 'Between you and me, my Maisie's not yet found the knack of cooking roast beef, let alone Yorkshire pudding. Growing up, I became used to good food on the table at all times. Only now with rationing and shortages I realize I enjoyed a privileged upbringing. Good old Ma can be relied upon for a decent hamper of grub from time to time. Shall I pour you a drop of port?'

'If it's all the same, I'd like a cup of tea. I'm thinking I'll save that bottle for Christmas. Not that I don't appreciate the generosity behind the gift.' Ruby was amazed when David had staggered in the front door of number thirteen with a large box containing food gifts from his parents' farm out in Wiltshire. Several times since Maisie had known David these hampers had arrived and they'd always been welcome. Ruby had managed to make time to chat with Mrs Carlisle at Maisie and David's wedding the previous summer and found that for all their wealth the Carlisles were a friendly bunch, just like their son, David. Unlike her daughter-in-law, Irene, she'd huffed to herself at the time. 'Young Freda enjoyed her dinner before she set off on her motorbike to goodness knows where,' she said as she put the full kettle onto the hob. 'Maureen and Sarah will have what's left when they get back from checking on Maureen's house and seeing if there was anything else they could salvage. I'm so grateful to you for helping Maureen.'

'That's not my doing, Mrs C. Bob and Mike had a quiet word with the landlord and he promised to make Maureen a priority. Work should start soon on rebuilding the roof and chimney stack. My thinking is that Mike knows the chap in a professional capacity, if you get my meaning.' He winked. 'He wouldn't want any bother now, would he?'

Ruby roared with laughter. 'I've heard it all now. Thank goodness for the strong arm of the law. I've always thought he was a bit on the slimy side.'

'Sit yourself down, Ruby, and I'll make that cup of tea, then I'll leave you to pack your suitcase. Are you sure you wouldn't like me to help you to the station?'

'I could get used to all this spoiling,' Ruby said as she sat down in her favourite armchair. 'I've done my packing and Mike is coming with us to Erith station, so there are enough hands to carry our cases, thank you very much. You must be at a loose end with your Maisie at the seaside with Betty?'

'There's no denying it. Do I look like a lost soul?' the handsome RAF officer said with a grin.

'It's like half of you is missing. We never see one of you without the other. P'raps you should have gone away with your wife. Not that I'm saying I don't like your company,' she added quickly.

'Too much work on, I'm afraid. In fact, I should get back home and make a telephone call to HQ in case I'm needed. You never know what's kicking off somewhere or other.'

'It's a shame we don't have a telephone but it seems a bit posh for the likes of us, although George said he could arrange it. I'm always surprised how you men can arrange things,' she said thoughtfully before adding with a grin, 'What it must be like to be man.'

'None of us can cook a decent meal like you, Ruby.'

'It's good to know I have my uses,' she smiled.

A loud banging on the door woke Ruby with a start. She'd put on her best coat and hat and sat down for a few minutes. She looked at the clock. She'd slept for an hour and was not only late getting over the road to meet Bob but had missed listening to the news. It was that heavy dinner, she thought as she gave herself a shake and picked up her case.

'I thought you'd left without me,' Bob joked as he gave her a quick peck on the cheek. 'My, but you look smart,' he said, giving Ruby an admiring look.

'You don't scrub up so bad yourself, Bob Jackson,' she

smiled. She did like to see a man in a smart suit and Bob was certainly looking the ticket.

'When you two have stopped admiring each other I think we'd best make our move. The train won't wait for the pair of you,' Mike said, picking up Ruby's suitcase. Bob offered Ruby his arm and they headed up the road towards the station on the other side of the small town.

Ruby pulled down the window above the train door and called to Mike, 'Don't forget to go over to mine for your dinners. Gwyneth knows to expect you. She's cooking for everyone while I'm gone, so an extra mouth is no odds.'

Bob joined Ruby. 'You need to pick the cabbage and carrots on the allotment and check the salad stuff. I don't want it going to waste, do you hear?'

Mike laughed as he waved back. 'I heard you both the first time you told me. Now, stick your heads back in and get settled before the train sets off.'

On cue the engine let out a long toot, and the carriages shook as the steam engine pulled out of Erith station and headed towards London, where they would change to a different line that would take them towards the South West of England and to Ruby's daughter and grandchildren in Cornwall.

The trip up to London was uneventful as the train stopped at stations Ruby recognized. She pointed out to Bob the large gypsy encampment at Belvedere and he told her of his time on the force and where he worked at different stations. Reaching the two stations that served the dockyard and the arsenal at Woolwich, they watched as women left the train chattering excitedly.

'They'll be munitions workers,' Ruby observed. 'It's not a job I'd fancy even if it did speed up the end of this war. You hear such things about what happens in those places.'

'These "things" wouldn't come from Vera by any chance?' Bob asked, trying not to laugh.

Ruby thought for a moment. 'Now you come to mention it, I do believe they do,' she said, joining in with his laughter. 'You know, she means well, Bob, and she is really fond of you.'

'A little too fond if you ask me,' Bob said, trying hard not to show how embarrassed he was by Vera's approaches. 'I've had trouble trying the fight her off at times. I'm not sure if it's my marrows she's after or something else.'

Ruby's roar of laughter caused fellow passengers to turn and look before returning to their newspapers or gazing out of the smoke-smeared windows. 'It's not your marrows, love, she's after all of you. Or to be blunt, she wants you living under her roof.'

'What?' Bob said, feeling none too comfortable discussing such things with Ruby. 'Rest assured I've done nothing to encourage her. I thought she knew that we . . . I mean I . . . what I mean is, we . . . Oh God,' he groaned, running his hand over his face, not really knowing what to say.

Ruby stopped laughing as she became aware of how embarrassed Bob was by Vera's attention. 'There's no need to be upset, Bob. At this moment in time any man would do. I won't say she's not jealous of our friendship, but what's more to the point is she doesn't want to take in any strangers. She'll be in trouble with the authorities before too long as she refused to have Gwyneth and young Myfi living with her. She knows it and that's why she's set her cap at you. For Vera, marriage would be more convenient than putting up strangers.'

'Oh my,' was all Bob could say as he mopped his brow with a clean white handkerchief.

'Now, don't you go worrying. I'll keep her out of your way. She'll soon find someone, or something, else to fixate on and then you'll be all but forgotten. Now, it looks as though we're about to pull into Charing Cross station and we need to retrieve our suitcases from the guard's van.'

Bob took their coats from the rack above the seats and helped Ruby on with hers. 'You know, Ruby, there is a solution to stop Vera with all these daft ideas.'

Ruby had a good idea what Bob was alluding to, but now was not the time or the place. 'What, you mean have her locked up for lunacy?'

'No. Me and you could get married,' he sighed as she stepped down from the train and thanked a young gent who'd helped her onto the platform.

'Ask me another time, Bob. One of these days I might just say yes if you catch me in a weak moment. Now, how do we get to our next train?'

Bob grinned from ear to ear as he collected their cases then led Ruby through the busy station and out to the main road, where he hailed a taxi cab to take them across London to catch their train to the South West.

'This is a bit grim,' Ruby said as they climbed into the

carriage. 'I'll be blown if I can see my hand in front of my face. We could end up in Scotland at this rate.'

'You'll be safe with me. There's no need to fret,' Bob said as he helped her to her seat. The blackout blinds had been pulled down, blocking out any view of the world outside of the train, with the only lighting coming from light bulbs in the ceiling of the train that had been painted blue, giving a strange glow to where they were seated. 'It's best if we travel by night as then we will arrive nice and early and Pat can collect us as planned before she starts her work on the farm.'

'That makes sense but I hope we don't have any air raids as I won't know where I'd be heading,' she said, reaching for her bag and delving inside.

'I think that's the idea. We don't want the enemy knowing where they're going either. Now, what are you doing, Ruby?'

'I'm looking for . . . ah! Here they are.' She rummaged in her shopping bag before pulling out a package wrapped in brown paper. 'I made a few sandwiches from the beef that David's mum sent up. Seemed a shame not to have a bite to eat during the journey. I've added a bit of that chutney I made last year, so mind it doesn't drip on your suit jacket. We'll never see it in this light.'

Bob pulled a large clean white handkerchief from his pocket and tucked it in the collar of his shirt, causing Ruby to nod approvingly. 'Tell me if I have chutney smeared round my face,' he said before biting into the sandwich.

Ruby leant back contentedly in the firmly upholstered

train seat, thinking she hadn't been so relaxed in a while now. Bob was good company. 'Did you listen to the news before we set off?'

Bob chewed and swallowed the food in his mouth. 'No, I was packing my case and forgot to turn on the wireless in time. Was you listening out for anything in particular?'

'Not really, I just like to know how the war's going. George has gone on at me about these Baedeker Raids. There was one in Exeter and he's worried we will get caught up in it if there's another. I never thought to ask him what happens if there's a raid while we're on the train. I wish I hadn't dropped off like I did. I can't help feeling I've missed something important,' she said. 'But I'm sure it can wait. There'll be a radio we can listen to when we get to where Pat lives.'

George continued to eat his sandwich. Ruby never failed to provide for her family and friends, and he was glad of the bite to eat as he'd forgotten about a meal before he left home. Staying longer at the ARP hut provided for the area in Erith that he covered, he'd written a few notes for Sarah and her colleagues just in case they forgot anything he'd taught them. He had faith in the young woman and knew that she would take her duties responsibly and could be relied upon in any situation. He smiled to himself in the darkness as he thought how she'd headed off in a raid and ended up helping those three children caught in a fire. It still shocked him how any parent could leave youngsters like that to spend time in a pub and not even head home when the air-raid alarm went off. He was glad Mike had sought them out and had more than a few stern words with the husband. With people like Sarah and Mike playing their part, he felt confident that Hitler would never defeat them. If things got sticky and he came marching up Erith High Street, he wouldn't know what hit him faced with the fortitude of the locals in Bob's hometown.

The train trundled on into the night as Ruby dozed leaning against Bob's shoulder. Carefully checking his watch, he could see that there was another three hours before they'd need to change onto a local branch line that would take them closer to the farm that lay deep in the Lizard Peninsula. Bob had enjoyed going to the library and finding information about an area of the country he'd never been to. Perhaps there would be time for him to visit some of the quaint fishing coves and look out to sea from the most southerly point in England? The farm wasn't far from the Helford River, a setting for the novel *Frenchman's Creek*. As soon as he realized the area where Ruby's Pat now lived had been used in a Daphne Du Maurier novel, he'd borrowed a copy and read it with interest. However, there was too much romance for Bob's liking, preferring as he did her earlier book called *Jamaica Inn*. Now, that was a very good yarn, he thought, as Ruby stirred and mumbled something before dropping off to sleep again. He patted her arm and let her sleep on. It felt right to have Ruby close, even though they were not alone, the carriage being full of other passengers. It seemed his idea to travel during the night was a popular one.

June 1942

Freda stood by the reception office of Margate Hospital waiting for the young nurse who had helped her upon her arrival. She was so worried about Maisie, who hadn't stopped crying since seeing Freda by the side of her bed. But her fears were also for Betty, who seemed to have vanished since being wheeled from the ward. Was she injured or perhaps she hadn't survived an operation? Freda did hope they would be able to tell her something even though she was not related to either Maisie or Betty. Hospital rules could be so strict and she felt so alone.

'Hello, did you manage to speak with your friends?' the nurse said as she pushed her way through the double doors leading from the hospital wards.

'I did, thank you, but I have a problem and wondered if you could help me?'

The young nurse thought for a moment or two before speaking. 'Look, it's quite late, but as the earlier flap seems to be over I'm sure I can spare you some time. Come through to the office, where we won't be interrupted.'

Freda settled herself in the chair that the nurse offered. She stifled a yawn. It had been a very long and tiring day since she'd set off for Canterbury on her motorbike. Having carried out her duties for the Fire Service and gone in search of her friends, Betty and Maisie, she was now feeling the effects of her first long journey on the bike and her worries about the two women.

'Now, how can I help you?'

'I'm worried about Maisie. Do you think she will lose her baby? Also, Betty Billington. I was told she was on the same ward as Maisie but I couldn't find her. Is she seriously injured? Please, tell me. I know I'm not strictly related to them, but they are closer to me than my own family and if anything was to happen . . .' Freda's voice broke as her fears came tumbling out.

'Please don't upset yourself,' the nurse said, reaching out to take Freda's hand. 'I know I shouldn't officially tell you, but I can't see how it would hurt. Mrs Carlisle's pregnancy is still progressing as it should. We are going to suggest that once she is home she has complete bed rest for a few days, but the baby is sure to be born fit and healthy.'

'Oh, thank God,' Freda said. 'I don't think she could cope if she lost another child. What about Betty?'

The nurse got to her feet and checked a folder that lay on a nearby desk. She frowned and turned the page over. 'If you will excuse me for a little while, I need to visit the ward and check the latest details. If you would like to make yourself a hot drink, the kettle hasn't long boiled and there's cocoa on the side table.' She pointed to the table, where Freda could see cups and spoons as well as a slightly battered tin of cocoa. After leaving the office she could be heard walking briskly away, the starched apron of her uniform cracking as she moved.

Freda half-heartedly made a hot drink for herself and the kindly nurse. She didn't really want a drink, but was aware she'd not eaten since being given a sandwich at the emergency canteen earlier in the afternoon. The last thing she wanted was to feel faint whilst on her journey home to Erith and to come a cropper. She'd got away with damaging her bike once but might not be as lucky a second time. If only she had one of her friends with her right now, she wouldn't feel so alone. Looking up at the large round clock on the wall, she became aware of how late it was. Ruby and Bob would be well on their way to Cornwall by now but perhaps Mike Jackson or David Carlisle could be contacted? They would be sure to know what to do. Even Douglas Billington would be able to help her, but then she hadn't seen him recently and, thinking about it, Betty had appeared rather sad in recent days. She closed her eyes and prayed like she'd never done before that not only would Betty be well but that she would find love with the man who shared her surname. She was still deep in thought as the nurse returned with an older colleague by her side. Freda could see by the colour of the uniform that she had a higher rank. A nursing sister perhaps?

'I understand you've been enquiring about Miss Billington?'

'Yes, sister,' she said in a wobbly voice. The woman looked stern and she suddenly felt very young and aware of her unkempt appearance. 'I'm worried about both my friends. I'm Freda Smith. Betty . . . I mean, Miss Billington is also my boss at Erith Woolworths and Maisie . . . well, we used to lodge together . . . and I was her bridesmaid,' Freda explained, trying hard to make sure the nurse was aware how close she was to both Maisie and Betty.

The woman smiled and suddenly didn't look quite so formidable. 'It is understandable and I'd feel just as you do in similar circumstances. Usually we would only give information to relatives, but you've accounted for yourself very well, Miss Smith, so I will allow my staff to inform you of the health of both your friends. I'll leave this in your capable hands,' she added, turning to leave the room.

'Thank you, Matron,' the younger nurse said, appearing more than a little shy.

Freda gulped, not believing she'd called the woman sister when she was a matron in charge of the whole hospital. She looked at the nurse, who held a buff folder in her hand. 'I feel a bit of a fool,' she mumbled.

'There's no need. I had no idea who was who when I first joined the nursing profession. Matron is a sweetheart really, unless we've done something wrong then she turns into a tyrant. She helped me to find out about your friend Betty Billington.'

'Thank goodness for that,' Freda said with a big smile on her face after she was told how Betty had been moved to another ward simply to sleep off her ordeal after being checked over by a doctor. Apart from a few cuts and bruises she was as fit as a fiddle.

'She will be released as soon as the paperwork is complete and we have a doctor's signature. Mind you, I'm not sure riding pillion on your motorbike is a good way for her to get home.'

Freda's face fell. She hadn't given a thought to how her friends would get back to Erith. 'Perhaps I could borrow your telephone and have Maisie's husband collect them both?' she suggested. 'But it would be hours before David was here and that's if he still has the use of the RAF transport. My goodness, what a pickle.'

The nurse picked up the telephone. 'We've still not been connected since the earlier air raids. Just as the Fire Service use motorbike messengers, we've been relying on the army to keep us connected with the outside world with their dispatch riders. May I ask a question?'

'Please do and if you have any idea how I can get two badly shaken women to the other side of Kent, I'd very much like to know,' she added with a worried look on her face.

'Why were they in Canterbury to begin with?'

'It was a day trip. Betty – that is, Miss Billington – was going to have afternoon tea with the manager of the Canterbury branch of Woolworths. She is the manager at the Erith branch. Both are on holiday in Margate for a few days. They are staying near to the seafront . . . Why, silly me, I don't need to arrange to have them back in Erith this evening. If I can arrange transport to get them both to the guesthouse where they've booked rooms, then I can head back home and let people know what has happened,' she said with relief. 'How long will it take to have them both released?'

'It could be a little while yet. I suggest you leave it with us to arrange transport for your friends. I promise we won't leave them to catch a bus. In the meantime you could be heading back to your hometown and informing their families what has happened. By now the bombing in Canterbury will be news and their loved ones could be worrying. You, young lady, will be the bearer of good news.'

Freda grinned. All thoughts of feeling tired had passed her by. She drank the rest of her cocoa and gave the nurse a hug. 'Thank you so much, you have no idea how much this means to me. Please give my love to Betty and Maisie and tell them to rest assured help is on its way.'

Freda knocked hard on the door of the house where David and Maisie rented rooms. There was no answer. She tried once more, before deciding that David must be at work and turning to leave.

'Are you looking for the young couple?' an elderly woman said as she opened the door. She frowned. 'Don't I know you?'

Freda sighed. She needed to go to Alexandra Road and get help but didn't want to appear rude. 'You may do. I'm a friend of Maisie's . . . Mrs Carlisle who lives here . . . I work at Woolworths.'

'That's where I've seen you then. I'm always in there doing my shopping. You can always find a bargain in Woolies. That's what I say to my 'usband, Stan. Even in wartime Woolies comes up trumps.'

'Yes, I'm sure you can,' Freda replied, edging away from the front door. 'If you'll excuse me . . .'

'Hang on a minute, dear. I have a message for anyone who should come knocking. Just wait there.'

Freda tapped her foot with impatience as she heard voices from inside the other flat. She was tempted just to go and not wait for the woman and her message – whatever it was.

'Here you are, dear. I was in two minds about whether to take it to Woolworths or not if no one came knocking by tomorrow morning, as I know Mrs Carlisle's friends work there. She mentioned it once when we were chatting.' She waited as Freda opened the envelope.

Freda scanned the few lines, aware the woman was waiting to know what was so important. 'Thank you, it's nothing serious,' she smiled and headed towards the door. She didn't like telling lies, but it was not her place to talk about Maisie's business to a stranger. The few scrawled lines on the page showed that David was fearing for his wife's safety after hearing news of the Canterbury bombings and had headed off to Margate to check Maisie had not been harmed. Freda sucked in her breath. The final few words in his note were most worrying and might well mean she wouldn't see her chum for a very long time.

16

Freda left her motorbike at the fire station and, after reporting to the officer in charge, set off to walk across town to Ruby's house in Alexandra Road. It was late and she was more than tired. So much had happened since she woke that morning. Although Betty had given her a key to her little house in Cross Street, Freda did not feel right staying there alone while Betty was away. She wanted nothing more than to have a wash and a meal and sleep in her own bed tonight. If only she'd been able to get to David Carlisle before he left Erith and reassure him that all was well with Maisie.

The front door opened before Freda had placed her key in the lock and she was swept into Maureen's arms and hugged tightly until she could hardly breathe. 'Oh, my love. I've never been so pleased as to see someone and that's a fact.' She pulled her into the front room, where Gwyneth sat with Mike Jackson. They all looked extremely worried. 'We've been that concerned since we heard what's been going on in Canterbury and then to read this.' She held out the postcard sent by Maisie and Betty that informed the women they were enjoying their holiday in Margate and how they intended to visit the Canterbury branch of Woolworths the next day.

Freda all but collapsed into the armchair that Mike had vacated. 'It's been a long day and I never want to experience again what I saw in that city. I do have good news. Knowing Maisie and Betty were planning to be at Woolworths, I tried to find them, only to be told they'd been taken to a hospital in Margate due to so many people being injured.'

'Isn't that where they are staying?' Gwyneth asked, as she poured tea into a cup and handed it to Freda.

Freda nodded and in between sipping the hot liquid explained what had happened since she'd left Erith many hours earlier.

'So they should be back at the guesthouse by now?' Maureen asked.

'And the baby is fine?' Gwyneth wanted to know.

'Yes, they will be and the nurse told me that although Maisie was distressed there should not have been any damage to her child. Both have a few cuts and bruises, but they were extremely lucky considering what has happened to some poor souls. I do wish I could have brought them home, but at least they will be comfortable in their digs. I stopped at Maisie's place to let David know but he wasn't home. He'd left a note with his neighbour in case any of us were worried. I'm surprised he never came here.'

Mike looked sheepish. 'David knocked on my door. Knowing Ruby was away, he didn't want to worry Gwyneth and Maureen. I did offer to go to Margate with him but as I'm on night duty later it would have been too much of a rush to get back. Besides . . .'

'Besides what?' Freda asked with a frown.

'I was worried that you'd not yet returned and I asked if you'd checked in at the fire station.'

'Cheers, Mike, I'm capable of doing a job without people checking up on me,' she said indignantly. 'They knew where I was as they'd sent me there.'

'I know but I was still worried. You're only a kid and doing a man's job,' he said quietly.

Freda glared at the policeman. 'They wouldn't have taken me on if they didn't think I was up to it. Next you'll be saying I can't do my job because I'm a woman. Honestly, Mike, you're so Victorian at times. Why, I'll be twenty-one in a few months.'

'That's almost ancient,' Maureen joined in, trying to lighten the atmosphere in the room. 'Now,' she said, getting to her feet and walking towards the kitchen, 'I'll find you something to eat and then you should get off to bed. We all have work in the morning and I need to find out what's going on with my house. I can't expect Ruby to put me up forever. We are bulging at the seams as things stand.'

Freda followed Maureen to the kitchen. 'There's something else that's worrying me,' she confided in the older woman.

'I'm a good listener,' Maureen said as she cut two slices of bread from a loaf and reached for the butter knife.

'It's David's note. It said he would never allow Maisie

to be in danger again and if it meant taking her away somewhere, then so be it.'

Maureen stopped buttering the bread to think. 'He is no doubt distraught to think he left her in a place where she could have been killed.'

'But she went to Canterbury with Betty. David only found the guesthouse. It's not as if he made her go to the city and on that day. Why, she could be in as much danger living here in Erith,' Freda argued.

Maureen shrugged her shoulders. 'Men react differently than we do. They have this idea they have to protect us, though usually it is the woman who is the stronger in a marriage. I do wonder . . .'

'What?' Freda asked as Maureen returned to making the sandwich.

'Well, his mother lives out in the country somewhere, doesn't she? Perhaps he means to take Maisie there. It will be safer . . . at least until the baby is born,' she added quickly, seeing the distressed look on the young girl's face.

'No,' Freda said, shaking her head in disbelief. 'No, Maisie wouldn't like that. Why, she's a town girl through and through. I can't see her agreeing to live on a farm out in Wiltshire, wherever that might be.'

'It's not a farm, Freda. From what David's mother told me at the wedding it's more of an estate.'

Freda wrinkled her nose as she thought about what Maureen had said. 'So, it's a posh house with lots of land and animals?'

'That's about it,' Maureen said as she spread fish paste

between the slices of bread and cut the sandwich into four neat squares, before handing the plate to Freda.

'Then she won't like that one little bit,' Freda said with a sniff as she bit into her sandwich.

'So yer see, I couldn't argue with David as he's right in a way. We've got ter think of our baby. I'm gonna hate living with his parents. They're decent enough and bloody good to me but it ain't home,' Maisie explained to Sarah, who was helping her pack a suitcase.

'There's ages before the baby comes and they do say that in the early months we should be more careful. Perhaps once David can see you are fit and well he will let you come home to Erith,' Sarah said, trying to comfort her chum.

Maisie sniffed and felt for a handkerchief in her pocket. 'I doubt it. He's angry with 'imself for letting me go and get into danger. I was having a bloody good time until Hitler and the Luftwaffe poked their noses in.'

Maisie sat on the side of her bed and started to weep. 'I'm so scared, Sarah. It's bad enough worrying if I'll lose this baby after last time, but at least I knew I'd have you and everyone else to hold my hand and now I won't even 'ave that. Whatever am I going ter do with meself?'

Sarah sat next to her friend and put her arm around Maisie's shoulder. 'Now, come on. Crying isn't going to help things, is it? I've had an idea how you can pass the time.' She reached down to where she'd left a large shopping bag and delved inside. 'Look, I have this pattern for some smocked summer dresses and wondered if you'd run a couple up for Myfi and Georgie? They'll be tickled pink to dress alike. I've unpicked an old dress I had from before the war. The fabric looks as good as new. What do you think?'

Maisie wiped her eyes and took the blue and cream material from Sarah. 'It does look like new. You've never been much good at smocking.'

'I've never been any good at sewing, let alone smock-ing. It's such a lovely pattern, though. The girls would look so sweet, wouldn't they?' She waited, trying hard not to breathe as Maisie read the words on the pattern.

'I was thinking of taking my Singer with me. David's borrowed the car again so he can take all my sewing bits and bobs. The RAF might as well give it to him the amount of times he's used it lately.' A smile broke across her pretty face before vanishing and she gave Sarah a troubled look. 'You've got to promise me a few things.'

'Anything, Maisie, you know that. Whatever you want me to do, I promise to do my best to help.'

'Blimey, you sound just like Freda with her Brownies,' Maisie said, giving a weak smile.

Sarah took her hand and squeezed it hard. 'What is it, Maisie?'

'I want . . . I want . . . I want you to come and help me when I go into labour. You've been there and know what it's all about. I'd rather it be you than any posh in-law or midwife. Will you do that for me?'

'Why, of course I will, you silly thing, I intended to offer anyway. You were there when I had Georgie and I want to do the same for you. As long as it's not in an

Anderson shelter,' she added with a grin. 'Things were a bit tight down there.'

'You can say that again. There are better places to 'ave a kiddie, but things didn't turn out so bad in the end, did they? There's something else. Will you write to me so I know what's 'appening here while I'm gone? I'm gonna be worried sick about you all as well as everyone at Woolies.'

'Of course I'll write and I bet everyone else will, so don't you worry yourself about that.'

Maisie gave a big sigh and went to the mantelpiece to take a sheet of paper from behind a small mirror. 'Here's the address.'

Sarah looked at the neat writing on the piece of paper. 'Where is Chippenham?'

'It's in Wiltshire. David told me his parents' place is close to a pretty village called Laycock that's near Chippenham. It sounds like the back of beyond to me, but there's not so much chance of bombing and he thinks I'll be safer there. David's only thinking of me, but I know I'm going to hate living there,' Maisie said as a small sob caught in her throat and she hiccuped. 'It's going to be hell.'

Sarah went back to her bag and searched inside until she found an envelope. 'This is for you.'

Maisie took the envelope and slowly opened it with a puzzled look on her face. She tipped out a pile of pennies. 'What's all this about? I'm not exactly short of money, you know. I did marry a bloke who has a few bob.'

Sarah laughed. It was typical of Maisie to state the obvious. 'There's something else in there.'

Maisie looked inside the envelope and a small sheet of paper fell out. 'Phone numbers?'

'Yes, I made a list of everyone in Erith who knows you, as well as Mum and Dad's number. Look, there's Woolies and that one is Misson's ironmongers and this is the police station. If you need to get in touch with one of us, then these are the telephone numbers you need to use. Even if there's been an air raid, chances are you can still get through to us with one of these numbers. I also had a word with Betty and we decided that if you can find a phone box, then you should use the pennies and we can chat in our lunch hour or tea breaks from Betty's office.'

'I wouldn't like to bother Betty. Not at work,' Maisie said dubiously. 'I know she's a friend but she's also the manager of Woolworths. I don't think we should bother her.'

'For heaven's sake, Maisie, Betty is beside herself with regret that she put you and your unborn child in danger by taking you to Canterbury. At least let her do this to make amends. Don't you understand that we are her only friends, or were until Douglas came along? This is something that she can help with, so please don't shrug away the chance to make her think she is doing something to help you. Please, Maisie?'

'I must go and see her before I leave. I don't want Betty thinking she played any part in us being in danger. That honour goes to Hitler alone. You're right. We are her friends and she needs us right now as well.'

It was Sarah's turn to be puzzled. 'What do you mean?'

Maisie sat back on the bed. 'What I mean is that Douglas isn't on the scene anymore. She sent him packing. For some daft reason she feels that she's too old to get attached to a man and take on his family. She's turned away from him and faces the rest of her life as an old spinster. If David hadn't been on at me to get packing and make my goodbyes, I'd have got around to telling you and Freda. Betty wasn't her usual self after our little adventure and she told me about Douglas when I suggested that we contact him to say she wasn't injured in Canterbury. That's when she confessed that not only hadn't she sent him a postcard, but that she had distanced herself from him at the Woolworths dance. She's adamant she's not changing her mind.'

'Poor Betty, she's so stubborn at times. Her and Douglas were made for each other. It's as if her Charlie arranged for them to meet. It's just a shame it took so long,' Sarah said sadly. 'She's been a different woman since he appeared on the scene.'

'You mean when we all but had him arrested,' Maisie guffawed, more like her old self. 'I think we should do something about Douglas and Betty before I leave Erith for goodness knows how long.'

Sarah walked to the window that looked out over the front of the house where Maisie and David rented their rooms. A few streets away were the busy shopping streets of Erith and beyond that the River Thames. She knew the town was as important to Maisie as it was to her. Even though Sarah had grown up in Devon, her heart belonged to Erith, where her nan and grandad had always lived. Her holidays as a child had been spent visiting her grandparents and she'd always thought of the riverside town as home. However was Maisie going to survive away from all that she held dear? If Maisie had decided to do something about Betty's romance with Douglas before she disappeared for the rest of the year, then who was she to disagree with her decision? 'How are we going to bring Douglas and Betty back together again?'

'We should convince Betty that she is not too old to find love and marriage. Then we need to get them together so that they have time to talk.'

Sarah thought for a moment. 'That's not such a bad idea, but what about Douglas? We don't know what was said when they parted. She may have hurt his feelings too much. You know how touchy men can be at times. Remember how Alan was before he went off to war? I couldn't say or do anything right. It could have broken up our marriage.'

'But Douglas isn't going off to war and you was as much to blame for the way Alan acted, so we can't compare your life to what Douglas and Betty are going through,' Maisie pointed out stubbornly.

'Ouch!' Sarah said. 'Don't hold back, will you?'

'I'm only telling you now as everything worked out fine.'

'So, what do you suggest?'

Maisie got to her feet and reached for the short-sleeved jacket that matched her navy blue skirt. 'I won't be able to do this up for much longer,' she said with a smile. 'Are you coming?'

'Where to?' Sarah asked as she followed her friend.

'We have to speak to Freda. She will most likely know where we can find Douglas. We need to convince him not to give up on Betty.'

Sarah smiled. 'Then we speak to Betty like you suggested and convince her she isn't on the shelf and has a romantic life ahead of her?'

'Well, that sounds a bit soppy but you're right. Let's go and find the third musketeer, shall we? There's no time to lose if I'm to head off to the wilds of Wiltshire tomorrow.'

Freda pushed open the staff door that led into the Woolworths store. Her eyelids felt heavy, as if she'd not slept in a week. The motorbike ride down to Canterbury and then the search for her friends had taken their toll, and now she didn't know whether she was coming or going. If someone had offered her a holiday in Margate, she'd have bitten their hand off regardless of whether there was an air raid while she was there. Just to be able to relax and breathe in the sea air would be delightful. If only. She sighed to herself as she straightened the skirt of the wine-coloured uniform and checked her buttons were done up correctly. She was so late this morning she wasn't even sure she'd dressed herself correctly.

Deep in thought, she didn't notice there were people standing close to the door and the first she knew was when there was a loud yelp of pain as the door swung outwards and met with a body.

'My goodness, I'm so sorry. Have I injured you?' was all she could think to say as she saw a man dressed in an

American army uniform rubbing his shoulder, while his friends stood nearby laughing at his discomfort.

'It's my fault, ma'am. I should be more careful where I stand,' a familiar voice said politely.

'Why, it's Sergeant Hank Marshall,' Freda exclaimed, unable to hide her delight at seeing the handsome American sergeant once more and wishing that she'd taken notice of Maisie, who was always reminding her that a dash of lipstick and brushed hair looked much more attractive than appearing in public as though she'd just been dragged through a hedge backwards. She ran her fingers through her short bobbed hairstyle, hoping to perform miracles with her appearance. 'What brings you to this branch of Woolworths?'

'I could ask the same of you,' he said in a deep drawl that made Freda's skin tingle in delight. 'Is that where you keep your motorbike?' he asked with a grin, nodding towards the staff door.

'N . . . no, I keep the bike at the fire station just up the road. This is my other job. I'm a Woolworths girl most of the time. But you haven't answered my question. Why are you here?'

One of Hank's comrades stepped forward and held out a small booklet. 'We are told that when we reach your shores there will always be a welcome found at any five-and-ten-cent store in good old England.'

'Oh, I remember now, the first ever Woolworths stores were in America.' She recalled Betty telling them about a famous building in America called the Woolworth Tower and showing them a photograph of it in the staff magazine *The New Bond*. Betty had enthused about it being the focal point of the company and about how she'd like to visit it one day. For Freda it had been a long enough journey to get to Erith from her home in the Midlands, so she wasn't so sure about journeying to America. It was so far away. 'I suppose your Woolworths stores are very different to ours, but you will find us just as welcoming,' Freda smiled at the young soldier. 'It must have been a big step to not only join up to fight in a war but to travel so far from home to a strange country.'

'I didn't expect to come over here and find the girl of my dreams inside a store,' Hank said gently, not bothering who heard him speak to Freda. 'There I was thinking you were a one-woman fighting team tearing around England defeating the enemy on your motorbike.'

Freda blushed. In the few times she'd met the American soldiers she'd found them loud and brash but quite harmless. 'You will find most women are helping the war effort when they aren't doing their day job,' she replied primly.

Hank's mates laughed loudly and one even whistled as they poked fun at him for being reprimanded by Freda. 'Well, that told me, ma'am,' he replied apologetically. 'I mean no insult to you and the women of this lovely country.'

'I'm sure you don't,' Freda smiled. Inside, her heart was giving another flip as he spoke with such sincerity. 'If you'll forgive me, I must get to my counter and work before I get into trouble with my boss.' She was aware that Betty was on the shop floor somewhere checking on her staff. It was Betty's first day back at work since returning from Margate and she didn't appear to be in a good mood.

'We wouldn't wish to get you into trouble, ma'am,' Hank said as he nodded to his comrades to move on. I wondered . . . and I hope this isn't too forward of me . . . would you care to accompany me to the cinema this evening?'

Freda froze. The last time she'd gone to the Odeon to see a film it had been with Ginger and that didn't turn out very well. She wasn't keen to put herself in the same situation once more. 'I don't know. It's not as if I know you very well, I . . .' she was lost for words. Although Hank was extremely handsome and she had dreamt about him often since they first met, she was afraid. Not having much experience of stepping out with young men, she could only rely on what her friends told her and Maisie's comments about some men she'd known having hands like octopuses came to mind. She was aware Hank was waiting for an answer with pleading eyes.

'Look, I'm not sure of the protocol when asking an English girl to accompany me to see a movie but if you'd like to bring a friend, I can do the same and then you will feel safe. What do you say?'

Freda felt awful. What must he think of her, knowing she didn't trust him? It must be written on her face. 'I'd love to come to the pictures with you. There's a film on at the Odeon that I've been longing to see.'

Hank beamed. 'Why, that's just fine. Where can we pick you both up?'

Oh my, Freda thought with a start. Even though Ruby

was away visiting her Pat in Cornwall she most likely would not want men appearing on her doorstep, especially soldiers, even if she had met them. It wouldn't be right. Besides, she needed to ask someone to accompany her and that could be a problem. 'It may be best if we meet outside the cinema,' she suggested. 'Do you know where it is?'

'I sure do, ma'am,' he said, taking her hand and shaking it until she thought her arm would drop off. 'Will seven suit you?'

'Perfect,' Freda said, retrieving her hand. 'There is one other thing,' she added seriously.

Hank's face dropped. 'You have a husband?'

Freda burst out laughing. 'No, but please will you stop calling me ma'am. My name is Freda.'

It was Hank's turn to laugh as he gave her a bow and then saluted her, making Freda's cheeks turn red once more. 'Until tonight, sweet Freda,' he said with a wink before joining his comrades, who slapped him on the back as they walked from the store.

'Friends of yours?'

Freda jumped almost out of her skin as she walked slowly towards the counter where she was covering for a colleague who had just heard her husband had been injured in North Africa. Turning round, she spotted Maisie and Sarah. 'Hello, you two, can't you keep away from Woolies?' she laughed as she went behind her counter. 'Can I interest you in in some darning wool or perhaps a knitting pattern?'

'Don't think you can put us off the scent,' Maisie said as she sat down on a chair thoughtfully provided for older customers. 'Who were those handsome guys? And what was that one saying to you to make you blush so charmingly?'

'For your information that is Sergeant Hank Marshall, he's part of the American army that's come over here to save us from Hitler,' Freda said proudly. 'He's invited me to go to the pictures with him this evening.'

Sarah was alarmed. She'd seen the state Freda was in after her disastrous evening out with Ginger. 'But you don't know this man, Freda love.'

'But I do,' Freda replied defiantly. 'He's the American serviceman who ran me off the road and damaged my motorbike.'

'It's the first time I've heard someone fancy a chap after he tried to kill 'em,' Maisie sniggered.

Freda ignored the joke and added, 'He's nice. He organized for my bike to be fixed and returned to me before I got in trouble with the Fire Service. If he hadn't helped me, I wouldn't have been in Canterbury and been able to find you and Betty. Speaking of which, you'd best buy something as she's heading in this direction and is in a foul mood today.'

'I do need some darning wool as it happens,' Sarah said as she started to hold up small skeins of wool to the light so she could check the colour. 'Mum said that Dad has poked his toes through almost every sock he owns and she doesn't like darning. I offered to do it for her even though I'm not that good at the job.'

'Leave some with me and I'll help out. Navy blue or grey?' Freda asked as she helped choose the colours.

'I'd better have some white sewing thread and embroidery silks if you have any, Freda. I've got a couple of orders to make summer dresses for Myfi and Georgie. I thought I could embroider their names on the pockets as I'll be twiddling me thumbs with nothing to do once I get to the mother in-law's place. Now we've bought something you can tell us about this Yank you've taken a shine to,' Maisie said, taking out her purse to pay for her purchases.

'Now, that's a sight I like to see. My staff here on their day off and buying our stock,' Betty said with a smile that didn't quite reach her eyes.

'Ex-staff, Betty. I'm not on the payroll anymore, remember?' Maisie pointed out.

'Oh, of course you aren't. I'm so used to seeing you girls together that I forgot you have left our employ. I do hope it won't be forever, Maisie? In fact, if you'd like a few hours each week helping out, I can find you something that isn't too strenuous to do,' Betty offered hopefully.

'Can't be done, I'm afraid,' Maisie said sadly. She loved life at Woolworths and although over the moon to be expecting a baby, she did miss shop life. 'David's packing me off to live with his mum until after I've had the kid. He reckons he can't trust me to take care of myself after our little adventure in Canterbury.'

'Oh my dear, I'm so sorry. I feel as though I'm to blame. After all, it was my idea we should visit the city for the day. So foolhardy of me. What can I do to help change his mind?'

Maisie shrugged her shoulders. 'It's a done deal, Betty. I'm all packed and ready to head off tomorrow.'

'I feel I've let you down, my dear. What can I do to make it up to you?'

'There's no need. Honest, Betty, it's not you, it's David. He's trying to wrap me in cotton wool and I can't win until he's got this kiddie in his arms. I'll be home by Christmas and we can make up fer lost time then. Besides, you can all visit me in Wiltshire.'

'Where's that?' Freda asked.

'A bloody long way away,' Maisie sighed.

'It's a beautiful county, you will love living there, and we will all write to you and send parcels to relieve the boredom. I promise,' Betty said generously.

'As long as it's gin and fags I'll be 'appy,' Maisie joked as Betty looked shocked.

'Now, why don't we all go out this evening to say goodbye to Maisie properly?' their boss suggested.

Sarah and Maisie looked at Freda expectantly. 'But I can't go with you. I've been invited to go to the pictures with Hank Marshall and I've accepted. Sorry, Maisie, but I really want to go. He's a sergeant in the American army,' she added as Betty gave her a puzzled look.

'Are you sure about this?' Betty asked. 'After last time . . .'

Freda sighed. 'It's very kind of you all to be concerned about me. I have to admit to being a little worried after last time but I won't be alone. Hank is bringing a friend with him and I said I'd do the same. I do need to ask Gwyneth if she can come along with me.'

'Oh dear,' Betty exclaimed. 'I've not long sent Gwyneth home. She is under the weather and I told her to get herself home and in bed until she is fighting fit.

The last thing we need is to share germs with those doing important war work. Is there someone else you could invite?'

The girls looked at each other. There was only one other single woman in the group. Sarah raised her eyebrows at Maisie, encouraging her to speak.

'It's like this, Betty, it only leaves you as you're still, er . . . still single. Even though we know you have Douglas,' she added quickly.

Betty didn't know what to say. The mention of Douglas had hurt her like a spear to her heart but she couldn't blame her friends for that. It had been her decision to not see Douglas again even though she had regrets. 'I'm flattered you should think I could join your outing to the cinema, Freda, but the poor men would think they were out with their mother. Had you not thought about the age difference? I must say I'm a little flattered,' she chuckled. The girls could be such a tonic at times.

'That just leaves you then, Sarah,' Maisie said.

'What? I have a husband and a daughter if you've forgotten. Why, I don't think Alan would be too impressed to hear I'd been out with another man while he was away fighting for King and country.'

Freda held her breath. She wouldn't have dared suggest anything that might cause a split between a man and his wife. Whatever was Maisie thinking – especially after what had happened in the past . . . ?

'Look, I don't see anything wrong in you accompanying your friend to the pictures. Make sure you tell the men straight off that you have an 'usband and then things will be all right. Then,' she added quickly, 'we could all meet for a cuppa at Mitchell's tea room tomorrow before I 'ead off to gawd knows where. After all, yer won't see me fer an age . . .' She nudged Sarah, indicating she should go along with her idea.

'All right, I'll do it, but I'm going to show them a photo of Alan so they know I'm not a good-time girl,' she said, glaring at Maisie and rubbing her arm where her friend's elbow had made contact.

'I don't think anyone would ever think you were a good-time girl,' Betty smiled at Sarah. 'Now that is all sorted out I must get upstairs and catch up on my paperwork. Perhaps you would be a dear and pop into the tea rooms and book a table, Sarah? Let's have lunch, it will be my treat. No, I insist,' she added as the girls started to protest. 'We won't get to meet together until Christmas so we should celebrate our friendship before Maisie leaves Erith. Freda, it looks as though you have a customer,' Betty added before heading off to do her work.

'Thank you very much,' Sarah hissed at Maisie. 'You've really put me on the spot now, haven't you? What were you thinking, shoving me in the arm like that?'

'I needed you to agree,' Maisie said, 'before Freda changed her plans.'

'You've lost me now.'

'For 'eavens sake. You'd never make a good spy, would you? Now that Betty thinks we are all meeting tomorrow she'll be looking forward ter her lunch and when Douglas arrives out of the blue, like he's going ter do, she will fall into his arms and all will be right again.'

'You've been watching too many soppy films. We still need to find Douglas and convince him to meet Betty.'

'A piece of cake,' Maisie grinned. 'Freda can fill in the details and Bob's yer uncle! There'll be wedding bells before the year is out. You mark my words.'

~

17

'You have a chutney stain on your tie.'

'We've travelled hundreds of miles through the night together. Ducked a bombing raid near Plymouth and stepped out of the station into a glorious sunny day, and all you can say is I have a chutney stain on my tie. You're some woman, Ruby Caselton.'

'And your one grumpy bugger first thing in the morning, Bob Jackson. Come on, we're late and our Pat'll be waiting around here somewhere.'

'I'm a creature of habit, Ruby. I just need a cup of tea and my breakfast and then I'll be as right as rain,' Bob said as he looked up and down the narrow country lane. 'I don't see any cars waiting, do you?'

'We are three hours late. What do you expect?'

'Now who's grumpy? Why don't we ask the station-master if there's been a message left for us? It seems the sensible thing to do at a time like this. It's not as if we know which way to walk. There aren't any signposts that I can see.'

'Sea? I can't even see the sea. I thought we were near the coast. There's not even a pond round here,' Ruby said as she sat on her suitcase and rubbed a foot. 'I shouldn't have travelled in my best shoes. My feet are killing me.'

Bob could see that Ruby was tired and she was also out of her comfort zone. With no family to organize or home to run she was lost. She'd expected her daughter Pat to be there with a big hug and grandchildren running around their gran's legs in excitement. Instead they had arrived to nothing. He felt a little deflated. 'I'll go see if I can find someone who can help us. There's a bench over there, why not rest your legs for a while?'

Bob went back into the one railway station building after settling Ruby comfortably on the bench and leaving their suitcases by her side. She was admiring the pretty pots of flowers on the window ledge, and thinking Cornwall wasn't such a bad place if only it wasn't so far from Kent, when she heard the clip-clop of a horse's hooves and spotted a horse and cart coming up the slight slope of the lane leading to the station. The scene looked like something she'd seen on the calendars she received as Christmas gifts from the girls. They were very popular in Woolworths, along with views of thatched cottages. She started to wonder if houses had thatch in Cornwall when the horse and cart came to a stop close to where she was sitting.

'Good morning, sir,' she said as the person controlling the cart walked towards her. He was certainly a strapping lad, she thought. Sun-bleached hair and the muscles that showed through the rough cotton shirt must surely attract the young maidens in these parts. However, it was strange that he wasn't in uniform.

'Good morning,' he said politely, wiping his hands down the sides of his trousers and holding one out to Ruby. 'I take it you'll be Mrs Caselton, Pat's ma? I'm Jago Trevellyn.'

'Why, yes I am,' she said, getting to her feet, the tight shoes being forgotten for the moment as she took his strong hand and shook it enthusiastically. 'Is Pat here?' she asked, looking expectantly at the cart in case she appeared from behind the bales of hay. 'She was supposed to be meeting us, but we are more than three hours late. We missed our link further up near Bristol and then there was an air raid . . .' She stopped gabbling as the young man smiled at her. My, he has a charming way about him, she thought. If only I was ten years younger . . .

'Pat did come to meet your train, but she had to get back as my pa needed the car. I was up this way so offered to step in and meet the next train. The few trains we have down this way don't usually have many passengers, especially now there's a war on. Did you travel alone? I thought your neighbour was coming down with you?'

'Oh, Bob, yes, he's here somewhere. He went off to find out if anyone knew how we could get to your farm. We thought perhaps it would be a pleasant walk after being cooped up for so long on the train.'

Jago roared with laughter. 'It's more than a walk to get to the farm, Mrs Caselton, but Rosie here will see us all right. Will you be calling your man so we can get moving? There's only two hours before I'm needed to milk the cows. Pat can't be expected to do it all on her own. Shall I put your suitcases on board while you give him a call?'

Ruby nodded and hurried off to find Bob. She found him chatting to the stationmaster. 'Our lift is here, Bob, get your skates on.'

Ruby introduced Bob to Jago as the younger man helped them up onto the long bench that ran the width of the cart. 'Mind where you put your hands,' she joked as the two men pushed and pulled until she was on board.

'There's a fair sight from up here,' Bob exclaimed as he held on to Ruby's arm so she didn't fall when the horse set off. 'Is that the coastline?'

Jago nodded. 'You're lucky we have a clear day. When the sea mist comes in you won't see more than a few yards in front of your face,' he explained.

'That sounds just like the pea-soupers we have back home.'

'Pat tells me that you're not far from London?' Jago asked and he gently shook the leather reins to make the horse move faster.

'Close enough to visit and far enough away not to get as many bombs as they do,' Ruby replied. 'My, but it's a beautiful part of the country you live in. Have you been here long?'

Jago thought for a minute. 'Around four hundred years. Trevellyn Farm's been in the family since 1560.'

'And you've always lived here yourself?' Bob asked.

'I was born on the farm, but until the war started I worked in the city of London. Pa's getting on now so it

was only right that I came home to run the farm as pro-
ductively as possible to aid the war effort.'

'Very commendable,' Bob said. 'It must have been a
big change for your family.'

'Pa still helps out as much as he can, but he was glad
to move into his cottage alongside Ma and for me to take
over.'

'Was your wife happy to move down here? Life in
Cornwall must be very different to what she'd been used
to up in London,' Ruby asked even though she knew she
was being very nosy considering they hadn't long met.

'I'm not married, Mrs Caselton.'

Ruby glanced at Bob and frowned. So her Pat was
living on a farm with a single man. No wonder she was
keen not to hang about in Erith at Easter. She too would
have raced back to Cornwall if there were men like Jago
Trevellyn waiting for her far away from her husband,
with open arms and no wife watching over them.

The journey to the farm took an hour as the horse
trotted along meandering lanes and either cows or crops
in fields behind the Cornish hedging. The sky was a
brilliant shade of blue and the sun beat down. Within
minutes of setting off from the station Ruby had removed
her coat and Bob had taken off his tie. 'I could get used
to this,' he said, holding his face up to the sun.

'Have you had many bombs down this way?' Ruby
asked, not believing that the Luftwaffe would be bothered with bombing fields when they could hit the
factories and shipyards in the main part of England.

'We've had our fair share,' Jago said grimly, 'and we
use our shelters just like city folk. They try to stop food

deliveries going up on the railway, but we won't let them win.'

'That's the spirit,' Ruby said, patting his strong back. 'My son, George – that's Pat's brother – told me as how the enemy bombed Exeter recently. It seems they are attacking places that are listed in some travel book.'

'The Baedeker Raids?' Jago said. 'There have been more over your way. Haven't you heard about them?'

Bob reached into his pocket and pulled out a folded newspaper. 'I was saving this for a convenient time. The stationmaster gave it to me.'

Ruby scanned the headline and gasped. 'Canterbury?' It was hard to read any more, what with trying to hold tight to Bob's arm in case she fell and with the sun in her eyes. 'Isn't that where our Maisie and Betty are? God, Bob, why did you not tell me earlier? Stop this contraption. We need to get back home in case the girls need us.' She looked round, frantically trying to work out how to get herself off the moving cart.

'Stay where you are, Mrs Caselton, or you may harm yourself. We're almost at the farm and you can telephone home and find out what's happened,' Jago advised as the horse turned left into a farmyard with hardly any need of guidance from his owner.

'You have a telephone?' Ruby asked incredulously.

'Not everything is four hundred years old,' Jago said with a smile, 'we do have some modern contraptions.'

'But we've not got one,' Ruby said. 'How can we find out what's happened?'

Bob squeezed her hand. 'Don't worry, Ruby. Once we've seen your Pat and got ourselves settled we can give Mike a ring at the police station. He's sure to know what's happening back at home.'

Bob had no sooner spoken than shrieks of excitement were heard as Pat's children raced to where Ruby had climbed down from the cart and was straightening her clothing. 'Look at you lot, haven't you grown? Why, I hardly recognize you all. One, two, three, four ... who is missing?' she asked, looking over the shoulders of the youngsters.

'Johnny and Ted aren't here,' the shortest of the girls explained as she looked shyly towards Bob and pointed. 'Who is he, Nan?'

'Don't point at people, Iris, it's rude,' Pat said, hurrying across the farmyard and hugging her mum. 'I thought you'd got lost, I've been that worried. Hello, Bob, it's good to see you again,' she added, giving Bob a peck on the cheek.

'But who is he?' Iris whined, draping herself around her mother's legs.

'This is Bob. He is Sergeant Jackson's daddy. You remember him, don't you?'

Iris nodded, suddenly very thoughtful. 'He will come and lock us up if we are naughty,' she said quietly to Bob. 'Will you lock us up too?'

Bob tried to keep a straight face as he bent down until he was face to face with the young girl. 'When I was a policeman many, many years ago my wife used to say the same to our little boy.'

Iris thought about what she'd been told, while Ruby and Pat burst out laughing.

'I promise I don't say things like that often,' Pat apologized to Bob.

'If it works, who am I to argue?' he said as he ruffled Iris's hair. 'Now, are you going to introduce me to these other young ladies?'

Iris took his hand and pointed at the next in age. 'That's Lily, and Rose and she's Violet. I'm Iris and I'm the youngest.'

'A beautiful bunch of flowers.' Bob smiled at Pat. 'Whose idea was that?'

'My husband, John's. His mother and her sister were all named after flowers and we both thought it was a lovely idea. Of course, I went and had two boys first so that put paid to our idea for a while,' she chuckled. 'Speaking of which, where are the pair of them?'

'I sent them off to deliver a message for me,' Jago said as he unhitched the horse from the cart. 'They should be back by now.'

'If you've sent them over to Isaac's place, you know they'll be an age. If the tide's up, they'll be messing about on the river.'

Ruby frowned. 'That's a bit on the dangerous side for two young boys, isn't it?'

'Wait until you see them, Mum. They're like grown men now. Johnny's fourteen and nigh on as tall as his dad, and Ted's not far behind. There's a year between them,' she explained to Bob.

'Time for them to be thinking about a proper job then,' Ruby said. 'If they was back home, your John would have them working on the farm by now.'

'You'll find the boys aren't allowed to be idle here

either,' Jago Trevellyn said as he started to walk the horse towards a barn on the far side of the yard. 'Pat perhaps you'll show your mum her room and I'll take Mr Jackson to his as soon as I've settled Jupiter. I'll not be long,' he said to Bob.

Bob nodded and picked up Ruby's case. 'Show me where I can leave this, will you, Pat?'

'Follow me, Bob. I've put Mum in the farmhouse and you have a room in the barn.'

'No offence, Bob, but you're a bit on the old side to be roughing it in a barn, even if you do go out on night-time manoeuvres with the Home Guard.'

'It's all right, Mum. The barn's been converted into a cottage and is used for farm workers. Since I've been here with the kids and Jago's back and running the farm, there's no need for help as I'm doing the work of a land girl and the boys are more than doing their bit around the place. I'm afraid you'll be sharing with the boys, Bob, but feel free to clip 'em round the ears if they play you up.'

'I'm sure there'll be no need for that,' he laughed. 'I'll help out while we're here. I've always had a hankering for being a farmer.'

'Help's always welcome, Bob. You can have your meals with us. Don't think you're not welcome. Cooking for an extra two people is nothing to me.'

'Does this Jago sleep in the farmhouse as well?' Ruby asked, watching her daughter closely.

'Of course not,' Pat answered indignantly. 'I'd not be able to look my John in the face if he knew I was down here sleeping under the same roof as another man. Whatever are you thinking of, Mother?'

'I'm not sure, Pat, I'm not sure,' Ruby replied thought-fully. 'Now, let's get a move on. I could kill for a decent cup of tea. The one we had when we changed trains was like dishwater.'

'The girls have been baking, so you'll be tasting their scones with a dollop of the clotted cream made here on the farm.'

'And the jam we made, Mum. Don't forget that,' Violet and Lily chanted together as they each held one of their nan's hands and led her towards the farmhouse.

'It should be somewhere up here,' Freda said as she walked briskly through the main shopping street of Bexleyheath. 'We can't hang about as I need to be back home to get ready for the pictures. I really don't want to miss the beginning of the B film. It's another Clive Danvers spy story and I've not seen it before.'

'You're always dashing about somewhere or other. You make me feel quite tired,' Maisie teased, knowing how much her young friend was looking forward to meeting the dashing American sergeant.

'I rather envy you your leisurely lifestyle, Maisie,' Freda grinned as she came to a halt outside the frosted window of one of the smaller establishments. 'This seems to be the right number.'

Maisie snorted. 'Bloody cheek. You'd be walking round almost starkers if I wasn't sweating over me Singer sewing machine fer most of the day. Are you sure this is where Douglas works?' she said, pressing her nose against the window.

'Let's find out,' Sarah said, pushing open the door and stepping inside.

'This gives me the creeps,' Maisie whispered to Freda as she stayed close to the door of the shop. 'If I'd known Douglas was an undertaker, I'd not have come with yer.'

'Don't be silly,' Sarah hissed as she rang a small brass bell that stood on top of a large mahogany desk. 'No one's going to hurt you here.'

'I had no idea Douglas was an undertaker. The card on Betty's sideboard just had his telephone number and business address. Not that it makes any difference to why we are here,' Freda said to Maisie, who seemed to be stuck to a spot close to the door. 'I swear if something creaked or went boo, you'd be out of this shop in a flash,' she grinned at her chum.

A door at the back of the small room started to open and Maisie froze. Freda tried not to giggle.

'Well, what a surprise. It is good to see the three of you,' Douglas said as he stepped into the shop. 'I hope you are not here on business and everyone is well.'

Sarah looked at her two friends, who seemed to have lost the power to answer Douglas as he stood there dressed extremely smartly in a black three-piece suit complete with tails. If he didn't have such a welcoming smile spread across his face, she'd have thought he was about to don a top hat and walk sombrely in front of a funeral cortege. 'No . . . no, we are all well, thank you, Douglas. But we wanted to speak to you about Betty. That's if you don't think we are interfering?'

Douglas thought for a moment. 'Does Betty know you've come to see me?'

'It was our idea, Douglas,' Freda chirped up. 'Please can you spare us ten minutes? Maisie is leaving Erith tomorrow and we wanted to put things right before she goes away.'

'Give me five minutes to get out of my work clothes and we can talk for as long as you want. There's a small cafe a few doors down. Go and order and I'll see you in there. Tell the owner, Janie, that the bill is on me. I'll have the bubble and squeak and an egg on top if she has any. Order whatever you want, it's my treat.'

The girls thanked Douglas, walked the short distance to the cafe and introduced themselves to Janie, who ran the establishment. 'I could eat a horse,' Maisie declared.

'If you order the meat pie, chances are you will be,' Sarah pointed out, trying not to laugh. There had been many stories of horsemeat being sold as beef and even though her nan had told her she'd eaten the meat often in the past, Sarah just couldn't face the thought of it. 'I think I'll have the same as Douglas if you have the eggs?' Sarah said, handing back the dog-eared menu.

'Just soup and toast for me, please,' Freda said. 'I'm not that hungry.'

Maisie grinned at Sarah. 'I think our Freda is just a little bit nervous.'

'I am a bit worried. I'm not sure I should be going to the pictures with you and the Americans. I reckon it will get out and then someone like Vera from up the road will find out and start spreading gossip about me.'

'Don't worry about it,' Maisie said. 'Why not explain to Maureen and then she can sort out Vera? I think I deserve pease pudding and faggots for coming up with that idea,' she said, lighting up a cigarette and beaming at her mates.

Douglas joined them just as the food was being brought to the table. He exchanged some pleasantries with the cafe owner before sitting down and taking a mouthful of tea from the mug that had been placed next to his plate. 'It's really good to see the three of you. I've not been down to Erith for a little while. Is everyone fit and healthy?'

Maisie coughed and almost choked on her food. 'Blimey, Douglas, that's choice coming from you. Are you touting fer business?'

'I fell for that one hook, line and sinker,' he grinned at Maisie. 'I keep forgetting I'm a funeral director these days. I still think of myself as an accountant.'

'That's rather an unusual change of occupation,' Sarah said. 'May I ask why you were an accountant first if you always wanted to be an undertaker?'

'I didn't,' he replied as he broke the yolk on his fried egg and dipped in a chunk of fried potato and cabbage. 'You could say I wanted a change and, believe me, owning a funeral business is far more exciting that balancing columns of figures every day. I inherited the business from an uncle. He's the Butterfield part of the business name. I have no idea who the Oborne part belonged to. No doubt long dead and of no interest to anybody.'

'Oborne and Butterfield has a nice ring to it. You didn't fancy changing the business to Billington's?' Freda asked. She'd got to know Douglas while staying with Betty and she liked the man. He was open and friendly. He was what Maisie would have described as 'what you see is what you get', but she couldn't understand what had happened for Betty to fall out with him.

'There's a certain amount of goodwill comes with a business like mine so I decided to keep the name as it was. I'm used to people coming into the office and calling me Mr Butterfield or Mr Oborne. I'm still balancing columns of figures, but these days it's for my own business.'

'Do you ... yer know ...'

'Do I lay out bodies and tend to the deceased, do you mean, Maisie?'

Maisie nodded, not sure what to say. The thought of what Douglas did for a living was making her skin creep.

'No, I'm purely the man who does the paperwork. You only see me in the official funeral director attire today as we are a man short due to him receiving his call-up papers and his replacement being off sick. The front office is as much as I'll do in the business. Do you want to know a secret?' he said, putting down his knife and fork and leaning closer to the three girls.

The girls nodded although Maisie was beginning to feel a little nauseous.

'The first time I visited the back room I passed out when I saw what was being done. I haven't got the stomach for the business.'

'Phew, thank goodness for that. I thought you was gonna tell us something awful,' Maisie said, fanning her face with her handkerchief, which made them all burst out laughing.

'I intend to hand the management over to someone

else once this war is over and those who know the job return to their rightful occupations.'

'A bit like Woolies,' Maisie said, lighting another cigarette and blowing the smoke away from the table. 'Once the men come home us women will be back on the shop floor and the men will be running the whole shop.'

Douglas frowned. 'I'd heard as much, but it doesn't seem fair when women like Betty have worked so hard and achieved positions of responsibility just to hand them back again. Why, it would be like snatching away her dream.' He looked at each of the girls in turn. 'Is this why you wanted to speak to me?'

'In a manner of speaking,' Freda said, aware that time was ticking by. 'It's just that we think we know why Betty pushed you away. She did, didn't she?' Freda asked timidly.

'I have no idea. It seemed that at one point we had some kind of future together then minutes later she was a different person and had no wish to know me.'

'Cutting a long story short, we think it's because she's aware of her age and that she is most likely too old to give you a family,' Sarah said shyly. Now that the time had come for them to share their thoughts with Douglas it felt as though they were interfering in something that wasn't their business.

Douglas ran his hand through his hair. 'I knew it was something like this. I just knew it. Rather than face Betty and asked her what was wrong I just walked away. I just didn't want to have her reject me. I'm such a fool. What can I do now? I doubt she'd even speak to me if I was to approach her.'

'That's what we thought,' Maisie smiled, 'so we've arranged for her to be alone and somewhere she can't easily walk away from you.'

'Can you arrange to be at Mitchell's tea room for one tomorrow?'

'I most certainly can,' Douglas grinned.

Bob rolled over in bed and stared out of the window into the night sky. Even after travelling through the night from Erith and a day spent investigating the farm followed by a hearty meal cooked by Ruby's daughter Pat, he found that sleep was evading him. He climbed out of bed and stood by the window. There was certainly a lot of sky in Cornwall and so many stars. With no chance of dropping off to sleep, he decided to head downstairs and make himself a drink in the small kitchen of the converted barn. If he was quiet, he'd not wake up Jago or the two boys, whose bedrooms were either side of his own.

The small stove in the corner of the room was still warm. Bob checked the kettle. Yes, there was just enough water to make a cup of cocoa. First sliding the kettle to the middle of the hob, he pottered about finding a mug and a tin of cocoa and a teaspoon and waited for the water to boil. The light of the moon came through the large kitchen window so there was no need to light a gas lamp. Taking his hot drink to an armchair by the stove, he sat quietly sipping the drink deep in thought, anticipating the day ahead. The plan was to help Pat with her chores before heading off to a nearby cove so the children could swim and spend time with their grandmother. Ruby had explained to him that rather than evacuate their children by themselves Pat and her husband, John, had agreed that Pat should go with them to Cornwall, where she would work on a farm and the children be safe from the war. The farm where John worked, and the tied cottage in which they lived, were close to the River Thames in Slades Green. With the enemy using the river to guide their planes to the capital city, the village was often a place where planes returning home would dump their explosives. Bob knew that Ruby missed her grandchildren something rotten although she hadn't been brave enough to make the journey to the South West of the country before now.

Deep in thought, the creaking of the wooden staircase along with whispered words startled him. It was far too early for the two lads to be rising to help with morning milking duties so what were the young scallywags up to?

18

'How do I look?' Freda asked as she spun around on the spot in the front room of number thirteen while Sarah clapped enthusiastically. 'I'm quite pleased with the alterations to this coat. Maisie was right when she said adding a new collar and cuffs would make a difference to it. No one would know that with Maisie's help I'd cut up an old coat I'd picked up from the jumble and edged it and changed the buttons as well.'

'Sorry, love, I was miles away,' Maureen said, looking flustered. 'Why, you look a treat. Is that a new coat?'

Freda looked at Sarah and could see that she too was concerned. Sitting down next to Maureen on the sofa, she took her hand. 'Is something wrong, Maureen?'

Sarah knelt down in front of her mother-in-law. 'You've been very quiet all day, Maureen. Are you poorly?'

'Don't the pair of you go worrying about an old woman like me. Go out and enjoy yourselves . . . And Sarah, you shouldn't think twice about what people say about you going to the pictures with Freda and her friends. You have my blessing and if that nosy so-and-so

Vera Munro says anything, she will have me to answer to. Now, get cracking, the pair of you, or you'll miss that Clive Danvers film and I know how much you admire him, Freda.'

'There's something else, isn't there, Maureen? Have you heard from Alan?' Sarah asked, thinking the worst had happened.

'Goodness me, no. I showed you the last letter he sent to me. He told me that everything was tickety-boo, whatever that means.'

Sarah smiled. That did sound like her husband. 'He does seem to be in good spirits, doesn't he? But I don't think you are, Maureen. Please tell us what is wrong. We may be able to help. After all, a trouble shared is a trouble halved.'

Maureen's hand shook as she reached into the pocket of her cardigan. 'This letter came from my landlord, Ken Barnham. He reckons that he won't be paying for the repairs to the roof and chimney as the damage is my fault, and that I have to pay the bill before I can move back into the house.'

'Why is he blaming you?' Freda asked.

'He says that I never took care of the property. Alan was a baby when we first moved into that house and we've decorated and done everything possible to make it a comfortable home. He's always been a pain in the backside where money's concerned, but we've never not paid the rent on time or not complied with what's in the tenancy agreement. He's just a mean, horrid man.'

Sarah took the letter and quickly read the words as Freda looked over her shoulder. 'How many hundreds of pounds does he want you to pay? Why, that's preposterous. I'm sure he can't do this to you. Bob was telling me that the government pays for repairs to homes damaged by enemy action. Granted Barnham hadn't pointed the chimney, but it was enemy action that made it come through the ceiling. You shouldn't have to worry about this.'

'But I am worried. I can't stay here at Ruby's for much longer. It's not fair on everyone and it also affects you, as where will Alan live when he comes home? Ruby can't squeeze another person into this house and the pair of you do need your privacy.'

Sarah blushed as she realized what Maureen was referring to. 'I don't think we should do anything rash. Why not wait until Bob is back from Cornwall at the end of the week? He is sure to be able to help. I'd ask Dad, but Mum said he's up to his neck in work at the moment and may as well sleep at Vickers for all the time he spends there. You have a bed here and as Ruby is away there's plenty of room.'

Maureen nodded but didn't seem to be convinced.

'And what you said about being an old woman,' Freda added, 'you're not at all old so that won't wash with us either.'

'You're both good girls,' Maureen said, giving them a watery smile. 'Now, off with you and enjoy your evening out. Don't you worry about me. I've got my knitting and there's a programme on the wireless that I want to listen to. So off with you right now.'

The two girls slipped out of the house, making sure to close the door quietly as Georgie and Myfi were already tucked up in bed and Gwyneth was upstairs reading. After Maureen's scare they'd all decided that the children would never be left alone upstairs in case there was a sudden raid.

'Maureen's right, you know. We're fit to bursting in the house and it only needs Alan to come home early and we're in a right fix,' Sarah said.

'I suppose I could ask Betty if she would put me up for a while until Maureen's house has been repaired.'

'Hmm, that is an idea but it's not fair on you as number thirteen is your home and we are the ones who have taken over. I think I should look into moving somewhere else along with Maureen. I'll ask at the council offices.'

'But you may be moved miles away. How will you and Maureen cope with getting to work and who will look after Georgina?' Freda said with alarm. 'Why, it would be worth me moving up the road to live with Vera rather than you going to live somewhere else.'

'Now, that is an idea,' Sarah said brightly. 'I don't mean you moving in with Vera but perhaps she would put me and Georgie up and possibly Maureen. She does have two spare rooms going begging. I'll pop down the road tomorrow morning and have a chat with her.'

'Rather you than me,' Freda giggled as they arrived at the Odeon cinema. 'Look, there's Hank and his friend over by the main doors.'

Sarah took a deep breath. Here we go, she thought to herself.

Freda introduced Sarah to Hank and he did the same with his friend, who smiled shyly to Sarah and stood next to her as they joined the queue filing into the sumptuous interior of the popular Erith cinema. The men purchased tickets and they walked up the wide carpeted stairs from where they were shown to their seats by a smartly dressed usherette. Even when seated Sarah was looking around to see if there was anyone she recognized who would naturally assume she had not long waved off her husband and was now in the company of an American soldier. There was a name for women who did such things and it wasn't nice.

'I believe you are married,' the soldier said as he sat to the left of her.

'Yes, that's right. My husband is in the RAF fighting overseas. We have a daughter.' She hoped she wasn't giving away vital information. Did 'careless talk' include chatting to an American serviceman called Chuck? She had a feeling that perhaps it did.

Chuck pulled out a wallet and produced two photographs. 'This is my wife, Jean, and here are our children, Sophie and Chuck Junior. We live out in Oregon. It's the first time I've ever left them,' he explained with more than a hint of sadness in his voice.

Sarah took a photograph of her daughter from her handbag and passed it to Chuck. 'This is our daughter, Georgina. She will be two in a couple of months. And this,' she said, taking out another small photo, 'is my husband, Alan. We were married the day war was announced. It was my twenty-first birthday.'

'A momentous day,' Chuck said as he took the picture and whistled. 'Gee, a pilot, that's one brave husband you have there, ma'am, if I may say so,' he said in admiration.

'You may,' Sarah said proudly as the lights were lowered slowly to indicate the first film was about to start. 'Alan flies Spitfires. I thought I'd lost him at one time.'

'Gee, those men are gods.'

'Alan has always been a god to me,' she whispered as she tucked the photographs away safely in her bag and settled down to watch the film.

Freda could hear Sarah chatting to Hank's friend about their families and was thankful her friend had accompanied her and that Hank had brought along someone who was a respectable family man. As the lights lowered and the screen lit up Hank put his hand over hers and she settled back to enjoy the film with no thought of her last visit to this cinema.

All four enjoyed the film and remained standing until the national anthem finished. Outside in the dark night Chuck shook Sarah's hand and thanked her for her company, adding that he wished her husband well wherever he was. Sarah reciprocated, hoping it wouldn't be too long before he saw his wife and family once more. They'd walked a little way away from where Hank was saying goodnight to Freda. Sarah noticed how tenderly he kissed her young friend. Someone would be walking on cloud nine tomorrow.

Bob huddled by the edge of a wall trying to catch his breath. The two boys had walked at a brisk pace until they'd reached the edge of a small inlet. He knew from studying maps of the area in the lead-up to their holiday that this would be part of the Helford River. He could hear waves gently lapping the shore and also murmuring voices. Whatever were those boys up to? The middle of the night was not a time for messing about on the river. Ruby would have a fit if she knew her grandchildren weren't safely tucked up in their beds. He could feel the start of cramp in his leg and tried to stretch it without attracting attention. Dressed only in pyjamas with his suit jacket thrown over the top, he felt rather ridiculous. A twig snapped underfoot and he froze.

'Don't move. Stay right where you are,' a menacing voice hissed in his ear as his arm was grabbed from behind. What felt like a gun was held to his back.

Bob held his breath for what seemed like an age before another person appeared and briefly flashed a torch into his face before swearing, whereupon Bob was dragged along a shingle beach and into a boathouse, where he was pushed onto a seat and his hands tied behind his back.

A bare light bulb was switched on and Bob could see a group of men who, in any normal situation, would have looked like simple fishermen going about a day's work – apart from it being the middle of the night and he couldn't see a boat, so what the hell were they up to?

Aware that a gun had been held to his back, he decided to stay put and not make a run for it. With the door to the boathouse closed, there was only one way out and that was into the river. Bob was not a good swimmer, especially with his hands tied tightly together.

'Does anyone recognize him?' a gruff voice asked.

'He's our nan's friend, Bob,' a boy's voice piped up. 'They've come to visit us on the farm. He must have followed us.'

'What have you got to say for yourself?' the man with the gruff voice asked, shaking his shoulder roughly. 'Why are you spying on us?'

Bob never knew whether it was nerves or the absurdity of the situation but he burst out laughing. His situation reminded him of one of the books Freda sold on her counter at Woolworths and she always had her nose in at home. 'I'm not a threat to you, whatever you're up to. I was just following those boys as they were out of their beds at such an ungodly hour. However,' he added with a serious look on his face, 'if you are up to no good, it's a pretty poor show to involve children. Does Jago Trevellyn know that evacuees are being dragged into your wrongdoings and that you are now holding a retired policeman against his will?'

The men fell silent, the only sound the splash of oars as a rowboat came close to the boathouse. Two men jumped out and dragged the boat free of the water's edge, assisted by several of the men who'd stood watching Bob.

'There was no one there to hand over the goods. We'll have to try again tomorrow night,' said a voice that Bob recognized. 'What have we got here?' he added as he noticed Bob for the first time.

Bob inwardly groaned. Whatever had they got themselves into coming to Cornwall? Would Ruby, Pat and the youngsters be safe once it was known he'd stumbled into a den of thieves?

*

'I feel ridiculous spying on Betty like this,' Freda said as she stood alongside Maisie and Sarah as they peered through the upstairs window of Woolworths that looked out over the main shopping road of Erith. They could see down to the large Mitchell's store opposite and the door that led into the popular tea rooms. Behind them Maureen was serving food to staff who were arriving for their midday break. 'What if Betty comes in here before she heads off to Mitchell's?' Sarah worried as she looked over her shoulder at the door, expecting her boss to walk in and catch them.

'She won't,' Maisie said confidently. 'Freda's the only one working up here today and she told Betty we'd all meet her in the tea room. Look, there she is crossing the road. I do 'ope Douglas arrives on time or our plan will fail.'

'How long should we leave it before we go over there?' Sarah asked.

'I'm thinking we ought ter cross over and peer through the window. It may be a way ter see how they're getting on. Let's give it a few minutes ter make sure Douglas arrives as planned, shall we?'

The girls were on tenterhooks as they watched and waited for Douglas to go into the tea rooms, but how would Betty react? Would she walk away? Perhaps she would be angry with her friends for interfering? Or just maybe she would be reconciled with Douglas, as they truly wished would happen.

'Look, there he is,' Freda squeaked, almost unable to speak with the excitement. 'Come on, let's go and look through the window of the tea rooms and see what's happening.'

The girls hurried down the staff staircase and rushed through the busy store to the street outside. Dodging around shoppers and a delivery van, they arrived at Mitchell's department store and the door to the tea room.

'Don't go in yet,' Maisie shrieked at Sarah, who had her hand on the door. 'Let's look in the window and see what's happening.'

'Sorry, I wasn't thinking straight,' Sarah said as her stomach growled. 'I was just wondering when we'd get to eat. I'm starving.'

'Come here, you two,' Freda called from where she was peering intently through a window crisscrossed with tape to save diners from shards of glass if there should be an air raid. 'It looks like Betty is smiling. I think everything is going to be all right.'

They watched as the couple spoke earnestly for a few minutes before Douglas leant over and gave Betty a brief kiss and she reached for her handkerchief and dabbed at her eyes.

A waitress arrived to take their order, but was brushed away as they continued to talk without taking their eyes from each other.

'I think our plan must have worked,' Sarah said with a huge sigh of relief. 'My goodness, look!'

In the middle of the busy tea room Douglas had knelt down on one knee and appeared to be proposing to Betty.

Maisie whooped with delight and hugged her friends.

'At least I can head off to the in-laws without worrying about Betty's love life. Come on, let's go in and have a bite to eat. I have to leave in a couple of hours and I want to say goodbye to Betty and Douglas and wish them all the best.'

The girls entered the busy tea room and were immediately spotted by Betty, who waved at them to come over. They felt a little sheepish as they sat down after greeting Douglas like a long-lost friend and confessing that they'd just spotted the proposal after admiring the single solitaire ring Betty was gazing at with delight.

'There's no need to pretend you've not seen Douglas in a while,' Betty smiled as she reached out and held his hand. 'He has explained everything.'

'Does this mean we have a wedding to look forward to?' Maisie said as her friends looked horrified.

'Honestly, Maisie, it may be a little soon for a question like that,' Freda said with a nervous laugh, but all the same she looked hopefully towards the Woolworths manager. 'After all, they've only just become engaged.'

'There's plenty of time for things like that,' Betty smiled. 'Let me enjoy the anticipation for a while.'

Douglas called the waitress over and ordered tea for five, cheese on toast and a selection of cakes to celebrate. The buns had very few currants and were a little on the small side but were enjoyed as much as if they were wedding cake and champagne at a posh London hotel.

'There's one thing, girls. Can we keep this our little secret for now otherwise I'll have the staff in a fluster when we return to work?'

'But you're wearing a ring on your wedding finger. Won't people notice?' Sarah asked.

'If Douglas is in agreement, I will wear the ring on a chain around my neck for now until we have a proper announcement.'

'And I'm going to miss all the fun,' Maisie said in a pretend huff before looking up at the clock. 'Oh my God, I'm late. David will think I've run off and left him,' she shrieked before kissing them all goodbye and rushing from the tea room.

'I'm going to miss her so much,' Sarah said, watching her friend until she was out of sight.

'Now, are you going to tell me what this is all about, Jago?' Bob asked none too happily as they walked back to the farm. His wrists ached from the rope used to tie his hands together and he was still trembling after the fear of being held at gunpoint.

'I'm sorry you were handled roughly, Bob, but you shouldn't have interfered in what doesn't concern you,' Jago said as he picked his way through a narrow pathway that skirted a field.

All Bob knew was that this was not the way he'd walked when following Pat's boys in the dead of night. Even as dawn broke he could not identify where he was until, after walking through a small copse, he found himself at the back entrance to the farmhouse. 'I'll leave you here and get myself dressed if that's allowed,' he said, looking Jago in the eye. 'Then I want some answers. You may do as you please, but when it involves two children

I'm honour-bound to inform their mother and their grandmother, who will be none too pleased that their boys have been put in danger.'

Jago sighed. 'Come in and have some breakfast first. Pat will have it ready by now and there'll be plenty as our guests did not arrive as planned.'

'You mean Pat knows what you're up to?'

'A select few are aware,' Jago replied, leading the way into the farmhouse.

Pat greeted him with a broad smile as she stood, frying pan in hand, by the Aga, her smile disappearing as she spotted Bob. 'What's going on, Jago? Where are our guests?'

Bob kicked off his shoes and left them by the door before washing his hands at the kitchen sink. All the time his mind was churning over thoughts of smuggling and that Ruby's family was involved. He might have retired from the police force, but he still believed that wrong-doers should answer for their actions. For guns to be involved meant this was not simply a few bottles of brandy on the black market. He needed to bring these people to task without hurting Ruby's family. Accepting a mug of tea from a now silent Pat, he took a sip of the hot liquid before glaring at Jago. 'Are you going to tell me what this is all about or have I got to guess?'

'I don't understand how you've become involved, Bob?' Pat interrupted. 'Was it my boys? I told them to keep their mouths shut.'

Bob groaned inwardly. He had hoped that Pat and her two eldest children had become unwittingly involved, but it seemed from the way she spoke that they were as guilty as Jago. A sudden thought made him jerk upright in shock. 'You're working for the enemy, aren't you?' he said accusingly, pointing a finger at Jago. 'You're bringing in spies.'

Jago roared with laughter and sat opposite Bob as Pat slid plates heaped high with sausages, bacon and eggs towards them. 'Your accusations couldn't be further from the truth. Eat up and I'll explain.'

Bob, although wanting to know what was behind what had happened out at the boathouse, tucked into his breakfast, as he felt almost faint with hunger after his recent experience. 'I suppose all this grub is black market too,' he added grumpily, not wishing Jago or Pat to think he condoned what had happened just because he was a guest at the table.

Jago nodded to the two boys to leave the table when they'd finished eating. 'You can start loading the vegetables for market,' he said. 'I'll be out directly.'

Pat cleared the dirty plates and left them in the stone sink. 'I'll leave you to it, shall I? I can take a cup of tea up to Mum.'

Jago nodded and leant back in his seat giving Bob a hard stare. 'What exactly do you think we were doing down on the river?' he asked.

Bob felt uncomfortable. If Jago and his friends were up to no good, then what would become of him? The man must stand over six feet in his stockinged feet and was as strong as the bull that Bob had seen in a nearby field. His fair hair and blue eyes gave the impression Jago could be a good sort, but his current demeanour still worried Bob. In for a penny, he thought to himself. He could always yell for Ruby and her daughter if things got sticky. Surely they wouldn't let anything nasty happen to him? 'I could ask the same of you,' he replied, trying the same tactic. 'Perhaps it's you who should be explaining. After all, I was the one who had a gun to my back and ended up tied up just because I was following Ruby's grandchildren in case they came to harm. I expected them to be up to boyish pranks, not involved in smuggling, or worse,' he glowered.

Jago roared with laughter. 'As much as I'd like to be thought of as a ne'er do well, like some of my ancestors who were smugglers, I'm afraid you are in for a disappointment, Bob. We are the good guys as they say in the westerns that Pat's children seem to enjoy at the cinema.'

'Good guys, how do you mean?' Bob asked, leaning forward and putting his elbows on the scrubbed pine table, eager to hear what Jago had to say.

'I haven't always been a farmer. It took the outbreak of war for me to come back to Cornwall and take on special duties,' he explained.

'Well, farming is important in wartime,' Bob agreed, but wondered why a strapping lad like him wasn't serving his country elsewhere.

Jago held up his hand to stop Bob. 'Yes, I'm a farmer but I also work for the government to try to bring the war to an end. They moved me back to the family farm from my desk job to oversee things from this end. Do you understand? I can't say much more than that.'

Bob rubbed his chin as he thought about what Jago had said. 'Special Operations Executive?' he asked.

'How do you know about that? It's not the sort of thing a civilian usually has knowledge of.'

'I don't know much. As an ex-London bobby and with my work in the Home Guard I get to hear of things. Our unit back in Erith has recently received training in undercover work and sabotage and we know what to do in the event of an invasion. In a small way we are doing in Erith what you are doing down here. So, you see, we are on the same side. But what's all this smuggling lark about?'

'We're not smuggling. Well, we are in a way but we . . . well, let's say we work in the movement of men.'

'I don't understand. Do you mean you're helping German spies come into the country? Surely not! I know I'm tired and probably not thinking properly, but this sounds ridiculous.'

Jago smiled. 'There are times when we need to have our operatives enter enemy-controlled areas and it's not possible to drop them by plane. There are other times when we need to get them out of the country pretty quickly. The problem is there is a bloody big stretch of water between England and France, so that's where our fishermen come in.'

'French and English?' Bob asked, getting interested now that he knew his life wasn't in imminent danger.

Jago nodded. 'With so many inlets off the main river down here on the Lizard Peninsula we can hide away then slip out to sea and meet the fishing boats, and coming back it's easy to hide away and not be found.'

Bob thought of Sarah's husband, Alan, and how he'd been brought back home after his plane went down in enemy-occupied France. 'You're doing a bloody good job,' he said gruffly. 'But what happened last night? Why was I tied up and treated like a criminal?'

'We'd had a problem with a pick-up and thought there was a spy in our midst. Usually I use only men I've personally recruited, but I was sent a couple direct from the London office and the day after we lost someone in France and the tip-off could have come from here. My men had just received my signal when you appeared.'

Bob was thoughtful. 'Your team believed this old man from Erith was a spy? I suppose I should be flattered,' he chuckled. 'What happened last night?'

'We were to rendezvous with a boat to pick up two airmen, but there wasn't even a sighting of them.'

'Did you hang around and wait?'

'No, it's too dangerous. We will wait for fresh orders . . . if they come.'

Bob was contemplating this information when Ruby joined them.

'Whatever are you doing still wearing your pyjamas?'

'I, um . . .' Bob didn't wish to lie to Ruby, but was stumped as he knew she would not be happy with her family being involved in all this.

'I asked him to help me with a difficult calving,' Jago answered without batting an eyelid.

He's used to covering for himself, Bob thought with a slight chuckle.

Ruby tutted and turned to her daughter, who was watching the conversation with a wary look on her face. 'Is it too early to use the telephone to contact Erith police station? I thought someone would have got back to us last night. I hardly slept worrying if those girls have been injured down in Canterbury. In fact, I thought I heard voices in the middle of the night.'

'Most likely the chickens, Mum, they can make a right noise if a fox is about,' Pat added quickly, glancing at Jago for support.

'It would have been us, Mrs Caselton. We had to walk under your window to get to the barn.'

'Bob, why don't you make that telephone call for Mum while I cook her some breakfast. Fried or scrambled eggs, Mum?'

Jago showed them through to his office and cleared a chair of paperwork so Ruby could sit down and then left them alone. It wasn't long before Bob was through to the police station he knew so well and was chatting to Mike, who had just come on duty. After a few brief sentences he passed the receiver over to Ruby. 'Here you are, love. You chat to our Mike while I go and get changed. I won't be long.'

When Bob returned, out of breath due to hurrying, he could see she wasn't her usual self.

Ruby sat holding the telephone receiver, her thoughts many miles away with her family and friends in Erith. Her face had gone a ghostly white. 'They were down there, Bob, while all that bombing was going on. All three of them.'

'Three ... who else went with Betty and Maisie? Are they all right?'

'Our Freda was down there on that bloody big motorbike. What the hell she was doing there I don't know.'

'I'd think she was doing some work for the Fire

Service,' Bob said, quietly wondering still if the three girls were injured or not. 'What happened?'

'Freda's fine, but the other two ended up in hospital with cuts and grazes. Maisie was worried about the baby, which is understandable. So much so that David was down there in a flash and has whisked her off to live with his family in Wiltshire until the baby is born.' She turned to Bob with tears in her eyes and gripped his hand. 'I should have been at home while those girls were in danger, not gallivanting off down here where it's safe. Who knows what's going to happen next?'

Bob put his arms around Ruby and rocked her gently as she cried. Looking to where Pat stood in the doorway, he was angered that the woman he loved was so upset. 'Do any of us know?' he said pointedly as Pat bent her head and turned away.

19

October 1942

Freda twirled around showing off her new dance frock. 'No one would even guess that it was a hand-me-down, would they?' she grinned. 'Maisie would be so proud to know that her dressmaking lessons have created such a beautiful dress.'

'She'd be just as proud to know that it came from something that's been languishing in my loft since before Eddie passed away. I wore the dress to our Pat's wedding. It must be all of fifteen years.'

'Waste not, want not,' Maureen said as she stepped back to check the hem of the dress. 'That's just about it. You're ready to go to the ball. Best not let Vera see you in the dress as she is bound to open her mouth and say she recognizes the fabric. She could suck the joy out of anything that one.'

'You can always move back here,' Ruby said. 'Why, I've never seen so many changes like the ones that were made around here in the few days that Bob and I were away in Cornwall. It's almost like you were all waiting for me to disappear so you could upset the apple cart.'

'Nothing could be further from the truth, Ruby Caselton, as you well know. Why, if I could move into my house sooner, rather than the six months I'm being told, I'd gladly hold you to your offer to continue living here, but it's not fair on you, or your other lodgers, to be in the way. No, I can put up with Vera until Christmas, if that's what it takes. I'll only be at her house to sleep so it's not so bad.'

'Well, if it gets too much, you just come back here. I'm pleased Bob and our George put their boots up the backside of that landlord of yours. He had no right to make such threats. I reckon he was trying it on, picking on a woman on her own like that.'

Maureen nodded in agreement. 'I'll never be able to thank them enough for putting things straight. I feared I'd be out on the street the way things were going. Now the workmen are there every day putting things back to how they was.'

'Not quite the way they were,' Freda said as she unzipped her frock and pulled on her siren suit, before placing the poppy-red dress on a hanger and hooking it on the back of the door of Ruby's front room. 'Your house will be heaps better than ever before. Perhaps you should have a party to celebrate moving home, even if we do have to wait until Christmas. We could all bring something . . .' she said with a grin, waiting to see what Maureen thought.

'That's a wonderful idea. I'll chivvy along the build-ers. How about we set a date? I reckon the evening of

Christmas Day would be something to look forward to,' Maureen beamed. 'Bob and George will be here soon. They've gone to see how things are progressing. It will be lovely to sleep under my own roof again, as much as I've liked staying with friends,' she added quickly.

Freda took a pencil from the drawer of Ruby's sideboard and made a large circle around the twenty-fifth of December on Ruby's calendar. It was identical to the one that they'd all purchased the year before. 'Nine weeks to go and so much to look forward to; Maisie will have had her baby by then.'

'It seems strange not to have Maisie around,' Ruby sighed. 'I do miss her little ways. I'm not much of one for writing letters and the last one I received from her seemed kind of sad.'

'That reminds me. I have a letter to send and I promised to post Sarah's as well. I'll put them in the post box before I go to the fire station for my next shift.'

'Why, hello, Mike. Fancy bumping into you,' Gwyneth smiled as she walked across the shop floor of Woolworths. 'Was it something special you were looking for?'

Mike Jackson was mesmerized by the dark-haired woman dressed in her wine-coloured Woolworths uniform. It suited her perfectly. He could listen to her sing-song accent all day long as well as gaze into her velvety eyes. Giving himself a shake, he tried to think of an excuse as to why he was in the store. He'd taken to popping in on his way home from the police station on the off chance of catching Gwyneth. 'Just a few seeds for the back garden. I've taken up a bit of the concrete and we've room for some more vegetables.'

'You can never have enough of those,' she said with a grin.

Mike felt a complete fool. He could never think of something clever or entertaining to say when in the pretty woman's company. 'Er . . . Gwyneth . . .'

'Yes, Mike?'

'I was wondering . . . I was wondering if you'd like to take a walk with me later this afternoon? There's a fun-fair up at the recreation ground and I thought it would be a pleasant way to spend the afternoon.'

'Why, that would be grand, Mike. Myfi would love that.'

Mike's face fell. He hadn't given a thought to Gwyneth's daughter accompanying them. His only thought was having the woman he'd fallen in love with from afar alone for a few hours. Then he felt mean-spirited. Myfi was an adorable child even though she'd never uttered a word since coming to live in Erith. 'Why, yes . . . of course . . .' he stuttered. 'It would be lovely to see her enjoying her-self. Shall we say three o'clock? And I'll collect you both from Ruby's?'

'That would be wonderful and thank you, Mike, for thinking of us both,' she smiled as he turned away and walked straight into a group of women chatting at a counter.

'Someone's more than a little attracted to you,' Sarah said as Gwyneth stepped behind the Christmas goods counter and started to sort through a box of Christmas cards that were to go on display. Even though there was a war on Woolworths were fortunate to be able to bring a little cheer to their customers, as an agreement with Lord Beaverbrook meant there was a supply of paper to print books, cards and other goods to brighten everyone's days.

'Mike is sweet and I do like him, but I can't think of romance at the moment.'

Sarah stopped hanging Chinese lanterns from a chain that had been strung above their heads and climbed down from the stepladder. 'Perhaps you ought to tell him about your husband?' Ruby had encouraged Gwyneth to talk about her family problem with Sarah and Freda, as she knew they would be able to support her when she felt down.

'It is only fair that I say something to Mike,' Gwyneth agreed, 'otherwise I could be accused of leading him on. I do like his company, though, and under different circumstances who knows what the future might have brought?'

Sarah could only nod in agreement. She thought it was awfully bad luck that Gwyneth was not free to be courted by the friendly policeman. She wanted everyone to be as happy as she was with Alan. Her hand slipped to her throat and the silver sixpence that hung there on a slender chain. She thought of how he had given it to her at a time she believed she'd lost him for good. This time she knew he was safe even though he was away fighting for his country. His last letter, which was safely tucked under her pillow at home, told how he loved her and missed her. Roll on the day he was home and safely in her arms once more.

*

'Fancy stopping off for a pint, Bob?' George asked as they left Maureen's house in Crayford Road.

'It'll have to be a quick one as Ruby will be expecting us,' he replied, checking his watch. 'At least we can report that the repairs are on schedule. I'd like to put a bit of wallpaper up once the building work's finished. It'll make the house feel more like home and Maureen deserves that after what she's been through. I'll have a word with them in Misson's ironmongers and see if they've got a few rolls of something we can have. There's not much call for it, what with Hitler doing his best to turn our homes to rubble.'

The two men walked into the Prince of Wales pub close by to Maureen's home, and ordered two halves of mild.

'I've been wondering what went on while you were down in Cornwall with Mum,' George asked. 'She told me that Pat was fine and the kids are thriving, but you didn't look so sure.'

Bob took a gulp of his beer and wiped his mouth. 'Nothing much gets past you, does it?'

'So, something was going on? Mum mentioned a farmer called Jago. Is he interested in our Pat? I hope you had a few words with him. Pat's husband, John, is a good bloke. I'd not like anything to upset him or destroy their marriage. Our Pat can be a bit headstrong at times.'

Bob looked around the half-empty bar and pointed to a table in the corner close to a fireplace, where a wooden fire stand stood in front of an empty grate. 'Let's sit over there. I don't want anyone to hear what I've got to tell you.'

George frowned as he sat down and looked at Bob across the round oak table. 'What's up?'

'I'm only telling you this as I know you've got security clearance with your job. There's more going on down on that farm than you think.' Bob went on to explain what had happened and George kept quiet apart from exclaiming annoyance when Bob said that he'd been tied up at gunpoint and again when he was told his two young nephews were involved.

'It's a tricky one and no mistake,' George said when he'd digested what Bob had to say. 'It's dangerous but vital war work. We need to get our chaps back from the clutches of the enemy and there are times that some of our people will have to be sneaked into France by the back door. However, I'm not comfortable with those two boys being involved. If our Pat wants to be doing her bit, then she can, but those kiddies have got to come home to their dad. I've got an idea so leave it with me for now. Thanks for letting me know, Bob. So, what happened to the men they were trying to bring back home?'

Bob shrugged his shoulders. 'They didn't arrive while we were at the farm, although there was something going on a few nights later as I stopped the boys following Jago and sent them packing back to their beds, much to their annoyance.'

'Good,' George said. 'I'd have done the same. It seems to me that they are old enough to be doing something responsible. I may just be able to arrange an apprentice-ship for the older one at Vickers and the younger one is more than old enough to be working with his dad on the farm down the Green.'

'Why did they go to Cornwall?' Bob asked.

'It was John's idea. He wanted the kids to be safe and I don't blame him there. We'd have offered to take them in while we lived in Devon, but can you imagine my Irene running after six children all day long? So, they went to this farm where Pat could work and the kids would be safe.'

Bob smothered a laugh. He didn't wish George to think he was laughing at his wife, but the thought of Irene and all those children, who'd become almost feral running around the farm often without even a pair of shoes on their feet, made him want to laugh out loud. Even Ruby had cause to talk to her daughter about a little more discipline. Perhaps coming back to Slades, Green wasn't such a bad idea. 'What will you do?'

'First off I'll have a word with this Jago chap and see if I can get him onside to influence Pat to bring the children home. If she wants to go back, then she will have to discuss it with her husband.'

'Seems reasonable enough,' Bob agreed. 'Fancy another quick half?'

Gwyneth sent Myfi out to the gate to look out for Mike while she collected their coats along with the gas masks. Many people had stopped carrying them, but after witnessing the destruction caused when her sister was killed by enemy action she didn't want to take any risks where the child was involved. Myfi came running in and tugged at her arm, pointing towards the open front door.

'Oh, Myfi, if only you could tell me that Mike was coming. Is it that hard?'

The child gave her a sad look before skipping off to greet Mike as he tapped on the open front door and called out a polite 'hello'.

The couple took a leisurely walk through the town and up to the large recreation ground, where the travelling fairground was set up in one corner. With Myfi holding their hands they looked like any other couple on a day out with their child.

'Why, this recreation ground is very pleasant,' Gwyneth said. 'We have nothing like this where I come from.'

They sat down on a bench not far from the funfair and watched as Myfi ran to play ball with two little girls whose parents sat nearby. Bob pointed to row upon row of vegetables growing on allotments where men were working on their plots. 'Before the war this was all green grass. There was a football pitch and an area for athletics. All kinds of events were held here and families would come for the day with a picnic and end up at the Trafalgar pub in the evening, where the children and women sat outside on a bench while the menfolk were inside. It was a good life.'

'You miss your mother?' Gwyneth asked, looking at his sad eyes.

'She was a good woman. I do miss not having her around. She was part of the community and she lives on in the memories of our friends. That's why Dad being close to Ruby is pleasing. Dad was a good friend of Ruby's late husband, Eddie, and Mum knew Ruby very well. It's as if they are both looking down on Dad and Ruby and giving them their blessing to be friends . . . perhaps even more given time,' he added, looking at Gwyneth with a gentle expression that showed his love for the pretty Welsh woman.

Gwyneth took a deep breath. If she didn't explain her complicated life to Mike now, she might never get another chance. 'Mike, there's something I've been meaning to tell you. It's about my life before I came to Erith. Mike, my name's not Gwyneth and . . . and I have a husband.'

Mike, who was about to take Gwyneth's hand and profess his love, turned away and looked into the distance. There was silence between them until he spoke. 'I had a feeling that someone as lovely as you would be spoken for. Just my luck,' he added bitterly.

Gwyneth reached out and touched his arm. 'I'm sorry, Mike. If things were only different . . .'

'Are you saying you no longer love him?' he asked with just a hint of hope in his voice. 'Where is he? Has he abandoned you and Myfi?'

Gwyneth started to explain what had happened. Mike's police training had taught him not to interrupt when someone was pouring out their troubles. When she finally finished her story by saying how Vera wouldn't take her in and how wonderfully kind Ruby had been, there was another silence as she reached for a handkerchief in her handbag.

Inside Mike was aching and if he'd been in the company of Gwyneth's husband, he knew he wouldn't have been able to control his temper. 'Should I still call you Gwyneth?' he asked, unsure what else he could say.

'Yes, please. That's if you don't mind and if you still want to talk to me after what I've told you,' she replied with a tremor in her soft voice.

'Good heavens, Gwyneth, I could never stop talking to you – or wanting to be in your company night and day,' he added with a shy smile. 'What I've been trying to say to you for a while now is that I love you, Gwyneth, and in time I had hoped you would come to love me and that . . . and that in the future we would be together for the rest of our days.'

'Mike, I'd be telling a lie if I said I didn't have feelings for you, but to all intents and purposes I'm a married woman. In my book that means till death do us part. I made my promise in front of God in our family chapel and I'll not go back on my word . . . whatever the consequences.'

Mike couldn't have loved her more than at that moment. 'I'll respect your wishes. Perhaps we could just be good friends?'

She gave a delighted laugh. 'Most definitely, Mike. I'd like that more than anything. Now, shall we take Myfi to the funfair? I don't know about you but I'm aching to have a go on the flying boats. They've always been a favourite.'

'Mine too,' Mike said, taking her hand as she stood up. 'There is one thing. Can you tell me the name of the prison where Idris Jones is incarcerated and when he is due to be released?'

'That's two things, Mike,' she said, 'but I've nothing to hide. The last I knew he would be out of prison in December. A week before Christmas. He was fond of writing to say it would be his Christmas present to find me and "sort me out" after I had given evidence against him.' She gave a shudder. 'To my knowledge he is still locked up in the large Maidstone prison in Kent. I could never enquire about him because, as I told you just now, I've been living as my sister since she was killed. I've not corresponded with him and he would still assume I'm living with her and my niece Myfi.' She shrugged her shoulders. 'Now, that's enough gloomy talk for one day. Let us go and have some fun and I'd like to taste the roasted chestnuts. They smell delicious.'

Mike was thoughtful as he followed Gwyneth and Myfi towards the fairground.

Freda was more than a little nervous as she entered the dance hall. Even wearing her new dress she felt like a fish out of water. Where were Maisie and Sarah when she needed them? she thought with a wry grin. It was so much easier to act self-assured and a little more grown-up with her chums by her side.

'Hi, doll, we're over here,' Hank called from a table halfway down the crowded hall. The band was playing a jazzed-up version of a Christmas carol, which to Freda's ears didn't sound right. The dance seemed so brash and loud and not what she was used to at all. She made her way over to where he was lounging back on a chair with three other American soldiers and their partners.

Hank stood up and gave her a hard kiss on her lips that left her breathless as she took his seat. 'You know

Chuck and the guys and these are their girls. Sorry, ladies, I'm bad with names.'

'A good job too in case you talk in your sleep,' a sharp-faced woman who introduced herself as Ena retorted. One of the men kicked her under the table. 'Ouch! I'm only speaking as I find,' she said, emptying her glass and holding it out to Hank. 'I'll have another gin, thanks.'

'Freda?' Hank asked as he collected empty glasses.

'Lemonade for me, please,' which made the girls giggle a tad unkindly. 'I have an early start tomorrow,' she explained politely. 'I need to keep a clear head.'

'What exactly is it you do?' one of the women asked as the men headed towards the crowded bar.

'My job? Oh, I work at Woolworths in Erith,' she said proudly.

The women tittered and nudged each other as they passed around a packet of cigarettes, which Freda refused.

'What's so funny?' Freda asked, just a little hurt.

Ena shrugged her shoulders. 'It's not my idea of fun standing on a shop floor all day long and being told what to do by supervisors.'

'The money's not so good either,' another woman added.

'You should come and join us at the munitions factory in Woolwich. We have a right laugh, plus we get to see some real men,' added the third, as she eyed Freda up and down. 'We also earn enough for decent clothes too rather than hand-me-downs.'

Freda felt indignant. 'I can afford clothes but there's a war on and only so many coupons can be spared for new dresses. It's much better to make your own as well as make do and mend.'

The women howled with laughter. 'You don't need coupons when you know the right people,' Ena said with a wink to her mates.

'And know how to pay for them,' another responded slyly.

Freda knew she was out of her depth. These were not the kind of women she was used to socializing with. She smiled politely and wished for Hank to rejoin the group. However, he was deep in conversation with people at the bar and didn't seem to be in much hurry to return to her side.

'How long have you been seeing Hank?' Ena asked, blowing smoke in Freda's direction that made her cough.

'I met him when he came to my rescue early in the summer,' she smiled, thinking how he had helped lift her from the pile of compost and then arranged to fix her bike. 'We've met on and off when he's not been on duty.'

The woman who'd made the sly comments nudged Ena. 'D'yer hear that, Ena? Next she'll be telling us that Hank's sweet on her and set to walk her up the aisle.'

The women all burst out laughing as one added, 'With his own kids as bridesmaids,' which caused further merriment.

'Are you sure you're not getting him mixed up with Chuck? I know he showed my friend, Sarah, some photographs of his wife and family.' That must be it, she thought, trying hard to remain friendly with these loud females.

Ena cackled loudly and reached for a leather wallet

that lay in the middle of the table. Freda recognized it as belonging to Hank. Opening it, Ena pulled out half a dozen snaps of a smiling woman holding a baby with young children holding on to her legs. In another Hank smiled back at the photographer in his uniform with an arm around the woman, who was kissing his cheek. Freda picked up the pictures and looked closely. There was no doubt that it was Hank and the way he held the woman and the look of adoration in her eyes proved she wasn't just a friend or family member. For a few seconds Freda felt as though her heart had been ripped from her chest. Hadn't she lain in her bed dreaming of the handsome American and even imagining that, come the end of the war, she may accompany him back to America to visit his family? She half snorted to herself. His wife would love that!

Freda looked up to see the three women watching her intently. They were like a group of hyenas about to jump on their prey. Placing the photographs back in the wallet, Freda smiled at the women as she rose to her feet and shrugged her shoulders. 'Such lovely pictures. I must write to his wife and compliment her on her choice of husband and tell her how he is enjoying your company. Now, if you will excuse me, I must be leaving. I'm up at the crack of dawn to collect my motorbike and ride to the East End of London with special orders for the Fire Service. We Woolworths girls are patriotic through and through. You won't find us carrying on with other women's husbands and offering our . . . let me think . . . yes, offering our services to any man in uniform. Good evening, ladies.'

She swept from the table, a smile fixed to her face, and headed towards the entrance of the dance hall as the American Air Force dance band struck up the popular tune 'In the Mood'.

'Wait up, doll, where are you off to?' Hank said as he caught up with Freda at the door and grabbed her arm.

Freda pulled herself free and turned to face him. What was the point in talking to the man? At least she had found out the truth before committing to him and then never being able to forgive herself. She looked him up and down and slowly smiled. Hank took this to mean she was pleased to see him and moved in to pull her into his arms. Freda raised her knee sharply and he doubled up in pain.

'Sorry, Hank. I'm no longer in the mood,' she smiled before walking away with her head held high. She'd known that one day the self-defence trick Maisie had taught her would come in handy.

Maisie ripped open the envelope before sitting on her bed to read what her friend, Sarah, had to say. The days hung heavy since she'd left Erith to live with her mother-in-law in Wiltshire. Maisie counted every second, every minute and every hour of each new day before striking a line through on her Woolworths calendar. Each morning she woke hoping to see wintery weather from the window of her bedroom for then it would be time for her baby to arrive and she could return to Erith in time for Christmas. It didn't help that September had been as hot and sultry as summer and the heat had dragged on into

October, where leaves were slow to drop from the trees and flowers still bloomed in the formal gardens. On the Carlisle family's estate land girls and old farm hands still worked the fields in their shirtsleeves. Maisie had never felt so lonely in her life.

It seemed an age since Sarah had made her visit to Wiltshire and Maisie missed their chats and being able to confide in her chums. Somehow writing down her words was not the same. She scanned the pages of news from home. Maureen was living with Vera; that did make her chuckle. Freda had split with her handsome Yank and had been inconsolable for some days, although she was soon philosophical once Ruby had gone on and on about how many fish there were in the sea. Sarah mentioned Freda's parting shot to Hank and Maisie snorted out loud, but her laughter soon turned to tears. She missed her friends so much. Perhaps it was time to invite the girls for another visit. There was room for Betty and Ruby as well. It would be lovely to see them. She quickly scribbled a note, feeling much better in herself as she thought of her chums coming for a visit. Maisie sealed the envelope and wrote Sarah's address on the front. There was just time to take a slow walk to the village and catch the last post.

20

December 1942

Freda waited patiently as Sarah placed a customer's purchase in a brown paper bag and counted the change into her hand before thanking her for visiting Woolworths. 'Has something happened?' Sarah asked, seeing Freda's agitated face.

'Here's a letter for you. It was delivered just as I was leaving the house. I thought you'd want to read it,' she said, pulling an envelope from the pocket of her Woolworths uniform.

Sarah's face fell as she took the letter from her friend and tore it open. She gave an audible sigh of relief when she saw it was from Maisie. 'I thought . . . Oh, you know what I thought!'

'That it was from Alan? I'm sorry. I should have said it was from Maisie. I received one too. She's not very happy,' Freda said with a worried look on her face.

After scanning the page Sarah nodded in agreement. 'She's terribly lonely and doesn't fit in with the locals, and is petrified about the birth of her baby. She wants me to visit. Does she say the same to you?'

'No, she's given me some advice about men. Told me I did the right thing when I found out about Hank and if it had been her, she'd have blackened his eye as well,' Freda grinned. 'But seriously, I'd be frightened too after seeing what you went through.'

'Oh, Freda, please believe me, when it is time for you to have your children you will soon forget everything apart from the wonderful new life you'll hold in your arms.'

Freda sighed. 'I'm sure I will, but will Maisie? I feel she needs to be with David and her friends, don't you? I wonder if Betty would allow us to take a couple of days off and visit Maisie before the baby arrives . . . I'll ask her as soon the opportunity arises.'

Sarah wasn't so sure their boss would agree to them taking time off work. She served another customer and returned to where her friend was tidying a display of jigsaw puzzles at the end of the counter. 'I don't know if she can free us this close to Christmas. We are classed as senior staff and to have both of us take time off work together will leave a big hole in the staff work rota.'

'It doesn't hurt to ask,' Freda said, although she realized that Sarah was right in what she said. 'I thought it would be nice to be with Maisie so the three of us could celebrate my birthday together. With no news from Lenny in the past few weeks I feel as though everyone is deserting me.'

'No news is good news, Freda,' Sarah said sympathetically. 'I don't suppose a letter from a ship somewhere overseas is as easy to deliver as one we send to Maisie.'

'I suppose not,' Freda said, 'but it does feel pretty tame to be a year older and not celebrating the day. At least we can go to the pub and perhaps have fish and chips for supper. I'll settle for that. All the same, I'll speak to Gwyneth to see if she will cover a couple of our shifts and then Betty can't really say no, can she?'

Sarah nodded thoughtfully as she watched her friend pick up a box of books and head to the other end of the counter to continue laying out stock. Freda deserved a special treat for her birthday and an idea had just come into her head. She would have to get her skates on if her plan was to work, as the young woman's birthday was in three days' time. If only Alan was here to help. She'd have to ask Maisie's husband, David, he would know what to do.

'Are you ready, my love?' Douglas asked as he tucked Betty's arm through his, before inserting a key into the lock of an impressive double-fronted Victorian house just off the main thoroughfare that ran through Bexleyheath. Betty had visited the house on numerous occasions and had grown to love the home that Douglas had purchased after moving to the area with two young daughters upon the death of his wife.

'I'm as ready as I'll ever be,' Betty said with trepidation as she stepped over the threshold into the high-ceilinged hall. Even on a cold December day the house was warm and inviting. Douglas took her coat and placed it on one of the hooks on an ornate hallstand.

'Are you sure you don't want me to go in first and inform the girls?'

Betty laughed quietly and took his hand in hers. 'Douglas, my dear, I love Clemmie and Dorothy to distraction and I don't believe for one minute that they hate me, so why should this visit be any different to when I've come to see them in the past? Now, give me that bag as I have presents to hand out.'

Douglas's mouth twitched as he handed a large shopping bag to Betty. 'Presents will do it every time. I'm afraid my two daughters are more than a little spoilt.'

'No one would blame you, Douglas. It must be hard for two young girls growing up without their mother,' she said before opening the door to the front room and entering to greet his daughters. 'Clemmie, Dorothy,' she said with delight as the two girls rushed to greet her with hugs and kisses. 'Whatever have I done to deserve such a welcome?'

Dorothy, the younger by four years, eyed the bag that Betty had placed on the floor beside her. 'Daddy said you were coming for something special. We decided it must be Christmas presents as our tree desperately needs presents to go underneath it,' she said persuasively, glancing to where a tall tree sat in a tub in the large bay window waiting to be dressed.

'My goodness, it is certainly magnificent,' Betty said, going to admire the tree and breathe in the aroma of fresh pine needles. 'I do believe it is larger than the one we have in the window at Woolworths.'

'Do you own Woolworths?' Dorothy asked in awe, still not taking her eyes off Betty's bag.

'Don't be silly, Dorothy, Betty just works in one of the shops. Don't you?'

Betty nodded. If she was unsure of either of Douglas's daughters, it was eleven-year-old Clemmie, who could be extremely blunt in her speech and not as open as her younger sister.

'Yes, that is right, I manage the Erith store. That means I'm in charge,' she said to Dorothy, who looked puzzled.

'Our mother owned hundreds of shops,' Clemmie said proudly, looking to a portrait that hung over the fire-place. She had the look of her mother with her thin face, green eyes and turned-up fine nose. Clemmie had inherited more than her mother Clementine's name.

'Now that's not strictly true, darling, and you know it. Our Clemmie tends to exaggerate at times,' Douglas said as he ruffled the girl's fair hair. 'Clementine's family owned a chain of haberdashers that was patronized by the late queen. It was her grandfather's business and a long time ago, as Clemmie knows only too well. I fear she likes to dine out on that story.'

Dorothy sidled up to where Betty had sat down and leant on her lap. 'I'd rather tell my friends that I know a lady who is in charge of Woolworths,' she said proudly.

Betty laughed and thought that she'd at least won over one of Douglas's adorable daughters.

There was a polite tap on the door before an elderly lady walked in. 'I'll be off now, if that's all right with you,

Mr Billington? The dinner's in the oven and everything is tidy and tickety-boo.'

Betty smiled to herself. She recognized the saying as one that Alan Gilbert often used. For a moment she wondered if he was safe and gave a silent prayer that her circle of friends would make it through the war. She never wanted anyone to go through what she had when she lost her Charlie in the last war. There again, she now had Douglas thanks to the men's friendship.

'Thank you, Cissie, I'll walk you to your door. It looks as though we have another fog coming in and we don't want you losing your way,' Douglas said. 'I'll not be long, then we have something to tell you both,' he said, smiling at his daughters and giving Betty a tender look.

'No, I'll be fine. You stay in the warm with your family. I'm only a few streets away.'

Douglas protested and ushered the woman to where she'd left her coat.

'We have a pie for our dinner. Cissie made it specially for tonight,' Dorothy said.

'It's probably full of dead bodies,' Clemmie said spitefully. 'Did you know Daddy works with dead people?'

Dorothy looked fearfully at her sister. 'It's not true, is it?' she pleaded.

Betty was annoyed that the elder girl was both upsetting her sister and trying to provoke a response from her. 'My goodness, nothing could be further from the truth. Your daddy has a responsible job where he looks after the families of people who have gone to heaven. He helps them say goodbye in a fitting manner. There's nothing to be afraid of,' she said, putting an arm around the younger daughter, who looked to be on the verge of tears. 'As for Cissie's pie, I am led to believe it is full of chicken and vegetables and I for one am looking forward to a big slice,' she smiled to the little girl.

Dorothy thought for a while then asked, 'Are you going to be our mummy?'

Before Betty could utter one word Clemmie stamped her foot in annoyance and pointed at the portrait. 'How can she be? We have a mummy and we don't need another.'

Betty froze. She had no idea that Clemmie felt this way. The news that she and Douglas would impart this evening would not go down well with one of the girls.

As she thought carefully of how she would reply, the quiet wail of an air-raid siren broke through the silence in the front room. As the sound grew louder and louder Betty could hear other sirens join in and a cold chill ran up her spine. She was responsible for these two young girls until Douglas returned, but silently thanked the enemy for getting her out of having to answer his daughter's question. She preferred to wait until he was by her side. 'Come along, girls, you must show me to your shelter and tell me what needs to be done.' She ignored Clemmie's sulking face and headed to the kitchen, first picking up the bag she'd brought with her. She turned off the gas, wondering if the pie would spoil, then took a torch that was hanging on a hook on the back door. 'Hurry up and put your coats on, girls!'

'It's over here,' Dorothy said, directing the torch to the entrance of the Anderson shelter as beams of light pierced the night sky, searching for the enemy bombers

ELAINE EVEREST

as they approached from the Kent coast. In the distance could be heard the sound of ack-ack guns and Betty knew the planes were getting closer.

'Those big searchlights are up on Dartford Heath,' Clemmie said, slipping her hand into Betty's as they went down the steps into the underground shelter. 'Daddy took us to see them. They're very large.'

'They are,' Betty agreed, 'and there are many of them dotted around the area. They are there to make sure we are kept safe,' she added, reassuring the two young children.

Clemmie showed Betty where a tin of candles was kept as well as matches wrapped in a piece of oilcloth to keep them dry. Both the children had carried a blanket apiece, which they wrapped around themselves as they settled on a bench, while Betty lit a small lamp that gave off a little warmth within minutes.

'Now, what shall we do to keep ourselves busy?' she asked.

'We could look in your bag to see what you brought for us,' Dorothy suggested cheekily.

Betty laughed and delved into the bag, giving both the girls a brown-paper parcel. 'You can have these now and perhaps open the other ones later.'

Both girls tore the wrapping from their gifts.

'Books!' they both exclaimed.

'These were the books I read when I was a little girl,' Betty said. 'I hope you will enjoy them as much as I did. I know they are going to a good home.'

'These were yours?' Clemmie asked shyly as she ran

360

her fingers over the cover of *Little Women*. 'We've never been given books as presents before.'

'Mine is *The Tale of . . . P . . .* Can you help me?' Dorothy asked.

'*The Tale of Peter Rabbit*. This was my first book and one I adore as the paintings of the little rabbit family are so sweet.'

'I'm not very good at reading,' Dorothy said, 'but I do like pictures. Will you help me to read it, please?'

Betty frowned. The child was old enough to be able to read simple words. She'd make a point of helping her. 'Of course I will, but perhaps when we have better lighting so you can follow the pictures of Peter and the other bunnies. Shall we start with *Little Women*?'

The girls agreed and snuggled next to Betty as she began to read. '*Christmas won't be Christmas without any presents . . .*'

Soon they were engrossed in the story and they all jumped as the door to the shelter was pulled open. 'Well, well, well, what do we have here?' Douglas asked as he joined them.

'Betty is reading us a story,' Dorothy explained. 'These were her books and she's given them to us. I have one about a rabbit called Peter and Clemmie's is about sisters . . . just like us. It's very sad as they don't have any Christmas presents and their daddy is away at war.'

Douglas joined them on the bench, leaning his arm along the back of the wooden seat. 'Can I listen for a while? The planes have gone over so I would think the all-clear will sound soon. But we can listen to some more of the story.'

Betty continued reading aloud by the light of the hurricane lamp. Douglas's finger stroked her neck as his daughters listened enraptured by the story of another family living in another war across the other side of the world.

'This is nice,' Clemmie said as she kissed Betty's cheek. 'Thank you and I'm sorry I was rude to you earlier.'

Betty felt a lump form in her throat. Everything she had ever dreamt of was here in this Anderson shelter. She was truly a fortunate woman.

Sarah replaced the receiver of the telephone and gave a sigh of relief. Betty had given her a few minutes to make her telephone call after Sarah explained how she'd like to arrange a birthday surprise for Freda and had left her alone to give her privacy.

Not finding David Carlisle at home the night before, she wasn't sure what to do until she remembered she had his office telephone number in case someone at number thirteen needed him in an emergency. The emergency being his wife, Maisie, and the imminent birth of their child. David had never explained his RAF job to his friends and they all knew that in wartime it was important not to pry. Sarah knew he was often in London and hoped that he would be able to help her with her plan. True to form, David promised to drop by later that evening and let her know if he had succeeded with her request.

Now for her next problem . . . She hoped Betty would understand.

There was a discreet knock before Betty stuck her head around the door. 'Oh good, you are still here. I do need to have an urgent word with you.'

'I need a word with you as well,' Sarah said as she sat down in the chair that Betty indicated, 'that's if you can spare the time?'

'I'm sure I can. Now, I'm not going to be here for a few days and I need you and the other supervisors to cover for me. I know you can do my office work with your hands tied behind your back, but I would like you to sort out the work rota and give extra hours to the part-time staff. That would mean you as well. I wouldn't usually take time off so close to Christmas but this is important. Are you up to it?'

Sarah sighed inwardly as Betty told her the dates. That was when they'd promised to visit Maisie. There was no way that she and Freda could ask for time off now. 'Yes, Betty, you can rely on me and I would think that the girls would be grateful of the extra hours before Christmas. Thank goodness we held the old service-men's party earlier this year.' She spent half an hour going over work details before rising to her feet to return to the shop floor.

'Was there something you wanted to speak to me about?' Betty asked.

'Oh, erm . . . yes,' Sarah mumbled, thinking hard for something to say. She couldn't say how they'd wanted to visit Maisie. Not after Betty had said she was taking time off work – which did sound strange for someone who hardly ever spent time away from Woolworths. 'Nan said to invite you and Douglas to spend Christmas Day with us, and Maureen is hoping to be back in her house and we will all be going to her in the evening for a party. You will come, won't you?'

'I'd be delighted and I'm positive that Douglas will agree. However, there is a small problem. We will have his daughters with us. Would it be too much of an imposition to bring them along? We won't come empty-handed.'

'Of course, the more the merrier, you know that. I'll let Nan know.'

'What about Alan, will he be home for Christmas?'

'I don't think so. He did say he'd try, but there's no knowing with this war so I'll settle for a letter this year. Who knows, the war may be over by next Christmas.'

'Let's hope so,' Betty said with a beaming smile. 'At least we can enjoy this year without too many worries. In fact, we have much to be grateful for.'

Sarah left the office wondering what was making her boss so happy.

'What are you three plotting? You're up to something with your heads together whispering like that,' Ruby said as she caught Bob, Mike and her son, George, out in her back garden. 'Why, it's blooming cold out here. Come inside and chat, why don't you?' she said, trying to shoo them indoors.

'Mum, we're just trying to arrange about decorating Maureen's house,' George replied. 'We've only got a week before Christmas and there are two rooms to paper and three that need painting. We have the wallpaper and enough paint, thanks to Misson's ironmongers seeing us right. It's just the manpower we need now and to not let Maureen know what we are up to.'

'You know Maureen's under the impression she can move in this weekend, don't you? You did a good job chasing up that landlord of hers, so now she thinks she's all but home and dry. You'd best put your thinking caps on if you don't want to spoil her surprise. Why not ask David to give you a hand. He's in the kitchen chatting to our Sarah. She's excited about something or other.'

Bob watched Ruby return to the house and blew on his hands before rubbing them together. 'Gentlemen, we have a problem. I suggest we tell Maureen there has been a burst pipe and she can't move in until Christmas Eve. It means upsetting her, as she will have to live with Vera for another week. Brrr, we are going to freeze to death if we don't go inside soon. There's a limit to how long we can say we are out here having a cigarette.'

George agreed. 'I must head home or Irene will worry. By the way, Bob, I had a letter from our Pat. She's none too pleased that I'd spoken to that farmer, Jago, with my concerns and she's going to write to Mum. It seems he's told Pat that her family should come first and told her to come home to Erith.'

'I'll keep my head down when the postman delivers. Thanks for mentioning it, George. Perhaps we should warn Ruby?'

'No. She agrees that Pat should be home with her husband and those boys should have gainful employment, so let's just leave things be until our Pat's letter arrives. Now, I'll be leaving you to talk to Maureen. I suggest the burst pipe is in the kitchen. That way we'll all have the same story.'

Mike followed the two men into the house. He'd not added much to the conversation as he'd been thinking of how he could invite Gwyneth out for the afternoon the following day. It was her half-day and he too had the day off. If he offered to work the rest of the day at Maureen's, then he wouldn't feel guilty about taking a few hours off. However, he was nervous as Gwyneth had made it clear she was not interested in any other men as she took her wedding vows seriously, even though her husband, Idris, was a bully and a wife beater. Which reminded him that he had a call to make to Maidstone prison. He'd do it from the police station later this evening when he went on duty.

Mike walked into the kitchen to find Gwyneth and Sarah chatting with David. 'You look happy. Have you heard from Alan?' he asked.

'No, not since he said it was unlikely he'd be home for Christmas,' she replied, her smile slipping slightly. 'It's Freda's birthday tomorrow and David has helped me to arrange a surprise for her.' She waved three tickets in the air. 'We have tickets to see *The Dancing Years* at the Adelphi Theatre in London tomorrow afternoon. It's perfect as it's our half-day at work and he managed to get three tickets so Gwyneth can come too. She's never seen a London show.'

Gwyneth's eyes shone. 'And I will be able to see Ivor Novello. That has been a dream of mine for so long,' she sighed.

Mike agreed it would be a wonderful present for Freda but inside he was screaming. Would he never get to spend time alone with the woman he held so dear? He would have to do something or Gwyneth would slip through his hands and never be part of his life.

'Wake up, sleepy head, we have a busy day ahead,' Sarah said as she pulled back the curtains, letting the winter sun into the bedroom that the friends shared. With Alan away the girls had decided that they would again share a room along with Georgie, allowing Gwyneth a room with her daughter.

'It's a bit early, isn't it?' Freda yawned.

'Not when it's your birthday and you have presents to open before we head off to work,' Sarah replied, lifting Georgina onto the bed, whereupon she climbed onto her favourite auntie and covered her face in sticky kisses.

'Urgh! Get off, Georgie. Whatever have you been eating?'

'Tose,' the little girl giggled.

'Nan made her toast and used some of the jam she made. There's more on Georgie's face than went into her mouth.'

'What a waste of sugar,' Freda said, reaching for her dressing gown and putting her feet into her slippers, thinking how they'd all given up their sugar allowance so that jam could be made for future treats. 'Any snow?'

'No sign and I doubt we'll have any this Christmas. Nan reckons it'll be so foggy Father Christmas may lose his way,' Sarah said, forgetting that her daughter was listening which resulted in the little girl starting to cry. 'I'm so sorry, my love. Mummy was only joking. Didn't he tell you he would be visiting you with presents when we went to see him in Woolwich?'

The child's tears stopped as she thought about what her mother had just said. 'Pwesents?' she beamed.

'That child of yours seems to have learnt to say the right words. Toast and presents sound perfect. What else is there to say?' Freda laughed.

'And yours are waiting downstairs along with toast and jam so get your skates on, birthday girl,' Sarah said, kissing her friend on the cheek and retrieving her daughter, who had started to snuggle down to sleep on Freda's pillow.

'Happy birthday,' everyone declared as Freda arrived downstairs. Myfi stepped forward and shyly handed Freda a home-made card.

'She made it herself,' Gwyneth explained proudly. 'This is from the both of us,' she said, handing over a parcel. 'It's not much but it is made with love and a big thank you for becoming a good friend.'

Freda smiled her thanks and carefully opened the brown-paper parcel. The paper would be stored away by Ruby and reused at some time, as would the string. 'My goodness, this is beautiful,' Freda said as she held up a navy-blue cardigan with delicate flowers embroidered down each side of the button band. 'Whenever did you find time to make this without me seeing you?'

Gwyneth laughed, delighted that Freda liked her present. 'Remember all those times we had different lunch hours and tea breaks? I'd asked Betty if she would change the rota so that I could knit at work and you wouldn't notice.'

'Talking of Betty, here is her gift. She sends her apologies that she isn't here to celebrate your special birthday,' Sarah added, handing Freda a small box and a card.

Freda's hands shook as she opened the exquisite box to reveal a small gold locket on a chain. 'Oh, isn't this wonderful?' she said through tears that had started to form in her eyes.

Ruby came through from the kitchen carrying a tray, which she placed on the table. 'Have some breakfast,' she said, 'before the toast gets cold,' and then wrapped her arms around the young woman and gave her a big kiss. 'Happy twenty-first birthday, my love. This is from me,' she said, reaching over to the table and retrieving another small box.

Freda frowned as she picked at the string and carefully uncovered a small ring box. 'What . . . ?' she asked as a small silver band with a single red stone shone from inside the velvet box.

'You're like one of my family and on a special day family should have special presents. My Eddie gave this to me when we first started courting. It's not a proper ruby but the sentiment was there all the same. I want you to have the ring as I know you'll treasure it always.'

The threatening tears did arrive at that point and it took a little while for Freda to compose herself after checking that Sarah did not mind that her nan had passed something to her that should have stayed within the family.

'The women will all get something when the time comes for me to leave this earth. But this is for you and it's given with our blessings.'

Freda tucked into her breakfast while she opened her cards and whooped in delight, as there was one from her brother Lenny. 'He says he has leave and should be with us by Christmas Day and is bringing a friend.' Her face dropped as she added, 'But where can he stay?'

'Bob has a room going begging. I reckon they will be welcome there and everyone will be here for their Christmas dinner. The more the merrier.'

There was a present from Maisie and David that had been left the night before. The women all gasped at the pretty powder compact and laughed at Maisie's note that Freda should wash her face before using the powder as her cheeks were often smeared with grease after riding her bike.

'I'd better get myself dressed for work,' Freda said as she rose from the table. 'With Betty off we need to be there on time or the customers will complain.'

'You've not opened this,' Sarah said, holding out a flat package.

'I'm such a lucky person to have good friends like you all,' she said as she opened the gift. 'Oh my, this is so pretty,' she added as she folded back the feather-light tissue to disclose a pretty scarf. 'Look at the colours!'

'It's hand-painted silk. Why not try it on?'

Freda chuckled as she unfolded the scarf. 'It will brighten up my dressing gown. Whatever is this . . . ?' she said with a start as three pieces of card fell to the ground and were retrieved by Myfi, who held them out to Freda.

'Tickets for the theatre . . . and for this afternoon? What a wonderful day!'

'We thought you'd like that,' Sarah smiled. 'The three of us need to get off work pretty smartish so we don't miss the train to London. Happy birthday, Freda.'

21

Maisie heaved herself out of bed and forced her swollen feet into the practical slippers that her mother-in-law had given her. The dressing gown she pulled around her shoulders had been David's from when he still lived at home with his parents. Even that no longer reached around her swollen stomach. Her back ached, she couldn't be bothered to make up her face every day, and her hair felt greasy and unattractive. As much as she wanted this baby, she hated what pregnancy had done to her and wished more than anything that Sarah would arrive on her promised visit.

Taking herself downstairs, leaning heavily on the ornate handrail, she headed for the breakfast room, following the tantalizing aroma of bacon.

'There you are, Maisie dear. We thought you were having a lie-in this morning before your appointment with Doctor Joseph. I've just this minute asked Smith to prepare a tray for you in your room,' her mother-in-law said with a warm smile.

'I'd rather be up on me feet,' Maisie said, going to the sideboard, where cooked food was being kept warm under silver covers. Lifting a lid, she grimaced as she spotted devilled kidneys and tried not to heave. 'The baby's been on the move most of the night. I swear it's gonna be a tap dancer.' She found bacon and scrambled eggs and filled her plate, adding a sausage and two slices of toasted white bread.

'Still eating for two, I see,' her father-in-law observed with a smile. 'He's going to come out fighting fit.'

'I 'ope so,' Maisie grinned. She liked her in-laws immensely but still felt like a fish out of water. She just didn't fit into their country life. 'Has the post come yet?' she asked, hoping that there was something from her friends. If Sarah didn't hurry up, she'd not be here in time for the birth. David had permission from the Air Force department where he worked to head to his parents' home the moment he heard his wife was in labour. She just hoped there wasn't an invasion or something that would stop him being there to greet his first child.

Mrs Carlisle reached over to a silver tray that lay on the dining table. 'Here you are, Maisie. Two for you today.'

Maisie accepted the envelopes, immediately recognizing both Freda and Sarah's handwriting. She tore open Freda's first, wanting to know if she liked the present that she'd chosen for her friend's birthday. David had taken her out to Chippenham for lunch on his last visit and they'd chosen the gift together. Even then she'd begged David to take her home to Erith but he'd refused, pointing out that she only had a matter of two weeks before their child was born and then, after the required lying-in time, which David's mother had said should be at least one month, they could consider taking Maisie home to Erith. For Maisie it was far too long and she despaired of ever seeing the town and the people she loved again. At least Sarah's letter would confirm she was on her way to see her friend.

She frowned as she read Freda's letter. The young woman enthused about her present, which pleased Maisie, but in the next sentence she told of going to London with Sarah and Gwyneth to see a musical show in the West End. Maisie could feel the tears flowing down her cheeks. Not only had she wanted to see Ivor Novello in the musical, but it also seemed that Gwyneth had taken her place in the trio of friends.

'Why, Maisie, my dear, whatever is wrong? Has there been bad news?' her mother-in-law asked, coming round the table to comfort her daughter-in-law.

'No, not really, I'm just being a daft bugger and missing everyone,' she said, trying to compose herself.

'Why not read your other letter and then take a rest? Your appointment with Doctor Joseph isn't for two hours.'

I'm sick of resting, Maisie wanted to scream, but instead she smiled wanly at the older woman. 'I'm all right, honest. It's just knowing I'm missing out on me mates having fun,' she said, trying to dismiss the thought that she was no longer part of the group who worked at Woolworths and spent their lives together. Picking up Sarah's letter, she prayed that it was good news. She scanned the single page and gasped. Her friend couldn't visit as Betty was taking time off from her job and Sarah had to work extra hours.

'Is everything all right, dear?'

Maisie nodded and tried to stay calm. She had never known Betty to take time off work and to do so in the days leading up to Christmas was unthinkable. No, it must be that her friends had moved on and she was no longer important to them. Well, she wasn't going to take this lying down. If they wouldn't come to see her, she might as well go home and find out what was happening. She tucked into her breakfast as there was no knowing when she'd eat again and the one thing she needed to concentrate on was the child she was carrying. Going without food would not be good for her baby. They'd didn't say an expectant mother was eating for two for nothing. 'If you will excuse me, I'll go and get ready fer me appointment. Don't expect me back for lunch, as I want to do some shopping. It'll probably be the last time I'm able to do so.' She kissed her mother and father-in-law and headed up to her room to carry out the plan that was formulating in her head.

'I'm still walking on air,' Freda said as she joined Sarah and Gwyneth in the staffroom for lunch. 'Who'd have thought I would see Ivor Novello and in the flesh? It's a dream come true.'

'The costumes and music were wonderful. It's a rare treat for me even to go to London, let alone to see a show,' Gwyneth sighed. 'It was like stepping into a palace, the building being so grand. I can't thank you enough for including me in the trip. I know that if Maisie had been here it would have been her ticket.'

'Nonsense,' Sarah said as she tucked into the Woolton pie in front of her. 'If Maisie had been able to join us, I'd have purchased four tickets. Now, eat your pie up before it gets cold. We are due back on the shop floor in ten minutes. I've never known it so busy. Betty will be back tomorrow and I don't want her saying we can't run Woolies in her absence.'

'There's no fear of that,' Freda grinned. 'You are a strict boss. I wouldn't mind betting they make you a manager one day.'

Sarah shook her head. 'No, once this war is over my Alan will be the only one working in Woolworths. I want to be at home looking after his children and taking care of our home. That's been our plan all along.'

'You'd give up all this to stay at home?' Freda asked with a puzzled expression on her face.

'It's what Alan wants. Who am I to argue?' Sarah said, getting to her feet to show the discussion was at an end. 'Now, are you off to the fire station, Freda?'

'Yes, I'm on duty this afternoon. I'll see you back home for tea, but if I'm going to be late I'll drive round and let Ruby know.'

'Take care, won't you? This fog is getting thicker,' Sarah said with a worried look on her face.

'Unless there's an emergency I'll be in the station, but if I go out on the motorbike, I promise I'll take care.'

'I'll stick the kettle on while you put the decorating tools in the shed and clean yourselves up,' George said to Bob and Mike as he let them into his mum's house in Alexandra Road. 'I'm glad to see the back of that job, I can tell you. I hope Maureen likes what we've done. Shall we give her the key this evening before I head off home? That's if I can see to cycle back to Crayford.'

'That's a grand idea,' Bob said. 'The poor woman is at her wits' end living with that Vera Munro. I've offered to let her have our back bedroom, but she wouldn't dream of putting us out.'

'Bob, is that you?' Ruby called from the front room, where she had her feet up listening to the wireless.

'I thought you was at the WVS this afternoon, love?' he said, putting his head around the door. 'I won't come in as I've still got my overalls on.'

'We shut up shop early as the fog was getting worse. Some of the ladies were worried about getting home. I'll come out and join you. I want a word with my George.'

George raised his eyebrows. 'Mum doesn't sound happy. I'll get the tea made,' he said, disappearing into the kitchen.

The three men had just finished cleaning themselves up when Ruby appeared. 'I've received a letter from our Pat. She's none too happy. She's coming home with the kiddies. I understand you've had a hand in this, George?'

Even at his age George knew when his mum was annoyed with him. 'I had a chat with Bob after what happened while you were down in Cornwall, and we thought it was best for them all to be at home rather than in danger. I have arranged for the boys to have apprenticeships at Vickers,' he added as an afterthought, trying to please Ruby.

Beside him Bob groaned. Ruby knew nothing of his escapade in the middle of the night.

'It looks as though you have some explaining to do,' Ruby said grimly to Bob.

Mike looked up at the clock. 'I'll go and collect Myfi from school and leave you to it,' he said, slipping from the room as Ruby continued to stare at Bob.

George started to rise to his feet. 'Stay where you are, George, I want to get to the bottom of this,' Ruby said, still without looking away from Bob.

Bob started to explain . . .

'Mrs Carlisle, I would say that you will be welcoming your child into this world by Christmas Day. I'll contact the maternity home and warn them there will be a Christmas baby. I'm not usually wrong.'

'I'd rather have the baby at home if it's all the same to you, Doctor,' Maisie said as she put her feet back into her shoes and pulled on her coat. 'I don't want the maternity home put to any trouble.' Especially as I don't plan to be here, she thought to herself.

'Don't worry yourself. The maternity home is first class. Only the best for the Carlisle family.'

Maisie nodded her head in thanks and left the surgery. She'd packed with care, aware that to take a suitcase would attract attention from the staff working in the Carlisle household and that they might alert her in-laws. Instead she had taken a large handbag in which she made sure to put the few garments she'd knitted for her baby. Maisie left a polite note on her pillow explaining that she was homesick and missed her husband and begged their forgiveness.

It was a short walk to the train station but Maisie found it hard going, having to stop to catch her breath on more than one occasion. Reaching the ticket office, she asked for a single ticket to Erith. The ticket clerk explained she would have to change trains in London and asked for the fare. Maisie searched in her handbag but could not find her purse. Panic struck as she rummaged in her shopping bag and realized that she'd left her purse behind and only had a few loose coppers in her pocket. 'I'm sorry, I've forgotten my money,' she said with a wobble in her voice.

The ticket clerk tutted disapprovingly and took back the ticket that was almost within Maisie's grasp. Watching it disappear was like watching her last hope of reaching Erith vanish. By now the letter she'd left would have been found. There was no chance she could hurry back to the Carlisles' grand house and hide it away while she looked for her purse. Walking from the station, she wondered what to do. Perhaps she'd dropped her purse at the doctor's surgery? Hurrying as fast as her body would allow, she entered the surgery and checked with the receptionist. The lady went to check and came back with a broad smile on her face. 'Mrs Carlisle, you are in luck. The doctor has taken it and will drop it at your home during his rounds.'

Maisie thanked the woman and walked from the surgery as if she had the weight of the world on her shoulders. Where could she go with just a few bob in her handbag? If she used the public telephone to call David, he would make her go back to his parents' home. She stepped out into the road and a loud horn startled her, causing her to fall onto her bottom on the pavement as the sound of tyres skidded past her limp frame.

A pair of strong hands helped her to her feet. 'Are you all right, love? It's not a good time to go bouncing about on the pavement, you know.'

Maisie blinked taking stock of how she felt. Apart from a sore backside she felt fine. As she looked up, a group of soldiers had climbed down from the lorry that had almost killed her and had crowded around, looking concerned. 'I'm fine but I could do with a helping hand,' she said before bursting into tears, much to the consternation of the sergeant in charge of his men.

'Give the little lady some air,' he said in a loud voice. 'Drummond, break out the flask. We need sweet tea and make it sharp!'

Gulping the hot tea, Maisie started to calm down. 'I'm sorry, I just wanted to get home and I've lost my purse.'

'Where are you going, love? We could drop you off,' the kindly sergeant offered.

'Kent. I'm going to Erith in Kent.'

There was a stunned silence before the soldiers all started speaking at once. She heard them mention Woolwich and then Maidstone. The sergeant held up his hand for silence. 'Miss, your luck is in. We are on our way to Woolwich, which is in south-east London, then on to Maidstone in Kent. We would be proud to give you a lift as long as . . .'

Maisie, whose hopes had raised skywards, frowned. 'As long as what?' She knew what soldiers could be like.

'As long as you don't tell a soul or we'll be clapped in irons for the duration. After all, you might be a spy.'

'It's a deal,' Maisie said, holding out her hand to the sergeant. Christmas had come early.

Myfi took Mike's hand as they walked along Manor Road. In the other she held a folded piece of paper. 'Is that a Christmas card you've painted?' he asked.

The little girl nodded and stopped to show him her creation.

'Why, that's very good, Myfi. Is this for your mummy?'

Myfi shook her head and pointed to him.

Mike felt a lump forming in his throat. 'For me? It's the best present I've ever had.' He'd become very fond of the child in the months since she'd moved to Erith with Gwyneth. His life would be so dull without them living just across the road.

They walked on in companionable silence with Myfi waving back to other children as they called out happy Christmas. Not one child seemed to notice that Myfi wasn't calling back. They accepted the little girl as she was without questioning why she didn't speak.

Turning into Alexandra Road, Myfi became excited and pointed across the street. The fog was starting to thicken up and Mike was thinking it would be a quiet evening on his shift as not even a cat burglar would think about stepping out into the freezing fog. Myfi tugged at his hand and pulled free as he looked up and spotted Gwyneth through the swirling fog on the other side of the road. It wasn't Gwyneth the child was excited to see, though, but Ruby's faithful dog, Nelson, running up and down outside the house barking for someone to let him indoors. The girl had become extremely fond of the dog and the pair could often be found curled up in the dog's basket or, on occasion, at the foot of her bed.

Myfi ran across the road to her four-legged friend as the animal raced towards her . . . at the very moment Freda turned into Alexandra Road on her motorbike. Mike watched as the scene turned into slow motion as Gwyneth screamed and dashed out to shove Myfi from in front of the wheels of the motorbike. The little girl fell to the ground against the dog, who'd been clipped by the motorbike's front wheel, and Mike saw Gwyneth flung into the air from the force of the motorbike. Freda did her utmost to steer the bike for a few yards before wobbling and crashing to the ground.

Around him Mike could see those he loved injured and in pain. Gwyneth lay motionless in the road as Myfi screamed over and over, 'Mummy, Mummy, Mummy . . .'

Maisie felt as though every part of her body was aching. As good as the soldiers were in giving her a comfortable seat next to the driver of the lorry and bolstering up her body with blankets and spare uniform jackets, she knew that she would ache until kingdom come once she was at journey's end. When setting out on her journey she hadn't given a thought to how long it would take, especially as the soldiers stopped so many times en route for Kent. Each time they approached a depot she was helped down from the lorry and left alone, then picked up around an hour later. She would drop off to sleep and wake with a start, asking where they were. Each time they were a little closer to Kent, although she had no idea how close as the names of the towns and villages they passed through were not familiar to her. The sergeant and driver were both parents and spoke lovingly of their families and told anecdotes of when their own children were born, much to the amusement of Maisie, who found their light-hearted banter kept her cheerful as she thought of the impending birth of her own child. She began to feel guilty that she had no doubt frightened her mother-in-law by disappearing, but tried to salve her conscience by the thought she'd left a letter saying she was going home to Erith.

Maisie must have dropped off again as she was woken by the driver of the lorry gently shaking her shoulders. Rubbing her eyes and yawning, she could see that dawn was breaking although it was misty and cold. She shivered and pulled a blanket closer around her.

'Miss, we're stopping for a bit of breakfast. Would you care to join us?'

Maisie licked her lips in anticipation of some food inside her stomach. She was so hungry it almost hurt. 'Sorry, I can't pay me way so I'd best wait here for yer. Ta all the same,' she smiled.

'It's our treat, miss. What are a few eggs and sausages between friends?'

'Then I'd be delighted ter join you. Thank you,' she said as the men gently helped her to the ground and escorted her to a greasy spoon cafe set in the middle of nowhere.

'Where are we?' Maisie asked as she took a seat at the table.

'We're in Surrey, love,' one of the soldiers said as he passed her a mug of strong tea. 'Kent is just up the road there.'

Ruby and Bob sat side by side not speaking a word as hospital life at Erith Cottage Hospital went on around them. Bob reached out and squeezed her hand, and not only did Ruby not reciprocate, she didn't even acknowledge his existence. Maureen hurried in and hugged her friend. 'Any news?' she asked, sitting down beside her.

Ruby shook her head, still unable to comprehend what had happened in the road outside of her house.

'Vera's come up trumps,' Maureen said. 'She's looking after Myfi and Georgina at your house. That young girl hasn't stopped talking although she's very distressed still. Who'd have thought it would take an accident for her to start speaking again?'

'It'll be the shock,' Bob said wisely.

Ruby nodded her head. 'It can do funny things to people. Myfi stopped talking when she witnessed her mother being killed in an air raid. So, when it looked as though Gwyneth had met the same fate, the shock reversed what had happened. Has the doctor been?'

Maureen was shocked by what Ruby had said, but now wasn't the time to be asking about the injured woman's business. 'He's given Myfi a clean bill of health apart from grazes on her knees, but Nelson's not so good,

Ruby. George took him up to the vet and they're keeping him in overnight.'

Ruby, who was known for being the strong one in the family and the person to rely on in times of trouble, started to shake before crying silently into her handkerchief.

Bob too blinked a few times and rubbed his eyes. 'He's a strong animal, Ruby, he'll pull through, don't you worry.'

'Bob's right. From all accounts Nelson's already eaten some food out of George's hand,' Maureen said, patting Ruby's back until she felt better.

'He's as much part of my family as the rest of you,' Ruby said, giving a glimmer of a smile. 'Good or bad, that dog's been by my side these past years.'

'Is there any news on Gwyneth and Freda yet?' Maureen asked.

'I'm okay,' a wobbly voice said as Freda appeared from a side door with her arm heavily bandaged. 'I've twisted something or other, but apart from a few scratches I'll live. I'm not so sure about my bike, though.'

'It can be fixed,' Bob said. 'I had a couple of sailors help me get it into my back garden before I came up to the hospital. They said they'll let the fire station know what's happened to you.'

'Sailors? You mean our Lenny and his mate have arrived?' Freda said, a big grin appearing on her face.

'He's home and very worried about you. I've told him to stay there and that you'll see him soon.'

'It'll be good to see the lad again,' Ruby smiled.

'That's good news at least. God knows we could do with some,' Maureen remarked.

'Which reminds me,' Bob said, reaching into his pocket and pulling out a door key. 'I believe this should be returned to you now you can move back into your home.'

Maureen's eyes sparkled. 'You mean . . . ?'

'I mean you'll find your home papered and painted courtesy of all your friends.'

'I can't believe it,' Maureen said, clutching the key to her chest. 'You can all come to me Christmas Day for that party. That is, all of those who aren't still in here,' she said, thinking of Gwyneth.

Mike paced the floor outside the ward. He couldn't rest until he'd seen for himself that Gwyneth would be all right. It had been hours since she'd been brought in by ambulance. He'd seen his dad for a few minutes and was pleased to hear that Freda was being taken home, although he too was concerned that Ruby's dog was injured. Perhaps he could have done something to stop the accident, but it happened so quickly. One minute young Myfi was holding his hand and the next she was in the middle of the road. It was like a nightmare that kept replaying inside his head.

'Mr Jackson?'

Mike jumped as a nurse called out his name. 'Yes?'

'You can go in and see your friend for a few minutes. She told us you were her next of kin otherwise it wouldn't be allowed. She is very sore but fortunately no bones broken,' the nurse smiled, seeing how concerned Mike looked.

'Thank goodness,' Mike said, following the nurse into the ward, where a Christmas tree sat at one end of the long room and a group of people were singing carols. She indicated he should go to a bed surrounded by screens.

'Mike?' Gwyneth said, reaching out to hold his hand. 'Thank you for coming to see me.'

'He's been outside since you were brought in,' the nurse smiled, pulling the screens closed so the couple had some privacy.

'That was very kind of you,' Gwyneth said as he took her hand and sat in a chair by the side of the bed.

'I wasn't going anywhere until I knew you would be all right. You know I think the world of you, Gwyneth.'

'And I think the world of you, Mike. I hope you didn't mind me telling the hospital staff you were my next of kin. I didn't want Idris involved in all of this. However, I've decided I must face up to my problems and will revert to my real surname. Hopefully Idris will not bother me . . . that's if he ever finds out where I live.'

'It's an honour to be your next of kin,' Mike smiled, kissing the back of the hand he still held tightly. 'About Idris, I have some news.'

Gwyneth's body tensed as she waited to hear what Mike had to say. Was he already in Erith looking for her? Her whole body ached and she felt sleepy after the long day, but she needed to know what Mike had to say.

'I made some enquiries – in an official capacity, you might say. My job has some perks,' he smiled gently. 'Gwyneth, Idris Jones is dead. There was a fight in the prison and he was killed. Felled by a single blow from all accounts.'

A look of shock passed over Gwyneth's face. 'I'm sorry, I don't understand . . .'

'My love, you are free from the man. He will never again make your life hell.'

Gwyneth frowned, trying to comprehend Mike's words. 'But . . . I don't understand . . . why wasn't I informed . . . ?'

'My darling, you are living as your sister. They couldn't trace you. What with the war, it just wasn't possible. No doubt in time the news would have caught up with you.'

'But now I'm . . .' Gwyneth paused. 'I'm free . . .' she said sleepily as her eyelids fluttered.

'You are free, Gwyneth . . . I mean Gladys,' he stammered.

'I'll always be Gwyneth. I prefer the name,' she whispered, fighting hard to stay awake. 'Mike, do you realize . . . ?'

'Yes, my love?'

'I'm free to love you and to be with you . . . What a wonderful Christmas it is . . .'

Mike kissed her lips gently as Gwyneth fell into a deep sleep, while in the ward the choir burst into a beautiful rendition of 'Silent Night'. 'Sleep, my love,' he whispered.

'You can drop me right here, lads,' Maisie said gratefully as the lorry pulled up outside Erith Woolworths.

The soldiers helped her down to the pavement and handed her bag to her before waving and calling good-bye. Maisie was a little wobbly on her feet after the long bumpy journey. She felt as though her back was break-ing. I'll soon have me feet up in me own home, she thought to herself.

Outside the store was the familiar sight of a choir from the local seamen's mission singing 'Away in a Manger' while an elderly man on crutches rattled a collection tin. She would have to borrow a few coins from Freda and give them to the men. It had become a tradition to do so ever since the day she went for her interview at Woolies and they were outside singing in the snow. No bloody snow this Christmas, she thought as she looked around her at the foggy damp day. It didn't feel like Christmas Eve.

Pushing open the double doors to Woolworths, she felt the warmth hit her and struggled through the crowds towards the staff entrance. Once she'd seen Sarah and the rest of her friends she'd ask for a hand to get home and then have a long soak in the bath. Sod the line David had painted around the inside of their bath to stop her using too much hot water. After that she'd go to bed and sleep until Christmas Day.

As she reached the staff door Maisie heard her name being called out and turned to see Betty Billington hurrying towards her.

'My goodness, Maisie, you're the last person I expected to see. Whatever are you doing here?'

Maisie could see that her boss looked different. There was a glow about her and she seemed even more self-assured. If that were possible. Mind you, she felt dog-tired so perhaps her mind was playing games with her. She wriggled a little as she felt something warm trickle down her legs and looked down to where she could see her shoes becoming wet. 'Good gawd! Me waters have broke!'

22

Christmas Eve

Sarah rushed down the staff staircase from Betty's office after a white-faced assistant banged on the door and told her that not only had their boss, Betty Billington, arrived unannounced for work, but now Maisie was downstairs and from what she'd been told was in labour. As it was Christmas Eve, today was the busiest day of the year at Woolworths.

She found Maisie sitting on a seat close to the door that led to the staff area with Betty kneeling by her side. 'Maisie, what on earth . . .' she started to say until her friend groaned in pain. 'How long have you been feeling like this?' she asked, nodding to a colleague to move the inquisitive shoppers away.

'Most of the night, but I was being bumped about in an army lorry.' She tried to laugh. 'Don't look at me like that, Sarah, I wanted ter be with me friends and if you weren't coming ter me, I decided to come home ter you all.'

Sarah felt ashamed that she'd let her friend down by

not visiting her, and even the telephone calls hadn't happened as often as they'd been promised, but Betty interrupted before she could open her mouth to apologize. 'Maisie, you can blame me for your friends not being with you when you needed them. I took time off work at the busiest time of the year and for that I'm sincerely sorry. Please don't fall out with your friends over this.'

Maisie shrugged as another pain ripped through her body. 'Ouch . . . I ain't one to bear a grudge but p'raps we should talk about it later or this'll be the first time a kid's been born in Woolies.'

'We need to fetch a doctor,' Betty suggested.

'No, we need to get Maisie to the Hainault maternity home. It's not far from here, but we have to find transport and pretty quickly,' Sarah said, looking around her for inspiration. Through the glass front of the Woolworths store she could see a horse and cart pulling up outside. It was Pat's husband, John, delivering vegetables, and Pat was sitting by his side. 'Aunty Pat!' Sarah called as she ran through the doors and out into the street. 'Aunty Pat, we need your help.'

Pat jumped down and hurried over to her niece and gave her a hug. 'It's lovely to see you, Sarah. What's the problem?'

Sarah quickly explained and before too long the women had helped Maisie onto the back of the cart with Sarah climbing on beside her.

'I'll track down David and let him know what has happened,' Betty called after them.

It was only as the horse trotted off up Pier Road towards the maternity home that Sarah realized that

Betty was now wearing a shiny new gold wedding ring on her left hand.

Ruby gazed around her small kitchen. There was hardly any space to work, what with the hessian sack of potatoes delivered by Pat's husband at the crack of dawn, along with a wooden crate containing all kinds of vegetables taking up space on the draining board. 'I need to get myself organized,' she muttered.

Rolling up her sleeves, she checked a saucepan half filled with peeled Brussel sprouts and tried to calculate how many people she'd be feeding the next day. She was used to having many people around her table, but it would take considerably more sprouts to feed this lot. 'This'll take a month of Sundays, Nelson,' she said aloud before realizing her faithful companion was not with her. She felt tears prick her eyes. 'Stop it, you silly mare,' she scolded herself. 'It's only a blooming dog.'

'Cooee, Mum! Are you home?' a voice called out as the front door opened.

Ruby wiped her eyes and called back, 'I'm in the kitchen, Pat.' She hoped her daughter wasn't here to cause a ruction about having to return home from Cornwall to her husband. She'd had enough upset these past couple of days and would tell her so as well.

'Blimey, Mum, what's all this?' Pat asked as she spied her mum at the kitchen sink. 'Are you feeding the five thousand?'

'It feels like it,' Ruby said. 'How are you?'

'I'm all right, Mum. I was going to come round and

talk to you, but with what happened just now I thought I'd pop in with the news sooner rather than later.'

'News? You're not going back down to Cornwall, are you?' Ruby asked, throwing her knife into the sink in annoyance.

'No, you can rest assured that I'm home for good. I shouldn't have got so hot under the collar over our George speaking to Jago like he did. He was right. The children were living like wild animals and the boys should not have been up to no good so late at night,' she sighed.

'From what I hear it was hardly "no good" as they was doing men's work in a way, helping people to escape the enemy.'

'Bob told you?'

'I insisted Bob and George spill the beans after your letter arrived. I'm none too pleased with Bob for not telling me at the time, but there again I'd probably have interfered too much,' she said, checking to see if the pile of sprouts had grown any bigger. It hadn't.

'Anyway, I'm home now and you should forgive Bob. He did what was right at the time.'

'I'll let him stew for a while longer,' Ruby grinned. 'It doesn't hurt a man to think he's in the dog house from time to time.' Her heart lurched as she said the word 'dog', making her think of Nelson lying at the vet's all on his own. 'Now, what else do you have to tell me? You burst in here like the house was on fire.'

'It's Maisie. She's back and she's in labour up at the Hainault. John and me gave her a lift on the cart. I left our Sarah with her until David arrives. Not that they'll let him in until she's had the kiddie.'

'Blimey! I thought she was safe and living the life of luxury with David's family. I wonder what has happened?'

'I've no idea, but I reckon the way she's going Maisie will be a mum by the end of today.'

'A Christmas Eve baby. That'll be nice,' Ruby smiled. 'That'll be something worth celebrating. Now, who the hell is that?' she said as someone banged on the door.

'I'll get it. Why don't you put the kettle on then have a rest? I'll make the tea when I've seen who is at the door.'

Vera staggered in with a heavy basket on her arm. 'Happy Christmas,' she called out. 'I've got a few things here for tomorrow. My granddaughter can't join me for Christmas dinner, so I thought I'd bring these to you so we can have them with our meal.' She pulled out a bottle of sherry, a large plum pudding and a chicken complete with its feathers. 'They were given to her by her boss. He appreciates what she does for him, you know,' she said smugly.

Ruby winked at her daughter before eyeing the vegetables waiting to be peeled. 'Roll up your sleeves, ladies, or we'll still be preparing dinner on Boxing Day and I for one would like to go to midnight mass this evening.'

'Now, mind your step. The edge of the pavement's along here somewhere. Whatever you do, don't let go of my arm or I'll lose the lot of you,' Bob said as he tapped ahead of him with a walking stick. 'Thank goodness I held on to this after that time Mike broke his ankle.'

'Never get rid of a thing, that's my motto. You never know when it'll come in handy,' Ruby said, gripping onto Bob's arm as if her life depended on it. 'Are you all right there, Maureen, Sarah?' she asked, looking over her shoulder to where her granddaughter and the girl's mother-in-law were following close behind. 'I've never known fog be so thick.'

'I'm right here, Nan. It was a good idea of yours to tie our coat belts together. At least if we get lost, we'll still be together. I thought we'd never get to church this evening with the weather so bad.'

'Although we might end up at the bottom of the Thames if we take a wrong turn,' Vera muttered.

'Blimey, you're a ray of sunshine,' Bob called out.

'Vera? I didn't know you were with us,' Ruby said, thanking God she hadn't been having a moan about her neighbour. The woman could be a fool to herself sometimes but at least they were talking again. Ruby didn't like a bad atmosphere, although at times it couldn't be avoided when Vera was leading off about something.

'I tagged on behind Maureen. I'm hanging on to her sleeve.'

'Well, mind your step or we'll all come a cropper.'

'Blimey,' Bob muttered, 'I feel like a tugboat pulling along a load of cackling women.'

'Mind what you say or you'll find yourself floundering alone with your stick when we cast you adrift,' Ruby told him with a laugh. 'Where do you think we are now? I hope we aren't by the river. The ships sound close letting off their foghorns like they are. It's really mournful.'

'I feel as though we've walked all the way to London my feet are aching so much,' Vera moaned out.

'It's kind of romantic and reminds me of that song about the fog and London,' Sarah said wistfully.

'Now that is a romantic song,' Maureen said.

'*A foggy day, in London town . . .*' a male voice crooned from somewhere behind them.

'What the . . . ? Who is that?' Ruby called out as the rich male voice continued to sing.

'Alan! Oh my God, it's Alan,' Sarah shrieked, reaching out to find her husband in the swirling fog.

Alan picked up his wife and swung her around as Maureen detached her from the chain of people who'd tied themselves together. There were times, even in a thick fog, that couples needed to be alone. She reached in her pocket and found her new door key and slipped it into her son's hand.

'We're nearly home. I take it you'll be staying with us tonight under the circumstances,' Ruby said to Maureen as Bob opened the gate to number thirteen.

'If that is all right with you, Ruby? It was good of Freda to look after the youngsters rather than come to church with us.'

'If truth be known, she's still exhausted after the accident and she insisted on going into work today, even though she's only got the one hand in use at the moment. Young Lenny and his mate are sitting with her as Mike went on duty after visiting Gwyneth this evening. But she wasn't too tired to put on a little lipstick and her best blouse after she met that friend of her brother's. Our Freda will be all right in time. One day she'll meet the right lad and settle down. It may take a few years but it will happen. Why, look at how things have turned out for Gwyneth and Mike.'

'That's a love story in the making,' Maureen said as she sighed, thinking of what Mike had explained to them all about Gwyneth's past. 'And now young Myfi has started to talk.'

'And she's making up for lost time. I swear she's not stopped chatting since the accident, as if nothing in her past had happened . . . Who's that waiting on my door-step?'

'It's me, Mrs C. I have news. I'm a father. Maisie gave birth to a little girl just before midnight.' David Carlisle held up a bottle of champagne. 'I thought we'd wet the head of Miss Ruby Freda Carlisle. That's if it's not too late?'

'It's never too late to welcome a new baby into the world,' Ruby declared with a lump in her throat.

'We have another guest for dinner, Mum,' George called out from the hallway.

'Whoever can it be?' Ruby muttered to herself as she left the steamy confines of her kitchen, wiping her hands on her crossover pinny as she went through to the hall to welcome the new guest, whoever it might be. 'We have the world and his neighbour already sitting down to dine. The two chickens will just have to stretch a little further and I'll boil a few more spuds. Who have I for-gotten? I'd best borrow a few chairs from Vera,' she muttered to herself.

'Here's a hungry lad,' George laughed as he staggered towards his mum with a happy Nelson in his arms.

'We couldn't let him stay at the vet's on Christmas Day,' Bob said as he closed the front door and helped George place Nelson on the floor.

'Oh my!' Ruby declared as she knelt to give this special dog a big hug. 'Thank you both so much,' she said, looking up at her son and also at the man who meant such a lot to her. Nelson gave a loud bark and limped off to the kitchen in search of food. 'Don't you touch those chickens or I'll ring your bloody neck,' she called out as she hurried after him.

'That's Mum's Christmas complete,' George said to Bob. 'Best not tell her the vet begged us to take him home as he was howling the place down. I've got some bottles of brown ale in the front room. Fancy one? You look as though you could do with it. Was it that hard helping me carry the dog down the road?'

'Thanks, that'll hit the spot,' Bob said as he followed him into Ruby's best room. 'No, I've just got something to do and I'm not sure how it'll turn out.'

'If it's what I think it is, you have my blessing,' George said as he reached for a bottle opener.

'The King!' they all echoed, raising their glasses as George made the official toast.

'I'd like to make a second toast if I may?' George added and started to speak after murmurs of agreement faded. 'We've faced another year of war and for this family, and our dear friends, life hasn't always been easy, but we've confronted our challenges with fortitude. We welcome new friends to the fold and are thinking of those who cannot be here with us around this table. Please raise your glasses to family, friendship and a brighter 1943, whatever it may bring.'

'Friends and family!'

'Hello there, happy Christmas!' Betty called as she entered the front door, after letting herself in using the key tied to the letter box. 'Are we too early?'

'Come on in, Betty,' Ruby called back, 'we're just clearing the table. Dinner went on longer than we expected.'

The popular Woolworths manager entered the room followed by Douglas holding a pile of brightly wrapped presents. Behind him stood his two daughters shyly hanging on to his overcoat.

'Come on in, girls,' Freda said and she rushed forward to hug the two children. She'd got to know them well while staying with Betty. 'Let me introduce you to Myfi and Georgina and this is Nelson.'

'He saved my life,' Myfi said quietly.

Freda knelt on the colourful rag rug made by Maisie and told the children how Nelson had been such a brave dog. They were soon stroking him and giving him kisses on his black nose. Nelson lapped up the attention.

'Do you have something to tell us?' Ruby asked, giving Betty's hand a glance.

'Nan, you don't miss a thing,' Sarah scolded, although she too was dying to know what had happened.

Douglas put his arm around Betty's shoulders and announced, 'I'm proud to say that Miss Betty Billington did me the honour of becoming my wife yesterday. She is now Mrs Betty Billington.'

Amongst the cheers, hugs and jokes about Betty changing her name, Betty asked, 'Is there news of Maisie?'

There were more tears of joy as the visitors were told of the safe arrival of Miss Ruby Freda Carlisle.

'I don't think there can be a happier household in the whole world,' Ruby declared. 'Why, there can't be anything left to celebrate apart from the end of this bloody war.'

George smiled to himself and gave a sideways glance towards Bob, who seemed to be miles away.

Ruby stood looking up at the early evening sky. Already she could see stars appearing beyond the barrage balloons bobbing above the river. Thank goodness the fog had lifted, at least for today. Families had been able to visit loved ones and Christmas Day had taken on a little more cheer. She reached down to where Nelson was snuffling around her leg and patted his head. After enjoying a lunch as good as anyone else had enjoyed that day, he snored his head off in his basket with the youngsters by his side. The little girl was convinced that Nelson had saved her life when he broke her fall in the accident.

Friends and family had arrived at number thirteen to celebrate the special day, with Pat, John and their family popping by during the afternoon. The house had been full to bursting. Just the way Ruby liked it. The icing on the cake had been Betty turning up with Douglas and his two delightful children, and what wonderful news, she thought. Fancy her going off and getting married without telling anyone, Ruby thought with a smile. It takes all sorts to make this world go round!

'Ruby, whatever are you doing out here, love?' Bob said as he joined her in the garden. 'We're getting ready to head to Maureen's for the evening. It's going to be a right old ding-dong with so much to celebrate.'

'Our friends and family have been lucky this past year. Life could have been so much worse. No one knows where this war will take us,' she replied, taking his hand. 'Bob, I want to apologize for giving you such a hard time over that business with our Pat. You're a good man and I shouldn't have gone on so. My Eddie would have given me a right earful if I'd let off at him as much as I did with you. There was you threatened with a gun and all I could do was tear you off a strip. I'm fortunate to have you as a friend, even though I don't deserve you.'

Bob gave a big sigh. 'I've been putting this off for a while now, Ruby, but it's got to be said.'

'What's that, Bob? You're not moving back to Margate, are you? Because I'd have something to say about that.'

'Let me finish what I'm trying to say, woman,' he grumbled.

'Get on with it then. We haven't got all night. I don't want Nelson catching his death in this cold night air.'

Bob reached into the pocket of his jacket and pulled out a small ring box. 'Now, before you speak another word let me say my piece. I know I've brought the subject up before and it wasn't the right time. I feel that now it is, so before you open your mouth and I lose my nerve again, I'm asking if you'll marry me, Ruby Caselton?'

Ruby was lost for words as she looked at the gold band with a ruby stone in the centre. 'It's like . . .'

'Yes, it's like the one your Eddie gave to you when you were first courting that you gave to young Freda for her twenty-first birthday,' Bob said as he placed the ring on her finger. 'This one has a real stone. I thought it would remind us that we've loved others in the past and they are still very much in our hearts. We rub along very well together you and I, and I do feel we have a future together. Please say yes, Ruby.'

Ruby took another look at the ring on her finger. It was as if it was meant to be there. She knew that without Bob in her life she would be miserable and in her own way she loved the man. It wasn't the heart-aching kind of love of youth, but a tender, caring love that would last until the end of their days. 'Yes, Bob, I'd be honoured to be your wife,' she smiled as she kissed him on the lips.

Bob was speechless.

'Now, I'm not saying we are getting married that soon as these things need planning. I'm not even expecting a big wedding. But, there again, I don't hold with this running away on our own business like Betty and Douglas did either. So, what I'm saying is . . .'

Bob followed Ruby into the house as she continued to talk. He'd go along with whatever she decided. As far as he was concerned he'd won the hand of the woman he loved and nothing could change the way he felt right now.

Acknowledgements

~

This book sees me delve into the lives of my wonderful Woolies girls leading up to Christmas 1942. It made me think back to those long-ago Christmases of my child-hood, when Woolworths played such an important part in making everyone's happy. Who do we thank for this, I wonder? Family . . . friends . . . Woolworths? Whoever it was, thank you for my memories.

It is often said that the life of a writer is a lonely exist-ence. I beg to differ. The comradeship of fellow authors in the Romantic Novelists' Association is testament to the success of the association. New writers, bestselling authors, publishers, agents and editors – all are there to support each other in our chosen careers. Again, I thank you all for your friendship.

A big hug also for my agent, Caroline Sheldon, who is there to champion my corner and chat about our dogs – what more could one ask for? At Pan Macmillan my thanks are for my editor, Victoria Hughes-Williams, and her colleagues Jayne Osborne and Francesca Pearce. The editorial team, headed by Kate Tolley, are worth their weight in chocolate for the hard work they put into making my books shine.

A great big thank you for the people who tell the world about my books. Emma Draube and her staff at ED Public Relations are second to none.

Research plays a big part in any historical saga author's work. My first port of call has always been the online Woolworths Museum, which never ceases to make me stop and dream of days gone by – not only my own childhood in the Sixties but as far back as the 1930s and 1940s where my stories are currently set.

Mr Paul Seaton, you have worked wonders with your museum. Thank you, sir. www.woolworthsmuseum.co.uk

For local research I'm either visiting the London Borough of Bexley archives or reading one of Bob Ogley's wonderful non-fiction books set in Kent during years gone by. I'm fortunate to have these rich sources of information to hand.

Last but not least, I must thank my readers. Sharing your memories of Woolworths and chatting about the characters makes my work so worthwhile.

Elaine xx

If you enjoyed *Christmas at Woolworths*
then you'll love

The Woolworths Girls

Can romance blossom in times of trouble?

It's 1938 and as the threat of war hangs over the country,
Sarah Caselton is preparing for her new job at Woolworths.
Before long, she forms a tight bond with two of her colleagues: the glamorous Maisie and shy Freda. The trio
couldn't be more different, but they immediately form a
close-knit friendship, sharing their hopes and dreams for
the future.

Sarah soon falls into the rhythm of her new position,
enjoying the social events hosted by Woolies and her
blossoming romance with young assistant manager,
Alan. But with the threat of war clouding the horizon,
the young men and women of Woolworths realize
that there are bigger battles ahead. It's a dangerous time
for the nation, and an even more perilous time to fall
in love . . .

Coming soon in April 2018

Wartime at Woolworths

**It is March 1943 and life for the Woolworths
employees and their families continues.**

Maisie adores her baby daughter, but begins to wonder
about her own family who she walked away from some
years before. Have they survived the war? She is determined to track them down, never imagining the
consequences . . .

Sarah and her husband, Alan, are blissfully happy and
Sarah longs for them to expand their family, but dark
days lie ahead.

Freda too wonders about her family, and events mean
that she has to encounter her past.

Wartime at Woolworths is the next moving
instalment in the much-loved Woolworths series.